CAMBIUM BLUE

Cambium Blue

Maureen Brownlee

HARBOUR PUBLISHING

Harbour Publishing Co. Ltd.
P.O. Box 219, Madeira Park, BC, VON 2HO
www.harbourpublishing.com

Front cover illustration, bottom © Pictures Now/Alamy
Edited by Caroline Skelton
Text design by Carleton Wilson
Cover design by Anna Comfort O'Keeffe
Printed and bound in Canada
Printed on paper containing 100% post-consumer fibre

Supported by the Province of British Columbia

Harbour Publishing acknowledges the support of the Canada Council for the
Arts, the Government of Canada, and the Province of British Columbia through
the BC Arts Council.

LIBRARY AND ARCHIVES CANADA CATALOGUING IN PUBLICATION

Title: Cambium blue / Maureen Brownlee.
Names: Brownlee, Maureen, 1960-
Identifiers: Canadiana (print) 20210383372 | Canadiana (ebook) 20210383380 |
    ISBN 9781550179309 (softcover) | ISBN 9781550179316 (EPUB)
Classification: LCC PS8603.R6993 C36 2022 | DDC C813/.6—dc23

For Lesli and Ron
Again. Still. Always.

Prologue

Ravens circle and call. One, a cocky beggar, much bigger than the others, glossy black wings tucked, perches on a sign: ragged, blood-red brush strokes scrawled on a whitewashed slab of chipboard: No Scavenging! The sign is wired to a metal cross driven into the ground too close to the edge of the pit. It is already tilting. By spring it will teeter over the yawning, stinking abyss. Eventually the weight of a raven will tumble it down the bank. A sleeping flame will awaken to lick clean the paint and incinerate the wood chips. By then no one will care.

Winter

I

It was four a.m. Monday morning and she was afraid again.

Behind her at the kitchen table, Kurt was fumbling with a box of shotgun shells. The box was pastel-green cardboard, the shells waxy red tubes with shiny brass bases.

"I'll do it," he said. He was still wearing the clothes he'd worn to work on Friday: plaid mackinaw, grey woollen bucking pants, orange suspenders.

"Go ahead," she said. She was curled in the tweed armchair that was hers when Kurt was home. Across the narrow living room, where he usually camped out watching television on his days off, the black recliner was empty.

"I mean it, Stevie."

"So do I."

Of course, she didn't mean it. She didn't want him to blow his brains out, all over the kitchen, just to prove that he couldn't live without her—now that they both knew that she didn't love him, and possibly never had. She hugged her knees to her chest, ignored her reflection in the black window beside her. She knew what she looked like: splotchy, pale skin, red, puffy eyelids, plain brown eyes, plain brown hair wisping out from under a blue polka-dot handkerchief. Instead, she watched Kurt's wavy reflection in the blank screen of the television perched in the bay window. They'd fought about that too, when they arrived last fall for this perfect new life: a job at the sawmill for Kurt, home nights, weekends off, no more camp work, he'd promised. No more moving was what Stevie had promised her

11

tearful girls when she pulled them out of school. Things will be better, she'd told them. Except Kurt wanted to put the TV in the bay window, and Stevie wanted to keep it for plants. Except they shut the mill two months ago, laid everybody off. Except he went back to work for the Bentwells, who were going north for the winter, Mackenzie this time. Despite Kurt's promises, 1994 had turned out just like every other year.

He hadn't believed her, Friday night, when she'd said no. He'd slammed out the door, shouting that they *were* moving whether she liked it or not.

"Start packing," he'd hollered.

And so she had. Everything he could lay claim to was out on the deck. His suitcase, three bags of clothes, two boxes of saw parts, his toolbox, his fishing tackle. The stereo was there, and his cassettes. She'd set aside her Bruce Springsteen, her Madonna LPs, packed him all of Bobby's metal. She'd kept her clothes, the kitchen stuff and the girls' things. The furniture had been hers from the start.

She'd known that he would say she was overreacting. They'd moved before, a hundred times. It wasn't a big deal. It wasn't as if there was something to hold her here. Certainly not this dumpy three-bed-room trailer, with its grimy aluminum windows and putrid green shag carpet. Certainly not this crappy little mill town, with its dirt streets and sway-backed shops. She hardly knew a soul besides old Mrs. Marsonkowsky who lived next door. And yet, she would not budge. Not this time.

Kurt rapped a shell down hard on the kitchen table. The sound of brass on Arborite rippled across the room and down her spine. She sucked in a careful, quiet breath, eyes glued to his reflection. He stared at the back of her head, waiting for her reaction.

She didn't move.

He wouldn't do it.

She forced her weary brain to consider how she might explain it, again, if she wasn't so tired of explaining shit to men who never listened anyway.

I was fifteen...

The trail started there, didn't it? That party at Bobby Jeffers's house, three days shy of her fifteenth birthday. Bobby's parents away at a logging convention in Vancouver, Big Bob always was some kind of wheel, they went every year. Bobby had been celebrating. What? The Grizzlies—they'd won their tournament, and Bobby was high on having scored the winning goal. Stevie had arrived with her brother, Adrian, but he'd gone home without her. She'd been one of the stragglers: long past midnight, maybe a dozen of them left, the stereo turned down, the keg in the kitchen empty, the haze of tobacco and marijuana smoke waning. She'd been standing hip to hip with Bobby Jeffers, their backs against the kitchen countertop while Kurt Talbot, Bobby's right forward, play-by-played the last minute of the last period, the magnificent winning goal. She'd been pretending to listen, but all her senses were attuned to Bobby Jeffers's thigh leaning into hers. When he draped his arm over her shoulders, she nestled along his ribs, and without looking at each other, they merged. She cherished that moment: his heartbeat, hers, the delicious weight of his forearm, the whisper of his fingertips against her skin. Later, in the dark cab of his pickup, parked at the end of her parents' driveway, his touch roughening, Bobby had used his knee to pry apart her clenched thighs—

Kurt cracked open the shotgun.

Stevie whirled, stabbing a finger into the air. "You wanna know why? That, right there, that's why! I'm done being pushed around. You hear me? Done!"

"We're not done until I say we're done. I can't—you're all I have, you and the girls."

"Right. Which is why you're always happier without us, off drinking or hunting with the Bentwells, hanging out at the bar, drooling over the peelers."

"I don't have to do that. I can stop." His voice broke. "I need you."

"You don't. You never did. You're—" She stopped. They'd been over it too many times already.

Kurt sniffled, the empty gun across his knee, his hands limp against the barrel. She knew what was coming now: he'd work himself up about the mess that was his life, and then he would cry. Her breathing eased.

Bobby hadn't ever cried. Except the once. His face tinted red from the dash lights, his hands twisting the steering wheel. He had wanted her to say it wasn't true, wanted her to say it wasn't his. "He's going to kill me," he said, and they both knew who he meant. He tried to laugh but it came out strangled and harsh, and he slumped over the steering wheel and cried. She sat beside him, his leg quivering against hers, and she hadn't been able to think of a single thing to say that might comfort him. Or herself.

"My life is over," he had sobbed. "Over."

When he stopped crying, he sucked in one last, hiccupping breath, and banged his head on the steering wheel three times. "Fucking. Stupid. Idiot." For years, she thought he meant her.

He drove her home, held the driver's door while she slid out, and said he'd tell his parents if she told hers. He had never asked, then or later, how she felt about it. No one had.

Kurt rapped a second shell onto the tabletop.

Stevie laughed, a single, short bark. She stalked to the kitchen, snatched the shells from the table and crammed them back into the box. "I'm pretty sure you don't get a second shot," she said.

"Give those back."

"Not today." She took the shells to the addition, where the gun case lay open on the top of the chest freezer.

Kurt followed her, the gun abandoned. He caught her into a clumsy hug. "Stevie." He caressed her back. "What about the girls?"

Here it came. His other tired story. This notion that he was duty bound to Bobby's memory, to Bobby's children.

Bobby's children.

Never Stevie's children. Always Bobby's children.

She opened her mouth, closed it again. He would never understand.

Everyone had been so thankful to have her off their hands—the widow and the right-hand man, how romantic. The same relief on her parents' faces as the day she had walked out of the church on Bobby's arm. She hadn't told anyone—who was there to tell?—but she'd known from the start that it was a gamble. Kurt was a good provider, just like everyone said, happy to hand over his paycheque in exchange for a handful of twenties to take to the bar, but he had always been awkward and impatient with the girls. Some idea he had about being in charge never let him relax around them. He was constantly dismissing them from the dinner table for contradictory infractions: eating too fast, eating too slow, talking too loud, whispering. He wasn't exactly mean, just a bit rough when he was tired or when he'd had too much to drink. With Stevie's help, Brit and Peg had learned how to tiptoe around him.

She shrugged out of his embrace. "I'm going to bed," she said. "Since you care so much about the girls, try to be quiet on your way out. They have school in the morning."

He grabbed her arm. "I'm not leaving."

"Yes, you are, Kurt. This time, you are." She let him hold her and searched his face: three-day whiskers, bloodshot eyes, acrid whisky breath. There was nothing left. His grip relaxed. She held his gaze without blinking, watched him calculate her silence. She wanted him to understand: she wasn't negotiating. He dropped her arm. She went to the kitchen for the gun, zipped it into its case, and held it out to him.

"If I go, I'm not coming back." He was stone cold sober now and angry.

"That's right, you're not."

"You'll never make it without me."

"We'll see."

"There's somebody else."

"I told you, there isn't." The last thing she needed was another man. "Just go, Kurt. Get a room. You'll be in camp by next week. By spring you'll have forgotten us."

"You'll regret this."

Her fear pulsed, forcing the air from her lungs. What if she couldn't pay the rent? Feed the girls? She steeled herself, thrust the gun case at him.

He grabbed it. "See you around," he growled. "Bitch."

She waited, leaning against the woodbox, as he ferried boxes from the deck to his truck. Finally, the pickup started, backed onto the street, roared away.

She crept to the tweed armchair and huddled, her knees clasped to her chin. He was gone. It was over.

She heard a small thunk behind her, firewood collapsing inside the heater. Outside, under the overhang of the addition, there was enough wood to last another week, maybe two if she was careful. And it was only October.

Stevie held the phone to her chest and pointed Brit down the hall, to the bedroom where Peg was playing. She waited until Brit had closed the door before continuing her conversation.

"Kurt is gone," she said, holding her voice to an even tone. She'd practised this sentence, and a hundred variations, knowing that she would have to have this conversation eventually. She'd avoided it a few times, letting the machine pick up, but this morning Brit had been in the kitchen when the phone rang.

"Another camp job?"

"No, Mom. Gone. I kicked him out."

"What about the children?"

"They're fine. Kurt never..." She wanted to say *gave a shit*. "He never really cared about the girls."

"Stephanie! That boy has been nothing but good to you. Think where you were when he came along."

Where I was? Where were you, Mother, when that boy came along? Stevie swallowed the words, curled her lips between her teeth, bit down gently. It was clearer now: she could almost forgive her parents' feeble response after Bobby's accident. Before they'd even got the call, Vivian Jeffers had swooped in and taken charge. Stevie and the girls were already unpacking in the big Jeffers house in Deighton by the time her parents arrived.

"Is he still…helping out?"

"No, Mom. He's not *helping out.*"

"Why didn't you call us? I can't think what your father is going to say."

"We're fine. I work—"

"Work? Since when?"

"I got a job serving." She'd seen the help wanted sign in Betty's window the day after Kurt left. Started work the following morning.

"A *waitress?*"

Another long pause. *Yes, Beatrice, your daughter is slinging hash at Betty's Café in Beauty Creek.*

"And the girls?"

"It's mostly days, just a few nights, and my neighbour Mrs. Marsonkowsky takes them when I have to work late."

"A stranger."

"No, Mom, not a stranger. My neighbour."

"Maybe you should think about moving back here?"

"Our life is here now."

"But if you're just going to wait tables—"

"I'm not ever coming back to Deighton." It came out harsher than she intended.

"Oh, Stephanie…I don't know what to say."

"We're fine." It was a small lie. She'd already had to ask Betty for an advance to fill the propane tank for the furnace.

"What about Christmas?"

"Mom, it's *November.*" Stevie paced to the end of the telephone cord.

"Your brother is coming this year. It's our turn. It would be nice if you were all here."

"Don't count on it. I don't know if the cafe is open or what. Or how the roads will be. My winter tires aren't the greatest."

"There's always the bus. What if I sent you tickets for the bus?"

"I have to go, Mom. I'll call you about Christmas. But don't count on us." Stevie hung up the phone and paced, talking back to the churning in her chest. *Deep breath. Count to ten. You're fine. She's fine. Everything is fine.*

"Mom?" Brit called. "Can we come out now?"

"Yes."

"Are we going to Grandma's for Christmas?"

"No. We're not."

"What about Grandma J's?"

"No. Not there either. Remember how far it is? All the way to the other ocean?" Brit had been three when Vivian Jeffers slipped into a deep depression that not even grandchildren could relieve. Recovery had led her back to her childhood home in Newfoundland, a high school sweetheart, and a new life. "But I bet there's going to be a really, *really* big Christmas parcel for you. Because that Grandma J, she knows how to shop."

Brit giggled.

"For me, too?" Peg came down the hallway, ducked under Stevie's arm, clambered into her lap.

"Yes, for you, too. Two really, *really*, big parcels. Because that Grandma J…?"

"Knows how to shop!" they shouted in chorus.

Peg nuzzled her bare foot into Stevie's palm. It was so cold it burned. "Margaret Jeffers, how many times have I told you? Socks, child, socks!"

Brit shoved Peg into the kitchen cupboards and knocked her to the floor just as Stevie came around the corner from the living room. Peg wailed and Stevie gathered her up and glared at Brit. "What is up with you?"

Brit's eyes welled. She shoved past Stevie and ran to her bedroom. Stevie carried Peg to the living room and deposited her in the recliner with the Christmas catalogue and a blanket.

She found Brit flung across her bed, sobbing. "Oh, Brit, shh, it's okay." Stevie knelt beside her. Brit curled away. She had been standoffish for months. Stevie remembered how it felt, that desire to align with your school friends, to separate from your mother, but it still stung.

Eventually the sobbing eased. Brit edged closer to Stevie, wriggled into her lap. Stevie rocked slowly.

Finally, Brit wiped her eyes with the back of her hand and retrieved a brown envelope from her school backpack. Inside was an oversized green report card, with charts of subjects and skill sets, and letter markings in tiny columns. *G* for Good. *S* for Satisfactory. *I* for Improvement needed. There were no Is, mostly Ss, just one line in the written comments: *Brittany is demonstrating an acceptable level of proficiency in all subjects.*

"That's nice," Stevie said. "Not that I'm surprised. You are very proficient."

"But I'm not on the honour roll," Brit quavered. "I don't have enough Gs."

"Oh, pet, that doesn't matter. You're doing just fine. I'm sure of it."

"But why didn't I get Gs in writing and reading? I always get Gs in writing and reading."

It was true. Brit had been an early reader. "I don't know why."

"Will you go? Will you find out?"

Stevie closed the report card. She'd met Mrs. Pritkin, the grade two teacher, at the parent interviews at the beginning of the year. The thought of questioning her was daunting.

"Will you?" Another quavering sob.

"I will. I'll go tomorrow."

Stevie hung up her coat, donned her apron, and attacked the morning's accumulation of pots.

"How did it go?" Betty called from the grill.

"Okay, I guess."

"What did she have to say for herself?"

"She said she never gives kids high grades in the first report. She thinks they try harder that way."

"No matter how they're doing?"

"Apparently."

Stevie drained the old water, turned on the hot, squirted in dish soap, and clattered the stack of pot lids along the stainless-steel counter and into the sink.

"That's stupid," Betty called over the clamour.

"That's what I thought." Stevie scoured a crusty lid and tossed it to the middle sink where the hot water was running. Water splashed up around her. "Stupid cow," she muttered.

"What?" Betty crossed the kitchen to stand beside her.

"Nothing."

"At least you can tell Brit it isn't her."

"I guess."

"Good for you, anyway, for going in there. Lots wouldn't." Betty swung the tap to fill the third sink, reached past Stevie's shoulder for the bleach, doled out two capfuls, and swished it into the water around the lids. "Jeezuz that's hot! Where are your gloves, girl? Put on your gloves."

Stevie's eyes welled. She dried her hands on her apron, slid her red fingers into rubber gloves. She splashed a potato pot into the sink and scrubbed, her sniffles masked by the running water.

It wasn't what Mrs. Pritkin said. It was *the look*. The way she glared over her glasses at Stevie, perched on a child's chair in front of her. "Brittany's file says this is her fourth school. Is that correct?"

"Uh, yeah."

"This might explain some of the temperamental issues. Children do so much better with consistency."

"Temperamental?" Everyone always remarked on how easygoing her girls were.

The look. Again.

"Do you work, Mrs. Jeffers?"

What has that got to do with anything? "I do."

A knowing nod, another flip of pages in the file.

"Have there been any upsets at home recently?"

Upsets at home? Everyone in the whole effing town must know her business.

Betty turned off the streaming tap. Stevie kept scrubbing.

The bell at the front door tinkled. "I'll get this one, you stay here." Betty patted her shoulder, gave it a gentle squeeze. "It'll get better, you'll see."

The kindness was almost too much. Stevie hefted the pot to the next sink, splashed it down on top of the lids.

Upsets at home.

Brit's teary face, the day they left Prince George for Beauty Creek. Stevie had packed them up, plunked them into the back of the club cab, handed them each a pillow and a baggie of popcorn she'd made up the night before. Her wine glasses, the ones she'd got from saving little paper stamps from the grocery store, those she'd wrapped in soft cotton tea towels and a layer of newsprint, set them on the seat between her and Kurt. But her girls? Tossed in the back seat with their coloring books and day-old popcorn.

She swished the lids through their final rinse and stacked them to dry. She rolled the potato pot around in the water, watched droplets cascade down its glimmering sides.

Mrs. Pritkin was a stupid cow, but she was right. It was Stevie's fault. She was the reason Brit got Ss instead of Gs on her report card. Too much moving. Too many *upsets at home.*

No more.

She wiped her damp cheek on her sleeve and lifted the bulky pot onto the drain board.

She would do better. She would.

2

Nash Malone flicked off his lights as he turned onto the dump road. He lifted his foot from the gas pedal, let the pickup idle through the potholes. A sagging page-wire fence hemmed the road, channelling vehicles to the dumping ground.

He parked on the far side, close to the stack of metal discards. He sometimes found valuable lengths of copper pipe among the cast-off appliances and crumpled sections of furnace ducting, but a light coating of undisturbed snow told him that nothing new had been added over the weekend.

He pulled on his gloves and picked up a long-handled contraption from the passenger seat. He called the mechanical grabber Jiminy after his last dog, a golden retriever who had roamed the town, dragging home whatever took his fancy: children's toys, burlap sacks, plastic bottles, doormats, a plethora of other dogs' dishes and bones. Nash missed the old dog beside him on the pickup seat, greying muzzle tipped to the passenger window, swivelling to attend to whatever nonsense Nash had to share. He missed the sound of toenails on the floor in the night; he even missed the three a.m. walks. But he hadn't replaced the golden Jiminy. The town had grown cranky along with the old dog—nagging reminders about a dog tag becoming a surcharge on his taxes, the tag delivered by mail, though he still refused to attach it. Twice Jiminy had been collared by some vigilante dog hater and delivered to the makeshift pound at the back of the public works yard. Nash had bailed him out, the small fine a minor slight compared to the humiliation of having to put his money into the oily palm of the village clerk.

"Eh, Jiminy?" He squeezed the handle twice, the well-oiled cable and spring mechanism smoothly opening and closing. "You're not much company but at least you don't need a licence."

A feeble thread of smoke drifted up out of the pile and floated east, toward the timbered slopes of the Monashees. The Beauty Creek dump had been on fire for years. It slumbered winters, oxygen-starved but never extinguished, sustained by subterranean seams of peat moss. In early summer the sleeping flame would awaken and blaze up intermittently until the snow drove it back underground. In winter, the public works crew would ignite the top of the pile periodically to burn away a layer.

Nash strolled along the edge of the pit, gauging the best route into the spew of bulging bags, some already split open in their tumble from the garbage truck. Household refuse, vegetable peelings, and tin cans mingled with cast-off clothing and footwear. Broken kitchen gadgets peeked between layers of cardboard and plastic packaging and broken lengths of lumber. Using Jiminy as a crutch, Nash edged down the bank to a small covey of wine bottles. He scooped them into his tattered hockey duffle and then used Jiminy to slice along the seam of the nearest bag. Clothing spilled out, jeans and checked shirts, a nylon jacket, a green down-filled vest. He plucked up one of the shirts. He was partial to a checked shirt with pearl snaps and button-down collars. He set Jiminy aside, held the shirt against his chest, and then examined the tag. Small. His size. It was unusual to find men's clothing in his size. He took the shirt, and two more. He didn't need a new shirt, but he couldn't leave these for the fire. He left the jeans. He only wore denim in the summer. This time of year he preferred wool.

He kicked the clothing bag aside, sliced into the next, plucked out three pop cans. These days he mostly only bothered with bottles and cans. He could easily make ten or twenty bucks on garbage day, if he got there before the fire took off.

He breathed through his mouth, turning his face away from the smoke when it gusted. He was accustomed to the smell, burnt plastic crossed with rotting food and a backwash of fetid disposable diapers. The last of the season's lawn and garden clippings, well on their way to compost, added an earthy brine to the smoky air.

It was too late for bears, but the ravens were year-round company. There was a sudden commotion above him; a raven, perched on the sign at the top of the bank, called urgently, several times.

"You tell 'em," Nash muttered.

More idiocy from dog-licensing bureaucrats. No Scavenging! Not twenty feet from their brand new recycling bins. He scooped a six-pack of beer cans into his duffle bag, shifted the weight off his hip, took another careful step. What was he doing here, if not recycling?

Maybe he should run for council. "Hey, raven," he called, "would you vote for me? Run my campaign? Nash Malone for mayor!"

The bird cawed. Nash chuckled, plucked up a whisky bottle and brushed off the congealed carrot and potato peels. He heard a vehicle gearing down at the highway and then the distinctive clanging of the garbage truck. It would be Alvin Tilburt with his second load.

"Malone? You down there? Watch out, here it comes." Bagged garbage tumbled down the embankment. One bag landed at Nash's feet, spewing its contents. Ashes and bits of charcoal and one, no, two dusty wine bottles. He scooped them up.

"Malone? Come on up. It's coffee time."

Nash didn't bother replying. Alvin wouldn't hear him over the scream of the retracting hydraulic cylinders. He liked Alvin Tilburt well enough, though the man could talk the hind leg off a donkey. He hefted his duffle. It was far from full, but Alvin's mother made very good coffee.

Alvin filled a Thermos top and passed it.

Nash cradled the cup, blew gently across the steaming surface, and sipped. "Now that's coffee."

"Yeah, silly old thing. I tell her that I'll get a cup at the gas station, but she won't have it. Always brews me a pot."

Nash sipped again. Midge Tilburt was anything but silly. Without her business savvy Alvin would never have survived the precarious life of the independent contractor after they privatized him out of his secure village job.

"Cold, eh?" Alvin said.

"Always cold in December. You're just getting soft."

Alvin ignored the jibe. "Not much snow though."

"Supposed to be a bit of a blow coming our way."

"I heard that. Won't see much of you after that."

Nash nodded. He used to prefer the winters. No flames. Much less stench. But now, once the snow deepened, he only made the trip a couple of times a month.

"I'll be here by myself," Alvin whined. "I swear there's more garbage every day. And I've got Christmas right around the corner."

Nash savoured his coffee as Alvin unloaded his compendium of complaints: the garbage, the people who created the garbage, the things they threw out—Nash wouldn't believe him if he told, which he wouldn't because that was part of the job, not telling—and, a more recent tirade, the new village council and all their red tape and regulations. Recycling. He sneered the word every time he said it. He poured Nash a second cup of coffee and moved on to current events.

"Did you hear? Somebody's bought the Timberline Motel. Going to expand it, I heard. Put in a pool and a restaurant. Build on. Two hundred rooms." He emphasized the number, as if it signified something Nash should understand. "Bus tours," he added.

"Bus tours?"

"Yep. All them buses going from Vancouver to Calgary. Town's all over it."

"We're not on the road from Vancouver to Calgary."

"We are now. Them Japan tour buses, they want to go through Jasper and Banff, drive the Icefields highway. Makes a nice loop if you go this way. Some of them fly into Vancouver and out of Calgary. All of them drive through here."

Nash doubted Alvin's logic, but he wasn't prepared to argue it. "Who bought it?"

"The Timberline? Guys from Vancouver. Whistler tycoon types. An investor group is what I heard."

Nash snorted.

Alvin nodded. "We've heard that one, haven't we? Investor group? Remember the spa?"

Nash laughed with him. The spa. The heady boom that had been the early eighties, before everything went downhill: Americans demanding softwood tariffs, lumber prices into the toilet. An investor group from Edmonton had bought up the block of empty lots along the highway south of Beauty Creek and unveiled an elaborate plan.

"Nothing but a bunch of pretty pictures." Nash rolled down his window, hawked and spat away the taste of burned plastic.

"At least this bunch actually has a building to start with. Council is all for it. Which they should be. Give them something to think about besides recycling."

"Whose idea was that?" Nash gestured toward the sign.

"Doyle, naturally. His grand garbage plan. No, excuse me, his solid-waste management plan. It's the end of an era, Nash. We won't be able to burn much past next year, or that's what they're saying." A knowing nod. "By the end of '95, I heard. They'll put bins here and truck it to that new regional dump up past Deighton."

"Deighton! That's a hundred and fifty miles. More. That's crazy."

"Yeah, well, crazy as it sounds, it's going to happen sooner than later."

After Alvin had clanged out of the gate, Nash considered the snowy pile and decided he'd had enough for one day. He took the back road to town, a leftover habit from the days when he'd driven without a pink slip. He'd been ticketed twice, and they'd threatened to take his truck before he'd resigned himself to the inevitability of universal insurance. It wasn't that he was opposed to it in principle; he'd just been averse to giving any of his money to Ernie Halvers, the local insurance agent in those days. They'd fallen out as boys over a bitterly contested fishing hole.

Quick to anger, slow to forgive. Of all the Malone traits Nash had coveted in his childhood that was the one he got. It had never seemed fair that he was short and skinny and blue-eyed while his black-haired, brown-eyed brothers towered. Runt, they called him, and tousled his blond tresses. He had pestered his father for tasks, set his sights on being pulled from school at eleven to peel poles like Pete. But the call never came. On rare occasions, when one of the older boys was sick, Nash was pressed into service, but mostly he was sent to school with the girls, shepherded by his big sisters until they married, then shepherd himself to the little sisters who had followed him.

Main Street was quiet except a cluster of cars at Betty's Café. At the school crosswalk, he stopped for two tykes, a rosy-cheeked pair bundled against the cold, each carrying a plastic lunch kit. The little one kept an eye on his truck as her sister tugged her forward. Nash smiled to himself. Siblings. Some things never changed.

The bottle depot wasn't open yet. He switched off the ignition and felt the cold seep into the cab. He cleared his throat, heard himself doing it, sounding like old Mr. Barkley, the aged teacher that his brothers had mocked so mercilessly that he'd hopped an eastbound freight one February night without warning. They'd huddled in the cold classroom, the older kids spinning scenarios: What if they didn't tell anyone and came to school every day as if nothing was the matter? How long until an adult cottoned on? They knew it was impossible, though it had been fun to pretend for the half hour before Bessie Carmichael got scared and ran across the tracks to tell her folks.

June Fletcher rapped his fender, startling him. She was on foot.

"Where's your car?"

"Wouldn't even turn over. The battery's going, and I forgot to plug it in last night."

Nash admired June Fletcher's tenacity. She'd gone into the bottle business after her draft-dodging husband took advantage of Carter's amnesty and went back to California. There couldn't be much money in it, but she persevered, six days a week, fair weather or foul, in the musty, unheated building that had once been the showroom for

Cooper's Motors. She lived along the creek in a log cabin she and her husband had built when they first arrived. They'd planned to live off the land: grow a garden, plant fruit trees, maybe keep a cow and some chickens. Sadly, Beauty Creek didn't allow cows or chickens within town limits, and crab apples were the only trees that reliably produced fruit. Since neither June nor her husband turned out to be gardeners, they'd had to settle for the cabin. Didn't even get to have an outhouse, she'd once lamented to Nash.

The cavernous building was frosty. June wore quilted coveralls and thick leather mitts. Nash spilled his haul onto the sorting table; they funnelled tins to one side, bottles to the other, June counting and calculating on the back of a used envelope as they went.

When they had finished, she tallied it by hand. "Ten fifty?"

"Sounds right."

"Will we be seeing you at Betty's on Christmas Day?"

She'd been on him about this Christmas dinner ever since Miriam died. Christmas for loners, she called it. Christmas for losers, more like.

"Probably not."

She held out his change. "Are you sure? We have a lot of laughs, and Betty puts on a spread."

He opened his palm, she dropped in the coins. He pocketed them.

She held out his ten-dollar bill. "Two o'clock Christmas Day at Betty's, if you change your mind."

He tugged the bill from her fingers.

Nash dressed quickly, got the fire going, and plugged in the heater for the pipes under the bathroom sink. They were always the first to freeze, and he'd just as soon not have to resort to the outhouse. He wasn't supposed to have one in town, let alone use it, though it remained, upright and functional, tucked behind the woodshed.

He scraped frost from the window above the kitchen sink so he could see the thermometer. Minus thirty. They hadn't forecast this. He scooped coffee into the basket of the percolator. It was a recent find, shiny, stainless steel with nothing wrong but a broken prong on the plug. He'd spliced on a new plug and voila. While the coffee perked, he fried eggs for a sandwich and ate it standing over the heater.

In the northwest corner near the unused front door, his desk a tidy island in the cluttered room, his typewriter waited with a half-written poem. He'd stopped working on it weeks ago, stymied by one line that simply would not come. He wasn't much of a poet, just rhymes mostly, and when he got stuck on a line he could go for months without doing anything about it.

He brought his coffee to the desk, pulled out the poem without reading it, and dropped it into the bottom drawer to join other false starts. He rolled in a fresh sheet and sat looking at it.

Alvin had ambushed him at the post office. "You're to come for Christmas dinner. Mother insists."

"Does she now?"

"Yep. Says I'm not to take no for an answer."

It had rankled and Alvin had noticed. "Only if you want to."

Chagrined, Nash had relented. "Tell her thank you." To make up for his bad manners, he offered to bring something, thinking of dinner buns, a bag of spuds, maybe a jar of pickles. But no.

"A poem?" he'd repeated, incredulous.

"Mother loves your poems."

He'd put it off, hoping inspiration would strike, but now he was down to the wire. What kind of poem could he write for Midge Tilburt? A Christmas poem? A garden poem? Midge was a great gardener. It was one of the things he admired about the old girl: her steadfast determination to thwart Beauty Creek's unreliable climate. Midge planted sweet corn every spring, no matter how many times she plowed it under without harvesting a single ear.

He placed his fingers on the keys, tapped lightly. Thought about gardens. Gardening. His fingers drifted. He typed the beginnings of a title: *An Ode to ...*

He meant to type gardener, maybe sweet corn, but that wasn't what came out.

An Ode to an Outhouse.

He contemplated the unexpected direction. It could work: light and fun, with no dark undertones. Change. Yes, and a certain nostalgia for a shared past. But no longing. Neither Nash, nor Midge, he suspected, had any desire to return to a time before indoor plumbing.

The fire crackled and an ember popped onto the grate, fiery red cooling to black. He came back to the title. He doubted it was original. Was anything?

He tugged the carriage return twice. Typed one line, and then a second. They weren't any good but he kept going. He had to get them down so he could move on to the words that might come if he cleared a space for them.

He pondered a word, typed a poor substitute. It never got easier. In his imagination, poems simply arrived for transcription. Here, at the typewriter, it was more akin to gold panning, pan after pan of dull, gritty river gravel washed and discarded, and then—just as he began to flag—a rare flake of colour.

The first flush of inspiration petered out. He rested his chin on his palm. Outside, beyond his frosty window, the mountains emerged from the darkness. He watched until the light touched the snow-capped peaks and then put his fingers back onto the keys, forced himself on.

3

Maggie Evans hated mornings, January mornings in particular. She hated getting out of bed to an empty house. She hated the shivering interlude between throwing back the blankets and being dressed. She hated facing herself in the harsh bathroom mirror: the grey hair at her temples, the deepening lines around her mouth, the sagging skin below her tired eyes.

Most of all, she hated having to make her own coffee. In the good old days, before Mildred's desertion, Maggie would sleep until ten, shower, dress and get her first cup of coffee and some scrambled eggs at Betty's Café just before the breakfast cut-off at eleven. But at this ungodly hour, Betty's would be bustling, and the only thing Maggie Evans hated more than making her own coffee was making small talk before she'd had it.

While the coffee pot dripped, she totted it up again. It was unfair that Mildred had left her in a lurch, two weeks' notice and off to the oil patch with her husband. Maggie couldn't bring herself to change the store hours. The *Beauty Creek Chronicle*—All Your Office Supplies and Stationers Needs—opened every weekday at nine. Set your hours and stick to them, Hank always said. Easy for him to say. He'd been an early bird, tiptoeing out of the bedroom at five a.m. even though she'd told him, time and time again, that she didn't even hear him going. Despite decades of marriage, their sleep schedules had never synchronized.

Hank.

A tear welled. She wiped it away.

"Let me see that," her mother used to say, cupping a teary chin in her hand. "Nothing but a few drops of self-pity." She'd brush a rough thumb across Maggie's cheek. "There, that's got it." Maggie had always thought the slings and arrows of childhood deserved a modicum of sympathy. Fifty years on, with troubles barely approximating her mother's fourteen-hour workday without running water or electricity, Maggie could better appreciate that hardy pragmatism.

Someone had to open the store, turn on the lights and turn up the heat. She needed Felicia to work weekends, and Dwight, bless him, couldn't run the cash register. And the payroll savings were adding up. A few months more and she'd be close to current on the overdue accounts.

The coffee pot sputtered. She filled a travel mug, donned coat and gloves and toque. She started the car and then unplugged the block heater and scraped a porthole in the icy windshield.

She idled over the tracks and drove slowly along Main Street, mindful of the slippery patches lurking at the stop signs. The downtown core hadn't changed much since her mother's day: the hotel kitty-corner to the abandoned CNR station, a two-block strip of shops, the dogleg past Cooper's hiding the new development that sprang up after they built the highway bypass in 1975. There were too many empty storefronts: Pennywell's Variety, Baker's Plumbing, Tilson's Music— where Blake had taken piano lessons as a boy. The windows of Borden's Men's Wear were papered over. They weren't all casualties of the latest downturn; some had drifted away earlier. Most of the buildings were well past rustic, and each had housed multiple ventures through the years. Borden's had been a bakery, a sporting-goods store, a shoe store and the Sears outlet. She scrutinized the front of the *Chronicle* building, sandwiched between Halvers Insurance and the Beauty Creek Barber Shop. It looked a little tired; the cedar-shingle facade was fading to grey. She needed to have it sandblasted and refinished. Maybe next year.

She wheeled through the alley to the back of the building and braked hard to avoid two empty garbage cans lolling in her parking spot.

"Goddammit, Alvin!" She carried the frosty cans to the wooden rack at the back of the building. This was her payback for the placating editorial she'd written last spring after they revised the garbage bylaw. She'd opined that everyone would benefit from reduced costs if they just went along and set their cans out onto the street.

"Not the way it used to be," Mildred had huffed, as she typed the endless complaining letters to the editor. No one in Beauty Creek, except the new council, thought there was anything wrong with the old system where Alvin Tilburt bumped along the alley, plucking tins out of racks, returning them, lids intact, one after the other. Just when we build a rack at the back, people had fumed, they want the cans set out in front. In the business district it was only a matter of setting the cans at the edge of the alley, and putting them back after Alvin had emptied them, but even that was taking some getting used to.

Maggie retrieved the lids and banged them into place. "Not the way it used to be," she muttered.

The back door swung wide, and Dwight, shaggy haired and bleary eyed, emerged. "Who're you talking to?"

"Alvin Tilburt. I'm channelling Mildred this morning. Maybe she'll hear me and come back."

"That'd be a great story."

She grinned. He grinned back.

"What're you doing here this early?"

"Early? I've already covered a meeting," he said. "The Chamber of Commerce has decided to try breakfast meetings this year."

"Who does that?"

"That's exactly what I didn't say. Actually, they get a fair turnout." Another broad grin. "You should come."

She glowered. "Where are you off to?" He had a camera around his neck, lens bag slung over his shoulder.

"The elementary school. A ventriloquist. A talking dog, I'm told, who does children's stories with a just-say-no message."

She nodded her sympathy, tapped the camera bag. "Have you got film in here?"

"Yes, ma'am. Three rolls, one in the camera, two spares."

"Good man." She handed him her keys. "Take the car. It is too cold for walking."

She watched him drive away.

She'd hired Dwight a year ago, when Richard left.

"I'm awful sorry," Richard had said, "but Danny graduates this spring and the wife, well, she wants him to be able to live at home for university."

"I understand," Maggie said. Richard's wife had always hated Beauty Creek. Too small, too hick, too far from everywhere and, most outrageous of all, bereft of a shopping mall.

"It won't be until July," Richard said. "I could probably stay right up to September, if you needed me to."

Dwight had turned up in the middle of July. A twenty-four-year-old English major, he'd come north with a tree-planting crew because he thought he might get a story out of it. He showed her the raw blisters on his palms, said that even with the other planters covering for him, it had only taken the bosses a week to figure out that Dwight wasn't built for the bush. He hated the thought of scurrying home with his tail between his legs, and he had been a reporter for his college paper. "I'll learn," he had promised, his hair cut short and slicked down, his earnest brow furrowed with desire.

And he had learned. Dwight, it could be said, learned by trial and error, with the emphasis on error. More than once, he had gone off to cover a story without film in the camera.

"They don't know," he told her after he used his empty camera to shoot a careful staging of a cheque handover from the Ladies Auxiliary to the hospital. "I'll tell them I didn't have the settings right and they were blurry. I'll write a short article, there just won't be a photo."

"Oh, Dwight."

It had become a joke between them.

Oh, Dwight.

When he taped four hours of a public meeting without making a single note. "But I've got it here," he said, holding out the tiny tape recorder. "Voice activated. I bought it with my own money."

"But now you have to listen to it again. That's four more hours." She held up one of the black flip-top notebooks Hank had bought by the case. "Notes, Dwight. Reporters make notes."

Oh, Dwight.

When he'd misquoted the most prolific letter writer in Beauty Creek, they had to endure weeks of letters filled with pedantic critiques of every aspect of the *Beauty Creek Chronicle,* from its egregious use of grammar to its outdated design. Dwight and Felicia had been incensed when Maggie declined to refute the more outrageous criticisms.

"Editors don't respond to letters," she'd said, quoting Hank. "They print them. Maybe they edit them for libel or slander, but they don't respond. It wouldn't be fair."

She quoted Hank often. In the years since his death, she had gradually become an amalgam. Part herself, part Hank. Sometimes pure Hank would flow through her.

"A newspaper is a town talking to itself," she'd tell Dwight when he tangled with a contentious topic. "It isn't our job to know what's right. Our job is to moderate the conversation: give everyone a voice, let people decide for themselves. It's not our job to decide for them."

She kept a portrait of Hank on the wall behind the front desk, beside the plaque from the provincial newspaper association for 1983's best front page (in the circulation-under-2,500 category). The *Chronicle* was Hank's paper, even now. She knew she had shaped it in ways he might not have in the five years since he'd been gone, but he had shaped her in the thirty years before that.

"Stick to the basics, kid." He would tap his stained fingers, after transferring a smoking cigarette to his beanbag ashtray. "Who? What? When? Where? How? And"—he'd tap the thumb of the opposite hand—"Why? If anyone knows or has an opinion. Someone other than you. We don't make the news," he'd remind the reporter du jour. "We get it down. That's our job." Then he would grin, his perpetual boyishness shining through the thinning hair and sagging jowls. "Sometimes we might tweak things, this way or that, but we know when we're doing it."

Maggie flicked on the lights, started the computers, and cranked up the thermostat for the baseboards. The room would never get warm, but everyone had a space heater at their desk to keep toes thawed and fingers functional. She unlocked the front door and turned the sign in the window to Open.

At the front desk, she thumbed through the stack of typing that awaited. Submissions arrived by mail or by hand, write-ups from club meetings, hockey scores, school news, weddings, births, deaths. Each piece of paper had to be transcribed into a text file, a job that Mildred had dispatched effortlessly. Maggie had never been a typist, and it took her at least twice as long as it should.

She followed the directions on her cheat sheet to open the word-processing program. The machine hummed and burped. She held her breath and waited for the window to appear. Had she pushed the right keys? She sighed. She couldn't say she missed the finicky old typesetter and all the cutting and pasting that used to go into every page, but at least she'd known how to operate it.

She rested her elbow on the desk, pinched her nose between her forefingers. She remembered Hank doing the same thing: thumb and index finger, ink smudged over the yellowed nicotine tips. His little cough that became his more persistent cough that became the cancer that took him before his time.

They'd decided she would sell the *Chronicle,* one of the many decisions Hank made while he lay in that hospital bed, emaciated, oxygen tubes a permanent fixture, waiting for the end that took so long to come. She could go to the Okanagan, he thought, settle near the grandkids. Maybe she could take up photography again, open a small portrait studio.

But the *Chronicle* hadn't sold. Not that year. Not the next. Who had they been kidding? No one wanted Hank's little weekly. Eventually she stopped advertising it for sale, abandoned dreams of milder winters, and surrendered herself to the relentless demands of the *Beauty Creek Chronicle.*

"I've got to have something to keep me busy," she told anyone who asked.

She'd always understood that the drama of publishing a weekly was largely fabricated. Not much happened in a Beauty Creek week. But there was pleasure in an interesting cover story, a catchy headline, a remarkable photograph.

Hank had never doubted the importance of his newspaper. "In Beauty Creek, we're the paper of record," he would thunder. "In a hundred years, they will still be reading us." Of course, the very next day, he would turn around and berate the reporter who groused about changes to their copy. "It's not literature, for Christ's sake. It's a news-paper. They'll be wrapping fish in it by Friday."

Dwight banged through the back door and stopped at the coffee pot.

"Did you get the mail?" Maggie called.

"No, sorry." He parted the beaded curtain that separated the store and front desk from the production area in the back of the building. "Do you want me to?"

"Never mind, I'll do it."

At the post office, she scooped mail from the *Chronicle*'s box. A fluorescent pink flyer topped the stack.

"Progressive Communities!"

"Public Meeting!!"

"BEAUTY CREEK NEEDS YOU!!!"

She counted eight different fonts, six exclamation marks. The down-side of computers: nowadays everybody figured they were a graphic designer. Who needed a professional when the office temp had access to all these typefaces?

At the bottom of the flier, in yet another font, was the new village slogan: "Room for Growth." It was part of the Progressive Commun-ities initiative, the most recent bright idea from Victoria. There was a new gambit every time lumber prices tanked. While the sawmills sat idle, they gathered loggers around conference tables to *brainstorm*. As if they could dream their way out of years of politically expedient forest policy.

"Room for Growth."

Wasn't that the truth? She closed the box. Contemplated its number: 84. Beauty Creek had peaked at four-digit numbers. An optimistic bank of new boxes gleamed along the wall behind her. She imagined the other side, all those empty slots awaiting mail that would never arrive. Plenty of "Room for Growth" there.

The new mayor and the two new councillors Beauty Creek had elected along with him were enthusiastic, she'd give them that. They'd billed themselves as the forward-thinking ticket: growth with a capital *G*. Maggie wasn't sure just where the business, with a capital *B*, would be coming from, but a few more advertisers would not go amiss.

In fairness, no one could have foreseen the shutdown at the sawmill. They'd laid off everyone this time. Not enough wood in the yard, they said. The muttering around town was that they hadn't even applied for cutting permits. Cash flow, someone said. The people who might have known weren't talking. The mill workers applied for employment insurance. The mill had gone down before. They'd weathered it then, the stretch in the eighties, two years that time.

Maggie set the pile of mail on the counter above the new recycling bins, flipped through it. There were a few letters, a few bills and a couple of other weeklies from up and down the valley. The rest, a third of the stack, was government press releases.

"Advertising," Hank used to scoff about these earnest missives from public relations departments. "It isn't news unless they don't want you to know. The rest is promotion, and they can pay for that."

Maggie was a little less rigid. On a slow week, she wasn't above letting a press release masquerade as news. She wasn't as effective as Hank at motivating reporters to seek the local angles.

"This is the *Beauty Creek Chronicle*," he would roar. "Bring me the Beauty Creek news. Anybody wants to know what is going in Victoria or Toronto or Ottawa isn't going to look for it in the *Chronicle*."

Hank had loved Beauty Creek almost as much as he loved newspapers. When they bought the *Chronicle* in 1967, it had been a third-rate weekly, owned by a distant chain that made its living off lucrative government advertising packaged around a sprinkle of local news and a surplus of generic wire-service filler.

Hank had dumped the wire service and set about building a newspaper that served its constituency. He hadn't cared one whit about newspaper associations either. He had paid the dues grudgingly and only because membership was obligatory to qualify for government advertising and reduced postage rates. It was Maggie who had filled out the forms and sent in the front page that won their one and only award. "Prizes for independent newspapers, now there's an oxymoron," Hank had sneered. "Readers are the only prize we're after."

He'd have hated to see the dwindling circulation, as their readers dispersed across the country looking for work. Some kept up their subscriptions; she mailed newspapers to former Creeksters in every province, but the numbers were falling.

She fit the stack of mail into her shopping bag. An envelope dropped to the floor, plain white with a simple, clean bank logo. No screaming fluorescence for them. She picked it up, slit the flap with her thumb. Smiled. The screaming was inside.

"No Interest for Six Months!"

Attached to the bottom of the letter, perforated for her convenience, were two blank cheques. Ten years ago, when she'd wanted to borrow five hundred dollars to buy a second-hand car, the bank had needed paperwork in triplicate and, in the end, Hank had to co-sign the loan. Nowadays, the credit card companies were falling over themselves trying to lend her thousands on nothing but a signature.

Hank never would have lowered himself to manning the cash register in the stationery store. He would have signed those cheques instead. Two mortgages on the house, an operating line at its max, and too many credit cards had been Hank Evans's idea of financial equilibrium. His life insurance had paid off the second mortgage, the credit cards and the operating line, and left her with enough for the computers. So far, she'd managed to avoid saddling herself with another payment. Yes, the printer's bill was overdue but, with the savings from Mildred's salary, and the cash flow boost from the Christmas edition, she'd be able to clear it up. She tucked the blank cheques into the pile of mail. She'd shred them when she got back to the office.

Maggie double-clicked to open the Current Week folder. There was only a half dozen text files. January was always a slog. Nobody did anything, newsworthy or otherwise, in January. She double-clicked Stories Pending. Not much there, either.

Felicia jingled through the beads. "I've done the ads. Is there anything else you want me to do?"

"No. Unless you want to do a couple of the inside pages today. I don't think much more will come in." Even advertisers were feeling the post-Christmas crunch. Maggie had already dropped the paper to sixteen pages from their usual twenty. "What if we cram it into twelve pages? There's no stories here, and I know Dwight doesn't have much."

"Sure," Felicia said. "I can do that. Not many classifieds, I guess?"

"Hardly anything."

The front doorbell tinkled. The phone rang. Felicia took the customer, Maggie answered the phone.

"Mom?" It was Blake.

"Hello, son."

They'd had a pleasant, albeit short, visit at Christmas. She'd driven to Vernon on Christmas Eve, back the day after Boxing Day. He enquired about her trip home. She asked about Glynnis and the children.

"Uncle Dwayne called me last week," he said.

Hank's brother had retired to the Okanagan after a lucrative real estate career at the coast. He kept his licence current and was doing a booming business selling retirement homes.

Blake continued. "He said the newspaper here sold to a company from the Island, Brownsfield Newspapers. Have you heard of them?"

"I don't think so."

"Uncle Dwayne gave me the number. I called their office in Victoria and talked to Brownsfield, and he said they're interested."

"Interested?"

"In the paper, in buying the *Chronicle*."

Maggie swallowed.

"It's still for sale, right?"

"I guess. Maybe. I haven't thought about it recently."

"Dad said—"

"I know it's what your dad and I talked about."

"I thought you'd be glad."

"I…uh…What else did Brownsfield say?"

"That's all. That they're interested. I gave him your number. He said he'd call you."

"Did your Uncle Dwayne know anything about them?"

"He said that they paid a fair price for our paper. Kept most of their staff. Brownsfield told me he wants to put together an interior group, offer some package advertising."

One size fits all. Maggie could imagine Hank's scathing response.

"Mom?"

"I'll talk to him when he calls."

"It's promising, though. Right? It's time we got it sold. Got things settled."

Maggie squinted at Hank's portrait on the wall. There had been some confusion after the funeral. Glynnis had mistakenly assumed that there would be some inheritance from Hank's estate. *Estate.* It would have been laughable if she hadn't been serious. Maggie had laid it out for Blake, showed him the financial statements, the mortgage balances. Even when the paper sold, there would be no excess.

She thought he'd understood.

"I'll talk to Brownsfield," she promised. "If he calls."

Snow gusted in the halo of half-light cast by the bare bulb at the porch door. Stevie tucked another block of firewood under her chin. Her weary legs protested as she pressed herself upright.

"We'll never be done!" Brit collapsed into the snowbank.

Stevie sympathized. She was grateful that Betty had wrangled them another load of wood, but she wished she'd known it was coming. She'd have lifted out the two sections of removable fence and had the wood dumped in the yard instead of out here in the parking spot. They'd been moving it to the stack alongside the addition for an hour, and they hadn't made much of a dent in the pile. She, too, wanted to crumple into the snow.

"We're more than half done," she lied. "The last half goes faster. There's more small ones on this side."

"But I'm tired. Tomorrow's Saturday. Why can't we do it tomorrow?"

"By tomorrow it could have a foot of snow on it. It's not that hard. Pick up a stick. Carry it to the pile." She walked through the gate, shouldered her armload onto the stack, shuffled it into place. Brit came up beside her and tossed up a kindling stick. "Leave those for Peg," Stevie snapped. "You're big enough to carry a piece of firewood six steps. Come on, Brit, smarten up."

Brit stomped back to the pile. Stevie followed, squatted, filled her left arm, forced her aching legs upright. Brit lifted an oversized block. Dropped it. "Just pick up a piece you can carry and take it to the stack," Stevie hissed, "or I will warm your backside with that."

Brit snatched up a smallish chunk by her feet. "I miss Dad," she muttered.

He's not your dad. Stevie squeezed her lips closed over the words. She'd encouraged them to call Kurt Dad, pretending along with them.

"Me, too," Peg echoed. "I wish he'd come home and help with the firewood."

"Keep working," Stevie said. "Even if he was here, you'd still be stacking firewood, and there'd be no slacking, don't forget. Hop to it! Chop-chop!"

They rolled their eyes at each other, and Brit gave Stevie a small smile. Kurt had often accompanied his "Chop-chop!" with brisk handclaps, or taps on the backside if they were within reach. They'd all hated it.

Stevie tipped her armload onto the stack. "Time for a break," she said. "Brit, you get my wallet, and we'll drive over to Betty's and get ourselves a hot chocolate. Say thank you for the wood."

Peg perked up. Brit was hesitant. "What about the snow?"

"I think it's stopping. Besides, nobody said life had to be all work and no play. Right?"

It was snowing harder when Stevie returned to the woodpile, the girls bathed and bedtime-storied and tucked in. Just one more armful, she promised herself, again and again. The tumbled stack slowly yielded and the tidy row grew. She wanted to quit a dozen times, but she kept going until nothing remained but a ragged circle of sawdust fast disappearing under the fresh snow. She slogged to the backyard for the tarp that shielded the sandbox from the neighbourhood cats. She kicked away the snow and grabbed a corner with two hands and yanked. Her feet shot out and the back of her head smacked down hard against the wooden frame. She cried out and curled into the pain before flailing back to her feet. She jerked the tarp free and dragged it to the woodpile. She snugged it along the top, used firewood blocks to hold it in place and then got the sidewalk shovel and secured the bottom edge with snow. It wasn't pretty but it would hold.

Inside she boiled the kettle and brought a cup of hot tea to the tweed armchair. She thought about turning on the television but stared at the dark window instead. Her head throbbed and she heard Brit's lament: "*I miss Dad.*"

Stevie's head had throbbed then too, that first, terrible night after Bobby's accident. Alone in the unfamiliar bedroom at the Jeffers's house in Deighton, her mind had grappled with the unimaginable. Bobby was dead. All their futures—the this-Fridays, the next-weekends, the somedays, the maybe-whens, the in-the-springs, the next-summers— all gone.

Vivian's doctor had prescribed sleeping pills, but Stevie hadn't taken hers. She wanted to hear the girls if they woke. Near midnight, her restless sleep was broken by the sound of a diesel engine. She went to the bedroom door.

"We came when we heard." Men's voices, a rush of cold air down the hallway against her bare ankles.

"Come on in." Big Bob must have been waiting for them, knowing they would come.

"It's a helluva thing, Bob, a helluva thing." She recognized voices. Wade Givens, the faller. Jerry Dundern, the loaderman. Was the whole crew here? She pulled jeans on under her nightgown, tugged a sweater overtop, tiptoed down the hall.

At the back door, a pile of frosty coats and cork boots thawed on the tiles. She could hear voices in the living room. She paused beside the breakfast bar, strained to hear the words.

"…the corner at Twelve Mile."

"At the top of the hill, or the bottom?"

"At the top. It always ices up there. You know how it is, gets the sun, thaws, freezes."

"Where'd he land?"

There was a long silence.

Stevie crept down the short staircase to the enormous, sunken room. Big Bob was at the far end, standing behind the bar, the crew ranged around him, their backs to her. She huddled on the bottom step.

"He landed in the rocks," Givens finally answered. "We could see everything with this moon. We climbed down. He must have been going a pretty good lick because he didn't land for at least thirty feet. Then he must've rolled. Three times, we think. Rolling and bouncing."

Big Bob winced. Jerry elbowed Givens.

"No, don't stop, keep going," Big Bob said. "I want all of it."

Stevie sucked in a breath. Held it.

"We could see where they worked on him. In the snow. He must've got thrown out. Maybe the second roll. Thrown forward, onto the rocks." Another pause.

Big Bob didn't flinch, just nodded Givens on.

"I guess the truck probably landed on him."

Big Bob grunted, and every man froze, and Stevie kneaded the rough nap of the carpet with her bare toes.

Givens kept going. "It would've been fast, Bob."

"That's what McKearny said." Big Bob gripped the edge of the bar, rocked forward slightly. "That he was already...gone...when they got there. That they tried CPR but it was too late."

"They'd have been right behind him, they left at the same time."

"McKearny said Bobby passed them at twenty mile, gave them a big old grin. They didn't see him after that. Until..."

Feet shifted. Throats swallowed.

Stevie pressed her shoulder into the gap between two stair posts.

"What about on the road?" Big Bob came around the bar, stood inside the circle. "Did he brake? Did he skid?"

Givens blew out hard through pursed lips. "I don't know, Bob, I just don't know. There were no skid tracks. McKearny and his boys thrashed through the snowbank getting down there and back up again, so maybe there was something to see there. But...the way he landed? I'd say he went straight off that corner. If he'd gone off sideways, he oughta rolled sooner."

"But why would he? It doesn't make any sense."

"Nope."

"If the corner was slick, and he slid, he should've gone over sideways."

"You'd think."

"Could it have been the truck?"

Frank Gibbs, the bucker, spoke up. "That truck was sound, Bob. We went over it when we did the brakes in September. It wasn't the truck."

"So, he just drove off the corner? That's what you're telling me?"

Givens put his hand on Bob's shoulder. Not many men looked down at Big Bob Jeffers, but Givens towered. "We'll go out in the morning," he said. "We'll look again. We'll see what there is to see. This cold, this moon, everything will be the same as it is now. Whatever is there, we'll see it."

"You know, Bobby," Frank said. "He might have been fooling with the radio."

Stevie felt the words knife through her stomach, just above her pelvis, and she knew. Bobby had driven straight off the corner. She didn't need to see any tracks in the snow. She knew. She could feel him, leaning over her, his elbow resting on her knee, his fingers twirling the radio dial, seeking, his whole body tuned to the faint break in the static. On clear nights, they could pick up the American stations: Seattle, Spokane.

Some sound must have escaped her because the room suddenly tilted in her direction.

"Stephanie!" Big Bob crossed the room, gathered her under his arm and led her back to the bar. She was hugged down the gauntlet of unshaven men, and a glass was pressed into her hand. They encircled her, these men who had known Bobby his whole life. They'd been putting up with his hijinks since he was four years old and had to be rescued from the uppermost branches of the poplar that grew in the shop yard. Bobby had been hyperactive long before they'd had a word for it.

Stevie hoisted herself onto a bar stool, and someone said, "Remember the time..." and she sipped and listened to stories she'd already heard, and one or two she hadn't, and the bottle of whisky was emptied, and then another, and they moved away from the bar to the chesterfield and chairs that faced the fireplace, and someone built a fire and more drinks were poured, and they laughed and every so often Big Bob would drop his chin into his chest and rock back and forth, or Stevie would cry, and there would be murmurs about calling it a night, and they'd have one more for the road, and someone would think of another time when Bobby... They were still there at dawn when Vivian woke; she was hugged around the room, and settled by the fireplace with a big glass of whisky while Frank and Jerry went to the kitchen to make coffee and pancakes and where was the bacon? Stevie got bacon from the freezer and set the table, and when Peg woke needing to be fed, Big Bob brought her out and said, "Can I?" and Stevie said, "Sure," and heated the bottle.

After breakfast, after Frank and Jerry had loaded the dishwasher and washed the cast iron frying pans, they had gathered Brit and Peg and Vivian and Stevie and divvied them among pickup trucks, and the whole entourage drove the twenty miles to the Jackpine turnoff and up the winding road to Twelve Mile Hill. Bobby's truck was still there. Stevie hadn't known it would be and she was broken open by the sight of it, crumpled and whole all at once, upside down, black tires to the sky, what was left of the cab hidden in the snowy rock pile. There was a patch in the middle of the slope where something had gone on. She'd expected blood, but if there had been, someone had swept snow over it.

"Can I go down?" she'd asked.

Vivian had shaken her head at Big Bob, and he'd explained that there wasn't anything to see that they couldn't see from where they were.

"It's deeper than it looks," he had said.

The furnace kicked in and the curtain beside Stevie billowed. She put her free hand out and directed the warm air toward her face. She sipped her lukewarm tea and listened to the wind whipping snow against the window. Her headache had subsided. The girls were safe in their beds, the firewood was stacked and covered. She could do this. She could.

Brit and Peg were giggling at the front window of the Seashell Laundromat, drawing stick figures on the steamy glass. Stevie was too tired to reprimand them. She flopped on the bench seat near the dryers and pawed through the assortment of tattered magazines and coverless romance novels. A flyer fell at her feet: "Work at Your own Pace. Get Your Grade 12." She'd always been a sucker for that story. This one was a college outreach program, night classes at the Beauty Creek High School. The grade twelve teaser was the same old GED program she'd tried twice before. Study the text and take the exam. She'd never gotten far with it.

A timer buzzed and she tucked the brochure into her purse.

"Can *we* do it?" Brit and Peg bounded to the dryer.

"Sure." Stevie opened the door.

"They're still wet," Brit said.

"They can't be." Stevie reached a hand in, felt the dampness, sighed. She'd already used every quarter. "We'll hang them by the heater when we get home."

In the morning, over her cereal and coffee, she browsed the outreach flyer. It wasn't just GED. There were lots of offerings, from macramé to computers. One class description was especially appealing: "Beginner Keyboarding: one night a week for eight weeks." She read it three times. It promised to teach her basic computer skills along with keyboarding exercises, to make her *computer literate*. Whatever that meant.

The price, two hundred dollars, was exactly right.

In the predictably gigantic Christmas parcel from Vivian Jeffers there had been two cheques for Stevie: five hundred dollars for "whichever bill is keeping you awake at night," and two hundred dollars for "anything that catches your eye as long as it is just for you." Stevie had paid the propane bill the very next day, but the second cheque was still tucked away in her dresser drawer. She knew that Vivian would have been thinking about a coat or a new pair of boots, maybe a perm and a manicure, not a keyboarding class.

Peg trailed down the hall, bumped herself up onto her chair, poured cereal.

"Where's Brit?"

"She's crying."

"What? Why?"

Peg gazed mutely into her bowl.

Brit, damp eyed and sniffling, was still in her pyjamas. "Get dressed," Stevie commanded. "Right now."

Brit looked sideways at her and didn't move.

"Brittany Jeffers!" Stevie heard her own shrill hurry-up tone, tried to temper it. "Come on, you haven't had your breakfast and it's after eight."

Brit quivered, sobbed.

"What, kiddo, what?" Stevie folded down on the bed. Brit hunched away from her. Stevie closed one eye, took a breath. "Oh, Brit, whaaaat?"

Brit threw out a crumpled ball of fabric. Stevie recognized the blouse, a Christmas gift from Vivian. It was a plain white shirt, but it had pearl snaps and red ruffles along the shoulder seams, and Brit adored it.

"What about it?"

Brit snatched the shirt back, held it up for her to see. Ragged pink lines wavered down the shirt front, where the red ruffles had bled into the white.

"Oh, no!" The damp load she'd meant to hang up. "We can probably get it out."

Brit sniffed. Glared. "It's ruined, Mom. *Ruined.*"

"There might be a way. Toothpaste or bleach or something. We just can't do it this morning. What else have you got to wear?" Something crashed in the kitchen. "Pick something, and hurry. You'll be late for school."

Milk dripped between the leaves of the kitchen table and pooled on the floor. "Peg! You should have asked for help."

"You weren't—" *sob* "—h-h-here."

"Did you get any milk on you?"

"Just my pants."

"Go and change."

Stevie scraped the puddle of milk off the table into Peg's empty bowl. The cereal box was unscathed, but the college brochure was sodden. She tossed it into the garbage.

Betty sat down across from Stevie at the staff table. "Whatcha lookin' at?"

Stevie smacked the newspaper closed. She'd been looking at the adult-ed advertisement, the keyboarding course in its own starburst: "Registration deadline extended."

"What?" Betty took the newspaper, opened it back to the page.

Stevie touched a finger to the starred text.

"Keyboarding, eh? Well, why not?"

"Who would look after the girls?"

"Ask Mrs. M. If she can't, you can drop 'em off here to hang out with me."

"It's Wednesdays and that's a school night."

"Stevie, for heaven's sake. It says here that it only goes until eight thirty. You'll be home by nine. One night a week for eight weeks. What they give up in sleep, they'll get back in spades just by seeing you learning."

"That's a stretch."

"It isn't." Betty went to the counter, brought back the coffee pot. She spoke sternly as she filled their cups. "It isn't a stretch at all. My folks never cared about schooling. Made fun of people who had an education. Me, I wanted to be a chemist."

"A chemist?"

"I wanted to invent a new vaccine, save the suffering. Like Dr. Salk."

"Dr. Salk?"

"Dr. Salk. The polio vaccine? My Auntie May had polio. We'd go visit her, in the home at Kamloops." Betty clucked her tongue. "Poor Auntie May. Seemed like magic, back then, that little poke in the arm, and no more polio. So, yeah, I wanted to be a chemist."

"Test tubes and white rats?"

"You'll laugh."

"I won't."

"You will."

"No, tell me."

"Sometimes I pretend these old white aprons are lab coats, that my bubbling pots are beakers." She waggled a finger at Stevie. "You go on and sign up for that course. We'll sort out the logistics when the time comes."

"It's probably only a typing course, and I already know how to type. I learned in high school."

"Says here it's on computers."

"Yeah, but the keys are in the same place."

"Really? Nothing new to learn about it?" Betty pointed. "What's this? WordPerfect? What does that mean?"

Stevie admitted she didn't exactly know. Betty tapped the newspaper with her finger. "You care enough about it to be embarrassed. That's a clue you shouldn't ignore."

5

Alvin had departed for the day, Jiminy was in the truck box with the bottle bag and Nash was kicking snow off his boots when a beige Cadillac bumped its way around the landfill, wheeled toward him and then backed slowly toward the pit, stopping well clear of the edge.

Harriet Lemsky. Just his luck. She stepped out of her car, a tall, angular woman wearing her perpetual scowl. They eyed each other.

If he hadn't been there first, Nash might have moved out and left Fifth Avenue to Harriet Lemsky. She'd been a difficult neighbour from the start. The golden-haired Jiminy had figured largely in their first disputes: flower-bed incidents, missing cat food, missing cat-food dishes. Nash pointed out that Harriet's cats were as fond of his garden as Jiminy was of her flower beds, but Harriet Lemsky never believed that her cats ever left her front porch. Nash offered to bring her the evidence. A long, cool period had followed.

After Harriet's poor, bedraggled husband decamped with the receptionist from the hospital—to the amazement of the entire town—Harriet had turned on Nash with the clichéd fury of a woman scorned. She reported Jiminy every time he strayed. She took exception to Nash's collection of bike parts. If a shingle blew off his roof and landed in her yard, you'd think she'd been invaded. Nash built a tall fence along the side of the lot that faced her house, but the complaints kept coming.

She was perhaps the unhappiest human Nash had ever known. She appeared to enjoy her flowers and her cats, and the word around town was that she'd gotten a nice divorce settlement. From Nash's side of the fence, it seemed like a pretty sweet life, and yet she was always on the fight.

Their most recent skirmish involved one of Harriet's old cats that, as far as Nash was concerned, had wandered off to die. Harriet accused him of killing it, accosting him in front of Cooper's. He assured her that he'd had nothing to do with the cat's disappearance, explained that cats often wandered away to die when their time came. He had restrained himself and not mentioned the many natural predators, four legged or winged, that might relish a deaf, arthritic cat with bad eyes. He'd even patted the old girl on the shoulder. To no avail.

He wasn't the only one on Harriet's hit list. She'd commenced a campaign against Alvin after she'd caught him *snooping* through her trash. Alvin said the ravens had gotten into the can, and he'd just been picking up the spreading litter when Harriet came barrelling out her back door shouting for him to get his dirty hands out of her garbage. Ever since, she brought her garbage to the dump herself, in the trunk of her Cadillac.

Nash opened his truck door and bent to slap the last of the snow from his boot tops. Harriet slammed her car door and advanced purposefully across the snowy space between them.

"You get out of here, Nash Malone!" She pointed to the No Scavenging sign. "It's not allowed, you being here. No more. It's against the law."

"I'm going, Harriet. I'm going."

"I'll report you." Her finger stabbed in his direction. "You will be arrested."

He couldn't help himself. "I doubt that."

"I'll call the police. Every time I see you here."

"It's a village dump, Harriet. It's not a criminal offence. The police haven't got anything to do with it."

"We'll see. We will see."

Nash got into his pickup and drove away. Harriet was lifting a bag from the trunk when he came around the far side, across the pit. He banged his horn, a sharp, hard blast, and she jumped. He gave her another light toot and drove home smiling.

He parked in his spot at the north end of the woodshed and gathered an armful of firewood. The shed was half empty, just one full row across the back, a partial row in front of it, the floor littered with bark and wood chips. There had been a time when the shed would have been full, Miriam handing up split birch, Nash wedging it in against the rafters, their version of life insurance.

He eyed the old pine beside the back fence. The bark near the base had fallen away, revealing a maze of beetle trails etched in the trunk, evidence of their greedy forage through the tree's cambium layer. High above, swaying green branches belied an ugly truth: the tree was already dead. By fall, the needles would redden and drop, leaving grey-black branches, bleak against the sky.

Nash shifted the firewood in his arm and turned toward the street at the sound of a vehicle. The Beauty Creek Public Works pickup stopped in front of him. Howard Doyle stepped out.

"Malone."

"Doyle."

He was no taller than Nash, but Howard Doyle ate better. He was stout where Nash was thin, thick around the neck, bullish.

"I've just had Harriet Lemsky down at the office, Nash. Again."

Nash hugged his firewood.

"I'm gonna have to put my foot down. The dump is closed for scavenging. It's a liability issue and I, we, just can't have it any more."

Nash raised an eyebrow.

"It's too dangerous, Nash. What if you break a leg or cut your foot or, or, pick up some bug? There's new regulations. It's not just me, this is a province-wide initiative."

Nash snorted.

Doyle raised his voice. "The sign has been up for months. This is the second time Harriet's complained. It has to stop. *You* have to stop."

"It's a stupid sign, Doyle, and a stupid policy. People leave stuff out there for other people to take. I'm not the only one ignoring your sign. Nobody pays it any mind."

"New signs are coming, and we'll fence it in the spring. The regional district is even talking about an attendant. It's the way things are going, Nash. It's in the plan that council signed off on."

"The plan?"

"The solid-waste management plan."

"Which is what? A stone tablet handed down from God?"

Doyle didn't reply.

"About what I thought." Nash sneered. "Bullshit on paper. Doesn't mean a thing."

"If you don't stop, we will stop you."

"You and whose army?"

Doyle stiffened. "You'll be fined if I, we, catch you at it."

"Yeah, well, we know how that works out."

"This is your last warning."

Nash really missed his old dog now. If Jiminy were here, he would be barking and growling. It would have been fun to watch—Jiminy, who wouldn't know what to do with a squirrel if he caught one, suddenly fierce with territorial rage, and Doyle, fidgeting and backing toward his truck, watching the dog with one eye, Nash with the other.

"I mean it, Malone."

"I heard you the first time." *Officious little toad.*

Nash watched him drive away. "Solid-waste management, my arse," he muttered. "Bureaucrat!"

Nash swept a six-pack of beer cans into a clear plastic bag and shoved a wine jug across the table to June Fletcher.

"You had a bumper week," she said.

"I did." He didn't explain that he'd been to the dump every day last week, that it had taken that long for his ire to cool.

"Howard Doyle came to see me," June said.

Nash kept sorting.

"He wants me to stop taking your returns."

Nash stared at the bottle he was holding, a glass vodka cooler, two fuzzy, orange peaches on the smudged label. He slid the bottle across the table, swatted a tin into his bag.

"He says I'm abetting you. Encouraging you to keep scavenging, even though they've put a stop to it."

"Bah! All they've done is put up a sign." Nash gestured at the sorting table. "Why would they want to bury this? How does that make any kind of sense?"

"Agreed. They ought to do more to keep all of this out of the landfill. There's no argument for it. But I don't make the rules. I just try to live by them."

"You going to stop taking my bottles?"

"I might have to."

He sorted faster.

"Now, Nash, don't get mad."

He shook the bag, made space for a last arm's sweep of tins. Spun the plastic and knotted it. Across the table, June picked up her pencil. "How many?"

"Eight dozen." He didn't look at her. He carried the bag to the stack behind the table.

"With the glass, that brings you to fourteen seventy-five. Sound right to you?"

"You're the one setting the prices."

"Nash." Her voice softened. "I haven't said I would, only that Doyle was making noise."

"Makes no matter to me. I can always take my bottles to Kamloops when I go in the spring. You go on and keep Doyle happy. No skin off my nose."

June lifted out her cash box, counted his money, held it out.

"You can keep that, too. Give it to Howard Doyle next time he comes snooping around. Tell him I said it's an advance on my fine."

6

Maggie sealed the envelope on the last of the T4s, handwrote Mildred's Fort McMurray address. Their Beauty Creek house had sold. Mildred really wasn't ever coming back. She heard Dwight come in the back door. She'd sent him to pick up the mail, hoping there would be at least a few cheques. With the mill down, the January cash-flow crunch was worse than she'd expected.

Dwight stopped at her doorway. "You really need to get a door for your office, Maggie, and a proper nameplate."

There had never been a door, a leftover from the days of the central wood heater. Partitions that didn't reach the ceiling and no doors on anything except the completely enclosed bathroom that did double duty as the darkroom.

She might consider a door for her office. But a new sign? Never.

In the early years, she and Hank had joked about what title they might put on an office door if they ever got one. Publisher? Editor? Newsboy? Dogsbody? She'd gotten him the sign for Christmas, and he had howled with delight, nailed it to the wall with a three-inch spike, and there it stayed: shiny brass, custom engraved, the word *JANITOR* in sans serif type.

Dwight dropped the mail on the corner of her desk. She handed him his T4, he passed her a handwritten letter. "This one's from Harriet Lemsky."

"To The Editor," the letter began, in a flowing cursive script that belied its vicious tone. Maggie frowned as she read. Harriet had never really warmed to Beauty Creek, nor the town to her, and she'd always had it out for Nash Malone, but this was a new tactic.

"I see it's not a dump anymore."

"A sanitary landfill," Dwight quoted. "Keep going, it gets better."

"'...to invoke the mandated consequences for infractions to the democratically legislated rules,'" Maggie read aloud. "That's a mouthful."

"What are we going to do?" Whatever his failings, Dwight had a reporter's instinct for controversy.

"I'm going to think about it," she said. "This last part feels pretty close to libel."

"Because she names him?"

"Uh-huh."

"But it's the truth."

"Not quite. The truth is that Nash Malone collects bottles and cans and bicycle parts from the dump. Most of it he recycles, some of it he brings home. The libellous part is the suggestion that he is somehow"—she consulted the letter—"'immorally and capriciously creating a public health hazard.'"

"What's wrong with that?"

"*Capriciously*? I don't think that's the word she's looking for." She reached for her tattered dictionary. "*Capriciously*? It's a...No, wait, here we go. 'Capricious. Adjective. Erratic. Eccentric. Freakish.' There you go, Harriet's one up on me. That is exactly what she thinks of Nash Malone."

"So, we'll print it?"

"No. Capricious or otherwise, it's only her opinion that he's creating a health hazard, but she states it as a fact."

"If she said it was only her opinion, could we print it?"

"We could. But I might not."

"Why not?"

"Because it's mean-spirited. Because my name is on the masthead and I get to decide."

"But you print everything." He raised a cheeky eyebrow. "There's not something going on that you're not telling me about? You and Nash Malone?" He laughed, ducked, as her pen sailed toward him.

"Funny, Dwight." She tossed the letter onto her heaped file basket, looked over her glasses. "What else are you working on?"

He held up his hands, mock surrender. "All right, all right. I'm going. It's fire practice tonight and I heard they're going to burn that collapsing shed at Persky's old shake mill."

"Ought to be a cover shot in that," she said, and felt a small regret that she wouldn't be there, crouched in the darkness, waiting for the front-page photograph: volunteer firefighters in full gear, framed by leaping flames, maybe an arc of steaming water. "Don't scrimp on the film."

He left the building, whistling. Maggie sighed and thumbed through the mail. No cheques, plenty of bills.

"Nothing is ever as bleak as it seems," Hank would tell disheartened reporters. "Just tell yourself a new story." Lung cancer had been the only misfortune that Hank Evans couldn't turn into a better story.

Maggie settled herself at the desk behind the front counter with the ragged pile of submissions: minor-hockey news and a report from the district Lioness convention interleaved with the curling club's league scores and a long list of skaters who had moved up a level after the figure-skating club's trip to a test day in Clearwater. There was a short poem from Nash Malone, a delightfully sardonic caricature of a small-town bureaucrat. Unnamed, of course. Clearly he'd had another run-in with Doyle. She'd been sorry when Malone's old dog died. Some of his best poems had come out of his altercations with the village over that dog.

She powered up the computer, opened a new file and started on the figure skaters. It was tedious work but she took her time. In some skater's scrapbook, this clipping would eventually yellow with age, the least she could do was get the spelling right. She preferred working at night, alone, no one to bother her, the building creaking in the cold while she was safe and warm, the space heater at her toes and a hot cup of coffee to look forward to.

She had finished the typing and was shutting down the computer when she heard the back door. She expected it to be Dwight. It wasn't.

"Mayor Vanisle."

"Maggie Evans."

"You're up late."

"You too."

He stood at the curtain, beads sparkling around his shoulders. "I saw your lights."

Their eyes met. A long look. Maggie looked away.

Rufus Vanisle had arrived in Beauty Creek ten years ago. He and his wife had taken early retirement, sold their Vancouver condo, set out for the interior. They wanted to hike and fish and live in the country. Beauty Creek had appealed. Unfortunately for Rufus, the appeal had worn off pretty quickly for his wife. She'd left him two years ago; the current gossip was that they had since divorced. Maggie could have asked and he'd have told her. But she hadn't. She wasn't ready to know.

"You want coffee?" she asked.

"Coffee? At this time of night? I better not. Maybe some mint tea?"

They took their hot mugs to her office, slouched in the armchairs in front of the desk.

"You look tired," she said.

When old Mayor Jenkins keeled over from a heart attack in the middle of a council meeting—just as everyone had known he would—there hadn't been a rush to fill his seat. Rufus had been new enough not to know better, so he'd agreed to the hat-holding delegation that nominated him.

"It's been crazy ever since the election. I didn't realize what a mess things were in. Victoria keeps funnelling more paperwork our way... and Doyle. What's his story anyway?"

"He's been doing that job forever. Old Jenkins's wife's nephew, if I remember it right." She half smiled at his expression. "To be fair, Jenkins was sick for a long time and Doyle picked up the slack. It might have blurred the lines."

"That explains why he thinks he's in charge."

"He can be a bit of a stickler for the rules."

"Maggie Evans, queen of the understatement. Don't get me wrong, we need people like Doyle. They just shouldn't be in charge."

"He's not. You are."

"Tell him that. I don't know how we'll ever get rid of him." He hesitated. "This is off the record, right?"

She kicked his boot lightly. "We've always been off the record, haven't we?"

They'd had a moment, the two of them, in what Maggie thought of as her dark years: the dull, grey gap between Blake's departure for college and Hank's diagnosis. She'd bumped into Rufus at three a.m., in the smoky, foggy darkness outside the curling rink. It was the annual Businessmen's Bonspiel, mid-March, snowbanks melting, spring breakup just around the corner. Hank was regaling a table of drunks at the upstairs bar, and Millie Vanisle was on one of her extended vacations.

Since they'd been in no shape to drive, Maggie and Rufus had walked the dark streets and, when their fingers touched, they'd halted, haloed in the light that splashed out the front windows of Cooper's. Neither of them had been drunk enough not to know what they were doing, though Maggie had certainly been on the careless side of her inhibitions. They'd kissed, chaste to start, and then hungrily. It had been electric. Maggie had pulled away first, contemplated Rufus across the abyss that was her life. Beauty Creek was too small for secret love affairs. She knew it, even if he didn't.

Rufus set his empty mug onto her desk. "Maybe we should think about going on the record. You and I. One of these days." He spoke lightly, carelessly, but she could hear the question beneath it.

She grabbed the first thing that came to hand, plucked Harriet Lemsky's letter from the top of her teetering in-basket and asked, "What's this about? What're you guys doing out at the dump that's got Harriet in such a knot?"

He took the letter, scanned it. "Technically, she's right. The legislation says we're supposed to prevent scavenging."

"Why?"

"Why? Because Victoria says so. They enact legislation, they don't explain it."

"So, they want you to prevent scavenging at the Beauty Creek landfill while the City of Victoria dumps raw sewage into the Pacific Ocean?"

"That's it."

"It's ridiculous."

"Yep. Luckily we're a long way from Victoria."

She laughed.

"What?"

"That. *A long way from Victoria.* We might make a Creekster out of you yet, Rufus Vanisle, we just might."

She took the letter, tossed it back into her basket. "If you can ignore Victoria, I can ignore Harriet. I didn't want to print the damn thing anyway."

A contented moment passed. He nudged her boot. "Have dinner with me this week?"

Maggie pulled her feet in, stood. Went around her desk. Moved Harriet's letter into a different pile. "Did I tell you Blake found me a buyer?"

"For the *Chronicle*?"

"Apparently the Brownsfield Group is buying."

"Did they make an offer?"

"I haven't talked to them."

"Why not?"

She evaded his eyes. "I'm thinking about it."

"What would you do without the *Chronicle*?"

"Apparently they're keeping staff, so I might just stay and get paid every month to do exactly what I'm doing now."

"Or?"

"You mean, would I move away? Maybe. Blake and Glynnis would like me to come and babysit the grands."

"What do you want to do?"

She'd been asking herself the same question for weeks.

"Maybe you should consider other"—he winked—"attractive offers."

She didn't respond.

"What? We can't go on like this forever, we're getting too old for it."

"Who's old? I'm not that old. You sound like Blake. He thinks anyone over forty has one foot in the grave."

"You know what I mean. There's no reason for us to go on pretending. We're both free, single, consenting adults. Have dinner with me. Tomorrow's Friday, the new chef at the hotel will be cooking. Come on. We'll set the tongues a-wagging."

"Not yet."

"It's been years, Maggie. It's time. In fact, let's do it right now. Come, we'll get a slice of apple pie at Betty's before she closes."

"Not tonight." She touched the cover of her chequebook. "I need to get a start on these accounts payable before I call it a night."

After he'd gone, she paid bills until the bank balance called a halt. She forced herself to add up the unpaid invoices and then the meagre accounts receivable. The implacable numbers stared up at her. What was she going to do?

What do you want to do?

She dropped her pen, leaned back in her chair and tried to remember a time when she had known what she wanted.

When she'd left home at fifteen, nervous but resolute, she'd had no intention of ever coming back to Beauty Creek. That was what you did. You left and you kept going. The world, the future, was out there, somewhere.

She followed her brothers to her Aunt Lizzie's basement in East Vancouver for her final two years of high school. "Chin up," her father had said, on the platform that late-August morning, while her mother was inside grilling the station agent about how long they could expect to wait. "It will be difficult some days, but you are ready," he said. "Never forget—"

"I know," she teased, "the blood of voyageurs." It was a family joke, reserved for moments when their mother wasn't within earshot. Her stiff, English upper lip would purse when their father boasted about his checkered French Canadian genealogy.

"You all make fun, but it's there, in your eyes, in your smile." He touched his index finger to the dimple in her cheek. "You have the face of my mother, and, through her, the old instincts." His hands spoke, drawing ripples in the air. "The city, she is just another river. Some rapids, some shoals, some fast water, some slow. Listen to the river, and she will warn you what is coming."

Maggie had hated Vancouver, the raw stench of the briny ocean, the cruel social hierarchies of a high school with more people than all of Beauty Creek. Hated her aunt's horrible cookery and her haughty condescension about what she called Maggie's boondocks manners. There had been a succession of after-school and summer jobs to save her parents the burden of her room and board. But eventually she had learned to navigate the rapids. She found friends and a social circle. Working girls, they intended to conquer the city. They'd get office jobs downtown, date interesting men, go dancing or to the pictures on Saturday nights, attend openings and premieres, get art gallery memberships. Against the advice of her art teacher, Maggie gave up sketching and registered for bookkeeping classes. She went from graduation to a job in the accounting department at the *Vancouver Sun*. She met Hank, a junior reporter, at the Christmas party. They were married the next spring, a simple, civil ceremony, a small luncheon at the Hotel Vancouver. Her parents came on the train. Hank's parents drove in from the North Shore.

She'd known, then, what she wanted. They both had. Maggie would work until they started their family. A small family, they thought, one boy, one girl. Hank would rise through the ranks, get a byline and then a column. Maggie would do volunteer work while she raised their family, take her turn on the PTA, maybe even the school board. When they retired to the Island, she'd return to her sketching, dabble in oils. Hank would tend their gardens and raise goats.

Then she brought Hank home to Beauty Creek—June 1965—for her father's retirement party. She'd been nervous, afraid her brothers wouldn't like Hank, that the animosity would be mutual. She'd also been apprehensive of what Hank would think of her hometown. After seven years in the city, she'd heard a lifetime's worth of jibes about the backwoods. She was afraid that the town, in all its rough ordinariness, would somehow diminish her in Hank's eyes.

Instead, from the minute they stepped onto the wooden platform, Hank had loved everything about Beauty Creek. "Look!" he exclaimed. "Look at that!" A Creekster from birth, Maggie had been taking Wolverine Mountain for granted for a long time. Yes, she agreed, it was a postcard view. Yes, the air was marvellous. Yes, the creek did make a lovely sound. Yes, Cooper's store really was something. Yes, she did know that they sold gut lacing for snowshoes and crosscut blades alongside squat glass bottles of Devonshire clotted cream.

When Hank wanted to visit again at Christmas, she joked that she'd only go if they drove. "You need to understand how far it is, what the winters are like."

He had jumped at the challenge, and they had driven up through the canyon and on from Cache Creek to Kamloops and north. As the snow got deeper, and the air grew colder, Hank just got happier. For him, it was always about the story, and this would be a doozy. The heater in the Buick froze up somewhere north of Clearwater, so they dived into their suitcases for extra layers and drove on. They drove in darkness, wipers squeaking across the icy windshield, wheels scrunching over the snowy road. Hank occasionally swiped an ice layer from the window in front of his face as he peered out at the narrow track between the looming snowbanks.

They'd limped into her parents' driveway at two in the morning, her father coming to the door, hugging her tight, sighing against her shoulder, scolding her for worrying her mother.

The drive back to the coast had been equally eventful: a steaming radiator near the top of Messiter Summit, overheated brakes on their way down the canyon, an overnight stay in Hope for repairs. When they finally chugged into their West Twenty-Second driveway, Maggie had been quietly confident that they were back to stay.

She'd gotten a promotion and a pay raise that spring. They talked about buying a house, Beauty Creek nothing more than an entertaining story for dinner parties.

And then.

Coincidence collided with fate and dropped the *Beauty Creek Chronicle* into Hank's lap. Or that was how he told it.

Meant to be, he'd always say. This from a man who didn't believe in God, or destiny, or anything much beyond the impossible pursuit of objectivity in journalism.

He'd offered to run down a few leads for a fellow reporter who'd been up late with sick kids. In a file of clippings from an Edmonton newspaper, background for a story on the tar sands, were two brief paragraphs about an Edmonton tycoon divesting himself of newspapers to sink his capital into bitumen. In the list of weeklies that were on the block: the *Beauty Creek Chronicle*. If she'd had a nickel for every time she heard Hank tell the story, she'd be able to pay the printer.

"I was on the blower the next day. Called him up, made the deal over the telephone. He thought he'd put one over on me. I thought I'd got a hell of a bargain. Hard to know who was right."

What Hank had purchased, sight unseen, was a decrepit building, clad in tar paper and shiplap, a hodgepodge of archaic printing equipment, five hundred dollars worth of supplies and inventory, and a newspaper with a circulation hovering at 450, half subscribers, half newsstand. The paper sold for ten cents, an annual subscription was three dollars, or you could get two years for a five-dollar bill.

Maggie's reaction had been part of Hank's legend. "The wife thought I'd lost my mind," he'd say. He had already made the deal by the time he told her.

"The newspaper in Beauty Creek?"

"Yes!"

"But…why?"

He could be his own man there. That wasn't how he told it to their friends, but that was the phrase Maggie remembered. His own man.

"You'll be close to your folks," he said—as if she had ever once pined for her mother.

She'd tried to dissuade him. Did he have a clue what he'd be giving up? There was no movie theatre, no art gallery, no taxicabs, no social life beyond the beer parlour, the curling club and the legion.

"Pfft," he said. "Empty amusements for empty lives." Did she know how little they could buy a house for? Or, better, they'd buy a lot, build a house.

"I don't want to," she had eventually admitted. "I have lived there. It's the back of beyond, Hank. You have no idea. Besides, it's … it's …" What was it about Beauty Creek that she understood that Hank did not? "It's the past!"

"Yes! That's it exactly, Mags. It *is* the past. It isn't polluted with this ugly, modern"—he waved at their new dining-room set—"glass and moulded plywood and plastic. We can do something real there." Hank had grown up in Vancouver. To him it was as much a backwater as Beauty Creek, a smug, provincial city with pretensions.

"But—"

"And Creeksters don't care," he crowed. "That's the best part, don't you see? They know they're living in the past and they don't care. They're doing it on purpose."

"Not all of them." She tried to make him see that his idealistic version wasn't reality, that broken lives and broken dreams lived as uncomfortably in Beauty Creek as they did on Skid Row.

He swept aside her protests. "Let's just try it for five years," he coaxed. "We're young; we've got nothing holding us here. If you hate it, we can come back. I'll always be able to find work."

Maggie acquiesced, never doubting that they'd end up back at the coast after the first winter. But she'd been wrong. Hank had fallen in love with the idea of Beauty Creek. The difficulties, and there were many, just made him more determined. He never got over the idea that he had discovered the town, and that its progress was his life's work. He and his newspaper were going to put Beauty Creek *on the map*. Another story she could have retired on.

Retirement.

Was that what she wanted?

She eyed the pile of receipts to be posted, pictured a life without deadlines and unpaid bills—without a newspaper. She spun her Rolodex and stopped at Brownsfield's phone number.

What would Hank do?

Not that.

Dwight dropped a stack of mail onto the counter and handed Maggie a sheaf of typewritten pages. "Village Council Minutes."

She sighed.

"Do you want me to type them up?"

"No. Keep working on your captions for the peewee tournament. Felicia wants to lay out those pages this afternoon." She scanned the minutes. Doyle was a stickler for procedure, so they were easy to follow. Maggie let Dwight skip the meetings. Nothing newsworthy happened at them anyway, or that's what she told Hank's restless ghost. Instead, Dwight picked up the minutes from the village office and Maggie typed them up. Dull as they were, folks in Beauty Creek, who also skipped the meetings, wanted to know what went on. Occasionally there was an item that could be broken out into a news story.

"What's this about untidy premises? Has Harriet Lemsky been agitating again?"

"You won't like that one," Dwight called from his side of the wall, "but they're all in favour." His chair squealed as he rolled to the beads. "I asked Doyle. They gave it three readings at once; they'll do the final reading next month."

"What happens after that?"

He came the rest of the way through the curtain. "The village crew can clean up an untidy lot and charge the owner for the pleasure."

"Who's going to decide what's untidy? Not Doyle, I hope?"

"It's part of that new 'progressive communities' thing."

"I suppose they'll be after me next." There had been some muttering when she'd spruced up the front of the *Chronicle* building with a siding of cedar shakes. Not everyone loved cedar as much as Maggie did. Fire hazard, a few had murmured. Ugly, said others.

"Don't worry," Dwight said. "It's not about your building. They want the junk gone from that old industrial site on First Avenue. The rest of Persky's mill. Probably Nash Malone's place."

"Bah. I wish people would just leave him alone. It's not his fault the town moved in on him. When he built out there, his was the only house within half a mile. In those days..."

Dwight leaned away. Maggie knew the look. He didn't want to hear another one of her rants about what Beauty Creek once was.

"Pull up a chair, kid," Hank used to say to the new reporters. "You need to know the history of the place, if you want to understand it." He'd send them home with the back issues, quiz them on founding families, and then, lest they believe history began there, he'd lecture them on BC's more distant past. "This was a multicultural place long before the Europeans arrived. Seven or eight language families, each as different as Mandarin is from English. At least thirty distinct languages..." Maggie was content if Dwight got his stories in on time. But maybe Hank had a point. "Before the highway—"

"I know, I know. Before the highway, everybody lived along the tracks except a handful of farmers, Nash Malone, and the single guys from the section crew out at Bachelor Flats. Mail came on the train. Groceries came on the train. Company came on the train. Cars came on the train. The train, the train, the train... my kingdom for a train." Dwight mimed an elaborate bow.

She laughed.

"It's not just you," he said. "I had a few beers with Stan O'Leary at the legion the other night. He was on about how it used to be. Almost made me wish I'd been here for it."

"Stan O'Leary. That would have been a story. It was something special. Not all sweetness and light, don't get me wrong, but different." She tapped the tidy minutes. "Less regulated, no village council, no police, no building inspector."

Maggie and her friends had grown up outdoors, fishing and building tree forts along the ridge. On mighty excursions to the shores of the North Thompson, they panned for gold with pie plates borrowed from their mothers' cupboards. They hiked miles of track searching for agates in the railroad gravel and dreamed of the day they'd build a raft and float all the way to Kamloops. Maggie was the only one of her parents' noisy brood still here. Even her folks had eventually moved to the Okanagan, attracted by the sunshine, the shorter winters, the fruit trees.

Felicia ducked through the curtain. "Are the classifieds ready?"

Mildred would have had the week's ads typed up, proofed and formatted, ready for Felicia to drop in around the legal notices for timber-sale licences and storage liens. "I'll do them right now," Maggie said.

Felicia and Dwight were hunched over their respective keyboards when Maggie brought Felicia the floppy disk of classified ads. "It's past suppertime, you two."

"I already called home," Felicia said. "Dillon is feeding the kids. He makes a mean chili con carne. He mixes one can of mild with one can of spicy and heats it through." She took the disk from Maggie, turned back to her monitor.

Dwight, fingers poised, waiting for inspiration, hadn't moved.

Maggie returned to the stack of mail on the front counter. Another bank envelope. Another cash offer.

What do you want to do?

She caressed the blank cheques. *Why not?* She knew Hank would.

She walked to the curtain, called through. "Felicia? Do you remember that 'Office Help' ad? The one we ran when Mildred was away for her operation?"

Felicia wheeled in her chair. "I can find it."

"Run it."

Dwight and Felicia high-fived each other across the room.

Maggie laughed out loud, and she was still smiling as she began to type the council minutes.

7

Stevie scowled at the computer screen. They were learning how to format tabs and she was longing for her high-school typewriter and its simple, precise, *manual* tab stops. She took a deep breath and sat up straight, arranging her body the way she had learned in the drafty classroom at Deighton High. Elbows close to her body; forearms parallel to the keyboard. Wrists down. Feet flat on the floor. Fingers on the home keys.

She had loved typing and consistently got top marks. She never tired of the repetitive exercises, counting the words, calculating her words per minute. "Take your time," their teacher, Mr. Perkins, had always cautioned. "If your fingers learn only the correct stroke, they will know it forever." He'd been right about that. The lessons learned had remained in her fingers. The computer was new, the funny soft keys, no paper, text just appearing on the screen, none of the crisp chatter of a typewriter, but the letters were in exactly the same places.

At their first class, Carol, the business teacher at Beauty Creek High, started them out on simple typing drills. Stevie had felt a bit smug, the youngest in the group, fingers comfortable on the keyboard. It didn't last. Their next class, Carol began teaching them how to use the computer. Apart from the familiar letters, it was all new. The keyboard controlled everything. There were commands to make a blank page appear, commands to align the text, commands to print. Stevie's brain swam from trying to keep it straight: Control, Alt, Enter, Escape, the multiple functions of the F keys along the top of the keyboard.

Carol was helpful but tough. "You try it," she'd say. "What do you think you need to do?"

Stevie would sigh, and try, and her text would leap across the page or disappear into thin air. Tonight's lesson had been particularly humbling. She pressed the Tab key and her cursor shot all the way to the right margin. She groaned.

"That's enough for tonight," Carol called. "Don't worry if you didn't get it. It will come with practice."

Stevie shut down the computer, pulled the cover over the dark screen, and said good night to her classmates.

At the cafe, she left the car running, ducked through the blowing snow and went inside to fetch the girls. Betty was at the staff table, folding paper napkins around settings of forks and knives. Alvin Tilburt was at the table opposite, working his way through a slice of apple pie.

"Girls," Betty called, and Brit and Peg bounded from the back room.

"Out on a date, is it?" Alvin teased.

Stevie ignored him.

"You get him to come in next time," Alvin said. "I'll check him out. Some shady characters in this town." He laughed at his own joke.

Stevie blushed, bent to help Peg with her coat.

"Shady characters," Alvin repeated. "Sniffing around, waiting for a nice girl like you."

Stevie could feel the heat in her cheeks. Brit thrust herself forward, into the space between Alvin and Stevie. "My Mom goes to school on Wednesday nights." She stared Alvin down. "She's … she's … *learning.*"

"There you have it, Alvin," Betty said, with a smug nod in Stevie's direction. "Our Stevie is learning."

In the car, crawling along the snowy street, Stevie replayed it in her head. They were right. It was frustrating and slow but she was learning.

"Mom?"

"Yes?"

"Remember how I said we were working on a history project at school?"

"The one where the old people came and you asked them questions about the olden days?"

"Yes. We each wrote a report and next week we're having a kind of fair where the old people come and see what we did."

"That sounds nice."

"It's at night, so our parents can come too. It's next…"

Stevie braked gently, felt the wheels slide on the snow, braked again, eased up to the stop sign. "Which night?"

"Wednesday."

"Ah, Brit, no. I can't. You know I can't. I have class." She accelerated slowly.

"Couldn't you miss it one time?"

"No. I couldn't."

At home, Brit got out, slammed her door and stomped up the steps. Stevie helped Peg with her seatbelt. "I can't go," she said, to Peg's stern scrutiny. "I have class."

Both girls were quiet the next morning, dawdling over their cereal. Exasperated, Stevie lashed out, "Look, you knew when you asked that I wouldn't be able to. Why did you even ask me? Just so I'd feel bad? I'm only taking this stupid class so I can maybe someday get a job where I don't have to work at night. I'm doing the best I can, dammit."

Brit glowered. Peg left the table, carrying her empty bowl. Brit followed, muttering as she went by.

"What was that?"

"Nothing."

Stevie clenched her lips together. She'd heard it. *Dad would.* It was too much.

"He would not," she barked. "He wouldn't even be here. He'd be somewhere in camp. In Mackenzie or Fort Nelson. We'd see him once every three weeks for five days. And"—she couldn't help it—"he's not your dad."

Brit shoved Peg aside, and dropped her bowl into the sink. Peg cried out and scurried down the hall.

"Now look what you've done." Stevie grabbed Brit's shoulder, shook it. "That's it. I've had it. You can walk to school, miss. Right now, coat and boots and go. You can forget about after-school television, too, until your attitude improves." The words were out of her mouth, her finger wagged, imperious: her mother's voice, her mother's finger. She watched Brit, chin quivering as she pushed her feet into her too-small boots, her fingers struggling with her zipper, and Stevie wanted to go to her but she didn't.

Carol laid a folded newspaper on top of Stevie's typing exercise. "Did you see this?" An ad was circled: "Office Help Wanted."

"I've never worked in an office."

Carol laughed. "This is Beauty Creek," she said. "Everyone here does jobs they've never done before. You should apply. You're exactly what Maggie Evans needs."

"I've got a job."

"This one is full-time, and I expect it will pay more, and it's weekdays. No evenings."

"What about Betty?"

"Ask her, see what she says."

Stevie didn't have to. Two days later, Betty brought it up. They were making pies, in the midafternoon lull between lunch and the three o'clock coffee crowd. Stevie was peeling apples, Betty was rolling pastry.

"Carol thinks you should apply for that job at the *Chronicle*."

Stevie dropped a long curl of peel into the basin between her knees. That Carol, the nerve.

"I think you should, too," Betty continued. "You'll like Maggie Evans, and she will really like you."

Stevie cored the peeled apple with a spoon. "She'll never hire me." She sliced the apple into a glass bowl, plucked up another apple, twisted off its stem. "I've never worked in an office in my life. I've got no experience."

"You'd never waited tables when I hired you."

"That's not the same."

"You'll never know if you don't apply."

"I already know."

Betty draped pastry over her rolling pin. "Ready."

Stevie scooped a generous portion of Betty's secret mix of sugar, cinnamon and tapioca pearls over the sliced apples, stirred and tipped the filling into the empty shell. Betty covered it with pastry and pinched around the rim. Stevie went back to peeling.

"These are excellent apples," she said.

"Nice try." Betty set the finished pie aside, dusted her pastry board with flour. "Even if she doesn't hire you, it would be good practice to apply and go for the interview. You're too smart to work here for the rest of your life."

"I like working here."

"And I like having you here, but that's not what we're talking about."

"I don't have anything to wear."

"You don't have a pair of black dress pants and a white shirt?"

It was her daily uniform. "Yes, I have a selection of black dress pants and white shirts."

"That's all you need. As long as there's no ketchup stain."

They laughed. Betty flopped pastry into an empty pie tin, smoothed it against the sides with floured fingers. She picked up the tin and turned it slowly, holding a table knife steady along the edge, trimming away the excess.

"But I'd also need a resumé. And, maybe, you know, some actual experience for when she asks me what I know about working in an office."

"You tell her you can type. Carol says you're a whiz on the keyboard. You can proofread. You can run a cash register. Tell her that you'll learn anything she puts in front of you. That you'll show up on time. You don't realize how rare a thing that is, showing up when you've said you would."

Carol made the whole class type resumés. Stevie wasn't the only person who thought she had nothing to put on one.

"Just for practice," Carol said to the reluctant class, looking at Stevie with a completely straight face.

They began with the section on education. Stevie's was one line: "Grade 10, Deighton Secondary, 1987."

"No first aid? Or maybe a Superhost course?"

"No," she whispered.

The next section was worse.

"But I haven't got any work experience."

"You've never worked?"

"Babysitting when I was thirteen. A few odd jobs at different camps."

"Put it all in."

She did. The babysitting from high school, the six weeks as cook's helper at Big Bob's logging camp outside Mackenzie, when she'd gone north with Bobby the winter after they got married. She hadn't gone back after Christmas because Brit was due in January. After that she'd been home with babies, making Bobby's lunch when he wasn't away in camp, cooking supper, hanging diapers on the clothesline, watching soap operas. The years with Kurt had been more of the same. Stevie typed the paltry lines and knew she'd never get the job. Who was she kidding?

Next came the section for references. Carol said she needed two, one from an employer, one personal. The first was easy, Betty had been pleased to be asked. Stevie suggested Mrs. Marsonkowsky for the second, but Carol said it would be better if it was someone who knew her longer, someone with a bit higher standing in the community. "Maybe someone from Deighton?"

Stevie would have put it off, but Carol insisted she submit her resumé that week. "You can't get the job if you don't apply," she said.

Stevie steeled herself, dialled the Jeffers Logging number from memory. Bobby's father had a long reach, even in Beauty Creek they would recognize his name.

Big Bob's secretary, Pearl, was delighted to hear from her and was confident he would give her a reference. "You go on and put him down, hon. I know he won't mind."

On Monday, slogging through the lunch dishes, Stevie heard the unmistakable voice, booming. "Betty, how the hell are you? Been ages. I hear you've got my girl working here."

His girl.

They'd barely seen Big Bob after she'd let Kurt move in. He hadn't approved and he hadn't been shy about letting her know.

They greeted each other awkwardly and it was Betty who suggested they use the staff table at the back of the cafe. Big Bob got right to the point. "Come on home to Deighton," he said. "Pearl needs some help in the office, and your trailer is just sitting empty. I'll pay you proper wages and you won't need to worry about the rent. The kids can go to their dad's school, grow up with some of his friends around."

Stevie examined her pruned fingers. *Her trailer.* It hadn't ever been hers, or Bobby's, for that matter, even though Big Bob had made a big show at the wedding, as if he was making them a gift of it. Somehow his name was always on the title, and, after six months, rent became a regular deduction from Bobby's paycheques. For their own good, Big Bob had explained. "Important to pay your own way in life."

It had been brand new, that trailer, a doll house on wheels, with a built-in dishwasher and a bay window. Vivian had helped her choose furnishings. The black leather recliner had been Bobby's Christmas gift from his folks. Peg wouldn't remember living there, but Brit might.

"When are the kids off school for spring break?"

The kids. He couldn't even remember their names. "Not until March."

"That will work. We'll be off for breakup. I'll send a crew with a couple trailers and we can load you up. Have you back home by Easter."

"No," she said. "I can't."

"Not that week?"

"No."

"When?"

"I don't mean the date. I mean no, not that."

"You can't stay here."

"Why not?"

"Look around you. The place is dead. You won't have a job inside six months."

"I might."

"You won't."

"I need to find out for myself." Her shoulders crept toward her ears.

"There's nothing to find out. You've got no family here. No friends. Come home."

"This is our home now." She peeled a strip of soft skin from the side of her thumb.

"Stevie, don't be stupid. I know, I should have come sooner, and I'm sorry I didn't. I hadn't heard."

"Hadn't heard?"

"That the bum absconded."

"He didn't. I kicked him out."

"I told Pearl, when she said you called. I said, she's finally come to her senses. I knew you would. You always were Jeffers material."

Jeffers material? Who was he kidding? He'd never thought she was Jeffers material. He'd always thought it was her fault. That Bobby never got to the NHL. That Bobby never got out of Deighton. He probably thought it was her fault that Bobby died.

"This is our home now," she repeated, forcing herself to look him in the eye. "I promised the girls we wouldn't move again. I've applied for a new job. That's why I need the reference."

He was going to argue when something outside the cafe caught his attention. Stevie followed his distracted gaze; a loaded logging truck had pulled up across the street. "Well, if you're sure," he said, and pushed back his chair.

Fear rose in her throat like bile. *Sure?* When had she ever been sure? She watched him walk away. He opened the door, held it, turned back to give her one last chance. She knew she should move, smile, nod. She knew she should take his job—no resumé required—take the trailer, take the advice. Her mother would say it was the sensible thing to do. Everyone would. Stomach quaking, she watched him walk away. The door slowly squeezed itself closed behind him.

8

The headlights lit up the frosty willows along the roadside, a ghostly legion marching down the narrow corridor of light. There was no reason for Nash to have set off this early, but he'd been awake, the barren woodshed nagging.

Alvin had offered to bring him wood. "I got a couple loads out of Bolan's slash pile. Doubt he'd mind if I brought a load for you."

"I can get my own firewood," Nash had snapped.

"Suit yourself. There's plenty there. He's at Twenty Mile on the Little Beauty."

Nash drove steadily, the truck finally warming, the radio cutting in and out, the day dawning. When he pulled in to the landing, he was dismayed to find Bolan and his crew already at work. He'd gotten the impression from Alvin that they were done on this block. At least the slash pile was off to one side. He'd be well clear of them. He parked near the faded orange crummy that passed as an ambulance and got out. Bolan's oldest boy, JD, was climbing up into the loader. Nash lifted his chain saw out of the box, gestured at the slash pile. JD waved a gloved hand.

Nash popped the tailgate, set the saw down, and leaned into the truck box for his jug of mixed gas. He felt a breath of air cross his cheek, heard a sudden *pop* and the back window of his pickup disintegrated. He dropped to the ground. Across the landing, the skidder was powering away up the hill, bouncing across ruts, pedal to the metal. One of its churning tires had launched a missile. Nash struggled to his feet and popped the driver's door. Atop the rubble of shattered glass was a short chunk of pine, one end shredded by chained tires, the other end a blunt saw cut. He picked it off the seat. No more than a foot long, but a solid two-inch diameter.

JD panted up beside him. "Fuck that was close!"

Nash held out the length of pine.

"I saw it go by you. It damn near took your head off. You okay?"

"Yep."

"Dad's gonna kill us both."

"Alvin said your dad wouldn't mind if I took a load of firewood out of the slash pile."

"Well, no, he wouldn't, but on the weekend, man. Not while we're working. Shit. Are you sure you're not hurt?" He shook off his glove and raised his hand toward Nash's face.

Nash leaned away, too late.

"I thought so." JD displayed his fingertips, tinged with blood. "It did hit you. You better let me take a look."

Nash jerked backward, lost his balance, fell.

When he came to, he was on the ground beside the ambulance, the entire Bolan crew on their knees around him. JD had a paper package in his mouth, tearing open a compress, and Bolan himself was dabbing at his cheek with an antiseptic wipe. He tried to rise, but the faller on one side and the bucker on the other held him down.

"Not yet, old man," Bolan said. "We just about got you cleaned up. Set still."

Above the cluster of hard hats, and the steam from their breath, Nash could see the sky and dying trees on the hillside behind the slash pile; red pines springing from the discarded bones of the old forest, skeletons that would become the ash that would feed a new forest, for a new generation. There was a poem in that.

His vision blurred as he slipped in and out of consciousness. Now the pile seemed to be moving away from him, invisible horses skidding it off down a grease road. Nash heard the grunt as they hit their collars. Heard a teamster calling.

Gee, Tip, gee.

Now, haw. Haw, Tip, haw. Haw Blaze. Git up there, git up.

Nash could see the steam of breath rising above the pile, could hear the creak and groan of dead wood, and the ghosts of bush teams crying.

"Malone!"

It was Bolan, calling him back, out of the bewildering fog of horses and bones.

"Malone!"

"What happened?" Nash twisted against the hands restraining him. "Is everybody okay?"

"We're okay, Malone, but you got smacked pretty hard. You're gonna need a few stitches." Bolan moved his index finger back and forth in front of Nash's eyes. "You probably have a bit of concussion. But your eyes are tracking properly, so I'd say you're gonna live. If you let JD get a dressing on it, we'll get you into the crummy and I'll…"

Bolan's voice faded.

Haw, Tip, haw! The horses were coming at him now, two massive Percherons, eight thundering hooves, powering across the landing, lunging through deep snow, breath billowing.

"Malone!"

It was Bolan again, but he was far away. A cold wind was blowing. Nash shivered.

"Get that insulated blanket."

A cold wind flung snow into his face. Inexplicably, the horses were in front of him now, the reins through his fingers, the slash pile at his back. Nash urged the horses forward, faster. They had to stay ahead of the pile. They were on the top of the block; he could see the valley bottom, far below. The skid trail snaked off through the slash and pecker poles and Nash knew they would never get down alive. They were picking up speed; he could feel the frozen ruts in his backbone, undulating hollows, then a short rattle as they crossed a section of washboard. There had to be a way to cut the horses loose. He wrapped the reins around the useless brake, stepped down between them. He was a dead man anyway, why not try?

"Malone?"

Not now, Bolan.

The horses were running hard, Nash could feel the pile pressing on his back, crushing him. He fought to stay upright. He had to save the horses.

"Nash! Can you hear me? Open your eyes, Nash. Open your eyes."

The dull, grey ceiling of the Bolan crummy was ridged. There was a splotch of red chain oil right above him. It was the shape of a horse. Legs here, tail there. Mane flying. A red horse.

"Malone?"

Nash grunted. It was all he could manage. His tongue was thick, dry.

"We're nearly there."

Nash tried to move, but it was too hard. He had been crushed by the slash pile, a heavy log immobilized his legs, branches and debris criss-crossed his upper body. Beyond the jumbled mountain of slash, he could see the sky. The sun was coming up and a delicate pink orange was swelling out of the east. He felt the light warm his face. The slash pile dissolved into it, and Nash slept.

He came to just outside the town and was fully conscious by the time they got to the hospital, sharp enough to deflect questions about how he'd been hurt. "Doing firewood," he lied. "My own foolishness." The doctor, a young locum, took him at his word.

"Appreciate that, Nash," Bolan said, after he'd seen him stitched up, fitted with a blue nightgown and propped in a hospital bed for a night of observation. "Be no end to the workers' comp paperwork otherwise."

"Told him the truth. It was my own foolishness. I put you to a lot of trouble today."

"No worries. Breaks the monotony. Gives the boys a story, and a lesson. I won't have to be ragging on them about their hard hats for a couple days."

Nash saw lights in his driveway and went to the window. It was Bolan's crew cab, loaded to the nines with firewood. Nash shoved his feet into his boots. They could just take that wood along to someone who needed it. He might be slowing down, but he wasn't so old that he needed charity firewood.

He was too late. By the time he got outside, they were already backed up to the woodshed and were unloading. There was no way to refuse without being a bigger arse than he'd already been. He fidgeted at the periphery, watching the young bucker in the back of the truck tossing wood to JD, who tossed it on to Bolan, who was stacking. He envied them their easy camaraderie, the rough jesting, a circle of men who knew just what to expect from each other. Nash moved the chopping block out of Bolan's way.

"No need for this," he said, "but I appreciate it just the same."

"No worries." Bolan towered, a broad-shouldered, black-haired man smelling of pine pitch and chain oil and diesel fuel. "The boys suggested it. Friday afternoon, we always wrap up a bit early, we had the time."

Nash stuttered another thank you.

Bolan clapped him on the shoulder. "We all get a turn, eh? Sometimes we give, sometimes we get. That's what my old dad always said."

Nash had been tempted to take the stitches out himself, save the bother of a visit to the doctor's office, but the receptionist who phoned to remind him about the appointment had been so pleasantly insistent that he had yielded. No harm letting them do their jobs.

His was the first appointment, so he was alone in the waiting room when Alvin dropped into the seat beside him.

"Hey, old-timer!"

Nash winced. Inside a building, Alvin always sounded three times louder than necessary.

"Haven't seen much of you this last month," Alvin continued.

"Just keeping the fire going," Nash said.

"Yeah, cold, eh? Though nothing like the old days."

"True enough."

"What're you in for?"

"Nothing much. You?"

"Bit of gout. But you're okay?"

"Yep. How's your mother?"

"She's dandy. What'd you say you're here for?"

It was rarely this much trouble to get Alvin to talk about himself. Nash plucked a magazine from the coffee table in front of them.

Alvin whispered, "I heard from Bolan what happened."

Nash thumbed through the magazine without replying. He hadn't pegged Old Man Bolan for a blabbermouth. Probably the kid.

"He said you gave them a helluva scare. Was it really twenty stitches?"

Nash slapped the magazine closed, tossed it to the table. "Wouldn't have happened if you'd told me they were working up there."

Alvin was unfazed. "Thought you knew. Thought everybody knew."

"I didn't."

"Can I see it?" Alvin reached for the bandage.

Nash recoiled. "Don't touch me, you fool. What's the matter with you?"

"No need to bite my head off."

"No need to be so damn nosy."

Alvin huffed, shifted to the far side of his chair.

"Mr. Malone," the receptionist called. Not a minute too soon.

The doctor was the same locum who had done the stitching. He gently and expertly pulled the six stitches, paused to admire his own handiwork. "There won't be much of a scar. Have you had any pain? Dizziness? Nausea?"

"Nope." The dent in his pride would be the only lasting repercussion.

"Reflexes can slow a bit in old age," the doctor said. "You need to factor that into your decision making. Especially for high-risk activities."

The doctor went out. Nash tarried putting his shirt on, waited until he heard Alvin talking in the examination room next door. Then he donned his coat and hurried out of the building.

9

Maggie unlocked the door and made her morning rounds. She'd been advertising for weeks, but she was still working the morning shift. With the mill down, a lot of stay-at-home moms were job hunting, but only one resumé listed any computer experience, and even it was far from promising.

She flipped the front window sign to Open. The carpet in the main aisle was spotted with mud, so she dragged out the vacuum cleaner. She was plugging it in when the phone rang.

"Maggie?"

The bottom of Maggie's stomach dropped away. Blake's wife never called her. "Glynnis? Is everything all right?"

"Oh, yes, we're fine. I just wanted to call and say congratulations! Blake finally got around to telling me your news!"

There was a perkiness to Glynnis that had always irked. "My news?"

"About the man who wants to buy the *Chronicle*. I'm so happy for you. You've been waiting for so long for this."

Maggie had been meaning to call Blake. She had.

Glynnis babbled on. "I know Blake would never tell you, but he's glad too."

"Really?"

"Yes, because we have some news, too. You remember how we've been looking for a property out of town—we have to get out of this neighbourhood—and, we found one! It has a small cherry orchard and a guesthouse that would be perfect for you. It's not on the market yet, the realtor says the owners aren't sure if they are ready to retire, but it would be such a wonderful spot for the whole family! And, a mother-in-law suite that's a whole house, wouldn't that be something?"

Maggie paced to the end of the telephone cord. "Um, that's something to think about but, uh, the paper isn't exactly sold. Best not to count our chickens—"

"Oh, Blake is sure it will sell. They're buying up any old paper, as long as it's in the interior."

Maggie stretched her jaw.

"It will be great to have you closer," Glynnis continued. "I've been wanting to get back to work, but Blake worries about the kids. With you here, they could just get off the bus after school. They'd love it."

"Glynnis? Sorry, but I've got to go. There's a customer in the store. Tell Blake I'll call him. Love to the kids."

Maggie returned to the vacuum. Thrusting down the aisle between the shelves, she reached the end of the cord, shoved hard and ripped the plug from the wall socket. The powerful recoil spring whipped it across the carpet, whacking her ankle on its way by. She jumped, hopped two steps, fell into the cardboard greeting-card rack, and tumbled with it to the floor.

"Dammit... *Glynnis!*" She lay on her back, glaring at the ceiling. The tiles were beginning to sag, and the light fixture was rife with spiderwebs and dead flies. *Damn. Damn. Damn.*

It wasn't all Glynnis. That was too easy. Glynnis did the best she could. Three kids under ten, plus Blake, who, like his father, was a hard worker, but not much of a parent. This phone call was pure Blake. He'd always been a bit of a sneak, playing Hank off against Maggie, now using Glynnis to nudge her toward Brownsfield. *Little shit.*

It was midnight and Maggie was working through her bookkeeping backlog, when Rufus Vanisle tapped on her door jamb.

"I see you're hiring," he said.

"Are you thinking of applying? Because you'd make my short list. How well do you take instruction?"

"That could be a problem."

"Typing?"

"Sorry, no. Hunt and peck."

"Computer skills?"

"Ha! I wish." He smiled. "But, wait a minute, I'm pretty sure I heard from a very reliable source that you were thinking of selling."

She took off her glasses. "I said that, didn't I? And I thought about it, I really did, but I can't sell Hank's paper to a chain."

"You don't owe Hank Evans a thing. You've done your time."

"I know, but—"

"You're not doing him any favours by running yourself into the ground with this damn paper. You're not." His voice softened. "He's gone, Maggie."

"You think I don't know that? You think I go home to that empty house and I'm confused about that?"

"Of course not. I'm just—"

"Believe me, I know that I'm only one person." She threw her hand out, and receipts fluttered to the floor.

Rufus knelt, gathered them up, paused on one knee. "This isn't the time to talk to you, is it?"

"Probably not. I've got to get this paperwork done."

"I'll catch you another night." His voice was neutral.

Maggie dropped her head into her hands. She heard Rufus stand and wait for her to look up. She heard his boots against the carpet when he paused in the doorway to look back at her. She didn't move until she heard the back door close. She wanted to get up and go after him, she wanted to walk through the quiet streets with him, she wanted—

"Enough," she said out loud. She lifted her chin. "Enough."

She picked up a receipt. Barber Ellis. Paper supplier. Three hundred and sixty-nine dollars and eighty-five cents. When had paper gotten this expensive? Below it, the bills for darkroom supplies: developer, fixer, stop bath, more costly paper. Rufus was right. Blake was right. Glynnis was right. She should just sell.

Harriet Lemsky pounded the countertop with a closed fist.

"It is against the law," she shouted. "Why doesn't anyone see that? I am not the culprit. I'm not trespassing against everyone's privacy, rooting through their garbage, hauling home God knows what to stack in my back yard. I'm not the problem, why doesn't anyone see that?" She stalked down the aisle and slammed out the front door, setting the doorbell jangling.

Maggie retreated through the beads to the coffee pot.

Felicia came out of the darkroom. "What was that about?" she asked.

"Her letter we didn't print."

"Dwight showed me," Felicia said. "I'm glad you didn't print it."

"I just wish I had handled this better. You know what they say: the customer is always right."

"I don't think she's going to be much of a customer. Pretty sure I heard some hollering about subscriptions being cancelled."

"You could hear us in the darkroom?"

"They probably heard you over at the bank."

"Did I shout too?"

"Maybe. When she was shouting about where you could shove her subscription, and you said that in the olden days people did use newspaper in that very department and she was welcome to...? Your voice might have been raised, just a teensy bit."

Maggie raked her fingers through her hair. *Shit.*

"What's going on?" Dwight came through the back door. He set a film canister on Felicia's desk.

"Nothing," Maggie said.

"Yeah, right," Felicia drawled. "Just, you know, Harriet Lemsky."

"Uh-oh."

"It's fine," Maggie said.

Dwight turned to Felicia, who shook her head.

"What's Harriet going to do?"

The phone rang. Felicia answered it.

"Nothing. She's not going to do anything," Maggie said. "And we're not going to do anything but get this paper together. This will blow over. You'll see."

"It's Edith Hellman," Felicia held up the receiver, her palm over the mouthpiece. "For Dwight."

"Nooo."

"She loves you, Dwight."

He took the phone, and Maggie listened while he made conversation. He had grown adept at Creekster banter. He said goodbye, hung up the phone.

Maggie raised an eyebrow.

"Her amaryllis is blooming," he said.

"That *is* news."

"Do I have to?"

"You do. And put film in the camera. I don't want to hear about it later."

"I'll have to go in. Drink bad coffee."

"Ah, poor baby," Felicia crooned.

"Never mind, I'll tell her you want an Avon catalogue."

"Don't you dare!"

"It won't kill you," Maggie soothed, "and someday..."

"Yeah, yeah, someday she's going to know something newsworthy, and I'll be glad when she calls. I understand the concept. I'm just a bit dubious about Edith Hellman ever being a source of hard news."

Maggie sipped her coffee, examined the paste-up board where next week's paper was partially laid out. Stock pieces of design were in place: the masthead, the cartoon on the editorial page, the recurring ads, the business directory. The rest would slowly fill in as Felicia worked through the current ad orders. "It's looking a bit light this week," she said to Dwight. "Try to get us a vertical and a horizontal of that amaryllis. Maybe get Edith to pose with it."

The phone rang again. "For you, Mags," Felicia said. "Somebody called Brownsfield?"

"Tell him I'm not in."

Felicia frowned, but she lied effortlessly, jotted a phone number, gave it to Maggie without a word. Felicia would never make a reporter; her default instinct was to ask no questions.

Maggie took the number to her office, set it beside the phone. Hank always said that if you had to swallow a frog you ought not look at it for too long. She picked up the receiver, dialled.

Brownfield was pleasant and direct. "I understand your paper might be for sale?"

"It was, a few years ago, but it isn't at the moment."

"Your son said you were thinking about retiring."

He did, did he?

Brownsfield continued, "I hope you'll keep me in mind if you do decide to sell. We're prepared to make a fair offer"—he named a figure and Maggie was surprised how close it was to what Hank had set as his asking price—"and we're prepared to make commitments to your staff if that's something you're concerned about. Yourself as well, should you decide against retirement."

"You'd buy it and leave me running it?"

"Absolutely. Your town, your paper. It would only make sense. Is that something you would be interested in?"

"Not this week. Not in the foreseeable future."

"If you change your mind … at least give me first refusal."

"I'll do that," she promised. She hung up the phone. She should call Blake, tell him what she'd decided. He'd be disappointed. She pushed back her chair. She'd call tomorrow.

Dwight was at his desk scrabbling through papers.

"I thought you were off to get me Edith's amaryllis?"

"I was watching the store while you were on the phone. Felicia's developing my film."

"What else have you got this week?"

"Not much. Historical society meeting. They're planning a homecoming. June Fletcher is determined that 1995 is Beauty Creek's sixtieth anniversary no matter what Howard Doyle thinks."

Maggie chuckled. "The smart money in that fight was always on June. Doyle wouldn't stand a chance."

"He said the village would only put money up for a thirty-fifth because Beauty Creek has only been incorporated since 1960. June said that Doyle could stuff his money where the sun don't shine. Can I quote her? Can I?"

They laughed.

"What's so funny?" Felicia came out of the bathroom, sloshing the film-developing canister with one hand. She set a small kitchen timer on the light table.

"Howard Doyle versus June Fletcher," Dwight said. "Round one to June."

"No contest there." Felicia said. "Why would he pick a fight with June Fletcher? She's been here since there were mountains."

"Hey, she's not that much older than me," Maggie said. "Besides, she's right. We've been Beauty Creek since the CNR hauled the Burnette station down the tracks in 1935 and set it up across the road from Cooper's store."

She went to her office, came back waving a slip of newsprint.

"What's that?" Dwight asked.

She handed it to him. "It's from a special issue we did for the fiftieth. How the creek got its name. That's from a letter one of the railroad surveyors wrote to his wife."

Dwight cleared his throat and read aloud:

> I named it Beauty Creek because of the way the light
> fell on it this afternoon as I paused in my labours and
> gazed upon its shimmering countenance. It reminded
> me of you, dear one, a surface across which light will
> play. I have seen many other, grander brooks, but this
> trifling stream bespoke its name, and I could no more
> evade it than remove my eyes from the light that moved
> across its diminutive surface. Insignificant, perhaps,
> beside the Thompson or, before it, the mighty Fraser,

and yet where would they be, the mighty, without this rivulet and the hundreds like her? They would be as I am without you. Heartsick and lonely and diminished.

"When was this?" Dwight asked.

"1910? '12?"

"They had a way with words back then, didn't they?"

"Didn't they just?"

"Are we going to do a supplement for the Sixtieth?"

"We'll have to. Oh, Mildred, come home, we miss you!"

"We'll help," Dwight said.

"It's just that Mildred did most of the work on the last one. Getting photos from people and working with the historical society. It's a lot of work, to do it right."

Felicia's timer rang. She lingered over the clipping, tilting the developing jug back and forth.

Maggie said, "I hope that's not the developer."

"Nope, fixer." She started toward the darkroom. "Don't worry, Mags, I'm on it."

"Because we don't want a repeat of last week."

Maggie had been sloshing the developing canister and helping Ralph Phillips with his ad for the dress shop. By the time she realized she had missed hearing the timer, Dwight's photographs of the men's bonspiel were overdeveloped blobs beyond salvaging.

Maggie contemplated the anxious waif in front of her. She had big brown eyes in a round face, shoulder-length brown hair, tied back, and nervous hands. She had tried hard for the interview; Maggie would give her that. Black dress pants, well pressed, crisp, white shirt, buttoned to her throat. Clean hands, neatly trimmed fingernails. A few weeks handling newsprint would take care of them.

"From your resumé, it looks like you've moved around a bit?"

The girl rubbed her thumb across the back of her knuckles. "Yes."

"What brought you to Beauty Creek?"

"Work. My, er, husband worked at the mill."

"I see."

"But we're … He's … We're separated."

Trouble at home would mean trouble at work. Maggie scanned the resumé again. Not one applicable skill, beyond the keyboarding.

"Actually, we were never married." More knuckle rubbing.

Maggie had a raft of questions she wouldn't allow herself to ask. How old are you? Do you have children? What was not-your-husband's name? Who are your parents? Jeffers, that name rang a bell, loggers up by Deighton, she thought. She returned to the resumé. Why hadn't she finished school?

"I had my daughter when I was sixteen." The girl answered the unspoken question and glanced away.

Maggie smiled. So. She was brighter than her meagre resumé suggested. "But you've never worked in an office?"

"No. But I'm a quick learner, and I'm fast on the keyboard."

"I don't care about speed," Maggie said. The girl shrank. Maggie softened her voice. "I want accuracy. Can you do that?"

"Yes, ma'am, I can. I can do anything you want me to. I can. I promise I'll work hard. I know I'm not very experienced and I know I'm not … but I know how to work. I do. I will show up on time and learn anything you put in front of me."

Maggie was tempted. Why not? Hank would have hired her on the spot. "Thanks for coming in," she said. "I will let you know."

Maggie brought the thin resumé to the production table. "Have either of you heard of Stephanie Jeffers?"

"From Betty's Café? The waitress?" Dwight asked.

"That's the one. Do you know anything about her?"

"I know who you mean," Felicia said. "I see her sometimes dropping off her kids at school."

"She came here with one of Bentwell's crew," Dwight said. "But I have an idea she's single now."

"And you know that how?"

"I eat there a lot," he said. "I hear her and Betty talking. She lives over on Fourth. One of the mill trailers. She drives that beat-up orange Corolla."

"Not bad," Maggie said, "you might make a reporter yet, Dwight Osborne."

"A job and a car," Felicia teased. "Maybe you should pay even more attention. She's your age, isn't she?"

Dwight ignored her. "She's a good waitress," he said. "She's a bit shy, and she gets flustered sometimes, but she never mixes up an order. I can't say how she is about mornings though."

They all laughed.

"Her kids go to school," Felicia said. "She's used to getting up in the morning."

10

"Did you get it?" Betty asked, after the last of the lunch rush had gone.

"She said she'd let me know, but she hasn't called, so I guess not."

"What makes you so sure?"

The phone rang. Stevie picked it up. The meat supplier. She handed across the phone, went to the kitchen, brought Betty her ordering book. The cafe was empty, so she plucked up the sugar can and made her way from table to table, topping up the glass dispensers.

She wouldn't get the job for the same reason she always didn't get the job.

You didn't graduate?

Mrs. Please-Call-Me-Maggie Evans hadn't actually asked the question, even though Stevie had been prepared for it. It was always a question.

I had my daughter when I was sixteen.

She'd wanted to be honest about that, right off the bat, but she'd seen the way the woman's eyes had flicked away.

Brit, bless her, had been a full month late. The Deighton gossips could do the math on their fingers, but there would always be a bit of doubt. June to January. Was she? Wasn't she?

Not that it really mattered whether people knew or not. Stevie had figured that out the first time they moved to a new town. Even if they didn't raise their eyebrows, she saw their speculative looks and knew that they wondered what someone her age was doing with two little kids.

Among her mother's favourite parables had been the one about the master bricklayer who asks his apprentice to remove a flawed brick. Since it's a centre brick and will be hidden by the outer walls, the apprentice balks, insisting, "No one will ever know," to which the old master replies, "But *I* will know."

People meant well, Stevie told herself, when they laughed and said, "Boy, you sure started young." They didn't know how it seared, that crumbling brick in the middle of her wall.

She returned the sugar can to the shelf. Betty glanced up from her order book, mimed making coffee. Stevie dumped the oily leftovers and poured a pot of fresh water into the machine.

There had been other job interviews when they'd lived in Prince George. A new restaurant hiring a dozen people. Stevie hadn't been one of them. Another, a data entry position. That woman had suggested a computer class, had even given her a brochure for a twelve-week program. But Kurt had said no. Who would look after Brit and Peg? He wasn't paying for daycare while she went off to some la-di-da school. She'd even written away to the matchbook company that did home study courses in drafting and small engine repair and stenography. But Kurt said they couldn't afford that either.

"What're you doing?" Betty was at her shoulder. The coffee pot was half-full of tea-coloured water.

"Oh, gosh, I forgot the coffee. Sorry. Sorry." Stevie pulled the coffee pot out. Water streamed onto the hot burner and steam billowed. "Aah!" She thrust the pot back toward the water.

"Careful!" Betty caught her hand, swung it away from the boiling steam. "You'll scald yourself," she said, her voice a mild reprimand.

Stevie dropped the pot onto the counter, fled to the storeroom behind the kitchen. She slumped on the tall stool they used for reaching the top shelves and tried not to cry.

During the shadowy spring—when Brit was just a possibility and not yet a fact—Mr. Sanders, the English teacher who, everyone said, smoked grass and played bass guitar, spent an entire class explaining some theory he called "the butterfly effect." She remembered the little tap, tap of his chalk against the scarred blackboard as he scrawled the key points. How one butterfly flapping its wings somewhere in China could affect the wind that swirled outside their classroom window. One flap could turn an ordinary summer breeze into a hurricane. One little butterfly. One little flap. It had frightened her to think of it, that a Chinese butterfly's wing was what made Brit come into being.

Years later, she'd found a biology textbook in a box of books left behind in a closet. She'd skimmed the index and skipped forward to chapter ten where three dispassionate pages dispelled every myth she'd ever held about conception. She saw how little she had understood from the whispered snippets in the girls' locker room and from her mother's rare unguarded talk about women who had *more babies than sense*. Brit and Peg, she saw, were the result of hers and Bobby's combined ignorance, and Chinese butterfly wings had nothing to do with it.

The knowledge gleaned from the biology book had freed her from the monthly roulette, navigating Kurt's demands with only her sketchy knowledge of the rhythm method. Kurt said he wouldn't mind a boy or two, but Stevie knew neither of them was ready for that. She had conquered her own embarrassment and made a doctor's appointment.

"I've come about birth control."

"Do your parents know you're here?"

"I'm twenty-one," she said. "I have two kids."

He'd shaken his head, asked a few cursory questions, and insisted on the humiliating Pap smear before writing out the prescription.

At the drug store, more questions. No one thought she was old enough for anything. At home, she read the tiny print instructions on the pamphlet, unsealed the foil packet, rotated the plastic dial. She didn't tell Kurt. She hid the pills in her underwear drawer, continued to make him wear a condom some nights, an elaborate deception.

She had studied that biology textbook for weeks, moving on from reproduction to digestion and respiratory systems.

One night, after supper, Kurt noticed the book on the table. "What's this?" he asked, touching the cover.

"One of those books that were in the hall closet."

"Why's it out here?"

"What?"

"Why's it out here?"

"There's some cool pictures. I thought the girls might want to cut them out."

She'd been terrified he would open it and see her scribbled notes where she'd tried to answer the chapter questions. She couldn't have borne the shame of having to explain what she had really been doing.

She had been pretending. The same way Brit and Peg pretended to have a puppy, Stevie had been pretending to have another life: a life with textbooks, and a college with green lawns, and a dormitory and friends; a life without Brit or Peg or Kurt.

Betty knocked on the stockroom door. "Are you alive in there?"

Stevie scrubbed her hand across her eyes. Another lesson she'd memorized from the biology book: *Ten Rules for Critical Thinking.* Number seven. *Learn to tolerate uncertainty.*

"I'm fine," she called. "Sorry."

Betty popped her head through the door. "Nothing to be sorry about. Waiting is hard. But let's get that coffee going, shall we?"

Spring

II

Nash couldn't place the new girl at the desk. He circled the store, picked up a lined notebook, put it down, paced, picked up an ink pad. She watched him without staring. She was young, dark haired. A child. He was surrounded, these days, by children. He lingered at the shelves closest to the door, the poem in his pocket fighting a losing battle with his natural reserve.

"Hi, Nash." Maggie Evans came through the curtain of beads.

"Missus Evans."

"I wish you'd call me Maggie. We've talked about that Missus business."

"We have," he agreed. It was true what she always said, he'd known her since she was a girl, but the imperative to give a married woman her full title was too deeply imbedded. He approached the counter, clutching the ink pad. Maggie took it from him, but made no move to ring it in.

She gestured toward the new girl. "This is Stevie Jeffers, it's her first day. Stevie, this is Nash Malone. Poet laureate of Beauty Creek."

The girl smiled at him. "Nice to meet you."

He nodded his hello. He took out his poem, unfolded it and smoothed it on the desktop. Maggie took it from him, read it slowly aloud.

He pressed his fingertips against the countertop.

She looked up. "Wow," she said.

He breathed out.

"This last verse is powerful." She tipped the paper toward him, as if he didn't know every syllable by heart.

"…only moonlight, on a dying pine." Her voice caressed each word. He enjoyed hearing her read, but he was never sure if she did it just to placate him, so he could never respond except to nod.

"It will be in next week," she said, releasing him.

He was at the door when he remembered the ink pad she had taken from him and not rung in. He hadn't meant to buy it, and she had known. He picked up a package of lined paper and went back to the till. "Nearly forgot," he said. "I had an ink pad?"

Maggie paused at the beads. "It's right there. Stevie can help you with that."

The girl came to the till, took the paper and rang it in. She picked up the ink pad, set it down, fidgeted, went to the curtain and called through, "Which department does an ink pad go under?"

Maggie came back through the curtain and stood at the girl's shoulder. "What do you think?"

The girl flushed. Stammered, "I thought stationery, but I thought ink might go with newspapers, so I wasn't sure."

"What did we talk about? What should you do when you're not sure?"

The girl's cheeks flamed. Her eyes darted to Nash. He picked up the ink pad. "I'll just take the paper. I don't actually need this. I'll put it back." He was halfway to the shelf when Howard Doyle came through the front door. Nash drew himself up. Doyle halted, clutching an oversized brown envelope. His boots left a trail of sand and snow behind him.

"Malone." Doyle acknowledged him with a nod.

"Doyle."

The door opened again. June Fletcher stomped snow from her boots. Doyle pushed past Nash. Nash returned the ink pad, followed June to the counter.

"That's three seventy-five," the girl said.

Nash handed her a five-dollar bill.

Doyle was showing Maggie the contents of his envelope. "It's the new logo." He held it up. "Isn't it a beauty?"

"Pretty," Maggie said.

June Fletcher spoke before Nash could render an opinion. "What was wrong with the old one?"

"The consultant suggested we start our rebranding with this, associate Beauty Creek with a few select symbols. Keep our advertising consistent."

"Why's that?" June asked.

Doyle ignored June, spoke to Maggie. "I'll need this in our ads from now on. We'll also need new stationery."

"Oh, for Christ's sake," June said. "On the radio this morning they're saying the province is making noise about changing the processing rules, thinking about letting them haul our timber right out from underneath our noses, and our *chief executive officer* is ordering new stationery."

Nash covered his mouth to hide his grin.

Doyle stepped sideways, away from June, and drew Maggie with him.

June noticed the girl behind the till. "Who're you?"

"I'm Stevie. I'm new."

"What kind of name is that?"

"It's short for Stephanie."

"I see. Stephanie who?"

"Jeffers."

"Jeffers? Bob Jeffers? Up Deighton way?"

"He's, uh, was, uh, is, my father-in-law."

"Which is it? Was or is?"

"Is, I guess."

June scrutinized the nervous girl. Nash recognized the look. June carried a vast genealogical chart in her prodigious memory. She was tracking the girl's lineage. It took a moment. "The boy that died?" June queried. "That Jeffers?"

"Yes," the girl whispered, "that Jeffers."

Maggie stepped in. "What can I get for you, June?"

June wasn't finished. "Are those your girls I see with Anna Marsonkowsky? Both of them?"

"Yes," the girl answered, her voice barely audible.

"You don't hardly seem old enough. How old are you?"

Maggie interceded again. "What was it you needed, June?"

"Just wanted to renew the ad for the Emporium for another six months." She glared at Doyle. "Assuming I'll have any customers left in six months."

Doyle glared back.

"Righto," Maggie said. "Will do."

Nash hoped he might escape unscathed, but June followed him out of the store.

"Haven't seen you for a while, Malone."

Now it was his turn to duck.

"You taking your bottles somewhere else?"

"No," he admitted, "they're just stacking up."

"Howard Doyle is an idiot," she said.

"You'll get no argument from me."

"You're no better. All the years we've been dealing and one wrong word and you cut me off."

"But you—"

"I said Doyle was talking through his hat at me. Never said I would listen to him. You ought to know me better than that."

"You said—"

"I was just trying to be neighbourly. Letting you know what Doyle was up to. You heard him in there. *Rebranding.* As if the town is a breakfast cereal. When they incorporated this village, it was for safe drinking water and a proper sewage plant. Maybe some dust control. Those days the chamber of commerce were the ones drumming up business. Now we got Howard Doyle calling himself a CEO."

"I think it's an *A*, CAO, for administrator."

"Whatever. Times are a-changing Malone. You and I aren't careful, they'll be wanting to spruce us up, so we don't scare off the tourists."

"Speak for yourself."

"Limited thinkers, aren't they? You and I *are* the attraction. Authentic, that's what I hear on the television, what everybody's looking for these days. Something real"—she nudged him with her elbow—"and it doesn't get more real than you and me, Malone. Eh? We oughta sell tickets. What do you think? We could team up. You could do dump tours. Every other Tuesday. Teach 'em how to pick bottles, bring 'em to me, and they can buy themselves an ice cream at Cooper's. Bring 'em in by the busload. What do you think?"

"I don't know." Nash grinned. "Probably need liability insurance for that."

June laughed. "Seriously now," she said, "you bring your bottles by. If they pile up in your backyard, you'll just give Doyle more ammunition. You need help with them—"

"I don't need any help."

"You know what your problem is, Malone?" She stepped forward, stared directly into his eyes. "You're a snob."

He stepped back.

"You think people that get help from their neighbours are weaklings," she said. "Lesser beings. You think you're better than that. You're no different than Howard Doyle in there, lording it over us. Couple of snobs, the pair of you."

She really had gone too far. Nash walked away. She called after him, "You're not careful you'll end up like crazy old Van Slyk, talking to yourself instead of other people. You'll end up buried under your junk, dead for a month before anyone misses you."

12

Maggie walked Doyle to the front door, shook his hand and thanked him for the order. She knew he liked to be deferred to, and it didn't hurt her one whit to do it. No point biting the hand that feeds you. Across the street, she saw June Fletcher haranguing Nash Malone.

Was that her future? Working six days a week, going to historical society meetings and grilling every newcomer about their origins? She shuddered. At the front counter, she picked up Nash's poem and read it a second time. It was dark and difficult: a slash pile, runaway horses, dying pines. Too bad. His light verse was much better.

She gave the poem to Stevie, watched the girl read the four short, dense verses. Had she made a mistake? Hiring from desperation often was. She'd had to fire a few production assistants before she found Felicia, and it had been excruciating. Stevie could type, that much she had already proven, dispatching what would have been a full night's work for Maggie in just over an hour, but she was such a timid little thing, and there was a lot to learn.

"I don't know much about poetry."

At least she was honest. "I don't always get them either," Maggie said. "But take extra time typing it, get every comma, every period. Don't miss a capital letter, or he will think you've done it on purpose."

"Coffee time," Felicia called.

The girl turned to her computer.

"She means you, too," Maggie said. "I hope you drink coffee."

Felicia had set cups around the work table and was pouring.

"Who was that woman?" Stevie asked as she added sugar to her cup.

Maggie chuckled. "That was June Fletcher."

Dwight wheeled to the table. "Did you get the third degree?"

"The what?"

"Did she grill you about your parents?"

"No." Stevie blushed.

"She'll get you next time. Be prepared. She'll want to know who your father is, who your mother is, your grandparents..."

Maggie watched Stevie fiddle with her spoon.

"He's not kidding," Felicia said, "and don't think she will take no for an answer. She's—"

"Incorrigible?" Dwight offered.

"Unstoppable. If you tell her she's being snoopy, she'll tell you she's *just interested in people*." Felicia's voice was a perfect imitation of June's.

Maggie smiled. It was true.

"So, what about it, Stevie," Dwight mimicked, "where are your parents from?"

Stevie blanched, and Maggie intervened. "What about you, Dwight?"

"Fourth generation Vancouverite," he said. "Which is odd, I know, because everyone always says that nobody in Vancouver comes from Vancouver. But my folks did, and their folks. We're not sure where the original Osborne came from."

Felicia's family, on both sides, were from Ontario. "Loyalists," she said. "Refugees from the American revolution, the ones who said they'd rather live under the rule of one tyrant an ocean away than a thousand tyrants next door."

"How did you get out here?" Maggie already knew the story, but she wanted Dwight and Stevie to hear it.

"I was an arty kid, always sketching and dabbling. My teachers thought I should apply to art schools. Emily Carr was on the list. I never thought I'd get in. I didn't really have a clue how it would be, living alone on the other side of the continent from my family and my friends. Everyone back home was sure I was living a bohemian, artist-loft-in-Paris adventure and I never had the heart to disappoint them, but I hated it. I wasn't much of a painter, though I did have fun in my desktop publishing classes, so it wasn't a total waste."

"Is that where you met Dillon?" Dwight asked.

"I worked after school at a dingy bar on Cambie Street. Dillon was doing his apprenticeship at BCIT. He was the best thing that ever walked into that bar." Felicia picked up her mug. "That's me in a nutshell. What about you, Mags?"

"My mother was English. Her folks immigrated after the first war. Dad's family was from Saskatchewan, by way of Quebec."

"You're French?" Stevie asked.

"Oh, if my mother could hear you! Sometimes, when he was very drunk, which hardly ever happened except at Christmas, my dad would slur some old French song, and tell my brothers that they were descended from voyageurs. But never when my mother could hear. To her, he was a Scotsman. Already a step down in Mother's estimation. She was very English."

"Voyageurs?" Dwight queried. "In Saskatchewan?"

"Yes, in Saskatchewan. Anywhere there were rivers and furs there were voyageurs. They were famous for their paddling skills and their endurance. Also for how much they loved to party. That's the part my brothers latched onto, much to my mother's dismay."

The front door bell jangled. Stevie stood.

"Saved by the bell," Dwight joked. "Literally."

Felicia watched Stevie hurry away. Maggie caught her eye, raised an eyebrow. Felicia shrugged.

Maggie slept late and left the house in sunshine. She skirted the puddles along the driveway and breathed deep the muddy perfume of spring. How long had it been since she'd had the time and freedom to walk the familiar path from home to downtown?

Downtown. She couldn't think the word anymore without smiling. She'd hired an exchange student two summers back, got a philosophy major from Hamilton. Giles. He had laughed aloud when she sent him to cover a meeting of the *Downtown* Business Association. He'd been a good kid, but it had been Maggie's only foray into summer students. They weren't around long enough to justify the training, and it was a lot of work to keep them busy. Everyone had been relieved when Giles's western summer ended.

Stevie was dusting shelves near the front door.

"Didn't I ask you to do the TV guide this morning?"

"Done."

"Already?"

"Yes, ma'am. And I did the tear sheets. Dwight showed me. They're on your desk, but I can match them with the invoices whenever they're ready."

One more system that needed to be computerized. She knew Hank's method was archaic, writing every invoice, every envelope, by hand. "When you're done here, come find me, and I'll get you going on the envelopes."

Stevie quaked. Maggie pretended not to notice. The girl cringed like a beaten dog every time a new task came up, even though she was the quick learner she'd promised to be. Maybe she would work out after all. It was a treat, being able to sleep in, stroll to work on a sunny day.

Dwight was at his desk. "Morning, Mags. Do you have a minute?"

"Sure."

"Stevie mentioned something June Fletcher said the other day. About the province letting them haul our timber away."

"Stevie picked up on that?"

"Do you want me to follow it up?"

"Sure, call Forestry. I expect it's just talk, wishful thinking on somebody's part."

"Because?"

"The timber is tied to the mill. It's called appurtenancy. It means they can't have the wood if they don't keep the mill running. Apparently, some people are agitating to have the government do away with that, let the timber go where it pleases."

"Can they do that?"

"I suppose. Stroke of a pen."

"What would happen?"

"It would be the end of our mill."

"Why?"

"They've got a newer one over by Quesnel. Ours is a relic. They'd mothball it and haul our wood over there."

"Ouch."

"But that'll never happen," Maggie said. "It wouldn't affect just us. Towns all over the province would lose their mills. Victoria would have a revolution on its hands."

"So, what will happen?"

"Eventually somebody will want our timber badly enough, and the mill will get up and running and we'll go back to living like there's no tomorrow. The logger's life, my dad used to say. There's no in-between, it's either champagne or beer, chicken or feathers."

13

Brit and Peg were at the kitchen table with colouring books when Stevie came through the door. It was their second week without Mrs. Marsonkowsky. Her daughter in Vancouver had fallen and broken a wrist and needed help. Six weeks, she'd said, no more.

"Whatcha doin'?" Stevie called as she kicked off her shoes.

"Mom, we're colouring. Silly."

Peg curled herself around the picture she was working on. She swirled something in her mouth. Stevie saw a shiny candy wrapper on the table.

"Where'd you get the candy?" she asked, hoping to hear that Peg had made a friend.

Peg tried to answer, Brit cut her off. "We played soccer today, Mom. I scored a goal."

"Wow. That's great. But you just interrupted your sister."

Brit avoided Stevie's eyes. "Don't get mad, Mom, okay?"

It was a longstanding deal: Stevie wouldn't get mad, they would tell the truth. In her calmest tone, she asked again, "Where did you get the candy?"

"This old man—"

"Brittany Ann Jeffers! You'd better be kidding."

Brit pursed her lips, scowled.

"Tell me exactly what happened, young lady. Every. Single. Detail. Was Peg there, too?"

Peg coloured furiously.

"Mom," Brit wailed. "It wasn't like that."

Like that. The scenario they had rehearsed since Brit was old enough to toddle away. If someone offers to give you candy?

Don't get mad.

She sat, scrabbled in the art box, chose a colouring book, a crayon, guilt clamped around her heart like a vice. She knew better. They were too young to be left alone, even for these few hours after school.

"It wasn't like *that!*" Brit repeated.

Stevie sipped shallow breaths of air through her mouth. She coloured over an already green leaf. What if someone saw? She'd have social services on her doorstep in a flash. The thought stilled her breathing.

"There were a bunch of us walking home, and Sally had to buy milk for her mom, so we went to the grocery store."

"The grocery store?"

"Uh-huh."

Another long pause. She could feel Brit watching, but she didn't respond, even though the grocery store was well off the route home from school. She should have put them in daycare, even though it would have cost nearly half her day's wages for two hours of after-school care. Even though they needed a $150 deposit and she had less than fifty dollars in her bank account.

"While we were waiting for Sally, this old man came in, and he bought us all candy."

"He bought *all* of you candy? How many of you?"

Brit counted in her head. "Seven," she said. "Eight, counting me."

"He bought you all candy," Stevie repeated, picturing the brightly lit entrance to Cooper's Foods, full-height, glass panes, shoppers in the line at the till. "How much candy?"

"We each got to pick twenty-five cents worth, and he paid the girl."

"He paid the girl?"

"You know, the girl who takes the money."

"Did she know him? Did the girl taking the money know him?"

"Everybody did. They call him the Candy Man. I kind of know—"

"He just paid for the candy? He didn't hand it to you?"

"Yeah."

They were all quiet, Peg watching intently now. Stevie put back the green crayon, selected a bright purple. She coloured the petals of the smallest flower, and the petals of the next largest flower.

Brit sniffled into the silence. "I'm sorry, Mom. I know we're supposed to come straight home, but everyone was going, and I knew you wouldn't be home until later."

"I understand." Stevie set down the purple crayon. "I'm not too happy about it, but I understand."

Peg scurried down the hall to the bedroom and came back carrying a small brown paper bag. She gave it to Stevie. Two toffees remained. "Sorry, Mom," she said. "Sorry."

Stevie reached out with both arms and gathered Peg in, lifted her onto her lap. Brit came around the table and Stevie opened an arm for her and they hugged and rocked amid the faint bouquet of butter toffee and licorice.

In the morning, dropping the girls at school, Stevie gave Brit a stern look. "No detours on the way home."

"Yes, Mom." Voices in unison.

Stevie watched them run across the parking lot, Peg trailing, Brit already in a beeline for her friends. Peg plodded to the main entrance, set down her lunch kit, used both hands to open the heavy door, retrieved her lunch kit and disappeared inside. What had she been thinking? They weren't old enough to be alone. She'd ask to leave early today, and then it would be the weekend. She'd have to figure something out before Monday.

The *Chronicle* building was dark. She unlocked the back door and stepped inside, greeted by the now-familiar aroma of newsprint and cedar. The back room was lined with rough cedar shelves piled high with wrapped bundles of old newspapers. They saved twenty of each issue, removing the old to make room for the recent, saving two of each issue for the historical society.

In the beginning, the job had seemed insurmountable. That first terrible day, mixing things up at the till, the inexplicable poem from the old man who smelled like burnt plastic, that awful June Fletcher grilling her about Bobby. She'd gone home and wept, certain that she'd be fired the next morning. It had taken weeks before she stopped panicking at each new task.

"Stevie," Maggie would sigh, looking over her glasses, "take a breath. Everybody learned sometime. Today, it's your turn."

In a small black notebook, Stevie made checklists. In the morning: lights, Open sign, make the coffee, turn on the photocopier and the cash register. Turn on the computers: first Felicia's, which was the hub, then Dwight's, and Maggie's, in her square office with no door and an old engraved sign that said JANITOR. Last, her own computer at the desk behind the front counter.

This morning, she plugged in the hand-held waxer on Felicia's light table. Felicia arrived Friday mornings and worked through the weekend: designing ads, prepping the layout, printing the half-toned photographs. By the time Stevie got in on Monday, Felicia would be arguing with Dwight over the front-page photo: which one, how big, where to crop it. Maggie would settle the argument when she arrived. They'd toss headlines around most of the morning as the pages on the layout shelf were slowly filled. Stevie spent Mondays proofreading. All the ads, the front page, and then as many pages as she could get to by three o'clock when Dwight drove the box of flats to the bus depot. If they were late, Dwight or Maggie would have to speed after the disappearing bus, though that hadn't happened in the six weeks since Stevie started.

There had been so much to learn, all of it new to her: photocopier, fax machine, advertising rates, subscriptions, 35 mm cameras, darkroom. Not that she had much to do with the darkroom, but she had learned to roll film, counting out short (ten frames) and long (twenty frames) rolls with the clunky black film loader. Felicia did the developing, which she'd threatened to teach Stevie last week.

"It's not hard," Felicia had insisted, as she paced around the table where Stevie was proofreading ad copy. "The chemicals are just recipes, a bit of this, a bit of that, the rest is water. There is, however, this highly technical sloshing." She flipped the developing tank, and Stevie heard the gurgle of the liquid.

"You leave her alone," Maggie had said, coming out of her office. "She has enough to do. Besides, if she's going to learn something new, it will be bookkeeping before the darkroom."

"Nice to be popular…" Dwight was hunched over his keyboard, tapping away at a story. "But hell to be the rage."

Stevie felt a brief, warm glow, remembering. It was followed, directly, by a stab of guilt. Her girls had been uptown, taking candy from strangers.

She set it aside, brought the sheaf of typing to her desk, drew herself together, elbows in, feet flat on the floor. She stacked the submissions at her left, put her fingers onto the keyboard and gave herself over to the task of translating handwriting to text. She did not look at her fingers, and she only occasionally glanced at the screen. Her fingers moved, her stomach relaxed. She finished the 4-H meeting report; next in the pile was a list of raffle winners from the hospital auxiliary bazaar. She typed the heading, pressed Command S, saved the file to the Current Week folder.

"Save your work." Both Maggie and Felicia had drummed that into her. "Save early and often," was their mantra. The computers were temperamental, and the power supply was finicky; any number of inexplicable blips could occur at any moment, and unsaved work would be lost.

"Morning." Felicia set a cup of coffee at Stevie's elbow. "Thanks for always making the coffee. It's nice to come through that door to the smell of fresh coffee."

"Back atcha," Stevie said. "I've served hundreds of cups of coffee, but I hardly ever get one brought to me. It's a treat."

Felicia gestured at the typing pile. "Anything interesting?"

"Soccer tournament. T-ball practice schedule. Stock-car club had a meeting. Their new secretary has the neatest handwriting I've ever seen."

"What's Dwight working on?" Felicia asked.

"Apparently that new motel is going ahead. Some investor group from the coast. The Progressive Communities Committee had a meeting. Something about visual enhancement. Plus, he thinks he got a cover shot of the winning goal last Sunday."

"Let's hope he had film in the camera."

At noon—still no sign of Maggie—Stevie put the Back in Ten Minutes sign on the door and walked to the post office. When she returned, Dwight was at his computer. "Did Maggie come in?" she asked Felicia.

"Haven't seen her. Why?"

"I need…I, uh, have to get home earlier in the afternoons. Mrs. Marsonkowsky can't…well, she might not be able to watch the girls after school for a few weeks."

"I think she counts on you to lock up." Dwight wheeled around to join the conversation.

Stevie's shoulders sagged. "I know."

"Just get the kids to walk over here after school," Felicia said, looking over her shoulder, her fingers flying through a sequence of keyboard shortcuts.

"Yeah. Right," Dwight scoffed.

"I'm serious," Felicia said. "Maggie won't mind. She's cool."

"That's a nice thought," Stevie said, "but I can't ask her that. How much more unprofessional could I get?"

Felicia chortled. "Look around you, Stevie. This is the *Beauty Creek Chronicle*. There's not a professional in sight."

"Speak for yourself," Dwight huffed.

"Seriously," Felicia said. "You should ask her."

Maggie arrived a little after two, and Stevie heard snippets of her murmuring conversation with Felicia about the Sixtieth supplement. She waited until Maggie was in her office, and then knocked lightly on the doorframe. "Do you have a minute?"

"Just one." Maggie had a blue-lined ledger open in front of her.

"It's, um, well, it's about a couple of things." Stevie heard herself babbling, tried to remain calm. Maggie hated a fidgety person.

"They'll tell you lies," Stevie had heard her tell Dwight. "Yesterday, on the way home from school, the girls were with some friends uptown, and some old guy bought them candy."

"Sit down a minute while I add this."

Stevie sat. Prayed the old man wasn't Maggie's uncle or cousin or something.

Maggie banged away at the adding machine, penciled a number at the bottom of a column and pushed the book aside. "His name is Nash Malone," she said, "but the kids call him the Candy Man. He's harmless. In fact, you've met him. He's the poet."

"That's him? Mr. Malone?"

"Probably. He lives over on Fifth, the house with the junk."

"I know it." The house was legendary, a double lot crowded with lean-tos and tires and mounds of bicycle skeletons.

"He collects most of that stuff from the dump, sells some of it in Kamloops, copper wire and old batteries and such. And he fixes up bikes. Do your girls have bikes?"

"Not yet."

"He's your man."

"But buying kids candy? Surely he must know that it's a bit strange, in this day and age."

"Poor old Nash. He got rooked into that. It was Miriam who started it—buying candy for whichever kids happened to be in the store. After she died the kids just pegged it on Nash. Sounds like he still hasn't figured out how to say no."

Stevie wanted to believe her.

"Trust me," Maggie said. "I would know. Folks think he's weird, and plenty think he's too messy for the town, or don't care for his lifestyle, or his politics, but there's never, *ever*, been a breath of anything about kids needing to worry about him."

"Thanks," Stevie said, satisfied.

Maggie wasn't done. "He went to Spain, you know?"

"Spain?"

"Spain. The Spanish Civil War?"

Stevie squirmed.

Maggie hesitated. Stevie knew the look. Maggie was deciding how much to tell her, the same way Stevie did when Brit or Peg asked a tricky question.

"Seriously," Maggie asked, "you didn't learn about the Spanish Civil War in school?"

"I don't think so. We learned a bit about the world wars, around Remembrance Day, but not much of that even." Maybe if she'd gone further than grade ten.

Maggie screwed up her face, tossed her hands out to the side, expressing her disgust with high schools, maybe the state of education in general. "The Spanish Civil War," she explained, "was an experiment. It was the war that might have ended the Second World War before it began. If the world had been paying attention."

Stevie had no idea what she was talking about. "What was the hypothesis?" she quipped.

Maggie frowned.

Stevie flushed. "Experiment, you said, so…hypothesis?"

Maggie didn't smile. "Fascism. Communism. Anarchism. Democracy."

Stevie's stomach twisted around itself. She didn't want to hear any more. It was an old, childish fear. Communists had nuclear bombs. Her mother always said that they would shoot one at the States one day, and the States would shoot back and the world would end. Her parents had discussed this so calmly that Stevie had understood it as a fixed reality, a terrifying inevitability that she could not escape. All she could do was avoid hearing about it, close her ears to words like fascism, communism, anarchism. Democracy was good. The rest were fatal.

Maggie's voice slipped through. "…Franco and Hitler and Mussolini had free rein. The democracies didn't do anything. No," she corrected herself, "they did do something, they got together and agreed not to help. They agreed to let the fascists kill as many people as they could…They didn't teach you any of this?"

"No," Stevie whispered. There was always so much to know. It had to be a character defect, some inner flaw, that Stevie knew so little while others knew so much.

"You're not the only one. Believe me, you're not." She raised an eyebrow. "Do you want to know?"

"I guess."

Maggie twirled to her bookshelf. "This will get you started." She held out a book.

"Hemingway." There was a name Stevie did know. During one torturous spring term her class had wrestled with *The Old Man and the Sea*. Forest children, five hundred miles from the nearest ocean, their idea of a big fish was a two-pound creek trout. They couldn't begin to imagine the creature that had dragged them through Hemingway's ocean for six interminable weeks.

"It's a classic," Maggie said.

Stevie clasped the rough, textured cover. *For Whom the Bell Tolls.* "I think I've heard of it," she lied.

"How old are you, Stevie?"

"Twenty-four last month."

"I'm fifty-four," Maggie said. "I've been alive thirty years longer than you and I barely know a thing. But if you hide from learning new things because you're ashamed or afraid, you'll miss half the fun of life."

It wasn't feeling much like fun.

"Try this," Maggie said. "When you don't know something, just say: I've never heard of that, tell me more."

Stevie's stomach eased. "I've never heard of that, tell me more."

An approving nod. "And, this is a tough one, takes years of practice: I. Don't. Know."

Stevie mimicked the delivery, pausing between words. "I. Don't. Know."

They sat a few moments in companionable silence. Maggie picked up her pencil, tugged her ledger to the middle of her desk.

Stevie hadn't asked about leaving early. She'd do it later. Next week. Maybe she'd think of something over the weekend. Maybe

Mrs. M would come home sooner than expected. "Thanks for the book."

"You're welcome. I hope you enjoy it."

Stevie was at the door when Maggie called her back. "Wait, another thing, and I'm sorry I didn't think of it and offer sooner. If you ever need to, your kids can come here after school and go home with you when you're done. If you want. They're more than welcome. Just clear off that spare desk beside the coffee pot. They can have it."

"Really?"

"Really." Maggie bent to her ledger.

Stevie floated across to Felicia's desk, touched her shoulder with the Hemingway. "Thank you."

"What?"

"You know what."

Felicia grinned. "We have to stick together, us moms."

14

Nash laughed when the letter arrived. A lovely, creamy, linen envelope, the fancy new logo. Now they were the *Corporation* of the Village of Beauty Creek. Just as June had predicted: a two-bit mill town masquerading as a conglomerate.

Inside, a brief paragraph instructed him to bring his property into compliance with Bylaw No. 275—copy attached. The bylaw, single-spaced legalese, section and subsection, was printed on the same expensive linen paper. Nash scanned it, flipped back to the letter, examined the watermark below the clerk's signature.

"Administrator, my ass." Howard Doyle could call himself anything he wanted, he'd never amount to anything but a dog-hating village clerk.

Nash laid the pages flat on his desk, used the point of his letter opener to remove the staple. He smoothed the creases with the side of his thumb and tossed the paper into the good-one-side tray beside his typewriter.

He'd left a half-typed poem in the carriage last night. His heavily edited draft called for a line that no longer worked and he'd been unable to bring himself to type it. He had hoped a good night's sleep would restore its previous lustre, but as he scanned the typed lines, he saw that it hadn't. The line had to go, and with it, everything in the stanza. He picked up his working copy, paced the room, mumbling, listening to hear where the poem might want to go today.

Stymied, he paused at the window and surveyed his back yard. *Unsightly.* He'd half a mind to send a letter right back to the Corporation of the Village of Beauty Creek. Unsightly, indeed. He dropped the poem on his desk, thumbed his worn thesaurus: "unsightly, adj., ugly, unattractive, horrid, hideous, repulsive, disagreeable, dumpy."

Dumpy. That stung.

He replaced the book and went back to the window. To the east of the woodshed, four lean-tos leaned, some more than others, but they were basically sound. Maybe the orange tarpaulin that the wind had shredded last winter could stand to be replaced. He could do that easily enough. He had some salvaged tarps … somewhere. Along the back fence there were collections of bike parts: frames, forks, handlebars, wheels. Admittedly, some of them might be too rusty to be serviceable. Strictly speaking, he might have a few more car tires than he needed, but they were neatly stacked into a waist-high fence that separated his garden from the street. At each end of the row, he'd filled one set of tire wells with dirt. He would set his geraniums out there, after the last frost. The rest of the tires had some tread left. Folks came by periodically, looking for a particular size, often finding it. Along the back alley, plywood leaned on the fence. He'd find full sheets occasionally: an eight-foot slab of half-inch plywood, tossed with the kitchen scraps. It staggered the imagination, what people threw out.

There had been a time when everyone came to him for something. They had kept him in tobacco in lean times, paid the electric bill some months. No more. Everybody wanted everything new nowadays. He'd watched the houses going up in the subdivision at Bachelor Flats, after they burned the old shacks. Not a half-inch sheet of plywood in sight, just two-by-fours and chipboard with vinyl siding over top. If that was new, they could keep it.

The breeze ruffled the loose threads on the orange tarp. Nash sighed. Maybe there were a few things that could go. He'd take a stab at it. Once the garden was planted.

Nash had dumped his load of rusted bicycle frames and was poking around the edges of the smouldering fire when he heard the garbage truck rumble off the highway. He hurried up the bank but he was too slow. He was panting at his truck when Alvin rolled up beside him.

"Heya, Nash."

"Isn't it Thursday?"

"Yep."

"It's not your day."

"Is now. If you'd been around, you'd know. They gave me an extra day. Where've you been anyway?"

Avoiding you, you nosy old bugger.

"You got time for coffee?" Alvin continued. "Mother made cinnamon buns."

Say what you would about Alvin, he never held a grudge. And the only thing tastier than Midge Tilburt's coffee was her cinnamon buns.

After Alvin dumped his load, they converged on the discarded chesterfield beside the recycling bins, upwind from the drifting smoke. Alvin poured coffee and unwrapped the sticky, sweet buns. "I figured you was laying low," he said. "I heard Doyle's gunnin' for you."

Nash snorted. It wasn't new, the whispers in the grocery store aisles, the conversations that hushed when he came through the door at Betty's Café. He'd grown a thick skin over the years, told himself that if they were talking about him, they were leaving someone else alone. It seemed like a small thing he could do, a kind of civic contribution—give the idle minds a target for their petty witticisms and conformist tendencies. "I've been here," he growled. "Takes more than Howard Doyle and his cronies to keep me home."

"You reading the paper? Harriet's on her high horse again."

"Nothing to do with me," he said.

There had been a rash of letters back and forth between Harriet Lemsky and June Fletcher. Harriet wrote to endorse the village plan for benches and flower boxes on Main Street. June fired back a lengthy diatribe on the folly of municipalities pandering to commercial interests with tax dollars. This brought an official response from the chamber of commerce, also praising the flower-box plan and reminding June Fletcher that there would be no tax dollars without private enterprise. June was back the following week with both guns blazing. It was June's contention that capitalism was a religion and, like all religions, should be divorced from matters of state. The chamber of commerce had—wisely, Nash thought—retired the field.

"I dunno." Alvin indicated a pile of rusted, steel beams and tattered aluminum siding. "That's the lot from Persky's old shake mill. They just scooped 'er up with the loader and dumped 'er. Took 'em three days. Five thousand bucks, I heard, is what they're billing him. Five thousand!"

Nash had heard the same crazy figure, waiting in line at Cooper's.

Alvin repeated his warning. "Word is you're next."

"They wouldn't dare."

"They might. Seems to me Doyle has the bit in his teeth with that new bylaw. You know he's just been waiting for an excuse. If you need a hand…"

"Reckon I can take care of myself."

"Yeah, yeah, I know that, but I'm just saying… if you need anything, there's no need to be a hermit about it."

"Sounds like you've been talking to June Fletcher."

"I just asked if she'd seen you around. She's worried about you."

"She should mind her own business."

"Nobody's… I'm just sayin'…"

"Well, don't." Nash threw the last of his coffee onto the ground, tossed the cup toward Alvin, stalked to his truck and spewed gravel as he sped away. "Just sayin'," he fumed.

Rufus Vanisle came around the corner to the meat department and halted beside him. Nash left off perusing the cold cuts. "I've been meaning to talk to you," Nash said after they had exchanged greetings. "About this cleanup business."

"Ah, that. I take it you got a notice."

"Yep."

"That would mean there have been complaints."

Nash glowered. Harriet, no doubt.

"Come on, Nash, you know what it looks like."

"What it looks like? What's it supposed to look like? Since when are there rules about what a man's property is supposed to *look* like?"

"You live in town, Nash. If you lived out in the bush, where no one could see, I suppose you could do whatever you wanted, but you have neighbours. You owe them a little courtesy if nothing else."

"Reckon that should work both ways. You could've come to my door, had a conversation with me, man to man, instead of hiding behind some mumbo-jumbo bylaw."

"You're right. I could have done that."

Nash waited.

"I can see that, from your perspective, that might have been a better alternative."

Oh, he was a politician, this one.

"But here we are, Nash, you and I, face to face. What if we stroll over there and talk about it?"

"Talk about what?"

"Your yard...the...visual aesthetics of it."

Nash scowled.

"I was joking, Nash. But, seriously, do you want to? Walk over there, right now, see if we can't find a solution?"

Nash plucked a package of ham slices from the display case. "Might be a few things there that could go, I'll give you that. Could maybe be a bit...tidier."

Vanisle jumped on the word. "Exactly. That's all we're looking for. Tidy. It's not too much to ask, is it?"

"I suppose not."

"I could probably get Doyle to send a crew over."

"No! I can take care of my own yard without any interference from Howard Doyle."

"No interference. Just a helping hand."

"Don't need charity."

"It's not charity."

"So, I tidy up, you call off your dog?"

"Dog?"

"Doyle."

"Yes, Nash. You tidy up and I'll get Doyle to leave you alone." Van-isle held out his hand. "Deal?"

They shook.

The sun was setting as Nash tamped the dirt on the last potato hill. He'd brought up the tail end of his table spuds from the root cellar last week, set aside a half dozen for planting and put the rest in the fridge. His main sack of seed potatoes he'd leave in cold storage for another few weeks. It was too soon for them, but he always tried to get a few hills planted for early eating. He could taste them already, the sweet ambrosia of a new potato, the size of a gumball, dug and cooked within the hour.

He heard a lawnmower start somewhere nearby. It was nearly dark. What fool would be mowing grass at this time of night? The mower stalled. Started. Sputtered. Roared. Ran a few minutes. Stalled again. Curiosity led him out of his yard, through the empty lot, to Fourth Avenue.

It was that slip of a girl from the *Chronicle*. His instinct was to retreat, but wasn't that just the sort of thing an old hermit would do? He walked up the street, stopped outside the fence and tipped his hat. He could be neighbourly.

She eyed him warily, her shoulders taut. A vigilant whitetail.

"Warm tonight," he offered.

She nodded without relaxing. He heard a squeal from the back-yard, children playing. Not a deer, a mama bear. "You've got yourself quite a job there."

Her shoulders eased. "I didn't keep up with it last fall, and now I've got this mess of dead grass. I'm afraid to burn it, it's been so dry. I thought if I could just mulch it up, it would go back into the soil."

Clumps of clippings dotted the freshly mown section. They'd need to be picked up and composted or they would choke out the new grass. "Looks like you're making progress."

"I guess I was a bit optimistic, thinking I could get it done before dark."

He wanted to offer to help. He could rake while she mowed, get a compost pile going. He squelched the impulse. Neighbourly was one thing. Nosy, interfering busybody was something else. "Better get on," he said.

"Bye." She squeezed the spring bar on the mower, bent to pull the starter cord.

The engine sputtered but did not fire. He watched her struggle to pull the cord again. "You've probably got some grass balled up under there," he called. "Try pulling it over onto that patch you've already cut. Give 'er a thump or two."

She followed his suggestion. A thick wad of grass fell out. She yanked the cord once more, and the engine roared. She mouthed a thank you. He touched his finger to his cap.

Take that, June Fletcher, he thought.

Summer

15

Maggie opened the chequebook. The credit card cash advance was long gone, and while they were still sending her blank cheques, she couldn't bring herself to use another. She was back juggling who to pay, who to put off. Mildred had called it the Hank Evans Accounts Payable System: start at the top and write cheques until your money is gone; next month start at the bottom, work your way up. They joked that it worked for everyone except those poor saps in the middle.

But first there was the payroll. In this, she was different than Hank. When the cash flow dwindled, he had sometimes asked reporters to wait a week. Maggie would delay her payables, but she paid her staff on time, an advance on the fifteenth, a full accounting on the third day of the new month.

"Maggie?"

It was Dwight at the door. "I know I already took my holidays for this year but it's always dead in July anyway, um, if I didn't, I mean, if I took it without pay, could I maybe, possibly—"

"Speak, Dwight. What?"

"Take two weeks off?"

"I don't—"

"Wait. Before you say no. Stevie said she can do a few stories, and you wouldn't have to pay me."

The chequebook under her elbow twitched. "What if Stevie wants some holidays?"

"She doesn't. I already asked her. She just wants to work. She needs the money, I think."

"What about evenings? She can't do meetings."

"Felicia."

"Felicia what?"

"I asked Felicia. She said Stevie's kids can come to her place if there are meetings."

Maggie stalled. "Two weeks. What are you going to do?"

He pulled a brochure from his shirt pocket. "A photography course. I've wanted to take one of this guy's courses since I was a teenager, but they were always in Toronto or New York. But he's coming to Vancouver. This one is, like, six blocks from my mom's house. I can sleep in my old room. She'll feed me. She worries about me, up here in the wilds. She tells her friends I'm working up north. I try to tell her that if you folded the map in two, we wouldn't even be past the middle of the province, but she's not having it. They think I ride a dogsled to work most days."

Maggie laughed out loud. She knew he wasn't exaggerating. For a lot of people at the coast, north was anything beyond the Port Mann Bridge. "I should pay you to do that course," she said. "Professional development and all."

"You don't have to. Since I can stay with my folks, it won't cost much."

"The *Chronicle* will benefit, it should pay the tuition at least. That's only fair."

"Okay, but when I get back."

She returned to the payroll, but something niggled. "Dwight?" She followed his voice to the front. He was leaning across the counter, telling Stevie about his photography course. Maggie interrupted. "One teensy detail, Dwight. Before you go, I'll need the rest of your Sixtieth interviews."

"I've got one finished and one that just needs some tweaking."

"That leaves one more."

"There's no one else to ask. I've either already done them, or they're away on summer holiday."

"What about Jake MacDonald or Wilhelmina Phelps?"

"Away. I'm doing that beetle tour with Forestry before I go. Could we use that instead?"

"Not really."

"There's Nash Malone," Stevie suggested.

Maggie laughed.

"No doubt," Dwight said. "Thanks, Stevie, but Nash Malone won't be giving me an interview. Couldn't we use the beetles?" he pleaded. "*Please.*"

"Three interviews, Dwight."

"But—"

"No buts. Proofed, formatted, ready to go. Before you leave town."

"I could try," Stevie intervened. "If you want. Nash Malone. We're kind of neighbours."

Maggie relented. "You can try, but get on it right away. I want it in the bag before Dwight leaves."

Maggie went back to her office. She could hear Dwight happily dispensing interview advice. She envied his enthusiasm. The *Chronicle* kept her busy, but she had given up most of her favourite bits. Dwight had her camera and notebooks, Felicia, the pleasure of a well-constructed front page. Maggie got the payroll, the bookkeeping and the editorials. She'd be glad enough when Dwight felt ready to write editorials. She hated the weekly necessity of articulating an opinion. She didn't want to care what people did or how they did it. All that did was get you into trouble.

Stevie came to the office doorway.

"That was nice of you," Maggie said.

"I hope I haven't bitten off more than I can chew."

Maggie hoped so, too. "You never know until you try."

"Um, about Nash Malone, there's one thing…do you know if… if he's—"

"If he's what?"

"A *communist?*"

"You've been reading that Orwell." When Stevie returned the Hemingway, Maggie had scoured her bookshelf at home for Orwell's *Homage to Catalonia.*

"No, it's just, I heard it at Betty's. Is he?"

"People say it, but that doesn't make it true."

"Is Nash Russian?"

"Old Man Malone was probably a Brit. He was here the same time as Cooper, before the railroad. Nash's mother, Alvira, was second-generation Irish. Her people came on the potato-famine boats." The girl didn't have Dwight's beleaguered look, so Maggie continued. "According to my mother, Alvira was working as a housemaid when Malone went back east to visit relatives. They wrote for a year, and he asked her to marry him, and she came west with his letters in her pocket, frightened half to death that he wouldn't be there to meet her when she arrived. Course he was, more's the pity. Mom said she'd have done better to get right back on that train the minute she saw that hovel he called a house."

"But? If he's from here, Nash, from our side, how could he be a communist?"

Maggie summoned Hank. "Here's the thing, kiddo, and you will never amount to anything in this business if you don't grab hold of this and never let it go. There aren't two sides to anything. There are six. Or sixty. Or six hundred."

Stevie blinked, rocked her shoulder against the doorjamb. Maggie could see she didn't understand. What was the other thing Hank used to tell reporters? "Stories don't have sides," she said. "They are round and filled with marbles."

Again, the pained look. A train called at the crossing, and they rolled their eyes at each other as the sound shivered through the building, two wailing howls, one short toot, another long blast. "Do you know what that whistle means?" Maggie asked, when they could hear again.

"No."

"There you go. Sometimes one of the marbles is inside a whistle."

16

Stevie was working on the classifieds when Dwight came back for film. She asked him, "Do you know what the train whistle means?"

"The train whistle?"

"When it blows, at the crossing by the hotel. Two long, one short, one long. What does it mean?"

"Is this a trick question? What's the punchline?"

"No, seriously, when he blows the whistle, what's the guy, the engineer, what's he saying?"

"Get the fuck off the track."

Stevie laughed out loud, clapped her hand over her mouth.

Dwight beamed, tossed the canister of film into the air, caught it, and departed, grinning.

Stevie jotted Nash Malone's phone number in a fresh black notebook. She dialled and hung up before the first ring. Dialled and hung up again. Reconsidered her prepared greeting. Tapped her fingers on the desktop. Picked up the receiver. Noticed chips in the pink polish on her index finger. She lifted the phone from the corner of her desk and set it in the middle of the green blotter. Wondered why they called it a blotter. Took a deep breath. Dialled the seven digits. Plucked up her pencil. Listened to the ringing. No one answered. She counted rings. Three. Four. Five. She hung up. Checked the number.

Felicia came to the copier, made a copy and asked, "What are you avoiding?"

"Avoiding?"

"I heard you dialling and hanging up and sighing."

"I have to call Nash Malone and set up an interview."

"So, call him."

"But then I will have to actually do the interview."

"One would follow the other."

"I don't know how to interview anyone. What will I say?"

"Best-case scenario?" Felicia gathered up her papers. "Not much. Ask a question. Then shut up."

Stevie waited until Felicia was back at her desk and then dialled again.

"Hello?" A deep voice, raspy and hesitant.

Stevie pressed her pencil into the blank notebook page. "Hi. This is Stevie. Stevie Jeffers? From the *Beauty Creek Chronicle*."

No response.

"We've met a few times. I type your poems. You helped me with my lawnmower last week."

"Uh-huh?"

"Um, we, I mean, Maggie, I mean, Mrs. Evans...we've been doing these interviews for the Sixtieth and..." Stevie drew a deep breath, and then rushed it out. "I was wondering if I might be able to interview you."

"For the paper?"

"Yes. We've been doing a different story each week. Last week was Mr. Holloway."

A snort. Stevie waited to see if there would be more. She didn't know what else to say.

"I don't think so," he said.

"Please. I'm...it's just...Mrs. Evans is giving me a chance and I want to show her I can do a story. Please. I could come to your house or you could come to the office. Whichever would be most convenient."

"I don't—"

"Couldn't we try? If you hate it, you can just tell me to get lost. Okay?" She heard him sigh. "Is that a yes?"

A grudging grunt.

"When would be a good time?" They painstakingly worked their way through dates and times and settled on a Thursday two weeks away. She hung up and realized she hadn't asked him for an address. That, he hadn't offered. It didn't matter, she knew the house. Everyone in Beauty Creek knew it.

It was a rectangular box of a house, like one of Peg's drawings. Two rectangular windows on either side of a rectangular door. A tilted metal chimney. Grey siding. Green asphalt shingles, overlaid here and there with fresh red patches. A wooden ladder nailed to the roof below the chimney.

Beside the house, behind the house, around the house, everywhere except for the garden plot and a rough square of mown grass along the driveway, there loomed the accumulation for which Nash Malone was famous. The back of the lot was a maze of junk piles covered with ragged blue and orange plastic tarps held in place by rough lumber and old tires.

Tales of Nash Malone's eccentricities had been a staple at Betty's. Stevie had heard, more than once, the story of the time Nash was spied riding his bike home from the dump, a bed frame strapped to his shoulders, dangling out around him like the hoop of a ball gown around the legs of a princess. Or the time he caught fire while digging through the pile. Second-degree burns. Less often, someone would tell a story about needing a part for their washing machine, or their pickup, or their kitchen mixer, and how they tried everywhere, with no luck, until someone suggested Nash. He wasn't very friendly, they'd say—not someone who'd invite you in for coffee—but he would listen to your dilemma and then, and this part of the story was always repeated with awe, he would set off into his backyard jungle and unerringly lead you to the very pile that contained the very part that was required.

Stevie was just about to knock when Nash Malone emerged, dressed for departure. He glowered down at her. She blanched, stuttered, "Hello. Hi. I'm Stevie Jeffers. We have an appointment?"

"At the *Chronicle*."

"I thought I said I would come here."

"I think I'd remember."

She stepped back.

"Never mind. Probably me," he said. "I get things mixed up some-times. Come in if you must."

It was a rectangular room, kitchen along one side, living room on the other, separated by a central wood heater. Two easy chairs, a coffee table between them, faced a picture window that framed Wolverine Mountain. There was a desk against the end wall, near the front door. Every available surface was piled with books and papers and magazines, alternating with tobacco tins and potted geraniums. There was a stale, slightly smoky smell that she couldn't place.

"Excuse the mess," he said.

"Oh?" she said. "This is nothing." He doubted her, she could see. "No, really," she insisted. "My Aunt Adeline, on my dad's side? Messiest house you've ever seen." They hadn't visited often, but occasionally Stevie's dad would insist, and away they'd go, Stevie and Adrian in the back seat, for the forty-five-minute drive down the valley. "A pigsty," her mother would say at least once on the journey, drawing a furious glare from her father. Adrian hated it too, but Stevie never minded. Adeline hugged you like she meant it, and she always had store bought cookies, thin pink wafers, layered with vanilla icing that melted on your tongue.

He surveyed the room, reassessing, and she was glad she'd told. Adeline wouldn't have minded.

Stevie unpacked her cassette recorder and set up the flimsy plastic stand that was meant to hold the microphone upright. It promptly fell over. She righted it, twisted the wires around until it stood by itself. Nash got cups and poured coffee, sat across from her. Stevie turned on the recorder and took out her notebook.

"Double whammy," he said.

"Pardon?"

"Notes and tape."

"Tape to make sure I quote you accurately. Notes to remind myself where on the tape to find it."

"I see."

Her fingers quivered. Standing on the doorstep, waiting for him to answer, she'd seriously considered running back to her car. Maggie doubted she'd get a story anyway. But here she was, inside the house.

Ask a question.

"So, sixty years ago was 1935," she said. She had practised in front of her bathroom mirror. "I was hoping maybe you could tell me what you were doing in 1935. Where you were. How it was for you. That kind of thing."

"1935?"

"Uh-huh."

"It's kind of hard to say," he said. "We moved around a lot in the thirties. I might have been in Vancouver. Or I might have been in Winnipeg."

"Really?"

"Yeah. In '35, that was the middle of the Depression."

She tried not to fidget.

"My older brothers left home first. Said they'd send money when they found work. They didn't. My mother would send me to collect the mail, I'd come home empty-handed. My brother Pete set off next, and I went with him. Course, we didn't fare any better. There weren't any jobs. We were..."

She waited.

"They called us the unemployed. Thousands of men without jobs, without homes. We were just like them," he gestured with his chin, "like the ravens."

Across the narrow street, on the crosspiece of a crumbling picket fence, a plump black raven perched.

He waited for her to speak. She resisted the pressure to fill the quiet space. *Ask a question and then shut up.*

"Scavengers," he explained. "We lived on what people threw away. On their scraps."

"Like dumpster divers?"

"Not the way it is now, what you see on the television. Now people throw away everything. Back then, it really was scraps. People didn't have as much stuff. They had a lot less to toss."

The bird on the fence sprang sideways from some unseen threat. "Just like them," he said. "Men would fight each other for a cigarette butt. For a bread crust. We were outcasts. Our families couldn't feed us. No town wanted us. Besides my clothes, I had a belt and a fish hook." A pause. "We were always hungry. Always afraid."

She'd typed those very words, and recently. "That's from a poem. Your poem. The last one you brought in."

"Yes." A small smile, a loosening. "Do you like poetry?"

"Oh, no." She heard herself say it, grimaced, went on. "I mean, I don't not like it, I just don't always get it, and it's…Even when I do understand, it's so…so…dense?"

"Distilled?"

"I guess, sort of like a rich dessert, like cheesecake. Sometimes it's too much. That line: 'always hungry, always afraid.' There's only four words but they mean something…bigger."

She was talking too much. *Ask a question.* "You were in the relief camps. What were they like?"

He poured milk from a small tin into his coffee and stirred. Set down his spoon. Picked it up. Stirred again. "Hard."

She nodded him on.

"But times were hard even before the Depression. My folks didn't have much. My father was set on making his fortune cutting ties for the railroad. My mother wanted him to be a farmer. There were so many of us to feed. To buy shoes for. It was always hard."

There was another long silence. He was watching the raven. Finally, Stevie had to speak. "Did you live here?"

"Yeah."

"In this house?"

"Nope."

She tried again. "What was Beauty Creek like?"

"Small."

She waited him out. The raven flew away. He turned back to the table. "Beauty Creek, what there was of it, was mostly over by the tracks. Same as those old photos you've been printing, that little cluster by the station. It was the only way in or out. Most everybody in Beauty Creek, and that wasn't very many, mind you, most of them were either working on the railroad or in the bush. Some tried farming but it's a tough country for that. A few trappers. Not much of anything. It didn't really take off until the fifties, when Bull Devers built his sawmill on the Little Beauty and brought them Albertans over."

Stevie jotted it down, but he was right. There was nothing here that hadn't already been covered in the anniversary special.

"You haven't touched your coffee. Do you take sugar?"

"Please." She picked up her spoon, glanced at her notes. "Can you tell me more about the relief camps? What they were like?"

"They were bad."

"How?" She lifted the spoonful of sugar toward her mug.

"In every way you can imagine," he growled. "Bad food. Bad bedding. Bad administration. Bad, wasteful work. Stupidity piled on top of ignorance on top of arrogance." He banged down his coffee cup.

Stevie flinched and her spoonful of sugar scattered across the tabletop.

17

Nash saw fear flash through the girl's brown eyes as she dabbed at the spilled sugar.

"Oh, no, look what I've done. I'm sorry."

"No matter. Bit of sugar."

"If you've got a cloth…" Her voice was trembling.

To soothe her, he picked up the bowl and sprinkled more sugar onto the table. With his index finger he drew a pair of rectangles, interlocked at one corner, in the scattered crystals.

"Afraid," he said. "Sixty years ago, in 1935, that's what this sign meant: Afraid."

"Be afraid?"

"Just Afraid."

She picked up her pen, scratched in her notebook.

"Talk about density," he said. "Sixty years ago, it only took those squiggles to say everything that was in that poem."

"Like another language?"

"More like a shorthand." He smoothed the sugar, traced another simple rectangle, made a dot in the middle. "We'd make marks however we could, use a piece of charcoal, scrape the paint on a mailbox, carve into a fence post if we had a knife. There were places to look for them. Once you knew what to look for." He tapped the table. "This one meant Danger."

He saw her shoulders relax. He sprinkled more sugar, drew a pair of interlocking circles. "Take a guess."

"A lake, two lakes. Water?"

"Nope. Don't Give Up."

"No, really, what does it mean?"

"That's what it meant: Don't Give Up. It was a pair of handcuffs. So, when you got nicked, you'd see this one on the cell wall. Don't Give Up."

She drew the circles in her notebook.

"Here, I'll draw." He held out his hand, she passed him the note-book. He said, "You go on and fix your coffee."

She brought the sugar bowl right to her cup and scooped.

He held up his drawing: three angled vertical lines, crossed through, a slanted grid.

"Not a Safe Place," he said.

She stirred her coffee.

He flipped to a fresh page, drew a rough oval with legs, tail, bobble head, pointed ears, and whiskers. He showed her.

"A cat?"

"Yes. And?"

"Farm? Milk? Cream?"

He laughed aloud at the last. "Close," he said. "A Kind Woman Lives Here."

"So, there were kind people?"

"Some. Yep. There are always some. Lots of people just didn't care one way or the other. They'd step aside and let us pass without ever meeting our eyes, as if we were contagious." He sketched again, a large X with a small circle on each side, round eyes in a grotesque face.

She shook her head. "No idea."

"Safe Camp," he said. "This was a welcome sign. There was another one, but I can't remember how it went, for places that would feed you in exchange for work."

"So, there was work?"

"There's always work, but there was no money to pay anyone to do it. Some people had a bit of money, and the ones who did, the ones with a job and a paycheque, they just kind of sailed through saying, Isn't it a pity. But the rest of us? The ones who weren't lucky? There was no work for us. It was the camps or starve."

She took back her notebook and made notes beside the signs. He could see she didn't understand. Hunger, perhaps. But starvation?

"Is that why… Is that how… people got to be … um … communists?"

Oh, for Christ's sake. He pushed back from the table. "This was a bad idea."

"I'm sorry. We don't have to talk about that. Another thing I wanted to ask you … to, uh, hear about, was Spain, the war in Spain?"

"I don't think so."

"Maggie, Mrs. Evans, gave me some books about it." She was rubbing her thumb hard across the page, smearing ink, as she babbled. "Hemingway. *For Whom the Bell Tolls.* Also, Orwell. I've been reading up on it."

Hemingway *and* Orwell. Nash stood. "Nope. This was a mistake. Don't know what I was thinking." He waited while she gathered her tape recorder, walked her to the door and closed it behind her. He watched through the window until she drove away. "Sorry, kid," he muttered.

He woke thrashing, sweating, kicking at the blankets, flailing at hands that were holding him down. Waning moonlight illuminated the bedroom doorway. He lay quietly, used his mind to relax the muscles in his shoulders. He unclenched his fingers, drew a deep breath and exhaled slowly. His heartbeat eased.

He slid out of the blankets, pulled on his shirt. He didn't bother with pants; the night air was pleasantly cool against his bare legs. In the kitchen he plucked an orange from the fruit bowl, peeled it as he paced, then nibbled away every lingering strand of pith. When he split it open, juice spurted against his palms, and he felt the dream uncoil its grip on his backbone. He popped a section into his mouth and chewed, savouring the tangy sweetness.

That damn reporter, dredging it up. He finished the orange, dropped the peel into the compost pail and rinsed his fingers under the kitchen tap. There would be no more sleep tonight. He went to the bedroom, pulled on his pants, stretched his back against the old ache. At his desk, he took a sheet of paper from his good-one-side stack. It was the Beauty Creek linen. It made him smile to roll it into the typewriter.

He should have shown that girl this ridiculous letter. Told her what he thought about that. Her countenance intruded, striking brown eyes dominating her round face, her small voice, asking, "What was it like … in the camps?" His fingers fluttered over the keys, tapping without typing. "Yes, Mr. Malone," he muttered to himself, "what *was* it like?"

He'd started writing poetry in the camps as a way to pass the endless days when they weren't building roads with picks and shovels, watched by silent machinery they weren't permitted to use. Some said it was to make the work go further. The agitators said it was to humiliate them, to reinforce the popular notion that they were useless bums whose circumstances were their own fault.

Poetry had given his restless brain something to do. Paper was often scarce, but he had learned that it was possible to create a poem and save it in his head, against the day when he could borrow a pencil and scribble it into the margins of a discarded scrap of newsprint.

He typed the line that came to him:

> The boy learned everything and nothing
> in the camps.

Despite the senseless work and the absurd rules, there had been time for reading and arguing, a kind of noisy camaraderie Nash had never known. Sometimes, in that first camp at Harrison Mills—ten or twelve of them crowded around a table, their empty tin plates pushed back—passionate arguments would break out between the socialists and the anarchists. Big Buck Timmins always egged them on, exhorting them to think for themselves, to interrogate every assumption. Nash had been struck by the contrast to the silent dinner table of his youth: his father, hunched, chewing, occasionally grunting instructions about the next day's work; his silent brothers nodding.

Born into the middle of the pack, Nash had learned early to keep his mouth shut and his eyes down. At the foot of the table his mother whispered to the youngest children to mind their manners, chew with their mouths closed, keep their elbows off the table. His father often deliberately smacked his lips, or laid his great arms across the table-cloth. A hard look would pass between his parents, and Nash's mother would always yield.

Nash had always wanted to talk to Buck about power in a family, and how it must be the place where men first learned to submit. But he had been something of a middle child in the camps too, so he'd never got the chance to ask what Buck thought about that original tyranny.

But first he learned from his mother.

It wasn't the right line. He knew it before he typed the last word. There was no density to it. Sixty-five years, if it was a day, and the experience was not yet distilled. It perplexed him still, that silent war between his parents: his father's fierce insistence on getting his own way every time; his mother's valiant battle against filth and fever, ignorance and poverty. Her example had taught Nash that physical dominance was only one manifestation of power. Knowledge was another.

He remembered his father waiting, helpless, while his mother doctored a ragged wound on his brother's leg. A broken branch, pro-truding, had ripped through Pete's calf when a deadfall crashed down. One minute, the steady rhythm of the crosscut saw, Pete doing most of the work, happy if Nash managed to keep the blade straight. The next, a sharp crack high above, Pete throwing himself sideways, and the mighty *whump* as the falling tree landed.

Nash remembered his mother touching Pete's face, pushing him down on the pillow, away from the wound. He was already a hulk of a man, but her quiet touch stayed him. "Lie back, son." Her voice the same soothing lyric Nash had heard used on a restless milk cow, a fevered child, a drunken husband. "Easy. Don't move. That's got it." She had stiffened when she lifted the torn pant leg but her voice remained calm. "Boil the kettle, Father," she said, without looking at her husband.

And, he did. All afternoon he took orders delivered in that gentle voice. Precious brandy was measured into a tea cup, held to Pete's lips. Bloody basins were taken outside and dumped far from the house, scoured with snow, brought back inside. The cotton sheet from the top shelf of the closet was torn into strips by hands washed and scrubbed with a brush.

The younger children were sent outside to play. The older boys were dispatched to the tracks to flag down the way freight. His father objected to that, having already lost a morning's work. His mother insisted. "If he's to live, he will need to get to the hospital, and soon." When Nash's father glowered, she repeated herself. "If he's to keep this leg, he needs more care than I can give him. Go on, boys. Tell the engineer we will be there as quick as we can."

She had Nash bring the medical book, from its place on the shelf next to the Bible. He held it open in front of her while she plucked splinters. After dousing the wound with a wash of carbolic acid, she covered it with clean rags and winced along with Pete as she snugged up the splint.

Pete had returned in a month, leg intact. He knelt in front of his mother and kissed her hand. He said the nuns at the hospital in Jasper told him he should kiss the ground she walked upon. She had hugged him to her, laughing, and Nash hadn't minded that Pete was his mother's favourite. It was enough just to be close to them, their affection spilling over, warming the room.

If he is to live. Nash turned it over in his mind. It wasn't bad. It had the makings of a first line. Or a last line. He typed it just to see how it looked on the page.

`If he is to live.`

The floorboards quivered. He heard the train call at the crossing. He tapped restlessly at the keys, pushed back his chair, went to the window. He couldn't see the tracks from his house but he could picture the dark mass, rattling across the bridge over the creek. He should have given Maggie Evans's child-reporter a riding-the-rails story. That would have gone nicely with the hobo signs.

If only she had asked, "What was it like...riding the rails?"

Noisy, he would have said. Steel wheels on steel rails, a hammering clacking, the screaming of metal on metal in ungreased axles, men shouting to be heard over the racket.

Smoky, he would have said. Always a small fire at the end of the car, where old men huddled, playing poker for tokens that might be twigs or buttons or pebbles. Someone would eventually crack the door, and the noise level would go up and the cold would seep in. Smoke or cold. Those were the choices.

Boring, he would have said. He once spent three days at a siding somewhere between Kamloops and Revelstoke, their freight cars shunted off to await some order that took its sweet time coming. Nash had taken his fish hook, found worms under the old ties that rotted by the siding, cut a willow pole and fished the river. Caught trout and gutted them and gave them to Old Bill. There was no butter or flour so Old Bill added a bit of water to his tin pan and steamed the fish. The tiny bones meant that they had to be eaten slowly and this suited them, abandoned there in the wilderness with nothing but Shorty's deck of cards to pass the time. They shared stories of fish suppers they had known, agreed that a sprinkle of salt would have been nice, and talked a long time, as hungry men will do, of the dessert that might have completed their meal. A silent man, whose name Nash never knew, set some snares on a faint trail he found by the lake but nothing came of it. They saw a few grouse, and someone told about a fella he knew that could take out a grouse's eye with a slingshot and railroad gravel, but no one had a slingshot so they ate Nash's bony fish. They all walked the track, from the western switch to the eastern one, scouring the ground for cigarette butts. If a siding was used by passenger trains, there were often fair-sized stogies to be found in the gravel. Nash had found a brown fedora once, barely worn, hanging on a branch just off the track.

The vibration under his feet eased, the whistle faded. Nash wandered back to his typewriter, sat, pored over the paltry lines. He bent to the bottom drawer of his filing cabinet and lifted out a tattered brown manila folder tied with a white ribbon. There was a layer of dust on the cover. He touched it with his finger, traced two interlocking circles. A dog barked somewhere nearby, and he jumped.

"Oh, for Christ's sake," he said. He swept away the dust, untied the ribbon, and pulled out a hefty sheaf of yellowed pages. He read the brief prologue and scanned the opening paragraphs, but he couldn't make himself read on. He leaned back, away from the page, away from the pale, lost boy he had been, hunched over his typewriter, fingers pounding, convinced that words would save him.

He shoved the wad of paper back inside the folder and tied the ribbon with shaking fingers. He felt a dull ache behind his eyes and rubbed his palm hard against his temple, down over his prickly cheek. All he needed was a shave, a haircut and a long, hot soak.

The boy conjures the river. When the heat, and the cold, and the dry, and the endless, barren Spanish plains overwhelm him, and he feels his skin wither and crack, he conjures the river. He listens for it, amid the cacophony of too many men, and not enough food, and almost no tobacco, amid the shouts of the guards, and the grunts of pain, and the coughing fits of his comrades, he listens for the river. He listens for the sound it makes, when you have lifted your paddle and laid it, dripping, across your thighs. The powerful, swirling silence as the inexorable current wears away at the desperate roots of a toppling pine.

The boy conjures the scent of the river. Under the stench of sweat and shit and rotting wounds and spent gunpowder, he smells the murky, spring river as it rises into the lower pasture, water pooling in the fields, grass greening.

He smells the river mud, feels it in his fingers, the blue clay he had dug in pails for his mother. She fashioned smooth drinking bowls and rough containers for her kitchen. When he was a child, she made him a horse, a grey-blue stallion whose back legs blended into a chunky base, and the horse reared, defiant, on the windowsill beside his bed for years. He was surprised the first time he helped butcher a Spanish horse, how the essence of the animal disappeared with the hide. When you are hungry, meat is meat.

18

Dwight came to Maggie's office door bringing the smell of the bush with him. She breathed it in: pine musk, a trace of wood smoke, and the earthy essence of mosses and mushrooms. She needed to get out of the office more.

"How was it?" she asked.

"Crazy. There were four of them and, wow, the drama!"

"Drama?"

"Yeah, I mean there was all this…stuff…going on between them. The regional bug guy was there, and the woodlands guy from the mill, Eggers. And Roger Mallard—"

"The district manager?"

"Yep, and you know him. He's a walking press release. I think it was mostly for my benefit, though he might have been showing off for the new forester."

"Because?"

"She's a, well, she's a she. But, boy, she's tough. Eggers was full of cheap shots about girls in the bush. I couldn't believe some of it, really, but it just bounced off her. Every once in a while, she'd wink at me, just to let me know that she had heard it before."

"And the beetles?"

"Right. The beetles. Mallard thinks they've got"—he consulted his notebook—"an opportunity to slow them down. He says they've got science on their side. They're using some kind of pheromone to attract the females—there were some jokes about that—they bait certain trees, and then they fall and burn them. They're going to be putting out some contracts this winter, for more fall and burn, to get to the trees that have been attacked. Mallard says they can nip it in the bud that way."

"Did he say how many contracts, how much money?"

"He didn't."

"Will they hire locally? Sometimes they get crazy about certification and nobody local can qualify for the work."

"I didn't ask, but I'm going to need to follow up with him anyway." Dwight jotted a note. "They're tiny, you know."

"Tiny?"

"The beetles. About the size of a grain of rice."

"Did you get a picture?"

"Too small, but the bug guy gave me some line art we can use. He was a downer, that guy. He says the pine is doomed."

"Doomed? From a grain of rice?"

"A lot of rice."

"Can't they just spray them or something?"

"Nope. Mallard thinks they can limit the spread. Maintain. The bug guy thinks Mallard is delusional. He said that it's an epidemic and it won't be over until they run out of food."

"Run out of food?"

"Trees. The bug guy said that in twenty years there won't be a pine left standing between Hope and the Yukon border. The bugs will die of starvation. And that's his best-case scenario."

"Best case?"

"He's worried they could adapt, develop a taste for spruce. Then we'd be"—a stage whisper—"*screwed*."

"Is that for the record?"

"Nope. That was on the ride home. Mallard and Eggers took off for the Little Beauty, so I rode in with the bug guy and the new girl. He had a lot to say that wasn't for the record."

"If we stick to what's on the record, what have you got?"

Dwight held up his notebooks. "I've got lots. Mallard should have been in advertising. He was selling the whole time."

Maggie knew what he meant. "They used to be rangers, now they're bureaucrats. There used to be one guy, thousands of miles of bush, room for everybody: loggers, hunters, outfitters, hikers, bugs. Nowadays everybody wants to control their little piece, and Mallard is supposed to keep them all happy. Not that it matters whether he can or not. If the mills keep consolidating, it'll end up controlled by some corporation from Timbuktu. Globalization, eh? It's all about shareholders now. Not about what's best for the bush or the people that live in it."

"That's Eggers! To him it's all"—Dwight flipped pages—"*standing wood fibre*. He looks at a tree, he sees two-by-fours. He says they need to log the pine right away, while it's marketable. He wants Forestry to build the bridges so they can get into the back end of the Wolverine. Says if it doesn't happen within five years, the pine there will be gone. He says what the bugs don't get, a fire will."

"More optimism. Will Forestry build the bridges, do you think? At least they'd be logging."

"Mallard wasn't making any promises. He's still talking about visuals, aesthetic values. Both the bug guy and Eggers were rolling their eyes at that."

Stevie arrived and hovered in the doorway.

"How was Nash Malone yesterday?" Dwight asked.

Stevie shrugged. "How was yours?"

"I've got enough for a feature."

Maggie drew Dwight back to the beetles. "Did you get a sense that they'd fire the mill up again? If Forestry built the bridges, will they log the pine? Surely they could log the stuff that's already been attacked. Eggers is right about that, why let it just fall down in the bush?"

"Uh, yeah, that's a whole other problem. When the beetles attack, they bring a fungus with them. It's actually kind of cool, they carry the fungus with them and the fungus spreads into the tree and makes it easier for the beetles to chew through the cambium."

"Why is that a problem?"

"It stains the wood, blue streaks all through it. The lumber buyers downgrade it. Which means that unless Forestry drops the stumpage fees—"

"Which will get the Americans up in arms again about unfair advantages."

"The thing is, there isn't anything wrong with the wood."

"Like cows," Stevie interjected.

Dwight smirked. "*Cows?*"

"Yeah, at the auction house, buyers will downgrade a steer for any little thing. A floppy ear. A patch of white on a red calf. They cull it out, pay less for it. Any excuse, my dad used to say, even though the beef came from the exact same herd."

"Something like that," Dwight reluctantly agreed. "They said the blue-stained wood is structurally sound. But Eggers said that doesn't last forever. If they don't get to the tree soon enough after it's been hit by the beetles it"—he consulted his notebook—"checks? Is that right? How it cracks as it dries?"

"That's the word," Maggie said. "I've heard that too, about bug-killed timber."

"So, what, they want to clear-cut it?" Stevie asked. "You know that's not going to fly. Didn't somebody say that the beetles are in the park at Mount Robson? They're not going to clear-cut in the park."

No one spoke for a moment. Dwight turned to Stevie, asked, "What about your story? How was Nash Malone?"

"I didn't get anything, really."

"No interview?"

"No, yeah, no. I tried. I got a few notes but—"

"But what?"

"He didn't want to anymore."

"What did you do?"

"I left."

"You left?" Dwight shook his head. "You can't leave. They always want you to leave. If you want to be a reporter, you have to stick it out, get the story. I was counting on you."

Stevie shrank. Maggie took pity on her. "Dwight's right," she said, "reporters get their stories. But those old-timers, like Nash, it's hard for them. They come from a time when people didn't talk about themselves."

Stevie nodded. "That's my folks. Their private lives are private. No talk about feelings. No politics. No religion."

"What do they talk about?" Dwight asked.

"The weather. The cows. The hay crop. The neighbour's hay crop. The neighbours in general."

"Ah, yes, the neighbours," Maggie said. "We used to print a gossip column every week. All the comings and goings. Who had company. Who was going to the coast to visit relatives. Who had been to Kamloops."

Dwight snorted. "So, you could talk about the neighbours, but not—"

"Money," Stevie said. "Absolutely no talk about money."

Dwight said, "My parents and their friends barely talked about anything else."

"Not a peep out of mine," Maggie said.

"You're not exactly an open book yourself, Mags," Dwight quipped.

Maggie smiled. "Touché," she said. She felt them waiting, and she was momentarily tempted to lay it out for them: the accounts payable, the printing bill. If she was ever going to get out of the bookkeeping, she'd have to share her secrets with someone. Instead, she asked, "If I let you in on one little secret, will you let me get back to work?"

"Yes!" Both at once.

She lowered her voice, her expression deadpan. "Sometimes, late at night, I hear a voice that I'm sure is Hank's."

They exchanged a glance, but neither spoke.

"He's pacing, and muttering, and if I hold my breath, I can just make out what he's saying." They leaned forward in tandem. "Whooo. Whaaat. Whhhere. Hooowww." She slapped her palm on her desk. "Gotcha!"

Stevie jumped.

"Ooh," Dwight moaned, "so bad, Maggie, sooo bad."

They left, laughing, and she was alone with Dwight's earlier words looping through her brain: *Not a pine left standing. From Hope to the Yukon border.*

Stevie came back to the doorway. "I'm off," she said. "See you Monday."

"Enjoy your weekend."

"Thanks. Felicia and Dillon are taking me out tomorrow night. We're going to do the town."

"Sounds like fun. You deserve a night out."

Stevie turned to go. Maggie called her back. "Next Wednesday, in the afternoon? The Progressive Communities Committee? Could you cover their meeting?"

"Me?"

"Yes. You."

"A second chance?"

"Yes. That was my fault, letting you tackle Nash Malone. This will be easier, I promise. Get a notebook. Take notes. I know you've heard me talking to Dwight."

"Whoooo. Whaaaat. Hoooow."

Maggie laughed out loud and rocked back in her chair. She watched Stevie depart, feeling glad that she'd taken the chance on the girl after all.

19

Felicia made a face at Stevie's reflection. They were sharing the mirror in Felicia's bathroom, Stevie curling her eyelashes, Felicia adjusting errant wisps of hair. Felicia was beautiful, blonde and blue-eyed in the way Stevie had always longed to be. But she was different than most blonde, blue-eyed girls Stevie had known. She never bothered with makeup, none of the little enhancements that Stevie had learned from Vivian Jeffers. Felicia didn't seem to care about any of it. She wore faded denim shirts and tied her hair back with scrunchies that even Brit wouldn't have been caught dead in.

Felicia's husband, Dillon, had been a millwright at the sawmill but got on full time with the railroad when the mill went down. They owned their own house, had two nice kids, a boy and a girl. Even a regular babysitter, who was now downstairs with the four children.

It had been Felicia's idea. A night out. A few drinks, a dance or two, a couple of games of pool. "When was the last time you did the town?" she asked.

"A long time ago," Stevie admitted. "Even before Kurt and I split, we hadn't been dancing for a long time. Kurt didn't like to dance."

Felicia picked up the mascara tube and dabbed at her eyelashes.

"Give me that." Stevie turned Felicia to face her. "Don't blink."

When they arrived at the hotel bar, Dillon opened the door and held it for them. Stevie hesitated and Felicia nudged her into the room. Eyes swivelled. In the space of one long, painful breath, Stevie took in the whole room, a wide space with low ceilings and open beams. Tables were scattered along the edges, the bar was off to one side, the dance floor and bandstand at the far end. There were two men playing pool. Their women, a blonde and a brunette, watched from a nearby table. Stevie felt their scrutiny. She didn't recognize them.

Four old-timers had a table near the bar. Stevie recognized them from every bar she'd ever been in. Either lifelong bachelors or long-term widowers, faded, unshaven, greying. They didn't stare, but they noted her arrival. They didn't know her. If they had, she'd have been called over to buy a round.

They found a table near the dance floor, ordered drinks. Whisky for Dillon. Margaritas for Felicia and Stevie. "You want pitchers?" the barmaid asked. "We got 'em on special."

Stevie and Felicia shrugged at each other. "Why not?"

The drinks came. They danced. The band played a mix of country and classic rock, familiar covers from the sixties and seventies. Felicia dragged Stevie from her seat, opened a space beside her and Dillon. Stevie was embarrassed, but it felt good to move. The drinks flowed. During the break, after they had refilled their glasses and called for another pitcher, Dillon asked, "Was your husband Bobby Jeffers?"

Was. After all this time, the word still flattened her. She managed a nod.

"I played hockey in high school," Dillon said. "Same league. I faced off against him a lot of times. We never could beat the Grizzlies. He was as fast as Gretzky, that boy."

Stevie nibbled at the salty rim of her glass. People always said that about Bobby, that he was the next Gretzky, because he was handy with stick and puck, quick to dodge a check. They'd have hated to know how little he cared about the game. Bobby had never wanted to play NHL hockey. Stevie slurped down her drink, refilled her glass. Bobby hadn't wanted to be a logger either, come to that. Bobby had wanted to be an engineer. Tears stung at the corners of her eyes. She took another big gulp, avoided Felicia's questioning eyes. She saw Felicia elbow Dillon and frown. The tears welled. She fled to the bathroom. She pushed into a cubicle, closed the toilet lid and sat, slumped against the side of the stall.

Bobby. He'd have been swapping lies with Dillon by now, telling uproariously funny stories about hockey trips. There would have been laughter around that table, instead of uncomfortable small talk and long, silent glances around the room, Felicia and Dillon dancing with her out of pity. Stevie closed her eyes. The world spun. "Stevie? Are you in here? Are you okay? Dillon feels like an asshole."

Stevie scrubbed her knuckles across her eyes. A mistake. They came away smeared with mascara and tears. She wiped it off with toilet paper and unlatched the door.

"Oh, Stevie, I'm sorry. Dillon didn't mean anything by it." Felicia caught her into an awkward one-armed hug. "You poor thing."

"Not Dillon," Stevie said, "too many Margaritas. I'm not used to it."

Felicia moved her into the light over the mirror, balled a tissue and dampened it. "Stand still." She dabbed at Stevie's cheek.

"You'd think I was a teenager," Stevie said, "running off to the bathroom to cry."

"Here, you do it."

Stevie folded the damp tissue to a clean spot, rubbed at the mascara. Felicia watched her in the mirror. Their eyes met.

"Is it awful?" Felicia asked.

People wondered, Stevie knew, but few asked. "I was pregnant when I married Bobby. That's why. We wouldn't have gotten married otherwise. We weren't, you know, sweethearts. We just did what everybody expected us to do. Then, Brit...it was so soon, and Peg right after. Bobby and I, we barely knew each other. He was always away, working in camp somewhere. Maybe if we'd had more time, but we didn't. He just drove off the road one day." She swallowed. "His folks, you can imagine, their only son." She'd never told it this way. "I think a lot of what I felt was their grief, their loss. Vivian's, especially. I mean, I never expected to be a widow at nineteen, and I was sad for Bobby, for the things he didn't get to do, but for me"—the words were there, it was just a question of whether she would say them out loud—"for me, it was easier."

Felicia shifted from one foot to the other.

"I know, that's an awful thing to say, but I think it's the truth. Then, Kurt." Stevie tossed the blackened tissue to the garbage can. "That was more of the same, me doing what other people expected. He'd come sniffing around right after Bobby died, and everybody loved the idea. Bobby's friend, Bobby's enforcer, Big Kurt Talbot, the right-hand man. It was stupid. I'd just gotten a get-out-of-jail-free card and I traded it for Kurt Talbot."

"Was Kurt abusive?"

"No." Stevie forced a laugh. "We were … He was … just not around much. Always in camp. Not done partying. I figured the girls and I would be better off on our own than with a guy who wanted to live like he was single." The door swung wide and music poured in. The blonde from the pool table pushed past, into the cubicle behind them. "I feel better," Stevie said.

"Are you sure?" Felicia asked. "We can call it a night if you want to."

"No, really, I'm fine." The last thing she wanted right now was to go home to her dark trailer. "Come on. Let's dance!"

They danced every fast number of the next set, and then collapsed in front of their drinks, laughing. Felicia nudged Stevie, lifted a finger toward a table on the other side of the dance floor. A sandy-haired man was slouched in his chair, tapping his fingers on the armrest, a half-empty pitcher at his elbow.

He was medium everything. Not too tall, not too broad, well put together, none of Kurt's towering bulk. He was wearing suit trousers and a dress shirt with a button-down collar. His hand rested on the edge of the table and Stevie noted the lack of rings. Not that that meant anything. He saw her looking at him, didn't look away. He raised an eyebrow and nodded toward the dance floor. Stevie didn't respond. She watched him check out Dillon and Felicia, come back to her. Once more, the raised eyebrow.

Felicia kicked her under the table. Stevie jumped and grinned, and Medium Everything stood. He came to their table, half bowed to Stevie, offered his hand. She took it, allowed him to pull her lightly to her feet. The band played a fast two-step. Stevie relaxed into the guiding palm against her back, let the beat move her feet.

"I'm Miles," he said, when the song ended. It sounded like Miles. She didn't ask him to repeat it.

"Stevie," she replied.

"Pardon?"

"Stevie. Short for Stephanie."

They watched the band tuning. Other couples wandered off, but he made no move to leave the dance floor, held her hand lightly, no pressure, a comfortable warmth.

An hour later, seated beside him on the bench seat of his pickup, he caressed the inside of her thigh with the same practised ease.

"So?" he asked. "Your place or mine?"

"Yours." Felicia had already offered to keep the girls overnight, and she'd kicked Stevie again when Miles offered to drive her home.

"Mine, it is." He put the truck in gear and dropped his hand back to her thigh. She was fifteen again, and nothing mattered but those warm fingers against her leg and the rumble of the engine coming up through the seat. She knew better, but she wanted to go home with this man she didn't know. She wanted to be held, touched, loved.

She had a condom in her purse. "Just in case," Felicia had said. Stevie had blushed, protested that she wouldn't need it. "Put it in your purse," Felicia had insisted. "You're twenty-four years old, you're single, you're hot and it's 1995."

They pulled up to a room at the far end of the Timberline Motel, he killed the lights and turned to kiss her. It was a long, awkward kiss, their bodies at the wrong angle, but they kept at it, tongues dancing, jaws swaying. He shut off the truck and shifted in his seat, and they kissed again. He opened his door, she lifted her leg over the gearshift and slid out behind him. They embraced, standing beside the truck, her arms threaded around his neck, his hands on her hips.

Inside, he didn't turn on the light. His lips were on her cheek, her neck, the hollow beneath her chin. She was on the bed, his fingers on her skin. She caught his fingers at her top button, held them a minute, her mind processing furiously. What was she doing? Who was this guy? His other hand caressed her cheek, a finger lazily stroking her lips. She could feel it in her backbone. She released his fingers, let them do their work. He unbuttoned her shirt, one-handed, his other hand now stroking her thigh, the back of her leg, moving higher, stopping, starting, tantalizing. He used both hands to unclip her bra, his head bent to the task. He held it closed for a moment, then slid it along her ribs, his wrists brushing her nipples. Stevie raised her arms, her bra and shirt pulled away in one motion. There was a delicious pause while his hands slid down her arms, a promise of sensation that only lasted a moment before his fingers were back at her breasts, and then away, now working at the zipper on her jeans, the button already undone.

Somewhere between her jeans and his, the promise evaporated, and he disappeared into his own pleasure, moving her this way and that, hurried now, rougher. Stevie insisted wordlessly on the condom and he complied, but she'd been left far behind by then. He came with a shudder and a moan, rolled away, and lay on his back, breathing hard. Stevie huddled into his shoulder, resting herself against his warmth. He held her casually with one arm and drifted off to sleep without speaking.

In the half light, she could see that he hadn't been here long. There were no signs of an extended stay, just a small suitcase on the dresser, a garment bag hanging in the open closet. He'd told Dillon that he was in town on business, was thinking of relocating.

She slid out from under his arm, gathered her clothes from the floor and tiptoed to the bathroom. She swabbed herself with a hand towel, wrung out in warm water, and then held a hot facecloth to her eyes and breathed in the steam. She needed to go home. She dressed quickly, switched off the bathroom light, eased into the room.

"Hey, what're you doing?"

"Nothing. Go back to sleep."

He sat up, reached for the light. She stepped to the bed, stayed his hand. "I've got to get home," she whispered. "Don't get up. I'll walk."

"I'll drive you," he said, without moving.

"No. No. It's only a couple blocks and I'd rather walk."

"Really?"

"Yeah." She dropped his hand, it fell to the bed. "I'll see you around."

She waggled her fingers over her shoulder, unlocked the door and stepped out into the dim parking lot. She paused beside his truck. Smelled warm engine oil, her sweat, his cloying musk.

Stevie stroked the dusty hood. She wanted to rap on the locked door, crawl back into the warm bed, sleep skin to skin. She touched her cheek, her fingertips gritty with sand. "Go home, Stephanie Louise," she whispered. "Go home."

The town was quiet. She took the creek path behind the motel, angled up to the street at the back of Nash Malone's place. His backyard loomed: monstrous, prehistoric shadows. She shivered.

Afraid.

Be afraid?

Just Afraid.

She slowed her step, faced the shadows. They were only piles of bicycle parts, lean-tos draped in plastic tarps. She lingered, staring at the patchwork yard: the worn house, the woodshed behind it, the mounds of junk.

Why was she afraid of everything? Why could she never stand her ground? She'd just done it again, hadn't she? Let herself get pushed into something she barely wanted. She'd let Medium Everything pick her up because Felicia wanted her to. Everybody wanted to hook her up with somebody. Nobody wanted her single. A single woman, a single mother? Always such a problem for everyone.

A coyote howled. The village dogs bayed. Stevie cut through the empty lot to her street and followed her porch light home.

The sprawling complex that Creeksters called City Hall was a haphazard maze of buildings. It housed the municipal offices, council chambers, meeting rooms, the library, the college outreach coordinator, and the volunteer fire department. A buzzer sounded when Stevie pushed through the main door. Behind the long front counter there was a narrow hallway leading to the back of the building. Across the hall was a closed door with a sign: MAYOR. She could hear men's voices, muffled.

She waited a few minutes and then rang the small bell on the counter. Mayor Vanisle came out of his office and glared down the hallway, clearly expecting someone else to be answering the door. Behind him, the second voice appeared. It was Medium Everything. He was wearing a navy business suit and a textured red tie. Stevie felt a crevasse open at her feet, wished she could just lean forward and disappear.

"Can I help you?" Vanisle asked.

"I'm from the *Chronicle*," she said. "I'm here for the Progressive Communities meeting."

"So, you're Maggie's new reporter. Welcome." Vanisle stretched across the counter to shake her hand. He pointed to the door behind her marked Council Chambers. "They're in there. Go right in."

"Thanks." She nodded to Medium Everything, whose name might be Miles. He blinked and swallowed, his Adam's apple shifting his red tie up, and then down. He nodded back, without a trace of recognition.

Mortified—was he pretending or did he really not remember her?—Stevie turned and went through the door.

> Who: The Beauty Creek Progressive Communities Committee (PCC). Ned Shoults (Councillor), Doreen Morris (Councillor), Rosetta Burton (Beauty Creek admin. assistant), Midge Tilburt (Tilburt Contracting), Ralph Phillips (Pam's Dress Shop and Chamber of Commerce representative), Harriet Lemsky (volunteer).
> What: Regular PCC meeting. Burton reports flower boxes and benches for Main Street are being built by public works with PCC grant money. Shoults/Morris have contacted MLA re: grants for paving. Cleanup letters??????
> When: Wednesday, June 21, 1995
> Where: Council Chambers

How: Mel's Hardware donated nails and stain for flower boxes. They will also supply dirt and bedding plants at cost. Midge Tilburt recommends geraniums and marigolds b/c pretty and easy to keep. Harriet Lemsky wants begonias. Midge = begonias will freeze first cold night. Midge = flower-box flowers shouldn't be finicky.

Why: Shoults = "tourism is Beauty Creek future" Morris = "not a mill town anymore" Harriet = "a town should be tidy" Midge = if province "throwing money around to pretty things up" ought to use it or "won't get any next time."

"These are solid notes." Maggie gave her a thumbs-up. "Show me your story."

Stevie moved aside so Maggie could lean in and read the four paragraphs on her screen.

"You're on the right track. Keep going."

"I'm not sure what to put in."

"Put it all in. Later you can cut bits out but, at the beginning, put it all in."

"There is something else, but they asked me not to print it."

"What's that?"

"They talked a lot about messy yards, some new bylaw where the village can make people clean up their property."

"We covered that last week, the cleanup at Persky's mill."

"They were talking about what they'd do now, about other people who haven't complied, but they asked me not to say. They said could it be off the record, and I didn't know so I said okay."

"What are they going to do?"

Stevie hesitated.

"You can tell me."

"They're going to send a second batch of notices and wait and see. But they didn't want that to get around. They want people to think they might enforce the bylaw, the way they did at Persky's. They think they will get better compliance that way. Midge Tilburt is dead set against the whole thing. She said the village should just mind its own business. The rest of them think it's no big deal. They spent half of the meeting arguing about it. Then it was like they remembered I was there, and that's when Shoults asked me not print any of it."

Maggie pondered. "Don't worry about it," she said, finally. "If there's a story in it, we'll hear about it soon enough."

"So, it is off the record?"

"Technically, if you don't agree to it beforehand, it isn't off the record. But technicalities don't mean much here. We don't want them clamming up every time they see you coming."

"I doubt they'll do that. I volunteered for a work bee, and they made me a member of the committee."

"Really?"

"Yep. I'm on the beautification sub-committee. They say we need to spruce the place up, get the tourists to stay an extra day. Plus, they want more young people. I hope it's okay?" Could a reporter serve on committees? She hadn't thought about that.

"Anywhere else that would be a conflict of interest, but this is Beauty Creek. I'm glad you're getting involved. We'll ensnare you and you'll never get away."

Stevie blushed. "I don't want to get away. If I never move again, it'll be too soon."

Maggie opened the till, rifled through the cash. "Did you do the deposit yesterday?"

"I did."

"Why's there so much cash?"

"We had a big run on renewals. Six people. Plus Betty paid for her visitor guide ad."

"In cash?"

"She said she'd had a big week, some surveyors, and the cash was burning a hole in her pocket."

"Bless her."

"You know how she hates the bank."

Maggie looked blank. Stevie hesitated. Was it a secret? No, she decided, Betty told perfect strangers her opinion of bankers. "She'd walk to Kamloops to pay a bill with cash if she thought she'd rook the bank out of a ten-cent service charge."

"Did she say what the surveyors were doing?"

"Darn. I should have asked her, shouldn't I?"

"You're learning."

Maggie closed the till.

Stevie asked, "Have you heard anything about some guy named Miles who might be starting a business in Beauty Creek?"

"Miles who?"

"I don't know his last name. He was meeting with the mayor."

Dwight called from behind the partition, "You mean Miles Kingston?"

"Dwight!"

"It's not as if I can help hearing you," he said.

Stevie followed Maggie to Dwight's side of the wall.

"Was it Miles Kingston?" he asked. "He's not real tall, medium build, brown haired…"

"Medium everything?"

"That would be him. He's the developer behind the Timberline Resort project. The public meeting next week. The one you're going to cover while I'm away."

"Well, that explains that." Stevie spoke without thinking.

"Explains what?"

"Uh, you know, why he'd be meeting with the mayor."

"Did you hear anything? That door isn't very soundproof."

"Dwight! We don't listen at keyholes," Maggie said.

He grinned, unashamed. "Absolutely not, but, if we happen to overhear something, we're duty bound to check it out. No?"

"Did you hear something?" Maggie asked.

"Nope. He didn't say a word."

Across the room, Felicia swivelled, and Stevie felt her questioning look. "I better get back to work," she said.

20

The second notice was nothing more than a photocopy of the original. Nash tossed it onto the truck seat along with the grocery store flyer and the Hydro bill. Obviously Doyle hadn't gotten the word from Rufus. He would, soon enough. Nash had kept his end of the bargain: he'd hauled two loads of bicycle bones away. Might even get another one today.

He pulled out of the post office parking lot just in time to see June Fletcher's car turn down his street. He made an abrupt U-turn, drove north on Main, crossed the highway and bumped through the ditch and over the right-of-way to the old haul road below Blueberry Ridge.

At the wide spot at Four Mile, where they'd dug into the hillside for gravel, he parked in the shade of a spruce tree. The berries wouldn't be ready, but he and Miriam had always made time for an early reconnaissance of their favourite patches.

He climbed two gentle switchbacks up the gravel bank, stopping twice to catch his breath. There was a time he'd have run up this hill; now he was just glad there was no one watching him dodder along. He used to be able to drive to the top, but they had decommissioned the road last year, gouged deep, impassable hollows. Water bars, Forestry called them. Something to do with erosion, they said. Nash thought they just didn't want civilians in the bush any more.

Above the gravel bank, the ground sloped upward to the bluffs, a rock face his mother had called the high-water mark. Miriam, who had the eyes for it, had sometimes found small fossils here, remnants of the inland sea that had carved this valley. Nash angled through the brush, following the line of an old skid trail, an occasional greying stump reminding him of the magnificent firs that once grew here.

The blueberries were disappointing, plentiful but tiny. The heat had come too early, stayed too long. Without a soaking rain, the berries would ripen without getting any bigger. Luckily, there had been a bumper crop last year, and Nash had plenty left in his freezer.

From the bluffs, he followed another skid trail and found a few shady patches where the berries might grow to a useful size. He was bushwhacking his way back to the truck when he came upon a surveyor's peg: a fluttering pink ribbon tied to a knee-high stake. There were more, and now that he was looking, he could see that a right-of-way had been slashed. He followed the ribbons down to the road, a general outline taking shape as he walked.

"Hell's bells," he muttered. "It's a subdivision."

Private land? Since when? They'd been picking berries here for years. He cast out through time and a sliver of second-hand information rose to the surface. In Bull Devers's day, you could get a quarter section off the government if you promised to improve it. He'd heard stories of how Bull manipulated the system to get wood for his sawmill. Was this one of those? Who would've ended up with the title? Bull had been gone for years, and his kids were back east as far as Nash knew.

It embarrassed him to think that he was traipsing around someone's private property looking for berries. Trespassing. He knew people who did that. He wasn't one of them.

June had left a plate of scones on his doorstep. Her speciality: dry, bland biscuits peppered with crunchy black currants. Thank God, he'd seen her coming, no need to eat one to spare her feelings. He could smother them with bacon grease and feed them directly to the ravens. He left the plate on the counter, took the mail to his desk. He scanned Doyle's warning letter again, shook his head and tossed it to his paper tray.

The unfinished middle-of-the-night poem was still in his type-writer. He averted his eyes; it was ridiculous, avoiding it like a child, but he had learned the hard way what it cost, courting those old memories. Even for a poem, it wasn't worth it. He tugged the page from the typewriter, slipped it into the drawer reserved for reject poems. One line floated up.

If he is to live.

He strode to the kitchen, grabbed the kettle, took it to the tap. Water splashed his fingers and a memory surged. His vision blurred. He fumbled to turn off the faucet and the heavy kettle slipped from his grasp and clanged into the sink. As he slid to the floor, the past engulfed him and he was there again, in that black, remorseless night, and the blood—the warm, slippery, impossible blood—was pumping out of Pete's throat and flowing across Nash's fingers like a stream.

"Help us," he cried. "Somebody help us!"

The railroad bulls backed away, turned on the other men. Everyone scattered. To be caught, having witnessed this? They all ran. The bulls followed, left Nash kneeling over Pete in the pebbled alley between the main track and the siding.

The old men had warned them, said that they should stay aboard, that the railroad police here were particularly malicious. But Pete had insisted. He'd heard there was a card game. The bulls had come out of nowhere, clubs swinging. Pete's knife was no match. They'd knocked it from his hand with one blow and the biggest cop had picked it up and slashed.

The freight rocked beside them, hissing and creaking. A shadow crept from the nearest car. Dirty fingers pressed against Pete's wrist. Pressed harder. Then they tugged Nash's shoulder. Thin, pale lips whispered, "Come, lad. There's nothing you can do here."

Nash shook off the old man's hand.

"They'll be back. They'll kill you, too. Is that what your friend would want?"

"My brother," Nash said, the words a ragged cry.

The train shuddered, the first tug of movement rippling down through the cars. "Come away, lad." The dirty fingers closed Pete's staring eyes. "Come." The pressure on Nash's shoulder was more insistent. He shrugged it off and slumped back on his heels.

Dirty hands ransacked Pete's empty pockets. Nash chopped at them.

"It can't, any of it, help him anymore, can it?" Pete's shoes were slipped from his feet. "Come away, lad. Come away."

Nash swayed, might have fallen, but the old man dropped Pete's shoes and grabbed Nash's collar and smacked him across the cheek, open-handed but hard. "You'll not lie down for these bastards. Get up. Right now."

Nash took Pete's knife from the ground. He slit the knot that held Pete's money belt. There was no money in it, just their relief cards and a photograph of their mother with the twins. He folded Pete's arms across his chest, touched his own fingers to the quiet cheek, drew two interlocking circles in blood.

He heard a sharp intake of breath behind him. The dirty hands were gentle now, helping him up, moving him to the open door of the freight car. Another ripple undulated down the chain of box-cars, wheels squealed forward an inch. Nash was beside the door-way when he realized what he was about to do. "Wait! No!" He pulled away from the helping hands. "I can't leave him. We have to bring him."

"Get aboard, lad!" Arms held him from behind.

"Don't you see? I won't know...Where will they bury him? Where? How will I find him again?"

"For Christ's sake, kid. Get on!"

"What will I tell my mother?" It burst from his depths: his heart, his gut.

In the dark doorway, a man appeared, another behind him. They jumped down beside Nash and his keeper. "Come on, Jack," one of them said. "He's right."

One man hurried to the far side of the yard, climbed the ladder to the top of a grain car. "They're coming," he called. "Be quick about it."

Pete was heavy, his torso slippery with blood. Nash lifted his shoulders, the quiet head against his chest. The other men each took a leg. The steel wheels shuddered, the slow gathering of power reaching back toward them. At the boxcar door, the bigger man elbowed Nash aside to take the shoulders. Pete's arms flopped. "Careful!" Nash ran alongside, cradling one limp arm. The lookout raced across the yard, threw himself onto the freight, grabbed Pete's arm, hauled him into the car. He extended a bloody palm to Nash. The train picked up speed. Nash grabbed the proffered arm, swung into the car. He stayed where he landed, on the floor beside Pete's body, as the lights from the yard faded and they rolled west into the darkness.

The next day, at a siding high in the southern Rockies, between Hillcrest and Blairmore, they scraped a hole into the ground, piled a cairn of rocks. Nash stepped off the distance from the eastern switch. A fledgling spruce shadowed the grave. He carved Pete's initials in the tender bark, further marked the tree by breaking off its tip. Someday, he would need to know this precise location.

Nash heard a train call. The vibration in the floor seeped up into his joints, rousing him. He was in his house in Beauty Creek, flat on the floor, his cheek cushioned by the kitchen rug. Miriam had braided this rug, not long before she died, with strips of denim salvaged from a bag of discarded blue jeans. The train called again. He'd been making tea. He'd had a little dizzy spell. He worked himself to a sitting position and decided he'd rest a bit longer.

After Pete died, Nash had floated aimlessly. East coast. West coast. It didn't matter. Hounded here, hounded there, he'd been gathered up in one of the Vancouver sweeps and given the ultimatum: jail or camp. He chose a return to the camps. The agitators had gotten themselves organized. The Relief Camp Workers Union produced a newsletter, championed revolution. If Prime Minister Bennett, way over in Ottawa, couldn't hear them, they raged, there was only one solution: they would take the fight to him.

Bereft and angry and guilty—he still hadn't written to his mother—Nash fell in alongside the giant swell that became the grand, doomed On to Ottawa Trek.

During the heady days at the beginning of the trek, he had jotted notes for poems, trying to record something of the hopeful anticipation that had buoyed those tired, broken men. He hadn't shared their enthusiasm—how would it help him? Pete?—but he'd felt it, in the laughter, the singing, the amicable marching. He'd seen it in the faces of the people who flocked to greet them, giant kettles bubbling over bonfires in Golden, sides of beef donated to the cause in Calgary. People who had nothing somehow found food for a thousand men.

He'd never managed a single decent poem. For Nash, the trekkers' optimism and hope was forever eclipsed by the frantic, anguished mothers who had harried the lines at every stop. "Have you seen my boy?" they pleaded, some thrusting out a faded photograph, some with only a description: about your height, brown hair, blue eyes, always whistling. "My boy, Willy? My boy, Sam?"

My boy, Pete?

As the train clattered through the prairies, Nash composed paragraph after paragraph, committing nothing to memory save the salutation: *Dearest Mother*.

The trek stalled in Regina, flared briefly and violently, and slowly disintegrated. Nash was shipped back to the west coast. Hopelessness added to the guilt that soured in his throat. He lost a year, most of another, starving on the treacherous Vancouver streets, his days a tangled blur of drink and danger, filth and fear. The letter to his mother remained unwritten: he had no paper, no pencil, no stamp, no words.

He was eighteen, living in a mildewed tent near the viaduct, when he heard about Spain: the Vancouver newspapers were suddenly full of the plight of the valiant defenders in Madrid, holding out against the despot Franco. The fascists, Hitler and Mussolini, were supporting Franco; the fledgling Spanish government was isolated, rebuffed by the western democracies who should have been its allies. The call went out around the world.

"You'll have to straighten yourself out if you want them to take you," Buck Timmins told Nash.

So, he had. On New Year's Day, 1937, he left Vancouver, along with four other men in shabby clothes, each with a cardboard suitcase and five dollars spending money to get them first to Toronto, and then across the border to the docks at New York. They recognized each other but pretended they didn't. As they rattled out of Vancouver, and the smell of the ocean faded, Nash changed seats so that he faced the rising sun. His weeks-old passport was in his pocket. He was on his way to Spain—noble, distant, suffering Spain—where he could make a difference.

Nash tilted his head, testing. The dizziness was gone, his eyes were clear. He pulled himself up the side of the counter, took a tentative step. He stretched his jaw, then his shoulders. He'd just overdone it up on the ridge, got a bit too much sun. He retrieved the kettle and set it to boil.

The boy never completely understands what drew
him, pushed him, bore him to Spain. The moment
of decision remains a kaleidoscope of contradictory fragments, constantly shifting.

He went to Spain to avenge his brother.

He went to Spain to escape his past.

He went to Spain to belong.

He went to Spain to stand apart.

He went to Spain to live.

He went to Spain to die.

In the end, all he could be certain of was the
journey.

Everything he thought he believed, everything
he thought he was fighting for, became a distant, childish memory, tinged with woodsmoke
and the scent of the rough pine poles they had
used to erect the tents in the camps. The slo-
gans, the songs, the chants remained only fragments of rhythm, snatches of a chorus he would
hum to himself, when the poignant notes of a
Spanish guitar defied the roar of the bombers
and drifted over the shattered stone wall that
sheltered him.

21

Maggie was surprised to see the village council chambers so crowded on a weeknight; she counted at least eighty people in the small room. She held the door for Rufus Vanisle, who was bringing extra chairs from the staff room.

"Quite a turnout." She had to raise her voice to be heard over the din.

"I know," he shouted, "isn't it great?"

Most people were at the front of the room, where the councillors' desks had been pushed together to hold an elaborate model of the Timberline Mountain Resort. Others were poring over maps and conceptual drawings that were taped to the walls. Maggie found Stevie in the crowd, and they took seats at the side of the room, where they could watch both the speakers and the audience.

Rufus tapped lightly with his gavel. When everyone was seated, he said, "You know why we're here, so I won't waste your time with long introductions." He indicated the medium-built man with sandy hair who was standing near the model. "This is Miles Kingston, of Kingston Developments, and he wants to say a few words about the Timberline project."

The crowd clapped politely. Kingston thanked Rufus and waited for the crowd to quiet. Maggie noted his expensive shoes, his crisply creased dress pants, his confident air. City slicker, she thought.

"This town has got so much"—Kingston eased the word out, as if he was unveiling a jewel—"potential."

Someone at the back of the room laughed out loud. Heads craned. It was Alvin Tilburt.

"I mean it." Kingston raised his voice, drew attention back to the front of the room. "You folks don't know what you're sitting on here. Your little Beauty Creek has the makings of a world-class destination."

This time there was a murmur of appreciation.

"But, potential isn't enough. Lots of places have potential. What you have to have, along with your potential, is *capacity*." Again, the extra emphasis, like a teacher drawing attention to a word that would be on the test. "Will you be able to attract a world-class clientele? Will you be able to provide them with the kind of visitor experience they are accustomed to?"

Alvin barked again. Maggie saw Midge give him a sharp elbow.

"My investors," Kingston said, "aren't just looking for potential. They are looking for capacity. They want a forward-looking place. Forward-looking people. People who aren't afraid to make a change. People who are ready to grab the brass ring. And what am I asking in return? Your support for a couple of zoning changes, a minor amendment to an obsolete community plan."

"Our Official Community Plan is less than five years old," June Fletcher shouted. "Who are you to say it's obsolete?"

"I'm not saying it wasn't valid when it was drawn up, but times have changed, haven't they? Look around when you drive down the valley, those red pines?" He appealed to the room.

Heads bobbed.

"When times change, forward-looking people adjust. I'll bet that I'm not the only forward-looking person in the room."

Kingston paced to the other side of the table. "You have to ask yourselves, what have I got to sell? Once upon a time it was beaver hides. Then the railroad needed ties. Then it was lumber. Lumber has served you well, but it's going. You don't have any minerals to speak of. So, what have you got? You've got exactly what the people who named the place could see, you've got beauty. Natural beauty. No matter where you decided to build, you'd be looking at a peak that was worth looking at. People will pay for that."

As he spoke, Kingston's gaze moved along their row, landed briefly on Stevie and jerked past. Maggie felt Stevie flinch, but when she caught her eye Stevie looked away.

Kingston thundered. "I know your chamber of commerce is on board. I know your village council is on board. What I need to know is: are you on board?"

Maggie saw people nodding. Someone started clapping. A few people stood, a few more, and then the majority stood and applauded. June Fletcher remained seated. Alvin walked out the door, shaking his head.

Maggie was watching Stevie and Kingston. She saw them exchange a look, a brief look, but definitely a *look*.

The clapping abated. "Just a couple of words," Rufus said, coming to stand beside Kingston. "I want to thank Kingston Developments for their interest in Beauty Creek, and I want to thank you for your interest and enthusiasm, and for coming out on such a lovely summer night. We've had a lean year, and I know we've all been waiting for something to come along. Now that it has, all we've got to do is roll up our sleeves and get behind it. There'll be another public meeting once the paperwork is sorted. I hope to see you here for that too."

Maggie nudged Stevie. "Our turn. Let's see what he's not telling us."

Rufus introduced her. "Mrs. Evans owns the local newspaper."

Kingston extended his hand. "A pleasure. I hope we'll be able to work together to get this project off the ground. If there's anything you need from us"—he fished a business card from his shirt pocket— "my direct line is there. Call me anytime."

Ned Shoults elbowed in, wanting to introduce his wife.

People started to drift out of the meeting. Maggie dispatched Stevie to collect a few quotable Creekster reactions, and returned to Kingston. "What's your timeline?" she asked. "I didn't see many specifics—"

"It's fluid. Depends on, well, depends on Rufus, here, and Ned. Depends on you too. If we get some momentum, we could be breaking ground by the spring. We'll be bringing some serious cash with the construction phase, probably fifty or sixty jobs. Once we're up and running, there will be our jobs, plus the spinoffs. Everybody has to eat and buy socks. Am I right?" He chortled, waited for her to join him.

"Does that mean you've got the money for phase one?"

"I wouldn't be here if we didn't. Not much point in all this noise if we can't at least get the thing off the ground." Another easy chuckle.

"I'm a bit confused about what's included in phase one," she pressed. "Are the cross-country ski trails part of that? Or is it just the hotel and restaurant?"

"Wouldn't be much of a resort if it was just a hotel and restaurant, would it? No, we have a whole package concept in mind, summer and winter, skiing and hiking, plus the spa experience. High end, very high end." He drew her over to the model, stroked the rooftop of the main building. "Two hundred units and that's just for starters. Two hundred more the following summer. You people don't know what you've got here. It's a gold mine. Vancouver is bursting with yuppies with spare cash, and they all want a wilderness getaway. We can sell them hiking in the summer, cross-country in the winter. We'll market all-inclusive packages, outdoor stuff, indoor gym, pool, steam room, massage, the works. Get one of those Vancouver chefs that's all the rage. Beauty Creek will be *the* place to be. All we have to do is get it off the ground. The planning people envision two choices. An every-man kind of place: that's phase one, with the hotel and what have you. Phase two is the more exclusive option. We'll build a lodge across the creek, same view but a bit separate from the town, so they can pretend they're the only ones there."

Maggie shuffled to the last page of the information package. "This rezoning application covers a big chunk of property across the high-way, up on the ridge. What's that about?"

"That's for the long term," he said. "Once the main development here in Beauty Creek takes off." He lowered his voice. "Off the record, I can tell you that we're also talking to Council about that nice parcel the village owns, along the creek. It has real potential. Townhouses, condos, I could sell anything with that view."

"You mean...?"

He held a finger to his lips. "But that's under wraps, for now."

Couldn't be much of a secret, if he was blabbing it to her.

"Speaking of selling, I hear your newspaper is for sale," he said.

It caught her off guard. "News to me."

"Little bird told me." He winked. "If you're serious, give me a call. I've got a few investors that are mad for newspapers."

Maggie didn't know how to respond. Blabbermouth Rufus, she thought.

June Fletcher had elbowed her way through the crowd and was bearing down on Kingston. "Don't you run off," she shouted. "I've got some questions for you."

Kingston gave Maggie a resigned eye roll.

"Have you got the money?" June demanded.

"I have investors."

"That's not what I asked."

"You don't understand much about development, do you? Things tend to progress synchronously, zoning and permits need to be in place before most investors sign on, the two happen simultaneously."

"Actually, here in Beauty Creek, we know plenty about development. Not so much about building, but more than we care to about developers."

"Is that a question?"

"Maybe not, but here's one. Tell us about your project down by Sicamous."

"What about it?"

"The plans look a lot the same."

"It's not unusual to transfer concepts."

"Except that one, what was it? Sunrise Village? That didn't go, did it?"

"There's still some interest."

"But I hear that most of the properties in the vicinity of Sunrise Village did sell."

"People will speculate."

"It's true, they will." June's eyes glinted. "Some of the people there speculated to me that you bought up most of the real estate around

Sunrise Village. And sold it at a tidy profit."

"Last I heard, there was no law against buying and selling land."

"True enough. Just not much benefit to the community from it. The profit waltzes off, doesn't it? Nothing for the local economy but a real estate commission."

"Look, I don't know what you're trying to insinuate," Kingston said. "I'm just here to help you people sell the only marketable commodity you've got left." He gestured to the window, the mountains beyond. "If you don't want it, I can go somewhere else."

"Seems unlikely you're going anywhere," June said. "Unless the numbered company that bought up the property across the highway belongs to somebody else."

Kingston didn't bite.

June's voice rose. "You have no idea what it takes to live here. You breeze in on a sunny weekend and think you know something about the place. Try it in February when there's only eight hours of daylight. Or the road is closed for three days at a time."

"What's that got to do—"

"This place is our life. This is where we want to live until we die. Take me. I get by now. I'm not making a fortune, but I'm making a living. But if the assessments triple? Taxes go up to pay for the improvements your world-class tourists think they need? What happens to us?"

"Think about what you're saying," Kingston said. "If your assessment triples, your property value will probably have quadrupled."

"So?"

He repeated himself. "Your property will be worth four or five times as much."

"So what?"

Maggie knew what it was that June wanted him to spell out. He obliged. "You'll be able to sell it for, hell, ten times what it was worth when you bought it."

"And go where?"

"Anywhere you want."

June groaned.

Kingston shrugged at Maggie. "You can lead them to water—"

"Damn straight." June thrust a finger into his face. "And they still won't drink the snake oil you're selling."

Kingston stepped back, waved a disparaging hand, and walked away. June whirled on Maggie. "I hope you got that down."

"I'm on it, June." Maggie bent to her notebook, wrote quickly, the whole exchange. *People will speculate.* That was a direct quote. Also, *you people.* He'd said that more than once. She probably wouldn't use much of it—why pour fuel on that fire?—but she'd have it.

June raged on. "Cookie-cutter plans. Cookie-cutter towns. You know how a cookie-cutter works, right? You put it over the dough and you press. You keep the shape and peel off the edges and toss 'em. That's what Kingston has in mind here. A cookie-cutter resort town with his cookie-cutter hotel spa in the middle of it. All us ordinary bits? We'll just get scraped off. That's what we are to him. Scraps. He'll brush us right off his pastry board and into the scrap heap.

"People that have lived here all their lives, people who get by without flower boxes and pavement, will get squeezed, and squeezed again. Oh, there will be cappuccino bars, and more restaurants than stray dogs, but the people that work in them won't be able to afford a house. They'll put us to work scrubbing their toilets, polishing their floors, changing their beds, feeding them and wiping their arses. But they'll pay us in shit. Minimum-wage jobs. Tips. And, when they can't find enough people to do that, they'll import them. Someday, someone will want to build a ski hill on Wolverine Mountain, and we'll end up just like Jasper and Banff, teenage ski bums living eight to a bedroom."

Rufus came up beside June, touched her arm. "You didn't have to bite his head off."

"Bite his head off? That was me being nice. Does he own the property across the highway? They're surveying up on the ridge, looks a lot like a subdivision to me. But you'd know that, down at the village office, wouldn't you?"

"They can't subdivide without a public hearing, June. There'll be an advertisement in the *Chronicle*. In due time."

"They have to be pretty sure of the outcome to be surveying before the hearing."

"Parallel processes, June. You heard what he said. They had the surveyors here anyway."

"But—"

"No buts. He's right, we don't have much left to sell but the view. That, and our location. We're on the right highway; we're positioned to pick up bus traffic. We're close enough to Jasper for spillover."

Maggie wanted to take up June's argument. What *would* Creeksters do when the assessments tripled, and the taxes with them? She heard Hank's voice, cautioning: *Not your job to know what's right. Your job is to get down the arguments.*

June huffed in exasperation and walked away.

Maggie closed her notebook. "He'd heard the *Chronicle* was for sale."

Rufus didn't blink. "It's not a secret, is it?"

"I guess not."

Across the room, Maggie saw Kingston pouring cream into a cup of coffee, Stevie at his shoulder. "Speaking of secrets," she asked Rufus, "have you heard anything about that?"

"What? Kingston and your girl?" He shook his head. "Doubtful. He's got a wife and two kids in Vancouver."

Stevie watched Miles Kingston stir cream into his coffee.

"You didn't tell me you worked for the newspaper," he said.

"You didn't ask."

He reached past her for a sugar cube, brushed his arm along her rib cage.

She flinched. "I hope Mrs. Fletcher didn't give you too hard a time."

"Nothing I can't handle."

She clutched her notebook.

"So, you're a reporter?"

"Yes." She was. At least until Dwight got home.

"I've got a couple of investors flying in tomorrow. We're going to do a helicopter tour on Saturday. Why don't you come along, get a bird's-eye view of what we've got planned."

"Uh, that sounds great, but I'll need to clear it with Mrs. Evans."

"We're leaving from the airport. Nine o'clock. Bring a camera. Who knows, after I get rid of the moneybags, I might be able to give you a one-on-one interview." He winked, and touched her arm again, and then strode back to the cluster around the model.

Maggie came across the room. "What did he want?"

"He said they're going to do a helicopter tour on Saturday. Asked if the *Chronicle* wanted to come along."

"Did he now?"

"Uh-huh. Some of his investors will be here, he said."

"Aerial photos would be nice. How do you feel about helicopters?"

"I don't mind." Stevie had never been off the ground in her life.

Maggie gave her a long look. "Take extra film," she said. "And... be careful."

Stevie ducked her head to avoid the question in Maggie's gaze. "Look at the time," she said, "I have to pick up the girls."

Felicia insisted she come in for tea, Dillon was on nights. It didn't take her long to ferret out the whole story. "So, he pretended he didn't know you last week, and he hasn't called, but now he's invited you on a helicopter tour? And you said yes?"

"You said it yourself. I'm single. He's cute. It's 1995. Why not?"

"You do realize he's probably married? Or something. He's too old for no complications."

"I don't want to marry him, silly. It's just for fun. Besides, it might rain."

"None in the forecast."

"If I go, can the girls come here?"

"Sure. They can stay overnight. Dillon will be home, and I'm back by three. That way, if your helicopter tour runs, you know, *late*—"

A tremendous crash sounded from the basement.

They flew down the stairs. In the den beside the playroom, the four children were standing in a sombre circle around a shattered table lamp.

"Whoops." Felicia broke the silence.

"It was me," Brit volunteered, her voice quivering. "I didn't mean to."

Felicia unplugged the power cord. "Don't worry about it, sweetie. Things break around here all the time."

"What were you doing?" Stevie demanded.

"We were playing puppies," Peg said. "Brit and I were the puppies, we were jumping off the couch—"

"Brittany Jeffers! You know better." Stevie reached out, open-handed, but Felicia stepped between them.

"In this house, we don't hit." She said it quietly, a simple, matter-of-fact statement, as if she was telling Stevie where to hang her coat. Without pause, she added, "Could you run up and get me a garbage bag? They're under the kitchen sink."

Stevie flushed, but Felicia had already turned away. "Come on, you lot, let's get this mess gathered up. Be careful with that glass."

When Stevie returned, the broken lamp was in a pile, and everyone was back in the playroom. There was laughter, and she heard Felicia asking, "So, what did we learn here today?"

"Use your head to think ahead." Four voices in unison.

Since when did Brit and Peg say that?

Felicia nodded Stevie into the room, linked arms with her, and said, expectantly, "Anything else?"

"Every ugh deserves a hug!" Felicia's kids shouted. Laughing and tickling, they dragged the adults to the floor. Brit and Peg hung back for a few moments and then flung themselves gleefully into the game.

When the giggling finally subsided, Felicia got out the vacuum while Stevie put the crumpled shade and the biggest pieces of metal and glass into the garbage bag.

"There we are," Felicia said, after she shut off the vacuum. "Good as new."

"Gather up your stuff," Stevie called to Brit. "Time to go."

"Ah, Mom—"

"Don't go," Felicia said. "Dillon won't be home until midnight. Stay and keep me company."

"Please, Mom, please."

Stevie wanted to stay. She wanted to go back upstairs with Felicia and drink tea and interrogate every single sentence Kingston said to her but the crushing shame in her chest needed to get home where she could hide her head and sob.

"I can't tonight," she said. "Come on, Brit. Chop-chop."

Stevie helped Peg firm the soil around a dazzling yellow begonia. Brit stood by with the watering can, Midge Tilburt at her shoulder with a steadying hand on the spout. Harriet Lemsky hovered. She had frowned when Stevie showed up for the planting bee with the girls, but Midge had instantly made them welcome. "Extra workers! Excellent. I need all the help I can get."

Alvin had coaxed the girls into the wheelbarrow for the ride from the public works yard to Main Street. The flower-box bench units had been installed, and they were beautiful: wrought-iron frames and spacious hexagonal cedar planters.

Harriet took the watering can from Brit and added one more sprinkle of water. "There," she said. A mix of dwarf flowers surrounded the magnificent begonia centrepiece, a profusion of colour.

"Just pray we don't get a frost," Midge warned. "These begonias won't take a lick of it. They're pretty enough, but I still don't think they're worth all this bother."

In addition to being delicate and expensive, Harriet's begonias had also been late. The flower boxes were supposed to be unveiled for Canada Day, but when the hardware truck arrived, there had been no begonias. So, the initial planting bee had begun with a confrontation. Stevie had thought Harriet and Midge might actually come to blows over whether they should use geraniums instead.

"Where would we get them?" Harriet had demanded.

"Everybody's got 'em. I've got spares. So do you. We just get a few from here and there. Slap 'em in the middle."

Harriet bristled. "The begonias are coming. They just missed the truck. They will be here next week for sure."

"After the weekend?"

"Yes, but—"

"That's stupid. We should just use some geraniums."

"It's not stupid!"

Stevie had interrupted to suggest a compromise. "What if we plant them with geraniums for now, and replace them with the begonias when they get here?"

"That's a good, practical suggestion, Stevie. Thank you. Let's do that."

"Be a lot of extra work," Midge had huffed, but she'd happily gathered and helped plant the geraniums, some from her own gardens, a few from her neighbours, even one from Nash Malone.

In the end, it hadn't mattered. A deluge of rain drowned the events planned for the Canada Day weekend, including Stevie's helicopter tour. Geraniums swam in the new flower boxes. Kingston's pickup disappeared from the Timberline Motel. Stevie's answering machine was stubbornly silent, and when Felicia asked, she had nothing to tell her. "Bastard," Felicia said. "Yep," Stevie agreed and rolled her eyes. She hadn't told Felicia the pathetic version: how she'd showed up at the deserted airport at the appointed time; waited for an hour; driven back to town, past Betty's, past the Timberline Motel, past the village office, searching for the white pickup, imagining what she might say when she found it.

Alvin Tilburt trundled up to the planter with a wheelbarrow of topsoil. He lifted a shovelful and Stevie gently scooped the soil around a marigold seedling that had been unearthed during the geranium-to-begonia swap.

"We miss you, down at the cafe," Alvin said. "The new girl is okay, but she's not you."

"You guys be nice to her." Stevie pretended to glower. She remembered how intimidating the morning coffee crowd could be.

"Don't you worry," Alvin assured her, "I'm keeping an eye on her."

Harriet elbowed past Alvin and repacked the dirt around the begonia. "There," she said. "Don't they look nice?"

Even Midge nodded. The flower boxes did add a cheerful air, somehow filling in the gaps, masking the blank windows of vacant shops.

"Next we get some pavement here." Harriet indicated the dusty street. "You won't recognize the place."

Alvin chortled. Midge shushed him. "Coffee and pie," Alvin said. "I was promised coffee and pie for this day's work."

"Betty invited us," Midge said to Stevie. "Come. Bring the girls."

"Thanks, I will. I'm just going to pop in at the *Chronicle,* say hi to Felicia." She watched them walk away, Alvin pushing the wheelbarrow, Midge with a shovel over her shoulder, Harriet talking, her hands waving.

At the *Chronicle,* Felicia was copying a graphic from a clip-art catalogue. Dwight was at his keyboard, fingers poised. The store was dark and quiet. The girls went immediately to their desk. The office gnome, who was probably Felicia, but might have been Maggie, often left colouring sheets in the desk drawers.

"You're back," Stevie said to Dwight.

"Yesterday."

"How was it?"

"Awesome. What're you doing here on your day off?"

"Just popped in to say hi. We were on flower-box detail."

"Flower boxes? The village ones?"

"Ah, darn, yeah. I should have gotten a picture. If you want one, Alvin and Midge and Harriet are on their way to Betty's."

"Thanks!" He grabbed his camera.

"Flower boxes, eh?" Felicia teased. "You are Creekster material, Stevie Jeffers, you really are." She waved her photocopies in the air. "Anybody want to cut something for me?" The girls clamoured, and Felicia gave them scissors. "You should bring these two by every Sunday. Cut my work in half."

Stevie hadn't intended to stay, but the girls loved helping Felicia, so she brought a flat to the production table and proofread the ads, methodically comparing them, word for word, with the original order. She had finished the page by the time Dwight returned.

"Did you catch them?"

"Yep. Alvin wasn't having any of it, but Harriet was delighted. Too bad nobody's paying for colour this week. Those flowers would look great."

Stevie set the flat back on the paste-up board. Tires crunched in the alley.

"Here's Maggie," Felicia said. "Maybe she'll spring for colour or maybe she can get the chamber of commerce to kick in for it."

When Maggie didn't appear, Felicia stretched to look out the window. Stevie followed suit, saw a white pickup pull away with Maggie in the passenger seat.

Dwight came up behind Stevie. "Did Maggie get a new pickup?"

"That's Miles Kingston's truck," Stevie said.

Dwight frowned. "What's Maggie doing with Miles Kingston?"

Felicia busied herself at her monitor. Stevie and Dwight turned to her.

"What's going on?" Dwight demanded.

"Nothing."

"You know something, Felicia," Dwight insisted. "I can tell."

"It's just something Dillon heard. Total gossip."

"What?"

"Kingston's maybe looking at buying the *Chronicle*. Apparently, some of his investors are interested."

"She wouldn't," Dwight said.

"She might," Felicia said.

"Fuck," Dwight said.

Felicia glared and jerked her chin toward Brit and Peg, but they were absorbed in their cutting. She asked Stevie, "Did you know he was back?"

Stevie blushed. "Nope."

Dwight frowned. "Why would she?"

Felicia said, "The committee—"

"The committee! I was supposed to meet them at Betty's for pie. Come on, girls, give Felicia her stuff. We have to get groceries too, sometime today."

They went out the back door, past Maggie's empty car. Stevie's stomach curled in on itself. If Maggie sold the paper...? *Fuck* was exactly right.

"Don't hang on the side like that," Stevie snapped, as Brit's weight careened the grocery cart toward the tower of discount toilet paper.

Brit glowered, jumped off the cart and marched away down the aisle. Peg trotted after her. "Don't go out of the store," Stevie called after them.

When she finished her shopping, they were hovering near the candy display next to the till. Brit ignored her. Peg skipped forward to pluck the bread from the cart and flop it up onto the carousel.

"Hi, Mr. Malone."

Stevie wheeled. Brit was gazing up expectantly at a smiling Nash Malone.

"Hello yourself, little miss," he said. "How are you today?"

"I'm good." Brit bounced to the side of his cart, peered in. "Oranges. I knew you would have oranges."

"You did, did you?"

"Uh-huh." She stepped onto the base of the cart, clung to its side, sent Stevie a cheeky smirk. "Want me to put them on the checkout for you?"

"Sure, if they're not too heavy."

"Oh no, they're not heavy." She dragged the unwieldy mesh bag up the side of the cart. Nash caught one corner, eased it onto the belt.

"We met at the school," he explained to Stevie.

"Oh."

"When Mr. Malone was as big as me there was no highway," Brit said, "and he only ever got one orange at Christmas. And not every year."

"At the school history fair, in the spring. She—"

"My mom couldn't come to the history fair. She had her computer class."

"She interviewed me, for the fair," Nash continued, "that's how we met."

"And you bought us candy that time," Brit added. "Mom never buys us candy."

"Brit!"

"I remember." Nash smiled at Peg. "This one likes butter toffee."

Peg wriggled against Stevie's leg.

"That's Peg, she's my sister," Brit chirped. "She likes toffee. I like licorice."

"But we're not having candy today." Stevie glared.

"I can do that." Brit wheeled Nash's cart out from under his hands, pushed it forward into the other empty carts with a loud clang. The clerk frowned.

"Brittany. Ann. Jeffers. Over here, miss. Right. Now."

"I don't mind." Nash gestured toward the candy.

"But I do." Flustered, Stevie paid the clerk, set her bags in a cart, pushed it out the door. "Brit! In the car. This minute. Do up your seatbelt and don't even talk to me." Stevie thrust the bags onto the back seat. Peg was struggling to clip her seatbelt. Stevie took a deep breath. "You have to put it in this way, pumpkin. Remember?"

"I don't see why you were rude to him," Brit said, from the front seat.

"Rude? Me? You were the one begging for candy."

"Is it because he smells funny? Because that's nobody's fault."

"It hasn't got anything to do with how he smells. Do up your seatbelt." She spun the cart, pushed off toward the store just as Nash Malone came through the door. Short of running away, there was no escape. And, the girls were watching. Stevie squared her shoulders. "I'm sorry if I was a bit short with you. I—"

"No need to apologize."

"I was just surprised and... I'm not having the best day."

"Maybe you need a butter toffee."

She chuckled. "Maybe. I didn't know that was you, at Brit's history fair."

"She's a bright wee 'un."

"I think so. I mean, thank you."

"It's good, what that Miss Jasmani does, that history fair. Kids need to learn about that stuff. Along with their alphabet."

Stevie agreed. She was glad that Miss Jasmani would be Brit's teacher in September.

Nash cleared his throat. "I guess I might have been a bit short with you, too... that interview."

"It's okay," Stevie said. "Now we're even." She hesitated. "It's not only kids who need to know. Lots of people in Beauty Creek need to know more about the old days. I wish you'd let me finish that interview."

He switched his grocery bag from one hand to the other.

She persisted. "Can I call you about it? Next week?"

"I suppose we could try again," he said. "If you're sure you want to chance it."

"You're a beggar for punishment, aren't you?" Maggie snipped the plastic tie from a bundle of newspapers. The scent of fresh ink billowed.

"It's those books you gave me." Stevie tore a perforated sheet of address labels into three strips, began peeling and sticking. "I'm kind of curious about how someone from Beauty Creek ended up in Spain."

"Me too. Hank tried to interview him once. In the early eighties, there was some kind of reunion. It was on television. A bunch of them went back to Spain." She snipped the tie from another bundle. "Nash didn't go."

"Did Hank get the interview with Nash?" Stevie asked. "I'd like to read it."

"Nash wouldn't give him the time of day. Some reporter from the CBC came around too, tried to get Nash to talk to him. He'd been everywhere, talking to the Spanish vets. He was a nice guy. Stayed at the house a few nights. He and Hank wrote back and forth for a few years."

Stevie attached the last local label, moved on to the out-of-town subscribers. "Did Nash ever talk to the CBC guy?"

"Nope. Lots did though. Waste of taxpayers' money, that was. He did those interviews, hundreds of hours, travelling all over the country, and the CBC never did use them."

"Why not?"

"Idealists make people uncomfortable," Maggie said. "Always have." She went to her office, came back with a thick hardcover. "I found this at home."

The Face of War. Martha Gellhorn.

"I've never heard of her," Stevie said.

"See? Not hard at all." Maggie's voice was dryly approving. "She was a war correspondent. You might not get through the whole thing, but some of it is about Spain."

Maggie grabbed another stack of papers, resumed counting. Stevie tore several lengths of butcher paper from the roll they kept under the light table and started wrapping bundles sorted by postal code.

When Dwight arrived to do the local deliveries, Maggie was at the front desk. He came to Stevie's shoulder. "Did she say anything about Kingston?"

"Not to me," she whispered.

23

The recorder squeaked a few times and then hummed along, little plastic wheels dragging the tape forward. Nash blew out a long breath, wishing he'd phoned and cancelled.

"What was it like?" the girl asked. "In Spain?"

He snorted. Her eyes darted sideways. "Sorry," he said, "that's a big question."

"You're right," she stammered, "that's a silly question. When did you enlist?"

He wanted to snort again, but he didn't. He could see little Brit in her, around the eyes, and in this frank questioning. "It wasn't a regular war that you went down to the recruiting office and signed up for. You...you let people know you were interested, and they got in touch with you. The right people, mind, otherwise you'd be in jail."

"In jail?"

"We weren't supposed to go. Non-intervention they called it. A two-thousand-dollar fine or two years in jail. Or both."

"Non-intervention." She made a note. "Who got in touch with you?"

"Some of the guys were communists, some were anti-fascists, though I probably couldn't have told you what either word meant. Most of the organizing, getting us there and such, was the commies." She kept writing, but he saw her shoulders tighten at the word. He was scaring her again. He softened his voice. "They were mostly just workers. Which is a bit of a joke, since most of us hadn't had a scrap of work for years. Sometimes I think half the boys went to Spain just because it was a job." He saw her shoulders relax.

"How did you get there?"

"To Spain? By train to Toronto and on to New York. By ship from New York."

"What was that like?"

"The ship? Don't ask."

He had thrown up his supper the first night at sea and vomited every few hours for days. The men in his cabin had draped cold cloths over his forehead and coaxed him to sip water and chicken broth. They brought clean basins for him to shit and puke in. Eventually there was nothing left, and they held him while the dry heaves wracked his body. He wept and wished for death, drifting in and out of terrible half dreams of foggy switching yards, burly railroad bulls, bloody bodies without faces, and his mother crying.

He had tried to stay awake. He knew he ought to have hidden his small collection of bills. Now it was too late. But, when he fought them, as they peeled off his soiled clothes and changed the sheets beneath him, the oldest of his bunkmates, a lumberjack from Quebec, grabbed him, locked eyes. "I will protect your stake with my life," he said fiercely. "With my life. I swear it." He spat, sideways, into Nash's puke bucket.

During the dark vacuum between vomiting, exhausted beneath the rough wool blankets, Nash felt quiet hands lifting the cloth and stroking cool water across his face. It was nearly worth the agony of seasickness, that feeling of being cared for. After years of vigilance, he was, inexplicably, safe.

"I'd never been on the ocean, never been out of sight of land," he told the girl. "I was pretty sick the whole trip."

"So, then you were in Spain?"

"Not quite. We landed in France."

After the missing days of the ship's voyage, there had been the miraculous joy of recovery. Waking from a deep and dreamless sleep, he was reborn. Striding along the Champs-Élysées, him, a skinny kid from the sticks. In the air, the smell of bread. Other men ordered cheese, spicy sausage, but Frenchie, who had returned his money as promised and stuck with him through customs and the train to Paris, would not let him eat or drink.

"Non," he said to the waiter with the wine jug. He rattled off something unintelligible. The waiter brought a chunky mug filled with a steaming, vile brew. "Drink it," Frenchie ordered. "Tomorrow you may eat."

They had been separated at Valencia. Frenchie had a talent with engines; he volunteered for the motor pool. Nash had no particular talent, so he joined the mass of foot soldiers that streamed on to Albacete, where the international brigades were headquartered.

"How did you get from France to Spain?" The girl's voice called him back. "Did you climb the Pyrenees?"

She *had* been reading. Did Orwell climb the Pyrenees? Hemingway certainly hadn't. "We did," he said.

"Was it awful?"

"Not especially. Other guys had it worse than me. I had a decent pair of boots. I got 'em off a young fella who'd been in one of them government forestry camps. Traded him for a bottle of hooch."

"You mean a relief camp?"

"No, they were different, the forestry camps. I couldn't get in; you had to have high school to get into them. They were for a different class of bum than me. But I got those boots, and they were probably more use to me than getting into one of those high-class camps ever would've been. The Pyrenees were hell on the boys wearing Oxfords."

She scribbled, frowned.

"Why would they do that? Climb a mountain in dress shoes?"

Why, indeed. "That was all they had."

He watched her stew. She contemplated her notes, nibbled at her index finger. She didn't understand, how could she? Last week, at the dump, an orange, industrial-sized garbage bag, bulging with barely worn boots, none with so much as a hole in its sole. "When I was a boy," he said, "I remember watching my mother take apart a pair of overalls that she couldn't patch anymore. She was taking out the seams, one stitch at a time, and saving the thread to use again." He repeated it, to make his point. "*The thread.*"

She jotted another note.

"That's why those boys climbed the mountains in dress shoes. They didn't have anything else, couldn't get anything else. Course they didn't know any better, most of them. City boys, been to school, they knew what anti-fascist meant, but not a lick of sense between them." He paused, remembering. "But they learned. They learned tout suite or they died." He saw her put quotation marks around a word and held up his finger. "That's not fair, what I just said. Even smart, sensible, brave fellas died. Stupid ones did too, but you couldn't survive just by being clever. I don't want you to go away thinking that."

"I won't." She moved to a fresh page. "So, you climbed the mountains..."

The light, he thought. I should tell her about the light.

The tape recorder clicked off. He waited while she changed the cassette.

Dawn had been breaking when they crested the Pyrenees. Moaning men fell, exhausted, across the frontier, into Spain. Nash had rested beside the boulder that their guide said marked the imaginary line. He could see the way they had come, France still in darkness behind them. Along the other shoulder, Spain, lit by the morning sun. Spain!

Trucks waited below to transport them to the stinking hilltop fortress at Figueras, where the international brigades mustered. Three days later, they boarded the train to Valencia. They were supposed to keep the blinds drawn, to hide their numbers from spying eyes, but they peeked through when the militiaman assigned to them left the car. They watched the sparkling Mediterranean come and go, through the orange groves, exclaiming to each other: Spain!

People in the fields raised their fists in solidarity as they passed. When they halted, peasants pushed baskets of oranges up through the windows. Everywhere, the warm, welcoming babble of Spanish. Friendly strangers grasped his hand to shake it, called him *compañero*, patted his shoulder.

On one of his patrols through their car, the militiaman sat beside Nash on the hard bench seat. "Where from?" he asked.

"Canada," Nash said. Speaking the word brought an unexpected wave of homesickness and he was unable to say more.

The Spaniard wagged his head, a kind of silent commiseration. "Si," he said. "Casa."

Nash swallowed the tightness in this throat. "Tu?" he asked.

"Madrid." More followed but Nash missed most of it, something about the sky and death. Death from the sky perhaps.

The girl closed the lid over the tape, pressed the button to begin recording again. "If you didn't enlist, how did you get in the army?"

He didn't answer. He wanted a different question, one that would bring them back to the light, to the sea, to the beginning of things—

"Was there a boot camp or something? What happened once you got there?"

"When I got there?" He sighed. "Jarama happened."

"Harama," she held up her pen, "H-A?"

"J-A...the J is pronounced like an H. J-a-r-a-m-a."

"Is that a town?"

"A valley. A river. A battle."

She went quiet, bent to her notebook. She had a neat schoolgirl part in her hair, smooth, ivory skin. She was so young. "You have to forget every movie you've ever seen about war," he said, "because Spain was nothing like that. On our side, we defenders of democracy, it was a peasant's war. There wasn't enough of anything. Guns. Bullets. Food. Uniforms. Lots of fellas didn't even have boots. They went into battle wearing"—the Spanish rolled off his tongue, though he hadn't said the word aloud in fifty years—"*alpargatus*. They're sandals, the soles are made of rope and they're pretty tough, but they're sandals. They went into battle wearing sandals."

He spelled out the word, watched her write it. When she looked up, he avoided her probing eyes. They died in their sandals, he wanted to snarl, and he hated this girl in front of him, and every person like her who had not been there, had not seen them, those brave, ridiculous soldiers. The lucky ones died instantly. Bullet to the brain. To the heart. A major artery severed, life's blood gushing. They grew tired and cold. Then they died, vanished, ceased. In poems, he had tried to find the single word that could distill that indescribable moment when life departed. Here, there was a man. Now, there is not. While he held them and babbled nonsense in a language they did not understand: *Hold on. You're going to make it. Hold on. The medic is coming. It's only a flesh wound, it went right through. Medico! Medico!*

Once, on the field, cradling a heavy head against his stomach, the quiet body warm under his palm, Nash had let himself crumple, laid his cheek on the cold, red ground while the fight went on without him. He had no idea how long he stayed there. It felt like a long time. He thought he might even have slept, in the middle of that battle, exhausted from the effort of telling the same lies, over and over: *You're going to make it, the medic is coming.*

"We got slaughtered at Jarama," he said. "Some guys didn't even have a gun. The idea was they'd get one, from one side or the other. This while Franco had Hitler's Junkers. Bombers. Heavy artillery." He leaned back, away from the memories.

Her face filled with a kind of sad recognition. She reached a hand toward him. It lay on the tabletop between them. The tape recorder wound relentlessly on.

"I heard that you were captured," she said, "held prisoner."

Held. Such an innocuous word. "I was in jail for eleven months. Then they sent us home." A sharp pain stabbed, just behind his eyes. "Don't ask me what it was like."

She nodded, offered a small, gentle smile, and he was soothed.

In the living room, the mantel clock struck, and they both jumped.

"Maybe we should take a break. Have a cup of coffee."

"That would be nice. Thank you."

He scooped coffee into the basket of the percolator while the girl scribbled in her notebook.

"Where was the jail?"

He filled the pot with cold water from the tap, pretended he hadn't heard her. The coffeepot lid chattered as he tried to fit it around the basket. The girl set her notebook aside, stood, stretched, paced around the living room. She stopped beside his desk. "I learned to type on one of these," she called.

He didn't respond.

She stepped to the bookshelf and picked up a framed photograph. "Is this your wife?"

"Yep." Nash crossed the room, took the photograph. The pair of them, shortly after they'd married, Miriam seated, him standing behind her.

"You're so young."

"It was a long time ago. My sister was a great one for taking pictures."

"I love your vest." In the photograph, he was wearing a fringed leather vest with a swirling beaded design.

"Miriam made that. For my birthday. She was handy that way." He pointed to another frame on the shelf. "She could tuft, too."

The girl gave him the photo, picked up the framed tufting, a delicate cluster of blue flowers with yellow centres, their petals mounded above a velvety background. "How?" she asked.

"Moose hair," he said, "but don't ask me how. Patiently. Very, very patiently."

"It's beautiful."

"She learned it from her mother."

"Here?"

"No. Miriam was from northern Alberta."

"How did she get to Beauty Creek?"

"The hospital...one of the nuns knew her at school. Got her a job in the kitchen."

She gestured at the photograph. "You're not smiling."

"People didn't smile in pictures in those days," he said. Her brown eyes softened, urged him on. He felt a lump in his throat. His voice came out harsh and ragged. "Wasn't too much to smile about."

Another silence. He couldn't believe he was telling her, but the truth tumbled out. "I used to get nightmares. Pretty bad. I'd go days sometimes without speaking, half off my head. Miriam would bring me tea and keep the fire stoked." He clenched the photograph. "What a pair we were. She got them too. She'd wake up screaming. Then I'd make the tea and keep the fire stoked."

"What was she afraid of?"

"She never said. I could never make it out. She always dreamed in her own language."

"What language was that?"

What was he doing? Nash banged the frame onto the shelf, strode back to the kitchen. The coffee was just coming to the boil. He felt the girl behind him, back in her seat at the table. He picked up the plate, where he had arranged a half-dozen chocolate-chip cookies.

The girl took a cookie, nibbled at it. "You must miss her. Your wife."

"Every day."

"Did she ever tell you what her nightmares were about?"

She left a big empty space for him to answer. "Our government has got a lot to answer for," he finally blurted.

He saw something mesh in her brain. She brightened.

"Was she at a residential school?"

He didn't want to answer. "Yeah."

"What year would that have been? When she was there?"

"Before I met her," he rasped. "The forties."

"Could she have been there in the thirties too? In 1935?"

"I guess. Maybe. Look, this isn't—"

"I think Maggie would be interested in that story. She's always looking for a local angle."

He could envision her scribbles: *Residential school. Nightmares.* He shoved himself back from the table. Glared. "Don't you go thinking you know anything about Miriam from … from that." He stabbed the tabletop with his index finger. "She's not a goddamned story!"

The girl shrank. "I … I don't think … I mean … I wasn't …" She flushed bright red.

"She's not yours." He stabbed the table again. "She's…she's her own."

"I didn't mean anything…I wasn't…" She laid down her pen, gave him a small smile.

He could see she wanted him to smile back. Instead, he glowered. "She ain't yours to write about. She ain't…" He stood. "This can't… I'm not…We're done." He fumbled with the tape recorder, turned it off. In the sudden silence, he could hear the percolator behind them, bubbling madly.

When they got to the door, she hesitated. "I'm sorry," she said again.

He closed the screen toward her; she backed onto the porch step. She was clutching the recorder to her chest. He shoved the door, it banged shut. He gathered the cookie plate, the clean mugs. They rattled hard against each other. He dropped them onto the counter and they clattered down. Through the window, he saw the empty driveway. She was gone.

The percolator burped. Nash unplugged it, and scrabbled in the cupboard for his Thermos. It was a battered old thing. When he found it, both the tops were gone, but he'd brought it home, and Miriam had scoured it clean and bought a replacement lid at the hardware store for two dollars, and it had accompanied them everywhere: berry picking, moose hunting, fishing, firewood, car trips to the city. He filled it with coffee, added milk and sugar. Miriam had never liked milk; he used to have to carry a tin with him, and he'd always grumbled about it. Now, he could do anything he wanted to the coffee. He screwed the lid down tight, plucked up Jiminy from the porch. The pile would be on fire, but he could still work the edges.

It is the uncertainty that breaks you.

Smashes you to pieces.

Your soul, your spine, your bones become mush inside your skin. Behind the habits of a soldier, the habits of a man, you become water. You have nothing left that is solid, nothing dry to stand on, no way to lift yourself out of the stream. You float.

It is silent.

Amid the smoke and explosions and screams (men, women, horses, mules children) the boy becomes the silent water. He floats. Lifts his gun, takes aim, breathes in. Exhales. Takes aim. Breathes in. Exhales. He floats. Moves. Keeps moving. Like the river.

Some men count. He has seen the notches, little half-diamond scoring along the edge of a gun belt, round cigarette-burn smudges on wooden rifle stocks. The boy does not count. He pretends that he does not remember, though his dreams are often filled with faces, mouths opened to shout, grimaces, smiles. They blur in his mind and mingle with other faces he has known. In his worst nightmares, his trigger finger is flexing over familiar faces. His brothers. His father. Once, horrifyingly, his mother. He woke, screaming, held down by his comrades. They soothed him, lyrical phrases he did not understand, and then, in broken English, earnestly explained that he had been trying to climb over the wall. He saw the distress in their tired, dusty faces, felt their hands on his skin, holding him down, holding him back, holding him there, with them.

24

Maggie wheeled into her parking spot, turned off the car, left the windows down, and eyed the back of her building. The door was scuffed at the bottom corner where they all kicked it when it stuck. A drunken pile of buckets leaned against the garbage-can rack. She'd needed every one of them to catch the leaks during the Canada Day monsoon. Did Kingston really have a buyer for this leaking boat of a newspaper? She hadn't been able to pin him down. Maybe she should have pushed harder, mentioned Brownsfield's offer. She sighed. Hank would have had it sold by now, for his asking price. She straightened her shoulders, popped the car door open. All she needed today was a can of roof tar, a good big brush, and a teenager who didn't mind heights.

Felicia was at her desk. "Leave it with me," she said. "Dillon will know somebody who can tar a roof."

"Where's Stevie?" Maggie asked.

"At Nash Malone's. I said I'd watch the front."

"I hope she has better luck this time. Has Dwight been in?"

"Yep, he's just picking up the mail. I should warn you, he was looking for some background and found that…" Three hard-bound back-issue books were sprawled on the table, the top one open to a front page. "Now that he's all hepped up about photography, he's wondering why you never said you were a photographer."

Maggie chuckled, touched the rough newsprint. "I remember this shot."

Dwight burst through the door, dropped the mail next to the coffee pot. "You've been holding out on me."

"What?"

"These photographs. You never told me you were a photographer, back in the day."

"A photographer? Hardly. I just helped out."

"But, these are your photos, it says so."

"Hank was a stickler about giving credit for photographs."

"But then they stop. What happened?"

Felicia gasped. She would never have asked such a direct question.

"I had Blake," Maggie explained.

"You had a baby and you couldn't take pictures any more?"

"Something like that."

Felicia glared at Dwight. Maggie closed the book, picked up the bundle of mail and took it to her office. Wished for a door she could close.

Something like that.

She thumbed through the envelopes. A few cheques, a few bills. That stupid photo: Stan O'Leary's boy, Raymond, sliding into home plate. The summer of 1969. She felt the old ache. Behind her on the floor, in the gap between the bookshelves, a camera bag was squashed beneath a stack of magazines and newsprint. She steadied the pile, found the strap and pulled. The leather was cracked and rigid, and the clasp was broken, but it was the same bag she'd let them take away all those years ago.

At first, Hank had seemed happy, ecstatic even, at her pregnancy, imagining their son's name beside his on the masthead, but as her stomach mounded and her ankles swelled, he began to withdraw. At the *Chronicle*, they argued over small details. It wasn't new that they would disagree; there had always been a lively give and take over headlines and photo choices, but now everything was an argument.

"Seriously? You're going to run it, like that?" He had been the one who taught her that a caption should never describe what the reader was already seeing in the photograph. She was proud of the photo, the bits of mud on the player's face, the grimace, and the triumphant hand on home plate. She hated to see it ruined with the inane caption:

"Raymond O'Leary slides home at last weekend's tournament in Clearwater."

"Leave it alone, Maggie," he had snarled.

"But that's exactly what he's doing. What about: Raymond O'Leary hit a home run to win the deciding game?"

He stomped off and didn't come back for the rest of the day.

"What's going on?" she cried, over their silent supper. "Why is this happening?"

"Don't be so dramatic, Maggie. It's not that big a deal."

But she knew it was.

A month later, he hired a reporter. For her, he said. "You need more rest. This will help."

"But we can't afford it."

"I got a loan."

"A bank loan?"

"An operating line. To smooth out the ebbs and flows. And, with a reporter, I'll be able to concentrate on the business side. Give you a break."

"I don't need a break."

"But you will."

It wasn't the first time that Hank had confused her with some other kind of woman. The kind of woman who hadn't been working since she was old enough to carry a kindling stick from the wood-shed to the box by the kitchen stove. The kind of woman who couldn't open a car door, or light her own cigarette, or carry a bag of groceries from Cooper's. The kind of woman who wouldn't be able to have a baby and keep taking pictures.

"You need to go by the bank," he said, "sign the loan papers, the personal guarantees."

"What if I won't?"

"Don't be stupid, Maggie. Just go by and sign the damn papers. Don't make me regret putting things in both our names."

"You said we'd be partners," she wailed. "You said we'd do it together."

"We are. I don't know what you're so upset about."

"You didn't ask me," was the closest she could come to articulating her despair.

"So what? You think the banker asked his wife if he could make me that loan? You think Gil Parkins asked his wife if he could take this job? Did you ask me if I wanted chicken for supper? People don't ask each other about every little thing, Maggie. Think about it. Nothing would ever get done."

But this wasn't about whether they'd have chicken or steak for supper. In her body, where she sometimes understood things that she couldn't put into words, Maggie knew that something had changed. She had trusted him and he had trusted her and they'd been going to make something and now?

Now, there was Gilbert Parkins.

By the time Maggie came back to work after Blake's birth, pushing the pram in the back door and parking it by her desk, Parkins had taken her place at Hank's side. She had hated him, and he returned her animosity tenfold, though his slights were always small, nothing that Hank couldn't shrug off as her overreacting. Parkins thought women had no place in a newsroom. She'd laughed when he said it. Newsroom. Where did he think he was? Chicago?

She would never figure out what it was that changed. Maybe Hank had always imagined his future this way and just never bothered to tell her. Soon, he stopped calling her by her name. At home he called her Mother. At the *Chronicle,* he called her Missus.

"Ask the missus about that," he'd tell Parkins when he needed petty cash for expenses. "I'll get Missus Evans for you," he'd tell customers needing their subscription renewed.

Worn out by the arguments, Maggie eventually gave up saying that she thought they had buried the front-page photo on page six. If she was called on to proofread, she marked missing words, punctuation lapses, and spelling mistakes. She said nothing about awkward phrasing and incoherent ledes. Hank Evans was the editor, after all. For a while he brought her his editorials to vet. He still counted on her Creekster knowledge to save him from stepping on the wrong toes, but as the months passed, even that ceased.

They might have gone along that way for years, if Gilbert Parkins hadn't dropped his camera and cracked its lens.

"Gil needs the spare camera," Hank said.

"My camera?"

Parkins was standing beside Hank, the pair of them towering over her desk. "The spare, yeah. Where is it?"

"It's here." The camera bag, its thick leather strap worn smooth by her hands, was on the shelf beside her.

Hank reached for it.

She grabbed the bag, cradled it on her lap.

"Give Gil the camera, Maggie. He needs it. You don't."

She couldn't bring herself to do it.

Hank seized the strap. She clutched it tighter. He pulled. "Don't be stupid, Maggie," he growled.

She surrendered the bag, clamped her jaw hard against her tears, gathered her coat and purse and pushed Blake's pram out the front door. The next day she stayed home. Blake played by the heater. Hank came home at suppertime. They ate without speaking. She stayed home again the next day, certain he would yield, ask her to come back. He didn't.

"Suit yourself," he said, when she threatened to stay home on production day.

"I will," she said. She'd stayed home that week, and the next, hoping he'd see that Gilbert Parkins couldn't fill her shoes. Instead, he'd hired the first of the many Mildreds, and her expulsion had been complete.

"*Nooooo!*" Felicia wailed from the production room.

Maggie leapt up, dropping the camera bag on her desk. "What is it?"

"It won't open this week's file." Felicia smacked the side of her computer. "Something is corrupted."

The dreaded icon, a small black cannonball with a short, burning wick, was frozen in the middle of the screen.

"What do you think it could be?" Maggie asked.

"Those free fonts we got last week. I used one of them. It's probably incompatible. It keeps crashing."

"How many times have you tried to open it?"

"Three."

"Give it up. Shut it down, restart. Build a new file. Don't bother with the pages you've already printed. How much did you lose?"

"Three or four pages. Why didn't I print them? I know better."

"I know," Maggie soothed. "It's frustrating. But it goes faster the second time around. And, deep-six those fonts."

Felicia groaned as she reached behind the machine for the power button. The screen faded to black.

Maggie returned to her desk. Ever the diplomat, Felicia hadn't mentioned the overdue updates for their design program. But it couldn't be updated without updating the operating system, and the operating system couldn't be updated without new computers. Archie Sims, the shaggy geek from the computer shop, had given her the astronomical quote. She'd asked Dwight to comparison shop while he was in Vancouver, but, even at city prices, it was beyond her budget. She sighed and thrust the camera bag back where she'd found it.

25

Stevie parked at the back of Betty's Café. She couldn't go back to the *Chronicle* without the story. Again.

There was no one in the kitchen, so she pushed through the swinging doors to the front of the cafe. At the booth nearest the door, deep in conversation, were Miles Kingston and Howard Doyle. They both looked up. She asked, "Have you seen Betty?"

"She was here a minute ago." Doyle held up his cup. "Since you're here, we could use a refill."

She filled his cup. Miles Kingston stared right through her, the familiar never-seen-you-before look. It rankled. "More for you?"

"Will it be better than the last one?"

"You never can tell."

"I guess I'll chance it." He held out his cup.

She took it. *Asshole.*

"Leave room for cream."

She thrust the cup toward him.

He recoiled.

She set the cup down hard, coffee splashed. "It's hot. Don't burn yourself." She returned to the kitchen, scowling.

"What bit you?" Betty came out of the cooler, carrying a box of frozen burgers.

"Nothing." She pushed Miles Kingston's blank stare away. "Do you know anything about Nash Malone?"

"Nash Malone? Why?"

"I've been trying to do a story, one of those anniversary interviews, and I got half of it, but I hoped you might be able to fill in some blanks."

"Why not ask Maggie?"

"I'm trying to do it on my own."

"I doubt I'd be much help." Betty wedged her cleaver between two burgers. "The one you need to talk to is Stan O'Leary."

"Old Stan? Fried onions on everything but apple pie?"

"That's the one. He'll be at the legion. Buy him a beer, he'll tell you everything he knows, and quite a bit he don't. Tell him I sent you."

The woman behind the legion bar gave Stevie the once-over.

"You a member?"

"Uh, no."

"You need to be signed in."

"I didn't…is Stan O'Leary here?"

The woman scrutinized her. "You one of his grandkids?"

"No, no, I just wanted to talk to him."

"Stan! Somebody here for you!"

He came to the door, a once-burly man, stooped and worn, industrial grey shirt and pants, thin at the elbows and knees. Expecting anyone else, from his expression.

"I'm Stevie Jeffers," she explained, "from the *Chronicle*."

No change in the dour face.

"I'm working on a story about Nash Malone and the Spanish Civil War. Betty said you would help me. She said you knew Nash back then." He brightened at Betty's name, but he still didn't invite her in. She floundered, grasped at Betty's exact words. "She said if I bought you a beer, you'd tell me everything."

He laughed and signed her in with a flourish, swept her to a table and called to Del at the bar for more beer. There was already a half-empty jug on the table so Del brought a glass for Stevie.

"Oh, no, just coffee for me."

Del snatched back the glass. "I'll start a pot."

Stevie clicked a fresh tape into her recorder. They were alone in the dim, quiet room. A beige cover draped the shuffleboard; two cues lay silent on the green nap of the pool table.

Stan topped up his beer, slopped in tomato juice from an open can. "Don't mind Del, you get used to her. Nash Malone, eh? Betty's right, I'm shameless. You buy me a beer and I'll tell tales on anyone."

Stevie pressed Record, and slid the machine forward.

"Don't know much about Spain though. I didn't know him 'til after. He'd been gone for years already. Him and his brother Pete. They lit out of here in '32 or '33. Nash was just a kid, must've been hard on him. Course everyone had it hard in those days. My folks had it hard."

Stevie plugged in the microphone, set it on the damp tabletop. Stan hadn't known Nash in the thirties. She was about to spend her afternoon hearing about Stan O'Leary. She was never going to get her story.

"Can you tell me what you do remember about Nash?"

"I don't know much about when he was over there in Spain, but when he come home, well, he was a mess. His little sister knew us fellas since we was kids, and she came to us, one by one. Said pretty much the same thing, I think, to every one of us guys from the ball team. She said, I can't help him, you have to." He sucked back a long swallow of the pale red beer. "He was so thin when he got home. That would have been the spring of '39. He was a walking skeleton. Really, I'm not kiddin'. Just bones held together by this...this papery, thin, white skin. He was translucent. Like an albino. I asked him, one time, how could that be? He was in Spain, right? So hot they nap every afternoon and don't come out till the sun goes down. How could he be so white? He didn't want to tell me, but I didn't let up because that's one of the things his sister said. Don't let up on him."

Another long swig.

Stevie adjusted the microphone, slid it past the jug of beer.

"He got captured, I guess, he never said how, but they held them in this castle kind of place, underground. He never saw the sun except when they opened the door at the top of the stairs. Once a day, they'd open the door, and there'd be a spear of light that would come right up to the bars, and he could put his hand out to it. He said he could feel it was warm, and he'd just sit there for the minute or two until the guards came down the stairs, looking for somebody to knock about. It only ever got as far as his knuckles, that sunshine. When he told me about that, he got all quiet and dismal, the way he would. So, I says, looks like they didn't feed you so good either, and kind of laughed, just to lighten things up a bit, and he sort of chuckled with me and— I'll never forget this, it was the darndest thing—he stuck out his hand, and he put it right on top of mine." Stan stretched his arm, laid his hand on top of Stevie's, his fingers cold and damp from the beer glass. "Just like that." He took his hand back, raised his glass, and held it in front of his lips. He set it down without drinking.

"We weren't never a touchy kind of people, and after that I thought, well, I thought maybe…maybe I was his sunshine now. Maybe we all were, us guys. I bullied the other fellas into it. Everywhere we went, Nash came along. If we were the sunshine, he was our shadow…this dusty, little skeleton trailing along behind. He didn't want to, but we wouldn't quit and eventually he put on some weight and started to get back some colour, and that summer he played centre field, and he couldn't catch a ball to save his soul, and he never hit a single run the whole season, but we didn't care.

"That fall. The war. We all tried to sign up. They wouldn't take me on account of my heart, not even my daddy's regiment. They wouldn't take Nash on account of Spain. That was a bad time. I thought we'd lost him, for sure. He just slipped backward into that dark place we'd dragged him out of. But we never quit on him, me and Rose. We lost a bunch of boys in Europe, so we weren't, by God, letting Nash go. We needed to save something. Vic got him a job at the mill, night watchman. I didn't know if he would make it, out there alone at night, but it turned out okay. He had lots of time for writing them poems of his. Miriam came along and they got married and, well, I didn't know if that was such a hot idea either, but they was made for each other, them two. And for years, they was just Nash and Miriam."

He emptied the glass, refilled it from the pitcher, added more juice.

"He was always a bit odd. He'd never come here, to the legion. Hated this place. Course he wasn't a vet, eh? Them boys in Spain fought Hitler and Mussolini before anybody else, but they was never vets. Still aren't. Government won't give it to them." Another long drink. "But there was years, years, when Nash was just this ordinary guy. Went to work, came home, kept the woodshed full, planted some spuds, picked berries, fished, got a moose in the fall. Then Miriam got the cancer. None of us was playing ball any more. They didn't have such a thing as old-timers' ball, back then. You just got too old to play, and the young fellas took over, and you sat in the beer garden and watched."

Stevie's coffee arrived in a plain ceramic mug. "Is there sugar?"

"At the bar. Spoons there too. D'ya want cream?"

"Just sugar."

"I'll bring it." A curt nod for Stevie to stay seated, and, when she came back with the sugar, Del set it down beside Stevie without interrupting Stan's story.

"Things were different in those days; people didn't have so much stuff, and the stuff they had, well, it was generally fixable. You could take a busted-up bike and another busted-up bike and put them together. So, that's what Nash did. He'd given up the mill job when Miriam took sick, he wanted to be home at night. He didn't have no pension yet, so he got by just putting stuff back together. He'd take old batteries and scrap iron to the junk dealer in Kamloops. A few bucks here, a few bucks there. He never was much of a drinker, him nor Miriam, and there was no kids, so he didn't need much. That's how Nash came to junk collecting, looking for bike parts and whatnot. I think it just got away on him. After Miriam, well, it was like he couldn't let any of it go to waste, like he was trying to save every thing that could be saved."

He poured the end of the jug, shook the last precious drops into his glass. Their eyes met as he set it back down.

"Can I get you another?"

"I wouldn't say no."

Stevie took the jug to the bar, waited while Del filled it, and then brought it back to the table. Stan was staring out the window when she set it down.

"Funny, isn't it…?" He didn't look at her. The microphone probably wasn't picking it up, but Stevie thought it didn't matter. There wasn't much she'd be able to use anyway.

"What's that, Stan? What's funny?"

"How you can be talkin' about one thing and see something in it that you never saw before. Me saying that, about Nash trying to save everything. They was trying to save the world. All them boys. That's why they went to Spain." He picked up the fresh jug, held it aloft as he spoke. "I heard some professor on the radio one time, and he was sayin' how if they'd won the war there, in Spain, how there might not've been a Second World War. Imagine that." The light from the window glinted through the pale amber. Stan poured a half glass, set the jug down with a thump. "But they lost, didn't they? All them boys."

26

The pile was smouldering. Nash tried to stay upwind but the breeze eddied and drove the black, viscous smoke into his face again and again. He got a dozen cans. A few bottles. It wasn't worth it. He made a wide circle around the fire. At the periphery, where Dave Lerbo's Cat had recently cleaned up, there were remnants from earlier times. He picked up a peanut-butter tin, tried to remember when they'd changed to plastic, tossed it aside. He poked at a half-buried wine bottle. It seemed intact. He bent and tugged. His head swam and he stumbled, caught himself, staggered and fell, one leg extended, his boot inches from the flickering fire.

Darkness enveloped him.

"Malone!" The voice was far away. "Mr. Malone! Can you hear me?"

It was young Hardy, the new cop.

"Can you sit up?" Hardy offered a hand, Nash took it, pulled himself up.

"Must've tripped," he said.

Hardy's eyes went to the scorched boots, but he didn't dispute the explanation. They climbed out of the pit, Hardy hovering at his side.

"Maybe I should give you a ride home."

"I'm fine." It was the truth, he felt better.

"I'd worry. Just let me drive you home. I'll get Alvin to come and get your pickup."

"No need to trouble Alvin. I'll take the back road. I'll go slow."

"How about if I follow you in, make sure you get home safely?"

It seemed a fair compromise.

Nash drove carefully, signal lights at every turn, full stops at every intersection. He waited on his doorstep until Hardy had driven away. Inside, he bent to take off his boots, thought better of it, and sat at the table instead, put his boot on a chair and unlaced it. The boot was blackened from its encounter with the fire. He rubbed at the soot. It came off on his fingers.

In Spain, blood had dried on his boots and stained the leather, dark splotches that he traced with his finger sometimes, on a boring afternoon when there was nothing to do but contemplate your boots. Some afternoons he thought about cleaning the boots: applying a thick coat of brown polish, rubbing it to a shine, forever concealing the irregular blots that represented men who had died beside him. On the left boot: Ricardo, Manuel, Jerome. On the right: Jacko and Davey. Blown to pieces. Their salty blood on his lips. Their death in his nostrils. But, when he was on leave, he left the boots with his kit and wore sandals, and never once asked for polish. After the Ebro was lost, during the dark months underground, interminable hours with nothing to do but trace the blotches on his boots, he had vowed that he would never clean them, that he would wear them as long as he lived. That he would never forget.

Another poem he'd never been able to write, the loss of those boots.

On the ship home, wearing a cast-off suit and dress shoes, he cached the boots on the shelf above his bed. The only thing he had left in the world, those boots. They'd burned the rest of his clothes when he arrived at the camp in France.

On the day the ship docked in Montreal, he grabbed the laces, tugged the boots down, and was dropped to the floor, poleaxed. Someone, probably the cheerful lad who did up their rooms, had cleaned the boots. Black polish, buffed to a shine.

Black boots.

Jackboots.

The boots of the enemy.

He'd lain on the floor of that swaying ship's cabin for an eternity, eye level with those gleaming, traitorous boots.

Nash heard children's laughter. On the street, three teenaged boys were pushing and shoving, one dribbled a basketball. Nash felt the *thump, thump* of the ball in the veins along his temples. He closed his eyes. The sound faded. He finished taking off his boots, poured lukewarm coffee from the Thermos and went to his desk. He rolled a fresh sheet of paper into the typewriter, set his fingers on the keys, unshackled his memory. Maybe this time he could get it right.

He'd left the shining boots on the ship's floor, exactly where they had fallen, and joined the river of brigadiers that flowed down the gangplank. They'd been dispersed throughout the ship, but Nash could pick them out. They had a way of walking, a way of standing, a way of wearing their ragtag clothes. Even in their ill-fitting suits, they were men in uniform: a returning army.

Half their number melted away after the ship docked in Montreal, the rest caught the westbound train. A crowd greeted them when they disembarked in Vancouver. The papers would say there had been thousands though Nash thought they exaggerated. Buffeted and pressed on all sides, Nash easily slipped unnoticed through the throng into the night. He could hear the speakers, the cheering, but all he could think about was getting away.

The familiar streets were a comfort. He stopped at the corner of Hastings and Gore, across from the First United. He'd eaten many a meal there in the hungry years. Gulls circled and cried, and he breathed deep the briny air. He was home. Free. Alive.

He walked for an hour, his cramped muscles loosening. He ducked into a cafe, took a seat near the kitchen, his back against the wall. A squat woman in a blotchy apron brought a paper menu.

"Coffee?"

"Please."

"We've got a roast beef blue plate."

"Just the coffee."

She sized him up, took back the menu. Brought his coffee and a slice of apple pie.

"Can't hardly afford pie."

"I know it," she said. "This 'un's on me."

He lifted the mug, breathed in the steam and the sublime aroma of cheap, greasy- spoon coffee. The pie was even better. Sweet apples. A whisper of cinnamon. The exquisite disintegration of good pastry, crumbling between his aching teeth. "It's delicious," he said, "thank you." She acknowledged the compliment with a nod and topped up his coffee, and something eased in his spine.

The woman said he could probably get work at the shipyard. They were hiring again. He told her he'd been trying to find work since 1933.

"My kid brother just got on at the shipyard," she said. "He's thirty years old and it's the first job he could ever get. I had him here washing dishes for his grub, but that's no work for a grown man."

The man at the hiring hall scoffed. "You don't look like you could lift a wrench, never mind."

"I'm tougher than I look," Nash said. "Give me a try. Fire me if I don't keep up."

"Fair enough."

At the end of the week, Nash joined the lineup at the pay window, took his envelope from the paymaster and folded it into his pocket. When he was alone in his tent, he slit it open. It was a cheque for more money than he had ever held, enough for a room—not just any room, a good room—and eats every night, enough for a haircut and a new shirt.

He had three pay envelopes before he cashed them. He had never been inside a bank. He took the bills from the teller's clean fingers, rolled them into a tight ball.

At the rooming house, the landlady scrutinized him, as he had known she would. He took out the bills which he had already counted out. "I'll pay a month in advance."

"Come into high times, have you?"

"A job at the docks."

"Dinner is at six. I don't feed latecomers. Fresh sheets on Mondays on your floor."

She gave him the key and sent him up the stairs. "Third floor, to your right, bathroom down the hall."

It was a small, narrow room. A single bed. A squat nightstand. A lamp. A shelf. Three pegs for hanging things. A towel rack. One towel. A plain wicker stool.

Fresh sheets.

He laid his pack on the floor, sat on the bed, felt the springs yield, but not too much. A white cotton sheet was folded back over the wool blanket, a white cotton case snugged around the pillow. He touched the pillow, saw his grimy hand against the gleaming white and snatched it back. He rummaged through his pack for his sliver of soap and picked up the towel. He locked the door carefully and went down the hall to find the bathroom.

The next time he cashed his paycheques, he sent most of the money home to his mother. The telegram came two weeks later. The boy who brought it waited for his tip. Nash had a penny in his palm but—scruffy shoes, dirty face, threadbare pants sucked tight by a brown leather belt—he gave the boy a quarter instead. "Thank you, sir." Beaming, the boy backed out the door, wheeled and was gone.

Nash held the telegram. It would be a death. He rubbed his fingers over the flimsy paper, took a deep breath and unfolded it.

His baby sister, Rose, met him at the station. She was grown, married with a babe of her own, a round dimpled face peeking out at him from under a lacy bonnet. Nash reached for the baby without hesitation. Rose set her in his arms and he rocked the bundle of blankets. He gazed into the dark eyes and tears streamed down his cheeks. Everyone pretended not to look, clearing their throats and fidgeting with their boots on the wooden platform. Eventually, the baby whimpered, and Nash gave her back, wiped his eyes on the sleeve of his shirt and shook hands with his new brother-in-law.

His mother had died a year earlier. The ending was peaceful, Rose told him. "She was asleep in her bed. I went to wake her, and she was gone." Rose was the only Malone left in Beauty Creek. She left a space for Nash to say where he had been, but when he didn't, she moved on. They'd let the home place go for back taxes, she hoped he didn't mind. He didn't.

She offered a small shack behind her house. He accepted. It would do. It hardly mattered. Nothing did anymore.

Nash typed steadily, rolling sheet after sheet into the typewriter. It wasn't poetry. He didn't know what it was, but it kept coming. He had seven single-spaced pages when he stopped to freshen his coffee. The headache was gone. He felt…young, hopeful even. He set down his cup, bent to the filing cabinet, pulled out the tattered manila folder and untied the white ribbon. The old manuscript would focus his recollections, if nothing else. He plopped the wad of faded pages on his lap and began to read.

Like every man who made it home, the boy brought
with him a rosary of polished moments, strung
on a scrap of twine. It frayed, that fragile
twine, and the moments fell off, scattered across
floors, into corners, under furniture. One by
one, they were lost. Even the few he managed to
keep eventually lost their shine. No amount of
polishing could bring it back.

Spain was lost to him. To all of them.

At the beer parlour, he listened while other
men prostituted their precious, polished moments
for pitchers of beer. He saw their confusion as
the stories became ordinary, lost their shine
and took on the dull patina of neglected brass.
He saw their longing for the original lustre.
He wanted to cover their mouths with his hand,
wanted to look into their eyes and say to them:
"Shhhh, shhhh, I know, I know."

But it was already too late for them.

27

Maggie tossed the bank envelope into her accounts payable tray. She didn't need to look inside; she knew exactly what it was. Her interest-free period was up, six months gone in a blink. She ran her fingers through her hair, massaged the knot at the base of her skull. Unless she wanted to pay the usurious interest rate on credit-card cash, she'd need to get the money elsewhere. Kingston's buyer still hadn't materialized, and she was beginning to suspect he was just stringing her along to keep her malleable about his rezoning applications.

She eyed her Rolodex.

Brownsfield?

Not yet.

The bank manager was pleasantly, patiently resolute. "I can't increase your operating line without more collateral, Mrs. Evans. I would, but head office..." He tapped the papers spread out in front of him. "The *Chronicle* is maxed out. Your inventory has substantially diminished. And, the building? You know the assessments tanked last year. I read the story in your paper."

"A slump," Maggie said. "We're a mill town, this is how it goes. It goes up. It goes down. It comes back up."

"Maybe, but it's going to be some time until it recovers. If it recovers."

"It will. It always does. There's Kingston's resort. That should bump our assessments."

"Not this year." He closed her file. "If ever."

"What have you heard?"

"Nothing you could print."

"But?"

"You didn't hear it from me but I, well, all I'll say is that we won't be investing."

"I've heard that a few places. Nothing for the record, but question marks. Projects that never quite deliver. Though Kingston always manages to come up roses."

"He does have a knack for getting in on the ground floor."

"He offered to buy me out. Did you hear that around town?"

"I didn't."

"He might just be blowing smoke."

"Are you thinking of selling?"

"Maybe. I got another offer, a while back, from the Brownsfield Group."

"I've heard of them. Did either of them mention a number?"

"Brownsfield did."

"Do you want to share it?"

She told him.

"That's fair."

"It is, but it's meaningless. Hank would get up out of his grave to have a heart attack if I sold the *Chronicle* to a chain."

"I wish I'd known your Hank. He must have been a character."

"He was that. I can't think of how many times we mortgaged the house to keep the *Chronicle* afloat. What about that? What could you give me against the house?"

"I'd need an appraisal."

"You can't just give me, say, twenty or so without the paperwork?"

"I'm sorry, no. We'd have to do a proper second mortgage, which means an appraisal, financial statements, tax returns. The works, I'm afraid. And…"

She waited, but he didn't finish the sentence. "I should probably think about this, shouldn't I?"

"You've been putting money in for a few years. There does come a time when you have to sit down and calculate whether you'll ever get it back. If things don't pick up, and they might not, how long are you prepared to go on?" He hesitated again.

"Go ahead, say it. I'm not getting any younger."

"You do need to think about your retirement. Do you really want to put all your equity in one leaky basket?"

Maggie came out of the bank into bright sunshine. Music was blaring from the front of Cooper's where they'd set up a sidewalk sale for the weekend. The Sixtieth Committee had gone all out, and their enthusiasm had carried the town with it. Every business was doing something special: their staff dressed in pioneer costumes, their front windows decorated. In the alleys, floats were being festooned with paper flowers and balloons for tomorrow's parade.

Even the weather had cooperated. Sunny skies were forecast right through the weekend. Camper trucks and travel trailers had been arriving all week, and every other house had vehicles with out-of-province plates parked out front. Blake and Glynnis and the kids were already unpacking at her house. It was going to be a good old Beauty Creek shindig.

She pushed away the banker's gloom. Sixty years. Did he really think Beauty Creek hadn't survived hard times before?

"Maggie!" June Fletcher, wearing a long calico skirt and a ruffled purple blouse, hurried toward her. She stumbled at the curb, and Maggie caught her arm.

"Christ! How did anyone work in a getup like this?" June yanked up her skirt and tucked it at her waist. She wore bright-red pantaloons beneath.

Maggie laughed aloud. Sometimes it was just so easy to love June Fletcher.

June took a pencil from behind her ear and consulted her clipboard. "Can you work the welcome table for a couple hours tonight?"

"Yeah, sure, I guess. What time?"

"From nine 'til closing? We're set up at the legion. I'm hoping to have someone on the table the whole night. Catch anyone who arrives late."

"I can help out, sure."

"Also, tomorrow night, at the dance, will you do a shift in the bar? I've got your gal, Stevie, down for a stint from nine 'til ten. Maybe you could work with her?"

"I could do that."

June trekked off. Maggie crossed the street to admire her own front-window display. She'd rummaged around in the garage at home to find the old tin sign from the original *Chronicle* building. Felicia and Stevie had added the rest: printing relics, a few type cases, and a poster from the 1966 Loggers' Bonspiel. She contemplated the type cases. There had been a collector, years ago, who'd wanted the old hand-operated press and its trays of type. He'd offered a pretty penny for them. Hank had declined, hoped he might get it running again someday. Maybe she could flog it, get enough to keep the wolf from the door until something turned up.

28

From his seat on the back of a gleaming red convertible, Rufus Vanisle waved and tossed a handful of candy. Brit and Peg leapt from the curb to gather it up. Stevie watched from her post beside a flourishing flower box, the *Chronicle* camera dangling around her neck. The high school band paused in front of them and marched in place. She stepped to the street and snapped a shot.

She could see the last of the floats approaching, followed by the horses and, in the distance, just coming around the corner at the hotel, the fire engine, its lights flashing. Sandwiched between tractor entries, the Timberline Resort float rolled to a stop in front of her. Miles Kingston, at the wheel of his white pickup, tossed candy. On the flower bedecked trailer, the elaborate resort model was nestled in a miniature forest, beside a bubbling blue stream, dwarfed by a massive papier-mâché replica of Wolverine Mountain.

Stevie walked to the back of the float for a close-up. She composed a perfectly centred vertical of the snow-capped mountain and the gleaming red-roofed hotel.

Kingston leaned through his open window. "What's going on up there?" The parade had stalled ahead of him.

Stevie checked the girls. They were poring over their candy bags. She walked forward to the driver's window. "I can't see anything."

He nodded at her camera. "Did you get some good shots?"

"I think so. That's some mountain."

"The art class at the high school. I threw a couple bucks their way."

"They did a great job."

He fiddled with his air conditioning dials. Stevie examined her camera.

He cleared his throat. "About the other day at the cafe—"

"Forget it."

"It's just, it's a small town. People will talk and I've got this to consider." He wagged his chin toward the float.

"Whatever."

"Hey, I like you, I do. Maybe you'd like to drive over to Jasper one day? I, we, just need to be discreet." The tractor inched forward. He put his truck in gear.

Stevie stepped back from the window, felt a queasy premonition as the float pulled away. *Discreet*.

The parade paused again. Brit came to stand beside her. "That's our mountain," she said, looking from the Timberline float to the peak beyond.

"It is. The kids at the high school made that. Cool, eh?"

Brit studied the scene, her brow furrowed. "It's not done," she said.

"Oh, I think it is."

"No," she insisted, "it's not. Look." She tugged Stevie's sleeve, pointed, as the float began to draw away. "See? Sillies. They forgot to put the town in."

The community hall was rocking, the floor springing beneath dancing feet. Stevie was pouring shots, filling plastic cups with ounces of vodka, whisky and rum. She was ridiculously resplendent, in a formal gown of royal-blue satin that Felicia had found in her costume box. Brit and Peg were somewhere in the throng, relinquished into the care of Felicia's babysitter, who had promised to watch over them through the first hour of the dance before taking them home to Felicia's for the night.

Maggie, dressed in gingham, was taking money and handing out the shots. Dancers mixed them, according to their own tastes, at a sticky side table crammed with pop bottles, Clamato juice and water pitchers. A five-gallon cooler of melting ice cubes squatted nearby.

Miles Kingston approached the bar. He chatted easily with Maggie, his eyes flitting over Stevie and away. She turned back to the shots.

"Stevie!"

For a second, she thought Kingston had changed his mind. But, when she looked up, he was walking away.

Instead, Kurt dodged Maggie and came around the bar. "Look at you. You're a princess."

"Hardly."

"No, you look nice. You do."

"You too." He did look good, in his faded denim, a slightly wrinkled white shirt open at the collar, cuffs rolled up over his tanned, muscular forearms. She asked, "Are you here by yourself?"

"Yep," he said. "You?"

"Yeah."

There was a lull at the front of the bar, and Maggie joined them.

"This is my boss, Maggie Evans."

"I've eaten at your restaurant."

"Not that boss! Mrs. Evans owns the newspaper."

"You work at the newspaper?"

"She certainly does," Maggie said. "She's Beauty Creek's newest reporter."

Maggie turned to help June Fletcher at the bar window.

"Dance?" Kurt asked.

"Seriously?"

"Yeah."

"I can't…the bar—"

"Go on with you." June came around the bar, took down an apron. "Dance with your young man."

Kurt held out his hand. Stevie took it, followed him onto the dance floor. He held her lightly. She raised her eyebrows. He grinned. "I've been practicing."

"I can tell."

"All winter."

Of course, he'd have spent his winter weekends in the bar.

"Not what you're thinking," he said.

"No?"

"In the kitchen at camp. The cook."

"The cook?"

"Don't worry, she's as old as mountains. I said I couldn't dance. She said, nonsense, anyone can dance. Somebody made a bet." He swung Stevie around. "Now, I can dance."

They danced three more, and it was true, Kurt could now dance. What's more, he was enjoying it. The set ended with a lively polka that left them gasping.

"Beer?" he asked.

"Sure."

There was a crowd at the bar. "I've got some in my truck," he said.

"Works for me."

She sat on the tailgate, enjoying the cold beer, the music drifting out from the hall as dancing resumed. They chatted easily about the winter, where Kurt's camp had been, how Stevie had come to work at the *Chronicle*, how the girls were doing in school.

"They've really settled in," Stevie said. She didn't mean to dredge up the old argument, but she felt it happen. She used her thumbnail to loosen the soggy label on her beer bottle.

Kurt finished his beer and cracked another. "Stevie—"

"No. Wait. Me first. I owe you an apology."

"You? For what?"

"I used you."

"But—"

"No. Just listen. I've had a lot of time to think about it. What happened, and why. What I might say to you, if I had the chance. I didn't know what to do after Bobby, and you were, well, *there* and I just glommed on to you."

"I didn't mind."

"You should have. I was drowning, and you were the closest thing."

"Thanks."

"But, that thing they say? How a drowning person will climb right on top of the person who's trying to save them? I think I dragged you under, too. That's why things got … well, you were there."

"You were just trying to get by. You were a kid."

"You were too."

"Bobby too, eh?"

"Bobby especially."

They were silent together.

"Are you still?"

"A kid?"

"Drowning."

"Some days."

"But not every day?"

"Not every day. Not tonight. Tonight, I'm floating."

"That would be the beer."

He stroked her wrist—rough, familiar fingertips—and she was tempted. He'd drive her home, he'd come inside, he'd be there in the morning. He'd never look through her. Never pretend she wasn't in the room.

She took her hand back. "You're right. That would be the beer talking, and I want to do my own talking from here on out. I'd better get back inside. I've got another hour to go on the bar." It wasn't true; her shift would be over by now.

"What about tomorrow?"

"Tomorrow?"

"Maybe you, and the girls, want to do something … with me?"

This was Kurt at his most endearing, earnest and uncertain. She steeled herself. "I can't, Kurt. I'm maybe not drowning, but I'm not swimming either."

"Maybe you just need to put your feet down."

"Maybe. But I have to figure that out for myself."

"We can't do it together?"

"You do remember the night you left?"

He avoided her eyes.

She said quietly, "I don't ever want to be there again, and I think that's where we'd end up, you and I." She felt him withdraw. She felt the old fear. "I should get back to the bar." She slid off the tailgate and fit her empty into the cardboard box.

He caught her arm. "Stevie," he pleaded.

"Don't. Please, Kurt, just don't."

"Fine," he snapped. "Do what you want. No skin off my nose."

She walked away, heard the tailgate bang closed, heard the truck roar off. In the dense shadow of a large pine, she paused and sobbed, once, twice. She stroked the rough bark, sucked in a deep breath and wiped away her teardrops. Music and light spilled out of the hall. But it was late, and there was no one there for her.

She'd had enough to drink that it seemed sensible to leave her car in the parking lot, so she cut across the ball diamonds. She remembered Maggie's story about Hank Evans trying to get Creeksters to name the ball park something besides "the diamonds." He had cajoled the chamber of commerce into putting up money for a sign and ran a contest in the *Chronicle*. Maggie said there weren't many entries, and the only one they could agree on was Beauty Creek Ball Park. The sign was only up for a few weeks before somebody painted over Beauty Creek with the word *High*. It was the HighBall Park for about a month, until other pranksters rechristened it the ScrewBall Park. That was when the sign quietly disappeared. Stevie smiled. It was the sort of thing Bobby or Kurt would have done, at the end of a party when they'd run out of whisky and stories, and were feeling bored. Maggie said Hank never lived it down; that it was the story that got the biggest laugh at his funeral.

Stevie came out onto Main Street at Third Avenue and sat a moment on one of the flower-box benches. Had it been a mistake? Telling Kurt to go?

"I. Don't. Know." She said it out loud and laughed and got to her feet.

She had just started down Fourth, headed for her porch light, humming, when Miles Kingston's pickup drew up alongside her.

"Give you a ride home?"

"No thanks, I'm nearly there."

He nosed the truck to the shoulder, got out and stumbled after her. "Hey, wait up."

Stevie kept walking. He grabbed her shoulder. She shook it off.

"Whatsa matter? You don't like me anymore?"

"You're drunk." She was almost at her gate.

"I'm not drunk. I don't get drunk. I saw you dancing. Who was that guy?"

"None of your business."

He tried to take her hand. She pulled it away, hissed, "You can't speak to me in public but now you want…what?"

"Don't be mad. I have an image I have to project. Protect. It's business. It's bullshit but it's necessary."

"Yeah? Well, you can shove your image."

"Aha! You are mad. Don't worry, I'll make it up to you." He reached an arm around either side of her, latched them onto the fence.

"Let me go!"

"One kiss, and I'll go."

"Stop it!"

"Come on, I don't bite. Unless you want me to."

"Go away." She twisted, broke his hold on the fence.

He encircled her, hugged. "Come on. You know you want to."

Stevie wriggled. His arms tightened. She thought about screaming. Who would hear? What would happen if they did? He tried to kiss her, she ducked. Her heart raced, blood pulsed in her ears.

"Sounds like the lady wants you to go." A voice came out of the shadows.

Kingston released her, staggered, caught himself.

Nash Malone was across the street, just outside the circle of her porch light, a rifle in the crook of his arm.

"Mind your own business, old man," Kingston snarled. "This is a private conversation."

"Not what I heard. I heard you being told to leave."

"Fuck off, old-timer."

"I don't think so."

Stevie slipped backward, through the gate. "He's right, Miles, you need to go."

"If I go now, I won't be back."

He stroked her arm, she snatched it back. He moved toward her.

"Don't you touch her." Nash stepped into the light.

"Don't tell me what to do."

"Go on, get out of here," Nash said.

Kingston backed away, sneered in Stevie's direction. "Cocktease."

Her cheeks flamed.

Nash motioned with the rifle barrel. Kingston lurched into the darkness, Nash following. A few minutes later, Stevie heard the truck rumble away. She waited, but Nash didn't reappear.

She unlocked the door, crept inside and curled into the tweed armchair. She gathered her knees into her arms and rocked.

Afraid.

Be afraid?

Just Afraid.

He'd drawn another hobo sign in her notebook, Mr. Malone, that first, horrible interview. She traced it on her thigh, the shiny blue satin smooth beneath her fingertips, a simple slanted grid: *Not a Safe Place.*

Kingston ought to have it tattooed on his forehead.

29

Nash put the gun into the cabinet at the back of his bedroom closet. Spun the combination lock. Let out a long breath. What had he been thinking?

Those damn brown eyes. The eyes of a daughter, a granddaughter. Except they weren't. Maybe she reminded him of Rose. He'd have taken it up with any man who'd treated his sister that way. "Silly old fool," he muttered. "None of your business."

There had been nothing in the newspaper of their interview. He'd watched for it, scouring the pages of the *Chronicle*. There had been an interview with Stan O'Leary that he'd especially enjoyed. Nash had forgotten that Stan helped build the new curling rink, donated the logs for the skating arena. He'd had a sizable string of logging trucks, Stan had, in his day.

A slight breeze stirred the window curtains, but it was still too warm for sleep. He wandered through the living room, nudged the window as wide as it would go, opened the front door so the night air could flow in.

He stroked the typewriter keys, but couldn't bring himself to sit. Instead, he went to the fridge and took out the bucket of blueberries he'd picked that morning. He spread a towel on the table and dumped half the bucket at one end, used his hand to roll the berries across the rough cloth, let it wick away debris and tiny green berries. Before scooping the berries into a freezer bag, he'd pluck up any with a stem remaining, pull it off. He worked standing, bent over the table in the bright circle of the kitchen light. He was lost in the easy rhythm of the work, when—gears slipping effortlessly into place—he solved the riddle of the brown-eyed girl.

Amancio.

Of course.

Why hadn't he seen it?

Chocolate eyes. Dark hair. Round face.

Amancio Delgado.

Like Nash, Amancio had been a boy lost in a family of brothers. "How many?" Nash had asked when they compared families, in the brief reprieve before their first battle.

"Too many," Amancio replied, eyes sparkling, and Nash had known that they would be friends, comrades, *compañeros.*

They fought and survived Jarama, where most of the men who had been on the ship with Nash died. They fought and survived at Brunete and again at Teruel.

On leave, Nash spent a week at the family home in Barcelona. There had been a tension between Amancio and his father that Nash did not understand, something beyond the normal tension between a man and his son, but Amancio's mother had been warm and welcoming. A gracious woman, tall and affectionate, she enquired of his mother, and when he stuttered an answer, she forced Amancio to translate. By the time the afternoon was over, Nash had confessed the whole sordid story: Pete's death, the lonely grave, the unwritten letter. Amancio was dispatched for writing paper, pen, stamps. "You must tell your mother," Amancio had translated apologetically. "She insists. She says a mother must know where her sons are buried."

Nash had returned to the front rejuvenated, his terrible burden relieved the moment he entrusted the stamped envelope to the postal clerk.

Then, Teruel was lost.

In the horror of the retreat, a young recruit overtook him wearing an unmistakable brown fedora, Amancio's vivid red scarf wrapped around the band.

"Where is Amancio?" he had shouted at the boy. "Donde Amancio?"

The boy pointed toward the distant rear guard. "Muerto," he said. "Muerto."

"Where? Show me!" He grabbed the boy by the belt, and dragged him back, toward the guns. "Donde?"

The boy was squealing now.

"Malone! What're you doing?" An officer intervened, one of the Americans.

"This is Amancio's hat," he shouted. "Amancio Delgado."

The officer caught Nash's shoulder, swung him around. "He's dead."

"Si. Si. Muerto." The boy loosed a spate of Spanish, tried to pry Nash's fingers from his belt.

Nash released the boy and he ran. Nash watched him go, twisting the hat between aching fingers. "I have to go back," he said.

"There's no going back."

There was a moment of dreadful reckoning, sound oddly muted, time suspended.

When he stumbled forward and the noise resumed, he heard the frantic neighing of a wounded horse, calling to its retreating companions.

Weeks later, he made the reluctant trek through the bombed wreckage of Barcelona to Amancio's home. He'd dreaded it, hoped they would have heard the news already, from someone with better Spanish. He entered the quiet courtyard. Knocked.

An officer answered the door.

"Ah, señor," Nash said. "I seek the family Delga—"

"Muerto," the man said.

"Muerto?"

"Si. Perfido."

Perfido? Nash worked it out. *Traitorous.*

"Perfido," the officer repeated. "Comprende?"

"Amancio?" Nash ventured.

"No, no. Padre y hermanos." The father, the brothers. Another long sentence followed, most of it a blur. The man repeated it, slowly, and Nash grasped enough to understand the officer was saying that

Amancio was lucky that he had not lived to see this day. He nodded his comprehension. "Madre?" he asked.

The officer shrugged. Who knew? Who cared what happened to the wives of traitors?

Amancio Delgado.

Nash sealed the last bag of blueberries, took them to the freezer. Then he went to his desk, rolled a fresh sheet of paper into his typewriter, and began to type.

A child, dark hair gleaming, sparkling white apron over a ragged dress, offered a bouquet of field flowers to the marching soldiers. The boy stepped out of the line, bent on one knee, and waited while she approached, her flowers thrust in front of her. The boy took the bouquet, and they gazed into each other's eyes, and the child stepped closer, reached up a tiny hand, and touched his face.

"Gracias, compaero," she said, earnestly repeating the words she heard the adults shouting. "Muy gracias."

He closed his eyes, his cheek resting against the small hand, and for that moment, he felt a warmth that spoke of sleep, or silence, or peace.

Then someone bumped him, and he looked away, and when he looked back, the child was seeking her mother in the crowd, and someone grabbed his tunic, and he was absorbed once again in the marching mass.

It was their final parade. They were being sent home, all of the internationals, in an attempt to appease Franco, to restrain Hitler and Mussolini.

Around him, people sang and cheered, and the feeling of the small hand on his cheek faded, and the horrifying truth pressed in.

His war was over. He could go home, could leave behind the guns and the bombs, the hunger and the fear. But the child, that beautiful, blameless child, could not.

He slipped out of the line, and melted into the crowd. He would go home when her war was over, and not a moment sooner.

30

Maggie watched the dancers from a table in the dim corner beside the coat room. It was the chicken dance and the few remaining children had flocked in from the playground to join the dancing, or to watch, wide-eyed, from the fringes. June Fletcher was leading, her skirt billowing around her red pantaloons. A gaggle of teens giggled and whispered. Maggie had been one of those girls once, she and her friends giggling at the old women who danced with each other while their husbands drank hard liquor somewhere outside the hall. Now, she was one of those old women. It didn't feel like she had dreaded it would, at sixteen. She didn't feel pathetic or lonely. She was content, here in the corner, enjoying the hubbub. She'd been on her feet since dawn, and as midnight approached her weary legs were happy to be resting on the seat of a chair.

Blake was across the room drinking with the boys from his high school class. Glynnis was on the dance floor with the kids and three other moms. Maggie looked for Stevie but didn't find her. She'd watched her earlier, dancing with that nice young man. Was he the not-her-husband who worked for Bentwell?

The music looped, grew louder. Maggie yawned. It had been a long day. She slipped along the back wall and out the door into the warm night, strolled away from the building toward the picnic tables between the hall and the diamonds. There was marijuana smoke in the air. Teenagers scattered from the grove of pines as she passed. Maggie grinned, remembering sips from a shared bottle of rum in the sultry darkness outside the old community hall. It was gone now, that sway-backed barn of a building her parents and their friends had built with donated lumber and the profits from box socials and strawberry teas. It had been condemned during the reign of a particularly dogmatic building inspector. She couldn't remember his name. The fire department had refused to burn the old hall, so the inspector had harassed the village into assembling a crew and lit the fire himself.

The *Chronicle* had been flooded with letters and they'd kept coming, in intermittent swells, throughout the construction of the replacement building. Creeksters had been proud of their hall, proof of their ingenuity and resourcefulness. People here, Maggie among them, still called this one the *new* community hall, twenty years on.

"Maggie!"

It was Rufus, carrying drinks. "Rum and coke," he said, proudly, "squeeze of lemon."

She took a glass, sipped. "That was a good day," she said.

"It was. The Sixtieth Committee did a helluva job. I haven't had this much fun since…I can't remember when."

"I saw you dancing up a storm in there." Rufus was popular at the monthly dances at Twilight Manor, where the women markedly outnumbered the men.

"Gotta do my part to keep our Creeksters dancing."

"You are a keeper, Rufus Vanisle." She took his arm, leaned in to his shoulder. "Beauty Creek is lucky to have you."

"Beauty Creek? What about you?"

"Me too."

"Does that mean you'll come back inside and dance with me? In front of everyone? Let Beauty Creek get a look at its future first lady."

"You're drunk."

"No. Just happy. Come, dance with me."

"Okay. Why not?" She laughed.

What *had* she been resisting? This was her home. These were her people. She'd dance with Rufus and they'd think it was just dandy.

She'd let Miles Kingston have the *Chronicle*. She'd marry Rufus, and they'd save their fading town. She drained her glass and walked with him, arm in arm, toward the hall.

Even with a faint hangover throbbing behind her eyes, it was a treat to have Blake and Glynnis and the grandkids around her breakfast table. There was noisy, exuberant conversation about the many wonders of the previous day: the parade, the carnival games, the children's races, the cotton candy. Maggie had already exclaimed over their ribbons— every child who ran a race got some kind of ribbon, but she admired them again as they were passed around.

"Was this for the potato race or the sack race?"

"The potato race, Gram."

"How did that one work, again?"

"We got a potato on a spoon and the first one across the line who didn't drop their potato—"

"All right, you runners," Glynnis interrupted, "I want you to run across to the park and play. Your dad wants to have Gram to himself for half an hour."

Maggie fortified herself with another cup of coffee, took it to the back deck. Blake followed her. She winced when the sun hit her eyes.

"Are you okay?" he asked.

"Just tired. Late night. Teensy bit more rum than I'm used to."

She and Rufus had come back into the hall just ahead of a very drunk Miles Kingston, and Maggie had ended up imbibing too many rum and cokes while Rufus and Kingston traded stories about clever Vancouver business deals. When the band finally packed up their instruments, Rufus had insisted on driving Kingston home. By then, Maggie had been relieved to come home alone.

"I hear you," Blake said. "We used to drink until dawn and be waiting outside Betty's for her first pot of coffee. Apparently I can't do it anymore."

Glynnis came through the door. Sat beside Maggie. Nodded at Blake. He shifted in his seat. Glynnis nodded more forcefully.

Blake sighed. "We wanted to talk to you, together, without the kids, because, we're—"

"We're thinking about separating." Glynnis rushed it out. "Maybe a divorce."

"A divorce?"

"Maybe not," Blake interjected. "But a trial separation."

"But why?" A minute ago they'd been laughing and chatting with the children. "I don't understand."

"We think we might have rushed into marriage and a family. Both of us have doubts."

"Doubts?"

"We're not sure we even love each other."

Maggie glanced back and forth between them, wordless.

"This will be hard for you to understand," Glynnis said. "You and Hank were soul mates. Blake and I ... we thought we might be, but we're not. There's just too many fundamental things that we can't agree on."

"Fundamentals," Maggie echoed.

"Things that we can't agree to disagree on," Gynnis explained. "We just argue all the time."

Maggie watched Blake while Glynnis talked. He was watching her mouth move, but his expression said that he'd heard it all before. Maggie recognized the look.

"So, we're going to try a separation. I don't want half a marriage," Glynnis said. "I want what you and Hank had."

"What Hank and I had?"

"The two of you, when he was sick, I've never seen love like that."

Maggie shaded her eyes. "Wait. Give me a minute, will you? I need to absorb this before I can formulate a thought."

Glynnis picked up Maggie's empty mug. "I'll get you more coffee."

Maggie squinted at Blake. "Soul mates? Your father didn't even believe he had a soul, never mind one that could mate."

"I know, but she's a bit right. You and Dad ..."

"Before he got sick ..." Did it matter? After all this time? It mattered. The truth always mattered. "When your dad got sick, I was sleeping in

the spare room and he was…he was mostly sleeping somewhere else."
She knew it would sound bitter, even though she wasn't. "*With* someone else."

"Who?" Glynnis banged down Maggie's coffee cup.

Blake silenced her with a tiny head shake. "It doesn't matter who."

He had known. Maggie digested that. She'd always thought it was
her secret.

"Go on, Mom," he said. "You were saying, when Dad got sick?

"I went with him to the oncologist. They said it could be six
months, it could be a year, but it was incurable. It was, well, it was as
if the hand of God took us both by the scruff of the neck and gave us
a mighty shake. We were in shock, but we were awake. He cut it off,
with her. Then there were treatments, and hope, and it's a game of
snakes and ladders, cancer is. Your dad said that when the doctor told
him, he could only think about telling me. That he knew he'd been
stupid. That's what he told me. I don't know what he told her. We
never talked about it."

"What did you talk about?" Glynnis, again.

"We talked about the weather. We talked about treatments. We
argued about whether we should tell you and Blake. I thought you
deserved to know; he thought you deserved to get on with your lives
without his illness hanging over your heads. We argued and mis-
understood each other. Every single day." She tipped her head back,
closed her eyes against the sun. "The last day…he'd had a rough night,
I wanted to plump his pillow for him, but he couldn't bear to move.
He snapped at me. I snapped back, and he barked at me, and I burst
into tears and went to the bathroom to have a cry, and when I came
out, he was sleeping." She opened her eyes, spoke directly to Glynnis.
"He never woke up."

There was a long pause.

"Nobody gets all good days," Maggie said. "You two are tired.
Who wouldn't be, three kids, mortgages, mothers-in-law? Maybe you
need to get divorced. Who am I to say? Just don't decide when you're
tired. Take some time. Will you do that? Do you really want to start

over with someone new? Because that's one thing I can tell you for free: you can trade partners every other year, and you'll never find one that you won't disagree with over something."

The children poured through the front door, crying and shouting. Someone had fallen from a swing, scraped a knee, bruised an elbow. Maggie stayed seated while Blake and Glynnis managed the chaos. She should have told them about Rufus. She should have told them that she would sell the *Chronicle*. If Kingston's resort took off, maybe she could squeeze a few more dollars out of him, enough to give Blake a share. Maybe that cherry orchard Glynnis was so keen on could save his marriage.

31

Stevie parked in front of Nash Malone's house. It was after nine, and she would be late for work, and Maggie would be annoyed, but this had to be done.

She knocked firmly.

He pulled the door wide.

"I just came to say thank you," she said.

"No need."

"I think there is."

"I've got coffee on. A fresh pot."

Stevie sat at the table. Nash poured.

"I...He...He followed me home from the dance. I had, uh, dated him once. I guess he thought—"

"That's none of my business."

"It's so embarrassing."

"You've got nothing to be ashamed of."

"Thanks. And, thank you so much for...you have no idea how grateful I am."

"It was too hot to sleep. I heard something. Thought it might've been the coyotes that got Phillips's dog. That's why I had my gun. It wasn't anything. Really."

"It was," she insisted, "it was."

"Enough," he said. "You're welcome. We're square. You've said your thank you. I've accepted it. No more about it. It's done."

"But I need to do something."

"Okay. Okay. Bake me a cake."

Her relief became laughter. "I will! What kind?"

"I was only kidding."

"You started it, so you have to tell me. What's your favourite cake?"

"All right, you win. There was a cake Miriam used to make, a kind of huckleberry upside down cake. Do you know it?"

"I don't, but if you've got the recipe?"

He shifted, reluctant again.

"Where's the recipe box? Point me to it."

"Her recipe books are there." He indicated the bookshelf. "On the bottom. I haven't a clue which one."

There was a stack of recipe books. Stevie set them in a teetering pile on the corner of the desk, handed one to Nash. "Check the cake section. You'll know it by the splatters."

"Splatters?"

"Batter. If it's a recipe she used, there will be cake splatters."

At the door, recipe book in hand, she paused. There was one more thing she needed to say. "I want you to know I get it now. I didn't before but I do now."

"What's that?"

"About Miriam…" She stumbled on the name. "About you not wanting to talk about her. I'd hate for Saturday night to be in the paper. I'd hate somebody I didn't even know sticking a microphone in my face wanting to get the *local angle*."

"You never wrote anything about Miriam."

"But I thought I could."

"You were just doing your job."

"Maybe. But I get it now, why some stories aren't mine to tell. Aren't for the newspaper, no matter what Dwight says about the public's right to know. The public don't have the right to know everything, do they?"

"Nope," he agreed. "They surely don't."

"Whose book is this?" Brit wanted to know, when Stevie picked them up after work.

"It's from Mr. Malone. We're going to bake him a cake."

"How come?"

How come, indeed. "For that interview he did for me."

"What kind of cake?"

"Huckleberry."

Stevie asked Felicia. Maggie. Betty. Not a huckleberry among them. She knew of only one other place to ask.

"Mom?"

"Stephanie! How are you?"

"I'm good, Mom. How are you?"

"Busy. Your father's been haying, and there's a crew to feed."

"Isn't it a bit late for haying?"

"It is. But we had all that rain in July. How are the girls?"

Brit and Peg had spent a happy three weeks at the farm in July. "They haven't stopped talking about the kittens and the calves, about what they're going to do next summer."

"We so enjoyed having them."

"I was thinking about coming up before the girls go back to school."

"That would be wonderful."

"Could we maybe go huckleberry picking?"

"Huckleberry picking?"

"Is it too late?"

"No, you could probably get some but…you never liked berry picking."

"I remember." Stevie had *hated* berry picking. Now she couldn't remember why. "I must have been such a pain sometimes."

There was a small intake of breath, a wordless interval.

"Mom?"

"You were just fine, sweetheart. You were just fine."

"Hardly," Stevie drawled, remembering sullen trips to the berry patch and bitter arguments on the drive home. She heard her mother swallow.

"Having the girls here, your girls, this summer. They're so bright and funny and affectionate. I'd forgotten"—she paused—"I'd forgotten how young you were."

"Mom."

"It's just...I should've done more, *been* more."

Stevie slid to the floor. It felt like a wall she had been leaning on her whole life had just collapsed. She twisted the coils of the telephone cord around her index finger. "I should have been more, too," she said. "It wasn't just you."

She listened to her mother breathing on the line. Neither of them spoke. Minutes passed.

"Mom?" Brit bounded up the porch steps, burst through the door and skittered to a stop at the sight of Stevie on the floor.

"It's Grandma." Stevie got to her feet, handed Brit the phone. "Tell her we'll come the weekend after next."

She held out the pan with two hands. "Huckleberry upside down cake," she said.

There was an uncomfortable pause. He'd forgotten. It had taken her a few weeks: the huckleberry expedition had been delayed, and there had been one failed attempt, a burned cake, a rock-hard berry layer that took three days of soaking to remove from the pan.

"A thank-you cake," she said. "Remember?"

"Right. Come in."

She kicked off her shoes, carried the cake to the kitchen table, and pushed aside a tobacco tin to set it down.

"You'll stay for coffee and cake?" he asked.

"I shouldn't."

"The coffee's already made."

"Just one."

He gave her the cake knife. She started to cut. He cleared his throat.

"Bigger?" she asked.

"I should think so."

She moved the knife, carved and served two generous rectangles.

He took a big bite, chewed, sighed.

"This is the one," he said. "It tastes just like Miriam's."

They chewed in contented silence.

"Remind me," she said, "I brought the recipe book. It's in the car. There's lots of good recipes in that book."

"Maybe you should keep it."

She grinned. "What must you think of us Jeffers girls. Brit cadging candy. Me after your recipe book."

"There's a word I haven't heard for a long time."

"Cadge?"

"Uh-huh."

"My dad."

Nash used his index finger to pick up the last of his cake crumbs. Stevie cut another slice, slid it onto his plate. "I asked him about Spain," she said, "when I was home. He didn't remember anything about it. He didn't know much more about the Depression. He said his dad wasn't very sympathetic, that his folks were hard on people who didn't measure up. My mom was always a bit like that. She's mellowing but she always used to say people make their own beds…" She paused.

"What?"

"I just saw something."

"Go on."

"It's embarrassing to say out loud, but I never make my bed, except when I change the sheets, and every time I leave the bedroom without doing it, I think of my mother." She licked her fork, set it on her empty plate. "Silly, eh? The sum of my rebellion."

"I wouldn't be so sure about that."

"Trust me. That's it."

"Some might say your life is a rebellion."

"Hardly."

"On your own. Two little kids. Don't sell yourself short."

"I can barely pay the rent."

"But you do."

"So far." She drained her coffee cup. "I better get going."

"What about your cake dish?"

"I'll come for it in a few days. Or you can drop it off at the *Chron-icle*. I don't need it right away. Or...you and I never did finish that Spain interview."

"I kind of hoped you'd given that up."

"Not unless you want me to."

He wavered. "I guess we could try again."

"Excellent! I can't this week, for sure, we're up to our necks in the back-to-school issue. Probably not the next couple weeks, maybe after Terry Fox week? Miss Jasmani is taking Brit's class hiking for Terry Fox Day. She wants to climb Wolverine Mountain. I told Maggie I'd go and take pictures."

"Is the whole school going?'

"Just Brit's class, ten of them, maybe eleven, depending. They said I could take Peg if I wanted to. What do you think? Would it be too much for her?"

"Brit won't have any trouble, but it would be a long haul for a wee'un. And..."

"What?"

"I try not to give advice."

"But you had a thought, and you know the trail. Tell me, I don't mind."

"It's only that it's easy to sour a kid on mountain climbing. Kinda like bed making."

She returned his grin. "Maybe you'd like to come with us."

"I don't think so."

"Miss Jasmani would love it if you came. Probably some history on that old mountain. I bet you know where it got its name. I'm going to get her to invite you."

"You don't need to bother. I'll only say no."

She took her dishes to the sink, touched him lightly on the shoulder on her way to the door. "I'm going to work on you. Think of it: hiking all day with eight-year-olds. I know you can do it," she teased. "You climb that mountain out at the dump all the time."

#

Nash took the cake to the counter. Bent to the bottom cupboard and rummaged for the plastic container that would hold a full-sized cake tin. What had Miriam called it? A cake saver. He smiled at the small triumph of having remembered.

His typewriter called. He'd been working on filling in gaps in the old manuscript, which, he'd been surprised to find, was not as badly written as he'd feared. He rolled in a fresh sheet of paper and tried to summon Spain, but his thoughts were drawn instead to Wolverine Mountain.

He'd made his first trip to the line cabin on the mountain when he was ten. It had been a struggle to keep up with Pete, four years taller and faster. He nearly came to tears at the last hill. Pete kept going, left Nash to fight his own battle with fatigue. When Nash finally straggled into the cabin, Pete already had the fire going.

Tucked in its small hollow near the creek, the cabin was nearly invisible. It was only six logs high, a squat rectangle of rough notched spruce crouched on a round of cedar: a shelter, a place to sleep or to ride out a storm.

Nash had been hesitant, unsure where to put his pack, how to handle himself in the small space. He wanted to do the right things so that he would be invited back; so that he might, finally, find the niche that was to be his, the space where he would know instinctively what to do, when. Where he, too, might be a man.

"Top or bottom bunk?" Pete asked.

Nash tried to see if there was a trick behind the question. A man, he decided, would take the least favourable bunk, which, for him, was the bottom. Especially when a big man slept above you, farting and moaning and thrashing on sagging springs. "Bottom," he said.

"Throw your pack on 'er, and come and get your coffee."

Nash held in his smile, took the steaming cup—he wasn't allowed coffee at home.

He'd made his final trip to Wolverine Mountain the year after Miriam died. He'd climbed alone, the last, long, hill still a struggle. He rested twice. There was no need to hurry. No one expected him home. No one expected him anywhere.

The first morning he woke before dawn, watched a star move across the empty space of a missing shingle, and felt the deep, implacable solitude of the mountain. It had neither missed him nor marked his return.

For three nights he slept dreamlessly. He gathered deadfalls and cut and split firewood to replenish the woodpile, cut shingles for the roof, scooped water from the stream, and sat silently on the stoop while the kettle heated. The jays came on the second day, swooped down on navy wings for the crumbs of his bread. He spoke to them, inquired of their families, the weather last winter, the patter of nonsense that a man will speak to a bird. When they chatted back to him, he felt a smile tug at his face.

On the fourth day he packed his few things, rolled up his blankets and hiked over the shoulder of the mountain to the next cabin on what had once been the Malone brothers' trapline. Nestled in the timber at the end of a small, swampy lake, the cabin was in the same condition as the last. He began again: swept out packrat dung, fixed the roof with shingles cut from the block of cedar in the woodpile, shovelled ashes from the stove, carried water, washed the single wavy window pane, whistled.

That evening, at dusk, seated on the crumbling cedar log that was the doorstep, whittling a new leg for the broken stool, he heard loons call from the end of the lake. The sound swept across the water and penetrated his heart like a bayonet. When the call came again, he wept: dropped his knife, fell to his knees, and sobbed.

Each time the loons called, his grief twisted up through his stomach and into his chest. His tears spilled over, ran down his cheeks and dripped onto the wood chips.

Long after the loons had quieted, he knelt, rocking. His damp cheeks dried. A coyote howled across the meadow. He stood. Stiff. Cold. Empty. He fell into bed without starting the fire and woke to a skiff of snow on the ground.

When he packed up and hiked out, he'd been sure he would never be back.

Nash slowed, came to a stop. His breathing eased. The top of the hill was just over the next rise. After that there was only one last small hill and then the easy descent to the alpine lake where the children would be eating their lunch by now.

They'd cornered him at the grocery store, the Jeffers girls, and little Brit had extracted a promise. He'd gotten the time wrong; they'd already set off by the time he parked beside the school bus at the trailhead. He could have gone home right then, but a promise was a promise. He'd shouldered his day pack and hiked the familiar trail. The creek was low, the poplars were turning, and the sun was bright on the yellow foliage.

He heard the child crying just as he topped the rise: a wild wailing interspersed with great, gulping sobs. He hurried forward.

Brit Jeffers was huddled at the base of a stump, shoulders quaking.

"Hey," he called. "Hey, now. What's this?"

She curled herself tighter, sniffling and hiccupping. He halted, well back, and squatted to her level. His knees protested but he maintained the crouch. "Are you hurt?"

"Nooo," she quavered. "My mom left me."

"Did she?"

"Yes."

More wounded pride than any real harm. He dropped one trembling knee to the ground.

"She hates me." More sniffling.

"I doubt that. I expect she likes you a lot."

"Not as much as my sister."

It settled on the trail between them. What could he say? He knew that it was true, that a mother could prefer one child over another. That a child could know. "Did I ever tell you that I had four sisters? And six brothers."

She scrubbed her cuff across her eyes.

"My mother liked my brother Pete the best of us all."

"Didn't you mind?"

"Sometimes."

"It's not fair."

"You're right about that," he said. "It surely isn't fair."

He heard a frantic shout from up the trail. It was the mother, coming down the hill, full tilt by the sound of it.

"She's here," he called.

"Oh, thank God! I thought that Mr. Todd was behind us. I didn't realize he had passed us until I got to the lake and he was there. Him and a few of the boys took a shortcut." She spoke over her shoulder to Nash as she knelt beside the sniffling child. "I wouldn't have left you without an adult, Brit. I wouldn't have. I thought you might rather walk with Mr. Todd than me."

She might not be the favourite, but she was clearly precious.

"Do you hear me? Brit? Look at me. Say something."

"I didn't care."

Nash smiled. Little miss bravado.

The rigid child was hugged close, and Nash heard the fierce whisper. "I will never leave you. Do you understand? Never."

Nash waited, on aching knees.

The mother stood. "We'd better get going. Miss Jasmani was worried about you."

"I'm too tired."

"Brit, come on. It isn't far."

The child didn't move. The mother tugged. The child resisted.

"Will I try?" Nash asked.

She stepped back, he inched forward.

"You've already licked the big hill," he said to the child, indicating the steep, rocky trail behind them. "This mountain is in you now." He watched her work out that it was a compliment.

"Because I got this far?"

"Because you didn't quit when it got hard."

The child sighed, an exaggerated huff. She stood and offered her hand. He took it and she helped him to his feet, and he let her lead him up the hill.

Fall

33

Just past dawn, Nash heard the rumble of a truck, gearing down at the corner, growling up the street. He came fully awake when he heard the backup horn bleep outside his window.

A second truck arrived while he was dressing, and by the time he got outside there were three gravel trucks, one backed up against a pile of bike frames, the other two idling on the street. The public works pickup wheeled into the yard just as he stepped through the door. The steps were damp; there had been a light frost in the night.

Howard Doyle got out of the pickup holding a piece of paper.

"Morning!" Doyle shouted over the rumble of the waiting trucks as he came up the short path to the steps.

Nash glowered down at him.

"Now, Nash, you got our letters, three warnings."

"I talked to Rufus—"

"The last one was registered mail and you ignored it. It's all lined up. We have to. We can't have this eyesore in the middle of town."

"Hardly the middle of town."

"It will be."

"Your man Kingston's after those lots down by the creek. He afraid folks on their balconies will see how real Creeksters live?"

"This has nothing to do with that. We've had complaints."

"Complaints?" Nash nodded toward Harriet Lemsky's roof. "Plural? More than one?"

Doyle thrust the paper forward. Nash brushed it aside. "I already talked to Rufus about this," he repeated.

A second pickup pulled into the driveway, swung wide to go around the gravel truck and bumped into the garden, one tire crushing plants, the other spinning on frosty grass. Three young men emerged—shiny white hard hats, Beauty Creek logos—and came to stand behind Doyle.

"That's my garden you just drove through, Teddy Meyers," Nash said, to the tallest boy.

He flushed. "Sorry, Mr. Malone. I thought I had room to get around."

Nash turned back to Doyle. "You need to talk to Rufus about this."

"Mayor Vanisle is in Vancouver this week." Doyle scuffed his toe against the bottom step, looked up, hardened. "You've gone two months past the deadline we gave you. This is all legal and proper." He turned to the boys. "Get at it."

The boys watched Nash.

Doyle grabbed Teddy Meyers by the arm, swung him toward the yard. "Get to work. This garbage goes back to the dump. Where it came from." He swivelled to give Nash a triumphant sneer, tossed his missive onto the step, and strode to his pickup. As he backed onto the street, the village loader bounced down the alley and into the yard.

Nash bent to retrieve the letter. It was just a copy of the earlier ones. "Final Notice" was stamped in red at the top of the page.

But he had talked to Vanisle.

One of the boys yanked a tarp off a pile. The strips of lumber that held it in place tumbled down. "Wait a minute!" Nash shouted, but they didn't hear him. Teddy grabbed a bicycle frame, heaved it into the steel gravel box. Nash started down the steps, stopped. What he needed to do was call Rufus.

He tracked across the kitchen to the phone, dew from his boots leaving wet footprints. There was no answer at the village office. The office would open at nine, the machine told him. He ran his finger down the last column of Beauty Creek phone numbers, dialled Vanisle's home. No answer. No machine. The phone rang in his ear. Outside, youthful laughter and the clanging of metal on metal filled the silence between rings.

Mayor Vanisle is in Vancouver this week.

He hung up the phone. There had to be a way to reach Vanisle. Maggie Evans would know. He brought the directory to the kitchen table just as the police cruiser pulled into his driveway. Young Hardy got out, adjusted his hat. Good. Maybe he could put a stop to this nonsense.

"Mr. Malone? Nash? I need to know how you're doing in there."

Nash opened the door; Hardy came inside. Nash could feel the intense scrutiny, probing the room, noting every detail. He was embarrassed by the stack of dirty dishes at the sink, and the clutter on the kitchen table. "Just got up," he muttered.

Hardy shook off the explanation. "I feel pretty silly about this, Mr. Malone." He shuffled his feet. "But I'm going to have to ask for the bolts from your guns."

"My guns?"

"Your rifle. Your twenty-two."

"You're kidding."

"It's procedural, nothing to do with you in particular. Just standard protocol for something like this, where somebody might get"—he searched for a word—"agitated. It's only for a few days. Bit of cooling off time. Not forever."

Nash tried to speak. Felt a quiver in his fingers, a kind of helpless fury. It moved into his throat. Wordless, he motioned the boy to follow him to his gun safe. It took three tries to get the combination lock to release. Hardy pocketed the bolts, handed the neutered weapons back.

"Doesn't seem right," Nash finally managed. "Aren't they trespassing?"

"I agree, it doesn't seem right, but they have the authority. I checked."

"I talked to Vanisle about it," Nash said. "I talked to him."

"What did he say?"

"He said he'd take care of it."

"When did you talk to him?"

"July, maybe. Earlier this summer."

Hardy shook his head, a single, sad wag.

Nash thrust his shaking fingers into his pockets.

"You probably should go out there," Hardy said. "They can clean up, but you don't have to let them trash everything."

34.

Felicia was at the front desk with a customer when Maggie got to work. Stevie was in Deighton for Thanksgiving. She hadn't asked, but Maggie had insisted she take Friday, too.

"Are you sure?"

"Won't hurt me to get out of bed," she'd said.

Maggie hung up her coat and scanned the flats. Advertising had picked up over the summer. Kingston's resort had stirred up a little buzz. He'd taken her to lunch again, more vague promises, another mystery investor, but mostly he'd wanted to talk about his townhouse development. Did she think there would be much opposition? She doubted it. Beauty Creek was desperate.

Dwight burst through the front door. "I need film!"

"What's going on?"

"They're over at Nash Malone's place, hauling away his junk. Three dump trucks, the village loader. I shot the end of the roll I had, but the trucks were just leaving with a load. I want to go back, get them actually filling a truck."

"They're just scooping it up with a loader?"

"There's a crew there, dragging it out from behind the house, filling the loader bucket. It's a disaster zone."

"Did you see Nash?"

"No, I just stayed on the street. Howard Doyle was just leaving. He tried to shut me down. Said he didn't think it needed to be in the paper." Dwight chortled.

"Is Nash home?"

Dwight didn't know.

Maggie felt nauseated as she rolled the film. "Try to find out if Nash is there, how he's doing."

"I will." He held out his hand.

She placed the film into his palm. "This is going to be a mess."

Dwight closed his fingers around the canister. "They're not bulldozing his house, Mags, they're just hauling junk to the dump."

Maggie watched him drive away, paced several circles around the production table. "I should go over there."

"I'll watch the front," Felicia offered.

Maggie paced another lap. "I wonder if Rufus knows about this."

"He'd have to, wouldn't he?"

Maggie hoped not. "I'll be back," she said.

She drove to the village office. Doyle came to the counter. "Missus Evans."

"Don't you *Missus Evans* me. What the hell's going on?"

He screwed up his nose, pretended confusion.

"You know damn well what I'm talking about! What're you doing over at Nash Malone's place? Does Rufus know about this?"

"Mayor and council set policy. Enforcement is my jurisdiction."

"Answer my question. Does Rufus know about this?"

"The mayor can't be involved in every day-to-day decision. That's not his job."

"Answer me, damn it!"

"Yes, he knows. Perhaps not the specifics, but yes, the mayor knows, *and* the councillors."

"You're telling me they know that you've got dump trucks and the loader at Nash Malone's place today? Rufus knows that?"

"The mayor and councillors are in Vancouver this week for UBCM. You'd know that if you covered council meetings."

She remembered now, the Union of BC Municipalities annual conference. Rufus had asked her to come with him, weeks ago. She'd fobbed him off. She'd let things cool between them since the Sixtieth dance. One night of sitting mutely at his side had cured her of the momentary delusion that married life would be better than retiring to Blake's cherry orchard.

"You've put your foot in it this time," she said.

Doyle stiffened. "I have the authority. Besides, this is no different than Persky's mill, and no one had any trouble with that."

Maggie snorted. "I would've thought you'd know better. Persky came and went. He was only here, what, ten years? Nash is a *Creekster*. It isn't anywhere close to the same thing."

Doyle smirked. "I guess we'll see about that."

His smirk nagged at Maggie all afternoon. She grilled Dwight when he came back, but he didn't have much to add.

"They're nearly done," he said. "They're just filling the last truck."

"Did you talk to Nash?"

"I didn't. It didn't feel right."

Maggie understood his reluctance. On a good day, Nash Malone was a daunting prospect. "I'll do it," she said. "Later."

After Dwight and Felicia left, Maggie tried to proofread but she couldn't concentrate. She locked up and walked down Main to Fifth Avenue.

Not much remained in the devastated yard. The woodshed was still standing, and there was a small mound of bits and pieces beside the garage. Everything else was gone except two flower bins, made of tires, filled with the blackened, drooping remains of frozen geraniums.

She climbed the steps, knocked.

"Missus Evans."

"Maggie. Please. I guess you know why I'm here."

"Got nothing to say."

"Hank always used to say that it was better to get the facts out. That it kept the gossips on a leash."

"It don't matter to me what they say."

"It matters that the town knows what your side of things was. Is."

"None of their damn business, what my side of things is."

"But—"

"No buts." A pause. Maggie didn't fill it. He said, "Maybe I'll write a poem."

"And I'll print it. But, in the meantime, people need to know what went on here today."

"What went on?" he thundered. "Everybody in town knows what went on. Howard Doyle has been out to get me for years. Him and Harriet. That's what *went on*. Rufus Vanisle let him do it, and the municipal act lets them get away with it. That's what went on. Ask them what happened! Ask Doyle. Ask those hooligans he brought with him. Talk to young Hardy, get him to tell you what happened. They know. They were here. Ask your pal Rufus Vanisle. Ask him about his buddy Kingston of the posh resort. Ask him. He ought to know."

"I intend to." Maggie stepped back. Nash scowled.

She waited, but he didn't speak. "It shouldn't have happened," she said. "Not here."

"I got nothing more to say." He closed the door in her face.

Dwight was back at his desk when she returned to the *Chronicle*. "Do you think the mayor knew?" he asked. "Do you think he approved it?"

"We won't know until we get a chance to ask him."

"Do you think he set Doyle up? Why did it happen while him and the councillors are in Vancouver? So that Doyle can take the fall for it?"

Maggie hadn't considered that.

"What're we going to do?" Dwight asked.

"Not much we can do. Nash isn't talking. I refuse to quote just Doyle. We'll run one of your pictures with a caption. Wait and see."

"What about an editorial?"

"Saying what? We don't have all the facts."

35

Stevie set her quivering fingers on the keyboard. Drew herself together.
Heard Mr. Perkins's voice: *Eyes on copy. Elbows in. Sit up straight.*

She felt some of the tension in her gut ease.

Wrists down.

Nash Malone intruded: his pale, weathered face, the scar across
his wrist, the quiver in his fingers as he poured coffee, rectangles
drawn in sugar on the scarred tabletop.

Afraid.

Be afraid?

Just Afraid.

She focussed on the school sports report, typed the heading:
"Juniors Fare Well in Regional Tourney."

How many trucks?

Three. And the village loader. Voices from the coffee klatch at Betty's.

The cafe had been buzzing when she dropped in on her way to
work. The morning coffee crowd was out in full force; their table
was full but Hardy, in his off-duty uniform of blue jeans and ball cap,
hauled over a chair and made space for her in the circle of opinions.

"About time."

"They just scooped it up and hauled it away."

"Helluva thing, is all I can say."

"Not sure I want to live in a town that does such a thing."

"He got notices, same as everybody else."

"Threw them in the garbage, I heard."

"Nah, you got that wrong, he got them from the garbage."

General laughter.

Betty brought the coffee pot. Filled cups.

"Has anybody actually talked to him?" Stevie asked.

"I saw Howard Doyle Saturday. He told me Nash helped them load the trucks. That he wasn't even a bit upset."

"What a bunch of bull." Hardy raised his voice. "He was running all day trying to save stuff. Imagine if somebody showed up at your house and called everything you'd ever saved garbage and started throwing it into a dump truck." He banged down his coffee cup.

The table quivered.

"Sorry, Betty," Hardy said. "Guess I'm a bit peeved."

"We should all be peeved," Betty said.

Stevie brought her attention back to her typing. The headline was buried in the middle of the volleyball tournament report. While the juniors had not triumphed, they had come away with the Most Sportsmanlike trophy. It was the tenth year in a row they'd won it.

She would go see Nash after work. It was the right thing to do.

A thin thread of smoke trickled from the chimney of the bleak house, the barren ground and ragged ruts a new and terrible landscaping.

"Stay in the car, I'll only be a few minutes." Stevie cracked her window, pocketed the keys.

"But I want to come in. Mr. Malone likes me."

"Just stay in the car for five minutes. We don't have much time. I need to go back to the paper for an hour before supper. I'm not kidding, Brit, stay right here. Help your sister with her reading."

Nash pulled the door inward when he saw it was her. "I don't have anything to say."

"I'm not here for the paper. I just wanted to know how you're doing."

He snorted. "How do you think?"

She winced. "That was a stupid question. Is there anything I can do? Any way I can help?"

He sagged a little. "Come in. Read this poem I wrote last night."

She stayed in the doorway. He went to his typewriter, ripped out a sheet, thrust it at her.

She read the three short verses. "Holy cow!"

He plucked the page from her fingers, strode to the heater, lifted the lid, and dropped the paper into the fire.

Stevie gasped.

"Never write when you're angry," he said. "Or, do. Write it out, if you must, but, in the morning, burn it. Are you coming in?"

"It's…I've got the girls in the car."

"Bring them in. I've got cookies. I might even have some butter toffee."

"I don't want to bother you."

"It's no bother."

Stevie called from the steps, and Brit and Peg spilled from the car. "Shoes!" She corralled them in the porch. They kicked off their shoes and charged through the door, and it was as if they'd fallen through a portal: two completely different children came out the other side. They crowded back beside her and cowered silently in their seats at the kitchen table, surveying the room, awed.

Nash brought cookies, bent to offer them.

"You have a necklace," Peg said, pointing.

There was an awkward silence. Nash set down the plate of cookies, touched the thong beneath his collar.

"I forget that it's there, I've had it such a long time," he said. "Since I was a young fella."

"Young as me?"

"Not quite that young."

"Can I see it?"

"Sure." He lifted the braided cord over his head, passed it across.

Peg fingered the decorative centre knot.

"That there is called a monkey's fist. Sailors would tie it in the end of a heaving rope to make a lifeline. With that heavy knot at the end, they could throw it a long way: to another boat, or to a man in the water."

"Or to a girl?"

Nash chuckled. "Or to a girl."

Peg twirled it a few times. Stevie shot her a warning look.

"Were you a sailor?" Brit asked.

"No, I was never a sailor. My brother Pete made that for me when we were young fellas, riding the rails."

"Can I have it?"

"Peg!"

"I don't suppose I could give you that one. But I could show you how to tie your own."

"Now?" Brit asked.

"If your mom thinks you have time."

"Can we, Mom? Can we? Please."

"If Mr. Malone doesn't mind."

Nash went to the porch, rummaged, and came back with two sets of leather shoelaces. He half smiled at Stevie. "Lucky for us, that bylaw doesn't extend to the inside of my house."

Brit and Peg hovered as he took the laces from their cardboard backing. He gave them each a lace, tossed one down the table to Stevie, picked up the last one.

"Get a hold of your lace about here"—he grasped the lace near one end with his thumb and forefinger—"and make three loops." He wrapped the lace around his index finger three times. "Next, slide that off and wrap the other way, around the middle. Once, twice, and on the third, the end goes through."

Brit and Peg bent over their work, concentrating. Stevie felt something thick in her throat. She swallowed it down, focussed on her own knot.

"Now where?"

"Around the outside, three times. There you have it. Once, twice, and on the third?"

"The end goes through!"

"That's right. Steady now. Not too fast."

"Over or under?"

"What do you think?"

"Over."

"That's the ticket."

Nash looked up. Stevie mouthed a thank you. He acknowledged it with a slight nod.

"Look, Mom. Look!"

"I see it," she said. "What did Mr. Malone say it was called?"

Brit looked over her shoulder at Nash.

"A monkey's fist," he said. "Say you had a precious jewel, maybe a diamond or an emerald? You could tie it right inside that knot, slip it in there just before you snugged it tight, and you could carry it beside your heart."

"Can you tie my ends?"

He took the ends and tied a simple knot.

"Mine isn't working," Peg wailed.

"Here," Nash said. "You're nearly there." He spoke to Stevie over Peg's head. "This here's a hobo's knot. Funny what you remember any given day. I probably tied my first monkey's knot"—he winked—"sixty years ago."

While the girls put on their shoes, he went to his desk and brought back a folder tied with a white ribbon. "I've been working on something," he said. "I wonder if you'd read it for me. When you have time. If you have time. Tell me what you think."

"I'm not very good with poetry," she said. "Maybe you should get somebody better, maybe Mrs. Evans, to read it."

She saw him hesitate, knuckles white against the brown manila. She relented. "But I could try."

"It isn't poetry," he said. "I'm not sure what it is, but it's about Spain."

36

Nash closed the door. He clasped his empty, shaking fingers to his chest. His heart was raging. What had he done? He saw the car back onto the street. Too late now. He paced to the front door, into the bathroom, back to the window. What was the worst that could happen? She'd hate it. She'd lose it. He didn't have a copy.

"Quit yer sighing," Miriam used to say when he'd come home after mailing a poem, in those early years when he still imagined the writer he would become once he was published. "If you can't do nothing about it, you might as well do something else."

He picked up the cardboards from the laces and took them to the fire. As he bent, he felt the knot brush his neck. He had lied to the child. The knot Pete had tied was lost long ago. This knot he had tied himself. Once, and then again, rebuilding it each time the cord frayed, always the same knot, always one strand of red wool interwoven.

The Spanish train had wailed a mournful lament as they pulled out of Barcelona. They were travelling north, to freedom. After the endless months underground, escape had become their only victory, relief at being alive diluting the intense sorrow of defeat. Exhausted, filthy, wounds festering, lice feasting, their hair too long, their hearts breaking, they slouched on the hard seats, tense and silent, listening to the rattle of the wheels and the moans of the wounded.

Fed so long on dreams, they were starving now. Disbelieving. Unable to comprehend that Franco had prevailed. Nash had an aisle seat. Beside him, at the window, an American from Wisconsin. They had survived. Was it enough? Neither had the strength to ask. They dealt, instead, in the trivia of the moment.

"How much longer, do ya think?"

"It looks different, I can't tell."

Nash tried to summon something of the ride to Valencia, those first, extraordinary days. No one cheered this train onward. None dared raise the fist of solidarity now.

His bladder complained and he braced for the wretched trek to the end of the car, to the space between carriages where he could relieve himself.

Making his way down the swaying carriage, stepping carefully over bandaged ankles and shins, he noted the ashen faces, eyes closed, pain pulsing in the muscles along a jaw line, clenched fists tap, tap, tapping on a wooden seat.

"Almost there," he said to the boy on the stretcher nearest the door. He opened the door and stepped through.

"Leave it," the boy croaked. Fresh air stirred the loose end of a bandage. "Let the air in."

Nash stayed by the door a long time, watching the boy. There was a dark stain in the gauze above his right eye, and a dangerous scent wafted when the wind eddied. Nash averted his eyes when spasms of pain twisted the wasted body. A medic came out of the carriage in front of them. He knelt beside the writhing patient, dripped water onto the parched lips, dug into his satchel for a tablet, spoke soothingly, promising something. Nash knew it wouldn't be real medicine, they hadn't any, but shortly after administering the pill, the medic went on his way, and the boy slept. It was magic, Nash knew, something that the best medics had, in their hands, their voice. A certainty that overcame the pain, giving the patient just enough time to fall asleep, the sleep of healing or the sleep of death, either was preferable to the agony of consciousness.

Walking back to his seat, he had picked up a scrap of red woollen cloth from the floor, the remains of a sash. As the lonely miles clattered past, Nash loosened strands, braided them into a cord, tied a knot.

The trucks had broken the plants and compacted the soil, but they hadn't done much harm to the potatoes. Nash worked slowly, loosening the soil around each hill with his fork, scrabbling out the potatoes. They were a decent size, and there was only a touch of scab. When he had filled two buckets, he took them to the hose, rinsed away the clinging soil and spread them onto a sunny hummock. He'd move them to the shade of the woodshed later, to dry fully before he bagged them for the root cellar.

He was halfway down the second row when June Fletcher drove in. "There you are, you old coot."

He brushed dirt from his hands. "June."

"I'm here to talk you into doing something you're not gonna want to do."

"I guess we'd best do that over a cup of coffee."

She grinned. "Yep. We'd best."

She'd been right. He didn't want to.

"I can't."

"But you can. You need to."

"I don't think so."

"Doyle needs to be put in his place. You're the man to do it."

"Doyle has the bit between his teeth. I don't think you'll rein him in." Nash had already called a lawyer, picked at random from the phone book. The young fellow was kind, but he didn't think Nash had much recourse. He suggested small claims court. Nash doubted he'd bother. The cleanup bill—linen envelope, fancy new logo—was on his desk, still sealed. He might just burn the damn thing. What could they do to him? He'd been to jail. Didn't kill him.

"Nobody thinks that Doyle had any right to do what he did. They sure as hell don't think you ought to have to pay for it. I've got a petition for tonight's council meeting." June dragged out a ragged sheaf of photocopied pages, filled with signatures. "Three hundred and twenty-seven voters!"

"You don't say."

"A lot of people are up in arms about it."

"Been four people here since it happened, not counting you."

"That's not fair."

"I think it is. They're worked up at the idea of it, that Doyle could send the dump trucks and the loader into *their* back yard. They don't give a damn about me or my stuff. They're just worried about the precedent."

"That's not true. It isn't. People do care about you, even if you make it pretty near impossible. You keep to yourself, you always have. People figure you prefer it that way so they leave you alone. You can't run people off for years and then complain if they don't show up."

He didn't respond.

"Come to the meeting. Help me"—she shook her petition—"help us show Doyle that we won't put up with his bureaucratic nonsense. That Creeksters won't stand for it." She drained her coffee cup, took it to the sink, came back to stand beside his shoulder. "Promise me."

"When is it?"

"Seven o'clock tonight, Council Chambers."

"I'll think about it."

"I'll save you a seat."

He walked out with her, went back to his potato patch. Dug potatoes until five, had his supper, and went out to move the spuds to the woodshed. It took longer than he expected and when he came inside to clean up it was already past eight. June's meeting would be over by now.

37

Maggie sat down at her desk and flexed her clenched fingers. The level of her rage was inexplicable. She had wanted to strike someone. She hadn't felt this kind of explosive anger since her volatile menopause years, when she'd wake in the night and want to throttle Hank for breathing too loudly.

She pressed her shoulders up toward her ears, willed the rage down, felt it receding, an ocean current drifting out. She breathed in. Exhaled. Saw Doyle's smug face, Rufus banging his gavel. Her rage surged.

There was a knock. *Not now, Dwight.*

Not Dwight. Stevie.

"I just wondered what happened. I wanted to come, but my sitter bailed at the last minute, and Felicia's kids are sick, so we couldn't go there."

"Nothing happened. Doyle said it wasn't on the agenda, and they didn't have to deal with it. So, they didn't. Vanisle rapped his gavel, and they went on with the regular meeting as if we weren't in the room."

"What about June's petition?"

"She tried. She waved around her pages of signatures. Doyle said it wasn't a public hearing, she wouldn't be heard. That she could drop it off at the office for the next meeting if she wanted. Procedure, he said. Goddamn asshole." Maggie's rage welled, threatened to leak out her eyes. She wouldn't cry, not in front of the girl. "What are you doing here anyway?"

"You walked right by me when you came in. I came back to check the TV guide. I was kind of distracted this afternoon. I thought I'd better look over the work I did."

"Where are the girls?"

"They're with Dwight. He took them for chips and gravy at the cafe."

"Dwight?"

"I know, weird, eh? He said he was hungry, and they might as well come along."

"Did he say how his meeting went?"

"Only that they got done early. He was bummed that he had to cover the Girl Guides instead of June's petition."

"Well, he didn't miss a thing." Maggie pushed herself up. "I could use some chips myself."

Dwight and the girls were perched on stools at the horseshoe counter nearest the kitchen. Betty had just set down heaping ice cream sundaes.

"Hi, Mom," Brit piped.

"I hope it's allowed," Dwight said, "the ice cream. They ate their chips."

"Ice cream! On a school night. I don't know."

Brit beamed. Peg swivelled, her spoon in her cheek, checking to be sure it was a joke.

"How did it go?" Dwight asked.

"It just fizzled," Maggie said. "June wasn't allowed to speak."

"Was Nash there?"

"No. I think June expected him, but he wasn't. I wonder if Doyle would have been as officious if he'd had to look Nash in the eye. Bunch of cowards, hiding behind Doyle's rule book."

"And Rufus?" Dwight asked.

It perplexed her still. "He just sat there while Doyle shut June down."

"What about Tilda Cooper?" Betty asked. "It's not like her to get railroaded by Doyle."

"She's away." It would have been a different meeting if Councillor Cooper had been in her chair.

"What'll happen now?"

"June said it will be on the agenda, come hell or high water. That's in two weeks, the next council meeting."

Betty clicked her tongue. "Here in Beauty Creek. I never would have believed it. This is Doyle and that damn Kingston. I've had 'em in here, plotting. Bastards."

Dwight perked. "Did you ever hear them talking about Nash's place?"

"No. But what would it matter anyway? It's just shameful. I should have been at that meeting. I'd have spoken, by God."

Dwight chuckled. She glared at him, and he pretended to duck. "I'd have been there if you were speaking, Betty."

She smiled, mollified, and took Maggie's chip order to the kitchen.

"She's right," Maggie said. "I should have spoken too."

"Not your job," Dwight said. "Your job is to get it down."

Maggie didn't want to argue with Dwight. She turned to Stevie. "I'd like to hear the youth perspective. What say you, young Stevie?"

Stevie winced at the direct question. "I guess we all should have been at that meeting. But maybe we should have been between Nash's stuff and the trucks too. If we were going to do something, we should have done it sooner."

"That supposes we could read minds and know this was going to happen," Dwight said.

Stevie coughed on her water. "Come on, Dwight, we knew it was going to happen. Maybe we didn't think it would come to loaders and dump trucks, but we knew they were after Nash. Everyone in town knew. Lots of people are fine with it: they don't like him, or they're ashamed of him or they don't care. All the talk about tourism saving us, now that the mill is down. Progressive communities. Kingston's resort. Beautification. Me and those damn flower boxes. Did we really think it wouldn't have an impact? We need to think further ahead sometimes. Because, you're right, we don't have a crystal ball, and before we throw out the old and think we're going to make something better—"

Dwight tried to interrupt but she shushed him with a shaking finger. "They think, I thought, beauty is flower boxes and pavement. And that's bullshit. We don't need bureaucrats from Victoria telling us what's beautiful. Beauty Creek is already beautiful. Nash's yard doesn't add anything or take anything away from the way Wolverine Mountain looks with snow on it. Or the way that big block of poplars on the ridge changes colour in the fall. This whole progressive communities thing is just a trick to make Beauty Creek look like something that other people—people who can't see it for what it already is—can recognize. "

"Hear! Hear!" Betty slid a heaping plate of golden french fries in front of them.

"Well said, kiddo, well said." Maggie was impressed. She'd make a reporter yet, this one. Gumption, Hank would have called it. "You can teach them the rest," he'd say, "but it's no use unless they've got gumption."

After they'd eaten, Maggie returned to the *Chronicle* alone. She unlocked the back door, dropped her purse on the work table and faced the half-built newspaper. The flats marched along the paste-up board in their mismatched fashion, page one beside twenty-four, two with twenty-three, the four pages that would, back-to-back, become one sheet of the *Beauty Creek Chronicle*, Volume 52, Issue 37. She lingered in front of pages four and twenty-one. Page four, the editorial page, had the cartoon in place, and the constant masthead where the *Chronicle* proudly proclaimed its independence, where Maggie had left Hank's name as publisher. Above it, a blank space, reserved for the editorial. The editorial she had until Monday to compose.

When Hank put on his editor's cap, he had loosed his propensity for righteousness. You didn't have to agree with him. "Not a popularity contest," he'd growl. Every week, he'd cajoled or castigated or congratulated, depending entirely on his personal barometer to adjudicate the issues of the day. Maggie knew she was too hesitant. Her editorials, when she couldn't fob them off on Dwight, were more observation, less judgement.

But this.

This called for a blistering Hank Evans response.

The letters to the editor had begun arriving before Dave Lerbo's Caterpillar had finished filling in the hole at the dump, dug specifically to ensure that not so much as a bike pedal returned to Fifth Avenue.

June Fletcher had delivered hers in person. "I suppose you've heard," she'd said, thrusting the envelope forward. "I can hardly believe it. That Vanisle, who does he think he is?"

"You heard it was Vanisle?"

"Who else?"

"Rufus wasn't even here."

"He's the Mayor. The buck stops with him."

"But he's not even on that committee."

"Committee, shummittee. This is Vanisle and Kingston. Kingston's resort. Which is going to come to nothing because he's never going to find the money. I've asked around, he doesn't have the chops."

"Hard to be sure he can't do it, if he never gets a chance to try."

June snorted, indicated her letter. "I've put it all in there. Edit it if you need to. I already took out the part where I called them a bunch of drooling idiots. But I might have left in more than I should have."

"You do realize Beauty Creek needs this development. That it might be all we've got?"

"Horse feathers! Suppose he does get it built and every little thing he promised comes to pass. His international clientele comes a-flocking. Then what? We're supposed to fall over ourselves in gratitude because someone's going to overnight in Beauty Creek on their ten-day trip through the Rockies? Get their photo taken in front of Wolverine Mountain? Honestly? That's our destiny? Creeksters as a tourist attraction? Our lives some kind of carnival show?

"We'll only be popular for so long. Mark my words. Once they've homogenized Beauty Creek, they'll move on, lusting after the very thing they destroyed here. Sixty years from now, we'll be nothing but some black and white pictures on the wall at Kingston's resort."

Maggie meandered to the front of the store, shifted a few packages of copy paper to cover an empty space. The banker was right; her inventory was slowly diminishing, years of subsistence ordering taking their toll. "People are more likely to buy if the shelf is full," the stationer's rep was always telling her. People were inclined to buy their stationery from the city these days, ordering from the weighty catalogues that arrived free in their post office boxes. She could always write a "shop local" editorial. She had plenty to say about that.

She paced and muttered and eventually returned to her computer. Opened a blank text file, tried to get down her thoughts, but they wouldn't cooperate.

Was Stevie right? Were they all complicit? Praying some benevolent investors would save them? But why wouldn't they? Look at the provincial government, scrabbling around, desperate to find something else to sell, now that they'd pissed away the best timber. Encouraging everybody else to do the same. June was right, all they wanted were cookie-cutter towns, each of them feeding Victoria. Progressive communities. Bah!

What would Hank write?

She heard his gravelly, whisky voice asking, "What about our readers, Maggie?"

"Yes, Maggie," she grumbled aloud, "what about your readers?" What was the mood of Beauty Creek these days? Did she even know?

"Maybe you should write it," she'd said to Dwight earlier.

He'd laughed, held up his hands, palms out. "No way, Mags. This one's all yours."

38

The printer hummed and spat out three pages in quick succession.

"That's page four," Felicia said.

Stevie plucked up the pages, scanned them.

"Are these the right pages?" she asked, bringing them to Felicia's desk.

"Yep. Why?"

"It's a 'shop local' editorial."

"Yeah, I know."

"I don't get it. She was so mad about Nash Malone. Now she's not going to say anything?"

Felicia was engrossed in tweaking a headline. Stevie hovered at her elbow. "This is because of Kingston," she said. "She doesn't want his investors to think anyone in Beauty Creek has any opposition to their plan."

"Either way it's her call. Paste it up," Felicia said.

Stevie waxed the back of the page, used a razor knife to trim its edges. She lifted down the page four flat and aligned the copy. She felt a kind of roiling disbelief, an impotent fury. It had not diminished by the time Maggie arrived.

"Wow!" Maggie said. "Look at those letters."

The letters to the editor began on page four and went on to fill two full pages. Felicia had done her best to break it up, but the pages were dense with text.

"I left out the MP's column," Felicia said, "and I squeezed your editorial."

"I see that," Maggie said. "How's the proofing coming?"

"Oh, just hunky dory," Stevie drawled. She knew she'd overdone the sarcasm when both Maggie and Felicia gaped. She dropped her eyes to the page, pretended to read.

"Stevie?" Maggie stepped to the table. "Are you okay?"

"Never better. Just proofing, the *editorial*."

Maggie barked a laugh. "I know. It's lame."

"So, Nash doesn't deserve a—I don't even know—a defence?"

"He's got plenty of defenders. Those letters are six to one for Nash Malone."

"It's not the same as the editorial being for him."

"There's probably better points made in those letters than I could have come up with."

Gutless. The word floated to the front of her brain and spilled out her lips. "Gutless wonder."

"Pardon me?"

"You heard me."

Felicia wheeled back to her screen.

"I don't think I did," Maggie snapped. "Maybe you'd care to repeat it?"

Stevie snapped back. "You're always lecturing me and Dwight about our responsibility as journalists. Our ethical obligations. What about your obligations?"

"We gave it the front page. The story is covered, the whole story. There's no *ethical* reason I need to write an editorial that supports Nash Malone. If anything, there's a strong argument for not taking a side."

"I thought stories didn't have sides."

"They don't and neither does this. I don't have to have an opinion about everything."

"But you do have an opinion. Right? You do think that what they did to Nash was wrong."

"Yes, but—"

"Or maybe you don't. Maybe you and your buddy Rufus Vanisle and your new best friend Miles Kingston think it's justified, what they did. Maybe you think that the new improved Beauty Creek has no place for Nash Malone."

"Stevie. Calm down."

"Why can't you write that it was wrong? Why can't you at least give him that bit of respect? Why can't you?"

"He doesn't care what I think. What you think."

"I think he does."

"Stevie, I've known Nash Malone a bit longer than you have. You can trust me when I tell you that he could care less what I think."

"Maybe that's true. Maybe he doesn't care what you think. Maybe nobody cares what you think!"

"I can see you're upset. Maybe we should just drop this."

"You can drop it on your head," Stevie flared, pushing away from the table. The flickering ire had become a leaping, roaring flame. "Right beside Miles Kingston's stupid resort, right beside your stupid editorial and your stupid...stupid...job!"

Felicia and Maggie stared. Stevie fled. She grabbed her purse and left by the front door. Fuck you, Mrs. Please-Call-Me-Maggie Evans, she thought, as she marched away. *Fuck you.*

She had to call Brit three times to set the table. "Just for once, could you do it without making a fuss. Could you do that?"

Brit wrinkled her nose and, when Stevie turned her back, thumped down a plate.

Stevie jumped, shouted. "That's it, young lady. That is it! Just leave it. I'll do it. You go on, back to your television, and I'll just wait on you. Princess Brittania."

Brit locked eyes with her and slammed down another plate. It split in two. Stevie grabbed Brit's arm, swung her around, intending to smack her backside.

"Ooow! You're hurting my arm."

We don't hit in this house.

Stevie crumpled. "I'm sorry. I'm sorry. It's not you. It's me. Leave it. Just leave it. I'll call you when supper is ready."

Brit's eyes welled. She ran down the hall, slammed her bedroom door.

Stevie picked up the broken plate, put the pieces into the garbage can under the sink. What was she doing? She had enough saved to pay one month's rent. The propane tank needed to be filled. She'd just walked out on the best job she could've ever hoped for. Where would she get another?

"Mom?" Peg came down the hall. "Brit's crying."

"I know, pumpkin. I know. We had a little fight, but we'll work it out. Maybe you could set the table for me?"

Peg's brow puckered. Her loyalty to her sister was a mysterious force. Brit could treat her like dirt, and often did, but Peg would rally, every time.

"Why are you mad at her?" Peg asked.

"I'm not mad at her. I'm mad at the world."

"At the world?"

"Never mind, I'll set the table. You get washed, and tell your sister it's supper time."

Peg toddled down the hall, came back. "She's not hungry."

Stevie shut off the burners under their supper and went down the hall. Brit had a photo album on her lap. Stevie sat with her, and they paged through the wedding photos to the baby pictures. Bobby, just home from work, holding Brit's wrists, her tiny feet curled on his steel-toed boots, frayed red laces against her chubby ankles, as they waltzed around the kitchen.

"We're dancing. Right, Mom?"

"You are. Your dad loved to dance, especially with you."

Brit bent closer to the photo. Her shoulders swayed, a small movement, back and forth, two-four time.

Peg came down the hall and clambered onto the bed. Brit moved the album away.

Stevie gathered Peg up, carried her to the living room. "What did you do today?" she asked. They settled in the black recliner, and Peg toyed with Stevie's hair, and they talked about who had played with who at recess, and why James liked Sarah better than Ashley (Ashley was too bossy).

"Mom?"

"Yes, pet?"

"Is spanking hitting?"

"It is."

"Was it always?"

"It was."

Stevie tipped Peg's face up to hers, found the words. "I didn't always know that. But I do now."

"That's okay, Mom. Mrs. M says it's good to learn a new thing every day. Even when you get old."

Brit came out of her bedroom and they ate warmed-over scrambled eggs and beans and a desert of huckleberry jam on toast. After baths and bedtime stories, just as Stevie shut off their light, the phone rang.

It was Felicia. "How are you doing?"

"I'm fine." Stevie choked the words out. Why did kindness make her cry every time?

"You left your car."

"I know, I'll get it tomorrow."

"You don't really want to quit, do you?"

As if that was an option. "No."

"Because Maggie just thinks you were upset. She's sure you'll be back in the morning."

"Like nothing happened?"

"Not exactly. You did abandon us in the middle of production day. You might need to say you're sor—"

"Did you run it like that?"

"Run what? The editorial? Yeah. You didn't think she'd just whip out another one at two o'clock on Monday afternoon, did you?"

Stevie had hoped. She'd imagined one of Maggie's feisty editorials rolling out of Felicia's printer, Dwight laying it over the offending "shop local" copy, everyone relieved that Stevie had spoken up when she did.

"Oh, Stevie. Why don't you write something?"

"Write what?"

"A letter. An editorial. Write an editorial for next week."

"I can't write an editorial."

"Why not?"

"I can't."

"You can. What you can't do is keep on waiting for someone else to do things for you."

"That's what you think I'm doing?" Why did people always think they knew you?

"A bit. It's pretty common with women in your—"

"Women in my what, Felicia? My situation? My knocked-up-at-fifteen, single-mother-with-two-kids-and-no-job *situation*? You don't know me. You don't have a clue what I need to be doing."

"I didn't mean—"

"Yes, you did. You're just like everybody else, sitting in your comfortable life, judging me. Everybody's full of advice for women in my *situation*. And, they do think I should get someone to *do things for me*, just not them."

"Stevie. Stevie. It's me. Felicia. Your friend."

"I've gotta go. The girls are in the tub."

"Call me back."

"Yeah, maybe later."

She heard Felicia say her name again, the same gentle, pleading tone. She hung up the phone.

39

The ravens circled and called. Nash came out the door, stretched his shoulders against the pain in his back. He carried a battered tin pan, bacon drippings drizzled over chunks of bread crust. He walked slowly, stepped carefully over the ruts left by the village loader. He shielded his eyes, looked up, and clucked to three youngsters perched on the power line. They clucked back. An elder raven glided to the ground. She walked with him to the corner of the woodshed, head bobbing with each step, one eye fixed on the pan.

Nash heard the pan clatter down. He saw the raven flap herself up and away. He worked out that he had fallen. The view was hazy. He saw the big bird float down, and sensed her hopping in to peck at the scattered bread. He heard her call to her chicks, saw them come fluttering down, heard them chatting as the darkness closed in.

40

Maggie tallied the cash again. She was short by nineteen dollars. She'd already added the stack of cheques, twice. She tore off the adding machine tape and checked her numbers, one at a time, ticking them off as she went. It would have balanced for Stevie. She pushed the thought away. It had only been three days. Stevie would be back. She would.

Dwight swept through the beads. "Did you hear?"

"Hear what?"

"What's up?" Felicia was at his shoulder.

"Stan O'Leary says Nash Malone is in the hospital. A stroke or something."

"How bad is it?"

"Stan didn't know. He went to the hospital last night, but he couldn't get in to see Nash. He said Stevie was there."

"Stevie?" Maggie frowned. "What would she be doing there?"

"They're kind of friends," Felicia said.

"Since when?"

"Since she tried to do that interview."

"But she never got that story," Dwight said, dubious.

"He gave her a manuscript to read."

"A poetry book?" Dwight queried.

"Not poetry, a novel. About Spain, apparently."

Maggie was speechless. Nash Malone had given little Stevie Jeffers a manuscript to read?

"Where is she now?" Felicia asked Dwight.

"I don't know."

"I'm going to call her." Felicia went back to her desk.

"Did you know she was friends with Nash?" Maggie asked Dwight.

"Never said a word to me."

Felicia returned, her face sombre. "She said Nash is stable, for now. He can't walk and he can't speak, but the doctor said it was too soon to know if that's permanent."

"How's Stevie?" Dwight asked.

"She's pretty worried."

"She's got enough to do without taking on Nash Malone's troubles," Maggie said. "Did she say when she's coming back to work?"

Dwight and Felicia exchanged a look.

Felicia asked, "Do you want her to come back?"

"Absolutely. Don't we all?"

They nodded.

"You should call her and tell her," Felicia said. "She's at home."

Maggie felt Dwight watching her.

She sighed. "Okay. I will."

It was dark outside and Maggie was alone in the building when she heard a car door slam at the back. She'd locked the front door hours ago. Maybe she should lock the back door, too. She'd only just gotten rid of June Fletcher who'd needed to lecture her for an hour about her spineless editorial. She'd already grovelled to Stevie about it. It was easier the second time, though June hadn't been as quickly appeased.

Rufus came through the dim production room, tapped on the wall outside her office. "Anybody home?"

"If you're here to talk to me about my editorial, you'll have to get in line," she said.

"Actually, it was your front-page story that concerned me, the innuendo about Kingston Developments." He dropped into the chair in front of her desk. "I thought we were on the same page, you and me. I thought you understood how much Beauty Creek needs that development."

"There was no *innuendo*. Those were facts. You did hide behind procedure to avoid June's petition. Kingston does have connections to the numbered company that bought those lots along Beauty Creek, the ones right behind Nash Malone's house. Kingston does have a lousy track record. Those were direct quotes from the other places he was going to put *on the map*."

"It sends a dismal message to his investors. We need them to know that Beauty Creek is behind this. Nobody's going to sink money into a development that's controversial."

"You afraid June Fletcher will be out marching with a placard? Chaining herself to a bulldozer?"

"I wouldn't put it past her."

"And I will cover it if she does."

"There's no need to get snippy about it."

"Snippy? You think this is snippy? I've barely gotten started. Did you put Doyle up to this? Was it you?"

"Whoa, Maggie, whoa. It's me. Rufus." He changed his tone, wheedled, "Where's the Maggie Evans I know and love?"

"Gone. If she ever existed. Maybe you made her up from the start."

"Maggie, Maggie," he soothed. "Let's not fight. We're on the same side. You're just tired. And why not? This newspaper has been dragging you down for years. Miles tells me he's working overtime to find you a buyer. You'll feel differently once it's sold."

"Why are you so keen to get me to sell?"

"Because this place makes you cranky...and crazy."

"That's what you think? That I'm cranky and crazy?"

"Now you're putting words in my mouth."

"Those words just came out of your mouth."

"Maggie."

"And what if I do sell? Maybe I don't want to be Beauty Creek's future first lady."

"But—"

"Because I'm not sure I want to be Mrs. Anybody, ever again."

"You're upset."

She wasn't. Not really. "I'm not upset. I'm not cranky. I'm certainly not crazy. But I might be done with this little charade. We've been playing at this for years, Rufus. If there was anything to it, don't you think we'd have done something about it by now?"

"I've been trying."

"Not very hard." She shuffled papers. "I'd better get back to work, I have a lot to get through tonight."

"Have breakfast with me tomorrow."

She laughed out loud. "Oh, Rufus."

"What?"

"You really don't know me."

"You don't eat breakfast?"

"Never mind."

Rufus got to his feet. "That's it? Your final word?"

She felt for it. Tried to remember that first kiss. Couldn't. "I think so," she said.

Rufus waited for her to say something else. She didn't. He walked away.

After she heard the back door close, Maggie paced to the front window. Down the block, lights shone in the window display at Pam's Dress Shop. Pam Dubois left Beauty Creek in 1967, the same year that Maggie's parents sold out and moved to Vernon. The dress shop had changed hands several times, but the name had remained, along with some of the stock. It was an old town joke that there were dresses in Pam's that knew where they were when JFK was shot. Hank hadn't believed in holding on to old inventory; the *Chronicle* had a clear-out sale once a year.

Hank, again. Was it true, what she'd said to Rufus? Was she done being Mrs. Anybody? If that was true, was she done being Mrs. Hank Evans too?

What would that mean?

It would mean that it was time for her to run the *Chronicle* the way *she* would.

And what would that mean?

It would mean an editorial, for starters. Her own thoughts, her own words.

She went to the computer, composed herself, fingers on the keyboard.

We can't live in the past, she typed.

She backspaced it away, stared at the empty, glowing page.

She typed it again, faster, the words spilling out.

We can't live in the past.

We can remember it. We can cherish it. We can recreate it occasionally, but we can't live there. That is a plain truth of life.

Some of you will remember my husband, Hank Evans, long-time editor and publisher of this newspaper. He's part of the past that I can't live in any more. I thought I could. For years I thought that, by getting this newspaper out every week, I could keep on living in the past, where Hank Evans is still the editor and publisher of the *Beauty Creek Chronicle*, and Bull Devers's sawmill hands out paycheques every second Friday, and spring breakup never comes early, and we dance until dawn on that springy hardwood floor at the old community hall.

But I don't live there any more. None of us does.

That hall burned in the winter of '75. Bull Devers retired to the coast and sold the mill to the conglomerates, and we all know how that's working out. Hank Evans is dead and buried in the Beauty Creek cemetery these past five years.

The past has passed.

A day is going to come when Nash Malone's yard is a thing of the past. No one in Beauty Creek will even know what you're talking about. Who you're talking about. Or why it mattered. But that travesty they called a "cleanup" did happen. I let it happen. You let it happen. We shouldn't have but we did. The best we can do now is to get the village to tear up that outrageous bill (next Tuesday, seven p.m., Council Chambers—get there early if you want a seat). As far as I can see, that's the bottom line. A mistake was made, and Nash Malone certainly ought not be the one who pays for it.

But that won't take us back to the town we were before this happened.

No siree.

The same way I can't live in the past, I can't live in the future. I haven't got a clue what's going to happen in five years. Or tomorrow.

Where will Beauty Creek be in the new millennium? I don't believe the Timberline Resort, whether it happens or not, is going to save Beauty Creek. Investors require a return, which means that whatever real money gets made won't be staying here. Last I heard, none of the Kingston investors are planning to stake their future on Beauty Creek. They're just tossing a few spare dollars at an investment they hope pays more than the bank.

But what do I know about tourism developments? As anybody will tell you, I'm a mill brat. I was raised on logging and lumbering, huckleberries and moose meat, hard work and long hours, short summers and cold winters.

So, that's it. No past. No future.

The only certainty I can offer up, the one thing we've always known about living this far out, is this:

We are it.

No one is coming to save us.

It sounds bleak, but Creeksters have always been able to find silver linings. This is ours:

Whatever happens, we'll be in it together.

She saved the file. She'd come back to it tomorrow. Find a way to link that last sentence to Nash Malone's bill being forgiven because that was the point. She'd change some words, move sentences around, but the essence of it was there.

She shut down the computer, wandered to the paste-up shelf. The masthead drew her eye:

Publisher: Hank Evans

Editor: Margaret Evans

Reporter: Dwight Osborne

Office Manager: Mildred Barnes

Production Assistant: Felicia Hall

She peeled off the waxy rectangle and took it to Felicia's desk. She found a pen and marked her changes:

Publisher: Maggie Evans

Editor: Dwight Osborne

Reporter: Stephanie Jeffers

Production Manager: Felicia Hall

She went to the front desk, lifted Hank's portrait from the wall. She took down the old front-page plaque. Hank had been right about that; readers were the only prize that mattered. At her office door, she hesitated over the JANITOR sign. It still made her smile. It could stay.

She could stay.

All these years, she'd been leaving. Ever since she'd climbed out of the Buick and started unloading pots and pans into that first shack at Bachelor Flats. She'd never wanted to stay.

Now, she couldn't leave.

She'd call the real estate office in the morning, and get the appraisal paperwork underway for the bank. She'd buy a decent camera and never let the reporters touch it. She might not be able to live in the past, but she could sure as hell be there for the future.

Stevie had agreed to work the morning shift at the cafe. Betty was strapped, she said. The new waitress needed to take one of her kids to the dentist and no one else could cover. Mrs. Marsonkowsky would get the girls up and off to school. Maggie said she'd cover the front desk, as long as Stevie was back by eleven to label papers and get them to the post office.

It was both odd and comfortable, the cafe routines coming back, customers greeting her like an old friend, the cheerful backchat with the coffee regulars. When the last of them had trailed out into their day and she'd reset the tables, Betty asked her to pop over to Cooper's for a jug of pancake syrup and a litre of whipping cream.

She'd just grabbed the cream and was looking for the syrup when she bumped into Harriet Lemsky, coming around the end of an aisle.

"Hello, Stephanie. How are you?"

"Fine." She said it without smiling.

Harriet frowned. "You think this is my fault, this business with Nash Malone."

"I think you could have been kinder."

"Kinder?"

"Yes, kinder. I know he's old and weird but he wasn't doing you any harm. I think you could have tried to get along. Just because he's a bit of an outsider is no reason—"

"Outsider? Nash Malone?" Harriet stabbed a finger at her own chest. "I know what it is to be an outsider." Her voice wavered, she swallowed, went on, louder. "They called us names when we came here. DPs, they called us: dirty deportees. We were not invited into their homes except by the church people, and then only because their God required it. I know what it is to be different, to be an outsider. It is no excuse. No excuse for laziness."

"Nash isn't lazy! He's old!"

"No excuse for uncut grass and broken fences and garbage."

"There was no garbage. There were bike parts, and copper wire. A few old washtubs, some tires. There was no garbage."

"You can split hairs if you need to, but I know garbage. Filthy man." She shoved her cart forward.

Stevie grabbed the handle. "You do know he's in the hospital?"

"A heart attack, I heard. I am responsible now for his heart?"

Stevie gave way, watched the flowered smock move down the aisle. Her stomach roiled. She wanted to shriek, to strike out. She glared at the tins in front of her, made herself read the labels: brown beans in tomato sauce; kidney beans; lima beans. She swiped at her eyes, searched out the pancake syrup and carried it to the front.

Tilda Cooper was on the checkout. She reached across the turn-stile and patted Stevie's arm. "Well done," she whispered, "telling that old battle-axe what's what."

"I wanted to punch her, right in the…baked beans. For all the good that would have done. I don't think she even heard me."

"Maybe not today. But maybe next time."

"I doubt that."

"Okay, perhaps not Harriet. But some other people. Me, for one."

"You were there from the start."

"I wasn't. Progressive Communities wasn't one of my committees. I thought it was sensible. I mean, Persky's old mill needed to be dealt with before some kid got hurt. And why should Creeksters get stuck with the costs?" She made change, bagged the cream and syrup. "I never thought it would come to this."

Back at the cafe, Stevie was halfway through telling Betty the story when the doorbell tinkled.

Betty looked past her. "When it rains, it pours," she said.

Howard Doyle and Miles Kingston banged through the front door, took a booth.

Stevie sighed, picked up the coffee pot and two menus.

"Coffee?"

They pushed their cups forward. She poured. They took the menus without meeting her eyes. She returned the coffee pot, got her order pad, came back to the table, pen poised.

"I thought you and your pen were working for Maggie Evans." Doyle smirked.

"I am. I'm just helping out Betty this morning."

"I'll have the ham and eggs. Eggs over. White toast." Doyle spoke to the air in front of him, held the menu in her direction. "I'd have thought you *Chronicle* lackeys would be busy helping out your commie buddy."

She took the menu, ignored the taunt, asked Kingston, "What can I get for you this morning?"

"Same. Ham and eggs. Tell Betty not to burn my toast." He gave her his menu.

She jotted his order, eyes down.

Kingston murmured a question. Doyle replied. "Yeah, a dirty job but somebody had to do it."

Kingston chuckled.

Stevie turned away from the table. She stepped toward the kitchen, swung back, heart pumping. "Nash Malone is not dirty!" Her voice trembled. "And it is *despicable* of you to suggest it."

Doyle opened his mouth. Stevie raised her pen, thrust the nib toward his nose. "This kind of insinuation … don't raise your eyebrows at me, you know what I mean. So what if he was a communist? Better that than a fascist bully in a hardhat! He nearly got killed in Spain. Do you know he has shrapnel in his back? Do you know he can only sleep for two or three hours at a time because the scar tissue presses on a nerve when he lies down? Do you? That's when he works on pumps or bicycle chains. That's when he repairs toaster ovens and takes copper out of wire. Do you know that your trucks drove over his garden?

Crushed his potatoes. Do you even care? Did you even notice that garden?" Her voice broke. "You…you…you ought to be ashamed of yourselves. Both of you!"

Kingston rolled an eye at Doyle. Stevie flared. "And you," she hissed, her pen a stabbing sword. "We all know everything there is to know about the likes of you, Miles Kingston." Behind her, she heard Betty swing through the kitchen door.

"I guess we'll go somewhere else for breakfast." Doyle raised his voice for Betty's benefit. "Somewhere management has a leash on their staff."

"You do that, Howard Doyle," Betty replied. "Sight of you will put my customers off their feed."

Doyle slid out of the booth. Kingston followed. As his shoulders came level with hers, Stevie leaned in, her voice steady now. "You can pretend we're strangers if you want to, mister, but I *know* you. My pen and I will be watching."

Nash woke in a fog. Something was cutting into his wrist. He fought against it.

Alarms sounded.

When he woke again, he was tied to the bed. Lightly, soft padded belts, but cuffs just the same.

Someone was in the room. Round face. Brown eyes. Dark hair.

"Who did this?" she demanded to know.

He heard the nurse explain that it was to keep him from pulling out his IV. The doctor had signed the order.

"Are you his daughter?" the nurse asked.

"A friend," he heard her say. "I'm his friend."

Compañero. Through the haze he saw a leather monkey's knot dangling around her neck. He felt her hand on his cheek, a cool cloth against his brow.

He was safe. He could sleep. Miriam was home.

Howe Street was damp. It wasn't raining, but
moisture hung in the air, and the boy breathed
it in. It cloaked itself around him, lapping at
his ear lobes.

The boy twisted his shoulders beneath his
damp shirt. He sucked a minty penny candy, his
last, which he had unwrapped from a scrap of
brown paper before leaving his tent. His stomach grasped at the filaments of sugar that had
to sustain him until the midday meal at First
United.

The geese had already lifted off when he saw
them. They must have been poking around the
fountain in front of the courthouse. They were
silent, save the rush of powerful wings. They
swept past him, airborne, free, heading north.

He watched them go. The buildings swallowed
them, brown and black feathers lost against the
sooty bricks. There, now gone.

He kept watching.

He would have liked to have seen them silhou-
etted against the sky.

Maggie sat between Stevie and June Fletcher, in the chair they'd saved for her. Every other seat was taken, and Creeksters were crowded, two deep, along the back wall of the council chambers.

"They should have dealt with me at the last meeting," June whispered, practically wriggling with glee. "There were only half as many people. If they mess with this bunch, they'll eat them for breakfast."

Maggie watched Doyle. He fiddled with his papers, clicked the nib of his pen up and down, glanced at the clock as it ticked toward seven.

Rufus picked up his gavel, called the meeting to order.

The crowd was patiently silent while the councillors worked through the first few items on the agenda, but they sat forward when they got to "Correspondence," where June's petition had been lumped with the press releases and routine letters.

Ned Shoults whipped up his hand. "I move the correspondence be accepted"—he glared around the room—"and no further action taken."

"Seconded," said Doreen Morris.

There were mutters. Jeers. "That will be enough," Rufus declared. "I call the question. All those in fav—"

"Wait a minute," Tilda Cooper interrupted, "I'd like to amend the motion. I want June Fletcher's petition dealt with separately."

Doyle jumped in. "If you want to do that, you have to defeat this motion. Then you can introduce yours."

"Oh, for heaven's sake, I just—"

"Rules of order," Doyle said.

"If you insist." She glared at him. "I want to—"

"First we need a vote on the motion that is on the floor."

"Howard Doyle..." Tilda moved her glasses down her nose, glowered over them. "This village used to conduct its business at my kitchen table. It doesn't matter one *goddamn* whit what order we do it in. I want the petition, no, forget that, I want"—she waved at the assembled Creeksters—"what they want."

"Hear, hear!" someone shouted.

Rufus rapped his gavel. Doyle tried to speak. Tilda shushed him again. "I want Nash Malone's bill forgiven." The tiny silver chains that dangled from her glasses swayed. "In its entirety." She looked at the other councillors. "That's what I'll be asking you to support."

Someone clapped. More joined in.

Maggie's chest swelled.

"So, we'll be paying for it?" Harriet Lemsky called out.

"As we should, bunch of cowards that we are," Alvin Tilburt shouted.

Rufus spoke above the noise. "I call the question, on the motion to accept the correspondence and take no further action. All in favour?"

Shoults shifted in his seat. Tilda Cooper raised a finger in his direction. His hand stayed on the table.

Rufus spoke. "Opposed?"

All four hands went up. Shoults came last, reluctantly, after a furtive scan of the fractious crowd.

Rufus put up his hand.

"Your vote isn't required," Doyle said.

"Please record that it was unanimous." Rufus turned to Tilda. "You have the floor."

The crowd cheered.

Stevie sat the girls on the couch, knelt in front of them. "I have some sad news," she said. "Mr. Malone passed away last night."

"Where did he go?"

"He died, Peg."

Peg scooted forward, Stevie opened her arms. Brit leaned away. Stevie tried to gather her in, but Brit slid past her, ran through the kitchen and down the hall. Stevie scrabbled in the toy box for Peg's sock doll. "Will you be okay here for a minute?"

Brit was at her window, chin resting on threaded fingers. "I'm not being sad about this," she said. "Everything dies. So, why even bother? They'll just…die on you."

"It can feel like that sometimes."

"Just when you let yourself like them, they die." Brit glared out the window.

Stevie sat on the edge of the bed. Wolverine Mountain was clearing. As the clouds lifted, she could see that the snow was down into the timber. The lake would be frozen over, the little cabin shrouded in snow.

"Remember when we climbed the mountain?"

No response.

"Remember what Mr. Malone said?"

There was a long pause before the truculent reply. "The mountain is in me?"

"That's right. All your life long, Wolverine Mountain will be in you because you didn't quit when it got hard."

A sigh.

"Look around your room. Is the mountain in here?"

An eye roll.

"Is it?

"No."

"That's right. It isn't. Now, close your eyes."

Brit scowled, complied.

"Can you picture the mountain? The trail? The big hill?"

A half-hearted nod.

"Can you feel it? How it felt, under your feet?"

A chin bob.

"So, Mr. Malone was right. The mountain is in you. Keep your eyes closed. Can you see your dad?"

Brit's eyes flew open. "It's not the same."

"Come over here. Sit beside me."

She came reluctantly.

"We'll do it together. Close your eyes. Just try it, just once. Can you feel his feet under yours? Dancing?"

Brit closed her eyes. Stevie closed hers. Brit's shoulders relaxed and she melted into Stevie's side, and they swayed, remembering.

Eyes still closed, Stevie whispered, "It *is* the same. Someday, when you are grown and far from here, you'll be able to close your eyes and see Wolverine Mountain, feel it under your feet. You can't see Dad or Mr. Malone, they're gone. But they're in you. They always will be."

Stevie contemplated her reflection in the bathroom mirror. The blue eyeshadow wasn't helping her puffy eyes. She wet her finger and rubbed it away. She picked up the mascara tube, put it back down. Not today.

In the kitchen, the girls were dressed and waiting. Brit had supervised hair and teeth brushing and was using the lint roller on Peg's black leotards.

"Brit, are those shoes too tight?"

"They're fine, Mom."

"I thought you said they were pinching. At Thanksgiving."

"They're fine."

"We'll go to Pam's. This week. Get you a new pair." There was money in her bank account. Maggie hadn't just given her job back, she'd given her a title and a raise. Stevie took the lint roller from Brit and swiped a few times at her own skirt.

"Okay," she said. "Are we ready?" Her voice was too bright, too high. Peg glanced sideways to her sister. They clasped hands.

"Ready," they sang out in one voice.

Stevie picked up the crystal plate with the huckleberry cake, over-cooked and crumbling, but sliced and arranged and covered with plastic wrap. She checked her watch. Quarter to. Already.

"We might as well walk." It would be faster than fooling with seat-belts and trying to find a parking spot. It was only four blocks.

The girls hurried ahead, waited at the gate. Stevie bent to pull the door closed, the cake plate balanced on her arm. Her purse slid off her shoulder, the cake plate tilted, she grabbed for it, sped it on its way instead. It bounced off the step and shattered on the walkway.

Peg ran forward.

"Stop! There's glass!"

Peg skirted the carnage, clasped Stevie's skirt. Brit watched stoically.

"We'll just leave it," Stevie said. "We'll pick it up when we get home. Let's go."

Brit opened the gate. Stevie hesitated.

"Mom." Peg tugged her coat sleeve.

"It's okay," Stevie said, starting forward. "I wanted to bring some-thing. That's all."

Brit darted past her, back toward the porch. Before Stevie could call out, she was up the steps and through the door.

"Now what?" Stevie dragged Peg with her, stopped outside the circle of broken glass and shouted, "Brit! Come on, we have to go. We'll be late."

Late and empty-handed.

A raven swooped in from the south, perched on a picket. Brit came out the door, on the run. She leapt the scattered glass, landed safely beside Stevie, and handed up a plastic shopping bag.

Inside the bag, gathered from the fruit bowl on the kitchen table and the crisper in the fridge, their complete supply: three oranges.

Stevie laughed. She turned her back on the broken plate and left the cake for the raven. She gave each of the girls an orange, balled the bag and thrust it into her pocket and when they arrived at the crowded community hall, bearing their oranges like lavish bouquets, Stevie's heart was full and she was not afraid.

The river is not a memory anymore. It is inside you. It is no longer a place you are going to. A place far away, across an ocean, in a distant land that you no longer believe in. Somewhere on the road between Jarama and Teruel, the river flowed into you, in the night, and you became liquid.

You are already dead. That is understood. Acknowledged. There is nothing to go home to. There is only this sweet flowing moment. This terrible Russian cigarette. This beautiful Spanish orange.

The boy savours each carefully divided section. Then he gnaws the white pith from the peel. The other men tease him, tell him he is taking food from the mouths of chickens.

He laughs with them, and their laughter is the sound of the water as it ripples across the rocks below the bridge at Beauty Creek.

* * *

Acknowledgements

Readers familiar with life in the interior of British Columbia may wonder if some of Beauty Creek's characters are representations of real people. I assure you they are not. Through the long process of writing a novel, inspiration comes in many forms; pieces of history, geography, personality, events, and memory are gathered, incubated in my imagination, and then written into drafts, written out of drafts, chopped into bits, arranged, and rearranged until, eventually, the story I mean to tell emerges from the chaos (complete with fictional characters that I do my level best to make *seem* real). So it is with *Cambium Blue*. I drew inspiration from people and events, some real, some imagined, and concocted a tale.

That said, I would be remiss if I did not acknowledge the influence of Frank J. Blackman, historian, poet and Spanish Civil War veteran. This is not his story, nor is it meant to be, but this story could never have existed without him.

The Spanish Civil War has been exhaustively studied and it would be impossible to list all the sources I consulted during my research. For the big picture and timelines, I relied on Helen Graham's *The Spanish Civil War: A Very Short Introduction*; for the Canadian volunteers' stories, Michael Petrou's *Renegades: Canadians in the Spanish Civil War*, Mark Zuehlke's *The Gallant Cause: Canadians in the Spanish Civil War, 1936–1939* and William C. Beeching's *Canadian Volunteers: Spain 1936–1939*. The long-forgotten CBC interviews, recorded in 1964–65 by CBC producer Mac Reynolds, were finally broadcast, nearly fifty years later, in 2012 as *The Spanish Crucible*. Readers may be interested to know that the Canadian government never did recognize the Spanish volunteers as veterans. A monument to their sacrifice (paid for privately) was erected in Ottawa and dedicated by the Right Honourable Adrienne Clarkson in October 2001. It is engraved with 1,546 names below an inscription, taken from a speech given in Barcelona in 1938 to the departing International Brigades: "You can go proudly. You are history. You are legend."

I am, once again, indebted to the local historians whose tireless work has enriched my understanding of the British Columbia interior. I owe a debt of gratitude to *Yellowhead Pass and Its People* by the Valemount Historic Society, *The Robson Valley Story* by Marilyn J. Wheeler, *Upper North Thompson Reflections* by the Clearwater & District History Book Committee, and Ken Drushka's books: *Tie Hackers to Timber Harvesters: The History of Logging in British Columbia's Interior* and *In the Bight: The BC Forest Industry Today*.

I would like to thank editors Caroline Skelton, Lynne Van Luven, Sioux Browning and Suzanne Skagen for helping me make the story its best possible self; early readers Ron Baer, Lesli Brownlee and Kim Thorn for thoughtful critiques; Ellen Duncan for providing a crucial puzzle piece—even though it didn't make the final cut; Harbour Publishing for recognizing these characters and giving them a chance; Anna Comfort O'Keeffe for her reassuring emails—a balm during dark times; and my family and friends for kindnesses large and small, and for lending me support and understanding and patience during this book's long journey.

I also wish to thank the readers of my first novel, *Loggers' Daughters*. You made this one possible.

Photo Credit: Cynthia L Breden

About the Author

Maureen Brownlee was born on the western slope of the northern Rockies. A former journalist, she has also worked as an outfitter's cook, a trail guide, a bookkeeper and an employment counsellor. For ten years she was variously publisher, editor, reporter, photographer, graphic designer and janitor for a weekly community newspaper. She studied literature and creative writing at UNBC and the Open University. *Cambium Blue* is her second novel, her first was *Loggers' Daughters*.